罗尔德·达尔短篇故事品读及汉译探索
第3卷

An Interpretation of Short Stories by Roald Dahl and an Exploration of Their Chinese Translations
Volume 3

单　畅　王永胜　著
SHAN Chang, WANG Yong-sheng

哈爾濱工業大學出版社

内容提要

本书系对英国作家罗尔德·达尔“非儿童类”(个别篇章具有“儿童类”文学特点,但由于是罗尔德·达尔早期作品,也被收录进来,作为研究的对象)短篇故事(小说)进行研究所著系列图书中的第3卷,包括8部短篇小说。这些小说长短不一、难易各异,按照不同的主题分成四章加以编排,分别为“冷嘲热讽”“意识之流”“科幻色彩”和“匪夷所思”。每章收录两篇作品,先做引导性的介绍,名为“原作导读”,再给出小说的原文供读者阅读或作为翻译的参考,同时给出语言点及文化层面上的注释,以辅助理解,名为“原作释读”,最后给出探索性的汉语译文,名为“翻译探索”。

本书适合英语专业大学本科生及研究生阅读、研究、翻译之用(不少小说也可供高中生阅读、学习),也适合广大的文学爱好者阅读,更适合从事英汉翻译或外国文学研究的学者、教师等阅读、参考。

图书在版编目(CIP)数据

罗尔德·达尔短篇故事品读及汉译探索第3卷/单畅,王永胜著.—哈尔滨:哈尔滨工业大学出版社,2015.2

ISBN 978-7-5603-5107-0

Ⅰ.①罗…　Ⅱ.①单…　②王…　Ⅲ.①短篇小说－小说研究－英国－现代　②短篇小说－文学翻译－英国－现代　Ⅳ.①I561.074

中国版本图书馆CIP数据核字(2014)第303483号

责任编辑　田新华
封面设计　思　华　高永利
出版发行　哈尔滨工业大学出版社
社　　址　哈尔滨市南岗区复华四道街10号　邮编150006
传　　真　0451－86414749
网　　址　http://hitpress.hit.edu.cn
印　　刷　哈尔滨市工大节能印刷厂
开　　本　880mm×1230mm　1/32　印张11.25　字数400千字
版　　次　2015年2月第1版　2015年2月第1次印刷
书　　号　ISBN 978-7-5603-5107-0
定　　价　39.00元

前　言

对于罗尔德·达尔（Roald Dahl，1916—1990），中国读者耳熟能详的恐怕是他的一些儿童文学作品，国内外对他称呼最多的莫过于"儿童文学作家"。他的儿童文学作品的确十分畅销，已被翻译成多国文字出版发行，几乎家喻户晓。可以说，在儿童文学作家中，罗尔德·达尔是最为成功、最为知名的作家之一。达尔的儿童文学作品深受很多国家小朋友的喜爱，其中包括《詹姆斯与大仙桃》（*James and the Giant Peach*）、《查利与巧克力工厂》（*Charlie and the Chocolate Factory*）、《魔法手指》（*The Magic Finger*）、《查利与大玻璃升降机》（*Charlie and the Great Glass Elevator*）、《了不起的狐狸爸爸》（*Fantastic Mr. Fox*）、《特威特夫妇》（*The Twits*）、《女巫》（*The Witches*）、《好心眼儿的巨人》（*The BFG*，1983 年获"惠特布雷德奖"——Whitbread Award）以及《玛蒂尔达》（*Matilda*）等儿童故事。

然而，作为英国儿童文学作家的罗尔德·达尔还写过其他类型的文学作品，特别是那些"非儿童类"短篇小说（个别篇章具有"儿童类"文学特点，但由于是罗尔德·达尔早期作品，也被收录进来，作为研究的对象，也可以说"成人类"短篇小说，也就是说，为成年人写的文学作品。当然，这些作品中有些具有"成人"色彩——含有色情内容，但达尔"成人"作品中的"成人"内容大多是比较"隐晦"的。这样的"成人"作品，基本收录在他的《迷情乱性》（*Switch Bitch*）一书中）也同样精彩。称之为"非儿童类"，主要针对达尔"儿童类"作品耀眼的光环而言。其实，这些"非儿童类"短篇故事（小说）绝大多数是达尔转笔写儿童文学作品之前完成的，"儿童类"作品的耀眼光环或多或少掩盖了一些"非儿童类"作品的光芒，而在中国，这些"非儿童类”作品的“光芒”几乎没有散发出来,很少为中国广大读者所熟知。这些作品受到西方19世纪现实主义文学的影响,多数采用现实主义的创作手法。同时,达尔也从美国短篇小说家欧·亨利(O. Henry)那里汲取了一定的营养。就达尔作品本身对人物和景物的描写来看,可以说,他是“20世纪英国变形精神世界的一位工笔画家”[①]。同他的儿童文学作品一样,他早期的这些“非儿童类”作品同样具有结尾出奇、结局令人意想不到等特点,更进一步说,达尔的此类短篇小说这方面的特点尤为突出。这类作品充满奇思妙想,人物刻画细腻入微,其中不乏道貌岸然者、悲观主义者、心理变态者。此类作品也不乏荒谬、贪婪、邪恶、虚伪的成分,其中的人物大都在“机关用尽”之时,一不小心就“栽了跟头”,或者在“聪明绝顶”之际,反而被自己的“聪明”所误。

罗尔德·达尔的父母是挪威人,但达尔本人1916年出生在英国格拉摩根郡的兰达夫(Llandaff, Glamorgan,格拉摩根原来是英国南威尔士的一个郡——著者注),并在雷普顿公学(Repton School)接受教育。第二次世界大战爆发,他应征入伍,加入英国皇家空军,驻扎在内罗毕。后来,他加入了驻利比亚的一个战斗机中队,受了重伤。之后,又作为一名战斗机飞行员到希腊和叙利亚参加战斗。1942年,达尔作为英国大使馆的空军助理专员去了华盛顿。华盛顿成为他人生的转折点,因为在那里他开始了自己的创作生涯。随后,他被调到情报部。战争结束的时候,他成为英国皇家空军中校。他的第一批短篇小说共有12篇,都是根据自己在战争期间的经历写成。这12篇作品首先发表在美国的一些主流杂志上,后来编撰成书出版,书名为《向你飞跃》(*Over to You*)。

罗尔德·达尔所有受到高度赞誉的作品都被译成多种文字,成为全世界的畅销书。安格利亚电视台(Anglia Television)将他的一些

① 参见陈钰(1985)”,这里只不过将其中的“二十世纪”,规范性修改成“20世纪”。

短篇小说改编成电视系列剧,冠以标题《出乎意料的故事集》(*Tales of the Unexpected*)。他的作品还包括两本自传——《男孩时代》(*Boy*)和《独闯天下》(*Going Solo*),还有赢得很多赞誉的小说《我的叔叔奥斯瓦尔德》(*My Uncle Oswald*)以及《罗尔德·达尔倾心的鬼怪故事集》(*Roald Dahl's Book of Ghost Stories*)。最后一本是他自己编辑出版的。在生命的最后一年,他收集了一些奇闻轶事,并跟妻子弗利西蒂(Felicity)一道,整理了一些烹饪食谱,汇编成一本书。这本书1996年由企鹅出版集团出版,书名为《罗尔德·达尔的烹饪书》(*Roald Dahl's Cookbook*)①。

罗尔德·达尔于1990年11月23日去世。英国《泰晤士报》(*The Times*)称其为"我们这一代人中最为有影响力的作家之一,也是拥有极其广泛读者群的作家之一"(One of the most widely read and influential writers of our generation),并在写给他的讣告中写道:"孩子喜欢他写的故事,把他当成自己心目中最喜爱的人……他的作品将成为未来的经典之作"(Children loved his stories and made him their favourite ... They will be classics of the future)。据报道,在2000年英国的"世界图书日"(World Book Day)投票中,罗尔德·达尔当选为"读者最喜爱的作家"(Favourite Author)②。

对于20世纪的英国作家罗尔德·达尔及其作品,《爱尔兰时报》(Irish Times)的一篇评论,可谓一语中的:"Roald Dahl is one of the few writers I know whose work can accurately be described as addictive. Through his tales runs a vein of macabre malevolence, the more effective because it springs from the slightest, almost inconsequential everyday things. The result is a black humour of the most sophisticated kind."(罗尔德·达尔是我所认识的为数不多的作家之一,可以准确无误地说,

---

① 参见"Roald Dahl. *The Best of Roald Dahl* [M]. London: Penguin Books Ltd., 2006"。

② 参见"Roald Dahl. *The Collected Short Stories of Roald Dahl* [M]. London: Penguin Books Ltd., 1992"。

其作品令人沉醉、上瘾。他的作品始终贯穿着一条主线，这条主线令人毛骨悚然，充满恶意和凶险，但却更加行之有效，因为其来源是一些不起眼的、几乎微不足道的日常事物。结果，最为错综复杂的黑色幽默便应运而生了)①。

抛开后来"儿童类"作品的耀眼光环不说，罗尔德·达尔在20世纪中叶之所以蜚声世界，就是因为他所创作的这些"非儿童类"的短篇小说(当然，个别篇章具有"儿童类"文学特点，预示性地展露出达尔后来作为儿童文学作家的一丝"光芒")。但是，当时中国翻译出版业不是很发达，对他的作品译介得也不是很多。就算是有所译介，也处于零星的"散兵作战"状态，不成体系。在全球化浪潮滚滚而来的今天，研究罗尔德·达尔的这部分作品，并系统地加以翻译，如同打开尘封已久的大门，门内的景色依然会令当代中国读者惊喜不已。对于广大的英语学习者和文学爱好者来说，阅读达尔的这部分作品将会带来迥然不同的人生体验。其实，罗尔德·达尔这部分短篇小说的实质和绝妙，可以从英美主流媒体的评价窥见一斑：

"Roald Dahl is the prince of storytellers." ——*Daily Mail*

"罗尔德·达尔是位讲故事的王子。" ——(英国)《每日邮报》

"The absolute master of the twist-in-the-tale"

——*The Observer*

"绝对的大师，其故事的结局出人意料。"

——(英国)《观察家报》

"These stories pack their punch." ——*The Observer*

"这些故事蓄满了惊人之力。" ——(英国)《观察家报》

---

① 著者译自 Roald Dahl (1916—1990)的"*The Best of Roald Dahl*"(《罗尔德·达尔小说精品集》)一书的封底(back cover)。此书由英国"Penguin Books Ltd."出版公司于2006年出版发行。

"An unforgettable read, don't miss it." ——*Sunday Times*

"一次难忘的阅读体验,不可错过。"

——(英国)《星期日泰晤士报》

"Dahl is too good a storyteller to become predictable, so you never know whether the tyrant or the tyrannized will win in the end."

——*Daily Telegraph*

"达尔的故事讲得太精彩了,结局简直令人无法预测。因此,你永远都无法得知,最后的赢家是残暴的人,还是受到残暴对待的人。"

——(英国)《每日电讯报》

"Dahl has the mastery of plot and characters possessed by great writers of the past, along with a wildness and wryness of his own. One of his trademarks is writing beautifully about the ugly, even the horrible."

——*The Los Angeles Times*

"达尔拥有以往伟大作家的资质——善于营造情节、精于刻画人物,但达尔也拥有自己荒诞不经的一面,以及自己的一套挖苦讥讽的手段。其中的一个标志就是他对丑陋之人的精妙刻画,更有甚者是对恐怖之人的精妙刻画。" ——(美国)《洛杉矶时报》

"An ingenious imagination, a fascination with odd and ordinary detail, and a lust for its thorough exploitation are the... strengths of Dahl's storytelling." ——*The New York Times Book Review*

"达尔写作的影响力在于其独特的想象力,在于其对稀奇古怪和平淡无奇的细节的着迷程度,在于其对细节完完全全加以利用的欲望。" ——(美国)《纽约时报·书评》

"The mind of Roald Dahl is quintessentially nasty and wicked."

——*The Washington Post*

“罗尔德·达尔的思维具有典型的特点，那就是肮脏和邪恶。”

——(美国)《华盛顿邮报》

在此前提下，研究并翻译罗尔德·达尔的“非儿童类”短篇小说，将具有一定的学术价值和社会价值，会为中国文学的百花园增添一个品种，会为文学爱好者和翻译者提供一个可供参考的文本。

在历时三年多对罗尔德·达尔“非儿童类”短篇小说进行研究和翻译的过程中，共收集到长短不一的此类作品60篇，并站在一定的角度，根据著者个人的理解，细加编排，精心安排，详加注释，最终通过翻译，引介给中国读者。

本书在对罗尔德·达尔短篇小说的翻译探索中，采取了严谨的翻译态度，形成了以下基本的翻译思路：

(1)人名、地名按照一定的标准进行“异化”式处理(极个别人名作了“归化”式处理)，主要依据《世界人名翻译大辞典》(新华社译名室编，中国对外翻译出版公司1993年第一版或2007年第二版)以及《世界地名翻译大辞典》(周定国主编，中国出版集团、中国对外翻译出版公司2008年第一版)等，个别的人名、地名的翻译兼顾了流行的译法。

(2)绝大多数非国际化的度量衡单位，特别是英制的度量衡单位，采用“同化”或“归化”的处理方法，以便汉语思维者能形象化地加以理解。

(3)每一篇的题目都采用汉语四字格来处理，以求汉语的工整，发挥汉语四字格表达的优势，但同时最大限度地兼顾原文题目的字面意义。

(4)就汉语译文整体而言，尽量杜绝“翻译腔”，以保持汉语语言的纯洁性和规范性，但前提是确保对达尔小说原文的“忠实”。

(5)尽量完美地再现原文的风格，虽然做到这一点并不是轻而易举的事情。原文有些风格，在翻译中只能退其次而求之——基本上采用“归化”处理手法，照顾了汉语的通畅性。比如原文中很多非标准的英语表达，汉译时就没有在“风格”上充分得以体现，这也是以后有待继续探索的一个翻译问题。

当然，“金无足赤，人无完人”，匆忙且蹒跚的步履必将会迈出“不和谐”的步伐。在对罗尔德·达尔的“非儿童类”短篇小说进行研究、翻译并成书的过程中，不当甚至错误之处在所难免，还望读者不吝赐教，多多批评，特别是多做文学翻译方面的批评。

需要特别声明的是，本系列书中所引用的罗尔德·达尔原著内容以及所做的翻译探索，旨在学术研究，不做商业用途。涉及相关版权的地方，已经做了引用和标注。

著者

单畅　王永胜

2014 年 10 月 10 日于渤海大学

目　录

第一章　冷嘲热讽

冷嘲与热讽，抑或讽刺与嘲弄，是文学上一大创作手法，其功效不可小觑。冷嘲热讽的目的之一在于揭示虚伪，但使用的也许是荒诞不经的手法，创造的也许是荒诞离奇的效果。当然，即使是名曰"冷嘲热讽"的作品，使用的也不仅仅是讽刺这一种手法。反过来，即使某些讽刺类作品使用了其他类型的文学手法，也可以从中找到"冷嘲热讽"的影子。

根据某些成语词典的释义，"冷嘲热讽"一词出自清代袁枚的《牍外余言》：

"楚公子围为虢之会，其时子围篡国之状，人人知之，皆有不平之意，故晋大夫七嘴八舌，冷讥热嘲，皆由于心之大公也。"

可以说，在文学上，"冷嘲热讽"就是用比喻、夸张等艺术手法对某些不良行为、虚伪名声、愚蠢错误、致命弱点等进行揭露、挖苦、批评甚至攻击，以使读者在这些方面获得更加鲜明、深刻、直观的印象。冷嘲热讽往往是讽刺的代名词，鲁迅先生说，讽刺就是"一个作者，用了精炼的，或者简直有些夸张的笔墨——但自然也必须是艺术的——写出或一群人的或一面的真实来，这被写的一群人，就称这作品为‘讽刺’”[①]。但是,鲁迅先生又对“讽刺”和“冷嘲”做出了区别:“如果貌似讽刺的作品,而毫无善意,也毫无热情,只使读者觉得一切世事,一无足取,也一无可为,那就并非讽刺了,这便是所谓‘冷嘲’。”[②]

这样看来,本章所研究的英国作家罗尔德·达尔先生这两部作品无疑是用了“讽刺”之笔进行“冷嘲”,抑或“热讽”,同时衍生出某种“荒诞”的效果。

音乐“大师”博迪博尔先生因指挥“空乐队”而获得了极大的快感和满足感,但是,跟“钢琴大师”达林顿小姐的邂逅却是他始料不及的;品酒“大师”普拉特先生不能说没有一些真功夫,但是,结局却出人意料,“大师”的真面孔暴露无遗。

走进罗尔德·达尔的世界,去领悟《音乐“大师”》的境界,去体味《品酒“大师”》的精彩吧。

第一节 《音乐“大师”》*Mr. Botibol*

罗尔德·达尔的《音乐“大师”》(*Mr. Botibol*)收录在《罗尔德·达尔短篇故事集锦》(*The Collected Short Stories of Roald Dahl*)、《罗尔德·达尔第二辑:八篇故事集》(*A Second Roald Dahl Selection: Eight Short Stories*)、《完全出人意料故事集》(*Completely Unexpected Tales*)以及《更多出人意料故事集》(*More Tales of the Unexpected*)等书中,也被改编成电视系列剧中的一集——1980 年 5 月 24 日播映的《出乎意料的故事集》(*Tales of the Unexpected*)第二部中的第 13 集

---

① 参见《鲁迅文集·杂文集·且介亭杂文二集·什么是“讽刺”?》。

② 参见《鲁迅文集·杂文集·且介亭杂文二集·什么是“讽刺”?》。

(Episode 2.13),具有一定的影响力[①]。

一、原作导读

博迪博尔先生是一个很奇怪的人,他长相怪异——整个人看起来像是一件什么东西。这一点,从他进入一家餐厅后一位女士的叫喊中,听得很明显:“我亲爱的,*一定* 得看看呐,刚刚进来的是什么啊!”(“My dear, *do* look what's just come in!”)

故事开始的时候,博迪博尔先生到一家餐厅找克莱门茨先生——某公司的代理律师。克莱门茨先生约了他,要跟他共进午餐,以便谈谈收购他那家公司的价钱问题。这一次,令克莱门茨先生意想不到的是,博迪博尔先生接受了他的初始出价——低得可怜的一个价码。于是,克莱门茨先生要喝酒庆祝。尽管博迪博尔先生一再推脱说自己不会喝酒,但还是任由克莱门茨先生给自己倒酒,将自己灌醉了。喝醉后的博迪博尔先生向克莱门茨先生坦白说,自己的一生中从未尝过成功的滋味,哪怕跟女性丝毫温馨、幸福的时刻都未曾有过。

回到家后,博迪博尔先生打开了收音机,听起里面播放的一首贝多芬的交响乐。听着,听着,他突然来了兴致,把自己当成了指挥家,像模像样地指挥起交响乐队来了。这种假装指挥的做法令他感到十分惬意,于是,他决定第二天再指挥一次。但是,他想在自己家里建一座真正的音乐厅,安装上留声机来播放交响乐,这样他就可以淋漓尽致地指挥乐队了。接着,他对自己的管家梅森交代一番,要管家买酒,好在进餐时候喝。当然,当了多年管家的梅森对主人行为变化感到吃惊不已,但是,博迪博尔先生向管家解释说,自己很正常。

雇人将自家的音乐厅建好后,博迪博尔试验了一下,感到心满意

---

① 这部分信息以及本书以后此类部分中的资料都借鉴了克里斯廷·霍华德(Kristine Howard)创建并维护的网站“Roald Dahl Fans.com”(罗尔德·达尔粉丝网)中的部分信息,网址为:http://www.roalddahlfans.com/,由著者翻译整理。以后各章的此部分信息,若没特殊标明,其出处同此。

足,决定再在里面安装一架平台大钢琴——但要在弹奏时不发出声音的大钢琴。这样的话,他就既能"弹"奏鸣曲,又能指挥乐队了。

去商店买钢琴曲唱片的时候,一个名叫达林顿的女孩跟他搭话。女孩说,她十分喜欢他刚买的那张肖邦的唱片。令博迪博尔先生自己都意想不到的是,他竟然鬼使神差般地邀请那位女子到自己家里听唱片。第二天,女孩子前来赴约。他给她看了音乐厅,说出了自己内心的秘密并说服她当天晚上跟他一起"表演"——她弹奏钢琴,而他则指挥乐队。晚上"表演"前,他俩都身着盛装,愉快地共进晚餐,都喝了许多酒。晚饭过后,他俩走进音乐厅,开始"表演"起来。

博迪博尔先生对达林顿小姐在"哑音"琴键上的弹奏十分满意,印象深刻,还十分兴奋地邀请她第二天晚上再来弹奏。此时,达林顿小姐突然意识到,时间已经很晚了,自己第二天还要早起工作呢。匆忙之中,博迪博尔先生向她道别,希望她工作愉快,并询问她在什么地方工作。

"我教人弹钢琴。"

博迪博尔先生一下子跳了起来,好似有人用一根帽针从背后戳了他一下。他的嘴张得大大的。

"一点关系都没有,"她微笑着说。"我总是想成为霍罗维茨。你认为,我可否,明天我可否成为施纳贝尔呢?"

"I teach the piano."

Mr. Botibol jumped as though someone had stuck him from behind with a hatpin. His mouth opened very wide.

"It's quite all right," she said, smiling. "I've always wanted to be Horowitz. And could I, do you think, could I please be Schnabel tomorrow?"

闻听此言,博迪博尔先生惊呆了,一句话都说不出来。

二、原作释读

本篇小说中，达尔对人物的刻画十分细腻，人物的心态活灵活现。这一点，阅读中不难体会到，同时也不难体会：生活中随时可以找到博迪博尔这样小人物的影子。在对这篇小说的阅读和理解过程中，音乐方面的词汇和表达，应该是难点。

Mr. Botibol[①]

Mr. Botibol pushed his way through the revolving doors and emerged into the large foyer[②] of the hotel. He took off his hat, and holding it in front of him with both hands, he advanced nervously a few paces, paused and stood looking around him, searching the faces of the lunchtime crowd. Several people turned and stared at him in mild astonishment, and he heard—or he thought he heard—at least one woman's voice saying, "My dear, *do* look what's just come in!"

At last he spotted Mr. Clements sitting at a small table in the far corner, and he hurried over to him. Clements had seen him coming, and now, as he watched Mr. Botibol threading his way cautiously between the

---

① 本部小说原文出自"DAHL, R. *The Collected Short Stories of Roald Dahl* [M]. London: Penguin Books Ltd., 1992"。

② foyer: *Noun* an entrance hall or other open area in a building used by the public, especially a hotel or theatre（尤指旅馆或剧院等公共建筑的）门厅；休息厅

tables and the people, walking on his toes in such a meek① and self-effacing② manner and clutching his hat before him with both hands, he thought how wretched it must be for any man to look as conspicuous and as odd as this Botibol. He resembled, to an extraordinary degree, an asparagus③. His long narrow stalk did not appear to have any shoulders at all; it merely tapered④ upwards, growing gradually narrower and narrower until it came to a kind of point at the top of the small bald head. He was tightly encased in a shiny blue double-breasted suit, and this, for some curious reason, accentuated the illusion of a vegetable to a preposterous⑤ degree.

Clements stood up, they shook hands, and then at once, even before they had sat down again, Mr. Botibol said, "I have decided, yes I have decided to accept the offer which you made to me before you left my office last night."

For some days Clements had been negotiating, on behalf of clients, for the purchase of the firm known as Botibol & Co., of which Mr. Botibol was sole owner, and the night before, Clements had made his first of-

---

① meek: *Adjective* quiet, gentle, and easily imposed on; submissive 娴静的;温顺的;顺从的(e. g. I used to call her Miss Mouse because she was so meek and mild. 我过去叫她鼠小姐,因为她是那么温顺。)

② self-effacing: *Adjective* not claiming attention for oneself; retiring and modest 自我谦逊的;谦虚的(e. g. His demeanour was self-effacing, gracious, and polite. 他的行为举止显得谦虚、优雅和有礼貌。)

③ asparagus: *Noun* a tall plant of the lily family with fine feathery foliage, cultivated for its edible shoots 芦笋;石刁柏;龙须菜

④ taper: *Verb* diminish or reduce or cause to diminish or reduce in thickness towards one end(使)成锥形

⑤ preposterous: *Adjective* contrary to reason or common sense; utterly absurd or ridiculous 反常的;乖戾的;荒谬的;愚蠢的

fer. This was merely an exploratory, much-too-low bid, a kind of signal to the seller that the buyers were seriously interested. And by God, thought Clements, the poor fool has gone and accepted it. He nodded gravely many times in an effort to hide his astonishment, and he said, "Good, good. I'm so glad to hear that, Mr. Botibol." Then he signalled a waiter and said, "Two large martinis."

"No, please!" Mr. Botibol lifted both hands in horrified protest.

"Come on," Clements said. "This is an occasion[①]."

"I drink very little, and never, no never during the middle of the day."

But Clements was in a gay mood now and he took no notice. He ordered the martinis and when they came along Mr. Botibol was forced, by the banter[②] and good-humour of the other, to drink to the deal which had just been concluded. Clements then spoke briefly about the drawing up and signing of documents, and when all that had been arranged, he called for two more cocktails. Again Mr. Botibol protested, but not quite so vigorously this time, and Clements ordered the drinks and then he turned and smiled at the other man in a friendly way. "Well, Mr. Botibol," he said, "now that it's all over, I suggest we have a pleasant non-business lunch together. What d'you[③] say to that? And it's on me."

"As you wish, as you wish," Mr. Botibol answered without any enthusiasm. He had a small melancholy voice and a way of pronouncing

---

① occasion: *Noun* a special or noteworthy event, ceremony, or celebration (仪式、庆典等)重大场合(e. g. She was presented with a gold watch to mark the occasion. 为了纪念那个重大场合她被赠与一块金表。)

② banter: *Noun* [mass noun] the playful and friendly exchange of teasing remarks(友好的)戏谑;逗弄(e. g. There was much singing and good-natured banter. 充满了歌声和谈笑戏谑。)

③ d'you = do you

each word separately and slowly, as though he was explaining something to a child.

When they went into the dining-room Clements ordered a bottle of Lafite 1912 and a couple of plump roast partridges[①] to go with it. He had already calculated in his head the amount of his commission and he was feeling fine. He began to make bright conversation, switching smoothly from one subject to another in the hope of touching on something that might interest his guest. But it was no good. Mr. Botibol appeared to be only half listening. Every now and then he inclined his small bald head a little to one side or the other and said, "Indeed." When the wine came along Clements tried to have a talk about that.

"I am sure it is excellent," Mr. Botibol said, "but please give me only a drop."

Clements told a funny story. When it was over, Mr. Botibol regarded him solemnly for a few moments, then he said, "How amusing." After that Clements kept his mouth shut and they ate in silence. Mr. Botibol was drinking his wine and he didn't seem to object when his host reached over and refilled his glass. By the time they had finished eating, Clements estimated privately that his guest had consumed at least three-quarters of the bottle.

"A cigar, Mr. Botibol?"

"Oh no, thank you."

"A little brandy?"

"No really. I am not accustomed..." Clements noticed that the man's cheeks were slightly flushed and that his eyes had become bright

① partridge: *Noun* a short-tailed game bird with mainly brown plumage, found chiefly in Europe and Asia 鹧鸪;石鸡;灰山鹑

and watery[1]. Might as well get the old boy properly drunk while I'm about it, he thought, and to the waiter he said, "Two brandies."

When the brandies arrived, Mr. Botibol looked at his large glass suspiciously for a while, then he picked it up, took one quick birdlike sip and put it down again. "Mr. Clements," he said suddenly, "how I envy you."

"Me? But why?"

"I will tell you, Mr. Clements, I will tell you, if I may make so bold." There was a nervous, mouselike quality in his voice which made it seem he was apologizing for everything he said.

"Please tell me," Clements said.

"It is because to me you appear to have made such a success of your life."

He's going to get melancholy drunk, Clements thought. He's one of the ones that gets melancholy and I can't stand it. "Success," he said, "I don't see anything especially successful about me."

"Oh yes, indeed. Your whole life, if I may say so, Mr. Clements, appears to be such a pleasant and successful thing."

"I'm a very ordinary person," Clements said. He was trying to figure just how drunk the other really was.

"I believe," said Mr. Botibol, speaking slowly, separating each word carefully from the other, "I believe that the wine has gone a little to my head, but..." He paused, searching for words. "...But I do want to ask you just one question." He had poured some salt on to the tablecloth and he was shaping it into a little mountain with the tip of one finger.

---

① watery: *Adjective* consisting of, containing, or resembling water 由水组成的;含水的;似水的

"Mr. Clements," he said without looking up, "do you think that it is possible for a man to live to the age of fifty-two without ever during his whole life having experienced one single small success in anything that he has done?"

"My dear Mr. Botibol," Clements laughed, "everyone has his little successes from time to time, however small they may be."

"Oh no," Mr. Botibol said gently. "You are wrong. I, for example, cannot remember having had a single success of any sort during my whole life."

"Now come!" Clements said, smiling. "That can't be true. Why only this morning you sold your business for a hundred thousand. I call that one hell of a success."

"The business was left me by my father. When he died nine years ago, it was worth four times as much. Under my direction it has lost three-quarters of its value. You can hardly call that a success."

Clements knew this was true. "Yes, yes, all right," he said. "That may be so, but all the same you know as well as I do that every man alive has his quota[①] of little successes. Not big ones maybe. But lots of little ones. I mean, after all, goddammit[②], even scoring a goal at school was a little success, a little triumph, at the time; or making some runs or learning to swim. One forgets about them, that's all. One just forgets."

"I never scored a goal," Mr. Botibol said. "And I never learned to swim."

---

① quota: *Noun* a limited or fixed number or amount of people or things, in particular(尤指)定额;定量

② goddammit: *Interjection* (sometimes initial capital letter) (Informal: Sometimes Offensive) (used to express anger, perplexity, amazement, etc.) 该死的;要命的(表示愤怒、不满、困惑、惊讶等)

Clements threw up his hands and made exasperated[①] noises. "Yes yes, I know, but don't you see, don't you see there are thousands, literally thousands of other things like... well like catching a good fish, or fixing the motor of the car, or pleasing someone with a present, or growing a decent row of French beans[②], or winning a little bet or... or... why hell, one can go on listing them for ever!"

"Perhaps *you* can, Mr. Clements, but to the best of my knowledge, I have never done any of those things. That is what I am trying to tell you."

Clements put down his brandy glass and stared with new interest at the remarkable shoulderless person who sat facing him. He was annoyed and he didn't feel in the least sympathetic. The man didn't inspire sympathy. He was a fool. He must be a fool. A tremendous and absolute fool. Clements had a sudden desire to embarrass the man as much as he could. "What about women, Mr. Botibol?" There was no apology for the question in the tone of his voice.

"Women?"

"Yes women! Every man under the sun, even the most wretched filthy down-and-out[③] tramp has some time or other had some sort of silly little success with..."

"Never!" cried Mr. Botibol with sudden vigour. "No sir, never!"

---

① exasperate: *Verb* [with obj.] irritate intensely; infuriate 激怒;使气恼(e. g. This futile process exasperates prison officers. 这一无效程序使得监狱官们怒不可遏。)

② French bean: *Noun* (Brit.) a tropical American bean plant of which many varieties are commercially cultivated(英国英语)菜豆;四季豆

③ down-and-out or down and out: *Adjective* (of a person) without money, a job, or a place to live; destitute(人)穷困的;赤贫的(e. g. a novel about being down and out in London 一部描写在伦敦贫困生活的小说)

I'm going to hit him, Clements told himself. I can't stand this any longer and if I'm not careful I'm going to jump right up and hit him. "You mean you don't like them?" he said.

"Oh dear me yes, of course. I like them. As a matter of fact I admire them very much, very much indeed. But I'm afraid... oh dear me I do not know how to say it... I am afraid that I do not seem to get along with them very well. I never have. Never. You see, Mr. Clements, I *look* queer. I know I do. They stare at me, and often I see them laughing at me. I have never been able to get within... well, within striking distance of them, as you might say." The trace of a smile, weak and infinitely sad, flickered around the corners of his mouth.

Clements had had enough. He mumbled something about how he was sure Mr. Botibol was exaggerating the situation, then he glanced at his watch, called for the bill, and he said he was sorry but he would have to get back to the office.

They parted in the street outside the hotel and Mr. Botibol took a cab back to his house. He opened the front door, went into the living-room and switched on the radio; then he sat down in a large leather chair, leaned back and closed his eyes. He didn't feel exactly giddy①, but there was a singing in his ears and his thoughts were coming and going more quickly than usual. That solicitor gave me too much wine, he told himself. I'll stay here for a while and listen to some music and I expect I'll go to sleep and after that I'll feel better.

They were playing a symphony on the radio. Mr. Botibol had always been a casual listener to symphony concerts and he knew enough to iden-

---

① giddy: *Adjective* having a sensation of whirling and a tendency to fall or stagger; dizzy 头晕的;眩晕的(e. g. I felt giddy and had to steady myself. 我觉得头晕目眩,不得不稳住身子。)

tify this as one of Beethoven's①. But now, as he lay back in his chair listening to the marvellous music, a new thought began to expand slowly within his tipsy② mind. It wasn't a dream because he was not asleep. It was a clear conscious thought and it was this: I am the composer of this music. I am a great composer. This is my latest symphony and this is the first performance. The huge hall is packed with people—critics, musicians and music-lovers from all over the country—and I am up there in front of the orchestra③, conducting.

Mr. Botibol could see the whole thing. He could see himself up on the rostrum④ dressed in a white tie and tails, and before him was the orchestra, the massed violins on his left, the violas⑤ in front, the cellos⑥

---

① Beethoven: *Noun* Ludwig van Beethoven (1770—1827), German composer 路德维希·范·贝多芬(1770—1827,德国作曲家。)

② tipsy: *Adjective* slightly intoxicated or drunk; characterized by or due to intoxication 喝醉的;微醉的;由醉引起的;有醉意的(e.g. The wine has made him a trifle tipsy. 这酒喝得他有点醉意了。)

③ orchestra: *Noun* [treated as sing. or pl.] a group of instrumentalists, especially one combining string, woodwind, brass, and percussion sections and playing classical music(单复数相同)管弦乐队

④ rostrum: *Noun* a raised platform on which a person stands to make a public speech, receive an award or medal, play music, or conduct an orchestra 演讲台;讲坛;台

⑤ viola: *Noun* an instrument of the violin family, larger than the violin and tuned a fifth lower 中提琴

⑥ cello: a bass instrument of the violin family, held upright on the floor between the legs of the seated player 大提琴

on his right, and back of them were all the woodwinds[①] and bassoons[②] and drums and cymbals[③], the players watching every moment of his baton[④] with an intense, almost a fanatical reverence. Behind him, in the half-darkness of the huge hall, was row upon row of white enraptured[⑤] faces, looking up towards him, listening with growing excitement as yet another new symphony by the greatest composer the world has ever seen unfolded itself majestically before them. Some of the audience were clenching their fists and digging their nails into the palms of their hands because the music was so beautiful that they could hardly stand it. Mr. Botibol became so carried away by this exciting vision that he began to swing his arms in time with the music in the manner of a conductor. He found it was such fun doing this that he decided to stand up, facing the radio, in order to give himself more freedom of movement.

He stood there in the middle of the room, tall, thin and shoulderless, dressed in his tight blue double-breasted suit, his small bald head jerking from side to side as he waved his arms in the air. He knew the

---

① woodwind: *Noun* [treated as sing. or pl.] wind instruments other than brass instruments forming a section of an orchestra, including flutes, oboes, clarinets, and bassoons 木管乐器(指长笛、双簧管、单簧管和大管)(e.g. striking passages for woodwind and brass 由木管和铜管乐器合奏的动人乐章)

② bassoon: *Noun* a bass woodwind instrument of the oboe family, with a doubled-back tube over four feet long, played with a double reed 低音管;巴松管

③ cymbal: *Noun* a musical instrument consisting of a slightly concave round brass plate which is either struck against another one or struck with a stick to make a ringing or clashing sound 钹(一种乐器)

④ baton: *Noun* a thin stick used by a conductor to direct an orchestra or choir 指挥棒

⑤ enrapture: *Verb* [with obj.] (usu. as "be enraptured") give intense pleasure or joy to 使狂喜(e.g. Ruth was enraptured by the child who was sleeping in her arms so peacefully. 孩子安静地睡在怀里,鲁思心里乐滋滋的。)

symphony well enough to be able occasionally to anticipate changes in tempo or volume, and when the music became loud and fast he beat the air so vigorously that he nearly knocked himself over, when it was soft and hushed, he leaned forward to quieten the players with gentle movements of his outstretched hands, and all the time he could feel the presence of the huge audience behind him, tense, immobile, listening. When at last the symphony swelled to its tremendous conclusion, Mr. Botibol became more frenzied[①] than ever and his face seemed to thrust itself round to one side in an agony of effort as he tried to force more and still more power from his orchestra during those final mighty chords.

Then it was over. The announcer was saying something, but Mr. Botibol quickly switched off the radio and collapsed into his chair, blowing heavily.

"Phew![②]" he said aloud. "My goodness gracious me, what *have* I been doing!" Small globules[③] of sweat were oozing out all over his face and forehead, trickling down his neck inside his collar. He pulled out a handkerchief and wiped them away, and he lay there for a while, panting, exhausted, but exceedingly exhilarated[④].

"Well, I must say," he gasped, still speaking aloud, "that *was* fun. I don't know that I have ever had such fun before in all my life. My

---

① frenzied: *Adjective* wildly excited or uncontrolled 极度激动的;狂乱的;发狂似的

② phew: *Exclamation* (informal) expressing a strong reaction of relief(非正式)咳;唷;哦(表示松一口气)(e. g. Phew, what a year! 唷,又打发了一年!)

③ globule: *Noun* a small round particle of a substance; a drop 小球;滴(e. g. globules of fat 脂肪球)

④ exhilarate: *Verb* (usu. as "exhilarated") make (someone) feel very happy, animated, or elated 使高兴;使愉快(e. g. She was exhilarated by the day's events. 她为那天的事情感到高兴。)

goodness, it *was* fun, it really *was*!" Almost at once he began to play with the idea of doing it again. But should he? Should he allow himself to do it again? There was no denying that now, in retrospect[①], he felt a little guilty about the whole business, and soon he began to wonder whether there wasn't something downright immoral about it all. Letting himself go like that! And imagining he was a genius! It was wrong. He was sure other people didn't do it. And what if Mason had come in the middle and seen him at it! That would have been terrible!

He reached for the paper and pretended to read it, but soon he was searching furtively[②] among the radio programmes for the evening. He put his finger under a line which said "8. 30 Symphony Concert. Brahms[③] Symphony No. 2". He stared at it for a long time. The letters in the word "Brahms" began to blur and recede, and gradually they disappeared altogether and were replaced by letters which spelt "Botibol". Botibol's Symphony No .2. It was printed quite clearly. He was reading it now, this moment. "Yes, yes," he whispered. "First performance.

---

① in retrospect: when looking back on a past event or situation; with hindsight 回顾起来;事后看来(e. g. Perhaps, in retrospect, I shouldn't have gone. 事后想想,也许我不该去。)

② furtive: *Adjective* attempting to avoid notice or attention, typically because of guilt or a belief that discovery would lead to trouble; secretive 偷偷摸摸的;鬼鬼祟祟的;秘密的;遮遮掩掩的(e. g. They spent a furtive day together. 他们在一起偷偷摸摸地过了一天。)

③ Brahms: *Noun* Johannes Brahms (1833—1897), German composer and pianist. He eschewed programme music and opera and concentrated on traditional forms. He wrote four symphonies, four concertos, chamber and piano music, choral works including the German Requiem (1857—1868), and nearly 200 songs. 约翰内斯·勃拉姆斯(1833—1897,德国作曲家、钢琴家,作品多为非标题音乐,继承了古典传统;共创作了四部交响乐、四部协奏曲、室内和钢琴音乐、合唱曲以及近200首歌曲,包括《德意志安魂曲》(1857—1868)。

The world is waiting to hear it. Will it be as great, they are asking, will it perhaps be greater than his earlier work? And the composer himself had been persuaded to conduct. He is shy and retiring, hardly ever appears in public, but on this occasion he has been persuaded..."

Mr. Botibol leaned forward in his chair and pressed the bell beside the fireplace. Mason, the butler, the only other person in the house, ancient, small and grave, appeared at the door.

"Er... Mason, have we any wine in the house?"

"Wine, sir?"

"Yes, wine."

"Oh no, sir. We haven't had any wine this fifteen or sixteen years. Your father, sir..."

"I know, Mason, I know, but will you get some please. I want a bottle with my dinner."

The butler was shaken. "Very well, sir, and what shall it be?"

"Claret, Mason. The best you can obtain. Get a case. Tell them to send it round at once."

When he was alone again, he was momentarily appalled by the simple manner in which he had made his decision. Wine for dinner! Just like that! Well, yes, why not? Why ever not now he came to think of it? He was his own master. And anyway it was essential that he have wine. It seemed to have a good effect, a very good effect indeed. He wanted it and he was going to have it and to hell with Mason.

He rested for the remainder of the afternoon, and at seven-thirty Mason announced dinner. The bottle of wine was on the table and he began to drink it. He didn't give a damn① about the way Mason watched

① not give a damn:(informal) not care at all(非正式)毫不在乎(e.g. people who don't give a damn about the environment 对环境漠不关心的人)

him as he refilled his glass. Three times he refilled it; then he left the table saying that he was not to be disturbed and returned to the living-room. There was quarter of an hour to wait. He could think of nothing now except the coming concert. He lay back in the chair and allowed his thoughts to wander deliciously towards eight-thirty. He was the great composer waiting impatiently in his dressing-room① in the concert-hall. He could hear in the distance the murmur of excitement from the crowd as they settled themselves in their seats. He knew what they were saying to each other. Same sort of thing the newspapers had been saying for months. Botibol is a genius, greater, far greater than Beethoven or Bach② or Brahms or Mozart③ or any of them. Each new work of his is more magnificent than the last. What will the next one be like? We can hardly wait to hear it! Oh yes, he knew what they were saying. He stood up and began to pace the room. It was nearly time now. He seized a pencil from the table to use as a baton, then he switched on the radio. The announcer had just finished the preliminaries④ and suddenly there was a burst of applause which meant that the conductor was coming on to the

---

① dressing-room or dressing room: *Noun* a small room attached to a bedroom, used for dressing in and to store clothes(与卧室相连的)梳妆室

② Bach: *Noun* Johann Sebastian (1685—1750), German composer; German baroque organist and contrapuntist; composed mostly keyboard music; one of the greatest creators of Western music 约翰·塞巴斯蒂安·巴赫(1685—1750),德国作曲家

③ Mozart: Wolfgang Amadeus Mozart (1756—1791), Austrian composer 沃尔夫冈·阿马多伊斯·莫扎特(1756—1791),奥地利作曲家

④ preliminaries: business or talk, especially of a formulaic or polite nature, taking place before an action or event(尤指程序性或礼节性的)预备性事务(或对话)(e. g. She began speaking, without preliminaries. 她开始说了,没有任何客套话。)

platform. The previous concert in the afternoon had been from gramophone records, but this one was the real thing. Mr. Botibol turned around, faced the fireplace and bowed graciously from the waist. Then he turned back to the radio and lifted his baton. The clapping stopped. There was a moment's silence. Someone in the audience coughed. Mr. Botibol waited. The symphony began.

Once again, as he began to conduct, he could see clearly before him the whole orchestra and the faces of the players and even the expressions on their faces. Three of the violinists had grey hair. One of the cellists was very fat, another wore heavy brown-rimmed glasses, and there was a man in the second row playing a horn who had a twitch on one side of his face. But they were all magnificent. And so was the music. During certain impressive passages Mr. Botibol experienced a feeling of exultation① so powerful that it made him cry out for joy, and once during the Third Movement, a little shiver of ecstasy② radiated spontaneously from his solar plexus③ and moved downward over the skin of his stomach like needles. But the thunderous applause and the cheering which came at the end of the symphony was the most splendid thing of all. He turned slowly towards the fireplace and bowed. The clapping continued and he went on bowing until at last the noise died away and the announcer's voice jerked him suddenly back into the living-room. He switched off the radio and collapsed into his chair, exhausted but very happy.

---

① exultation: *Noun* the act of exulting; lively or triumphant joy, as over success or victory(尤指因成功或胜利而来的)狂喜;欢欣鼓舞

② ecstasy: *Noun* an overwhelming feeling of great happiness or joyful excitement 狂喜;极度兴奋(e. g. There was a look of ecstasy on his face. 他脸上显出狂喜的神态。)

③ solar plexus: *Noun* a complex of ganglia and radiating nerves of the sympathetic system at the pit of the stomach 腹腔神经丛

As he lay there, smiling with pleasure, wiping his wet face, panting for breath, he was already making plans for his next performance. But why not do it properly? Why not convert one of the rooms into a sort of concert-hall and have a stage and row of chairs and do the thing properly? And have a gramophone so that one could perform at any time without having to rely on the radio programme. Yes by heavens, he would do it!

The next morning Mr. Botibol arranged with a firm of decorators that the largest room in the house be converted into a miniature[①] concert-hall. There was to be a raised stage at one end and the rest of the floor-space was to be filled with rows of red plush[②] seats. "I'm going to have some little concerts here," he told the man from the firm, and the man nodded and said that would be very nice. At the same time he ordered a radio shop to install an expensive self-changing gramophone with two powerful amplifiers, one on the stage, the other at the back of the auditorium[③]. When he had done this, he went off and bought all of Beethoven's nine symphonies on gramophone records, and from a place which specialized in recorded sound effects he ordered several records of clapping and applauding by enthusiastic audiences. Finally he bought himself a conductor's baton, a slim ivory stick which lay in a case lined with blue silk.

In eight days the room was ready. Everything was perfect; the red

---

① miniature: *Adjective* [attrib.] (especially of a replica of something) of a much smaller size than normal; very small(尤指复制品)小于正常尺寸的;微小的;微型的;极小的(e. g. children dressed as miniature adults 穿得像小大人的孩子)

② plush: *Noun* [mass noun] a rich fabric of silk, cotton, wool, or a combination of these, with a long, soft nap 长毛绒

③ auditorium: *Noun* the part of a theatre, concert hall, or other public building in which the audience sits 听众席;观众席

chairs, the aisle down the centre and even a little dais[①] on the platform with a brass rail running round it for the conductor. Mr. Botibol decided to give the first concert that evening after dinner.

At seven o'clock he went up to his bedroom and changed into white tie and tails. He felt marvellous. When he looked at himself in the mirror, the sight of his own grotesque[②] shoulderless figure didn't worry him in the least. A great composer, he thought, smiling, can look as he damn well pleases. People *expect* him to look peculiar. All the same he wished he had some hair on his head. He would have liked to let it grow rather long. He went downstairs to dinner, ate his food rapidly, drank half a bottle of wine and felt better still. "Don't worry about me, Mason," he said. "I'm not mad. I'm just enjoying myself."

"Yes, sir."

"I shan't want you any more. Please see that I'm not disturbed." Mr. Botibol went from the dining-room into the miniature concert-hall. He took out the records of Beethoven's First Symphony, but before putting them on the gramophone, he placed two other records with them. The one, which was to be played first of all, before the music began, was labelled 'prolonged enthusiastic applause'. The other, which would come at the end of the symphony, was labelled 'Sustained applause, clapping, cheering, shouts of encore'. By a simple mechanical device on the record changer, the gramophone people had arranged that the sound from the first and the last records—the applause—would come only from the loudspeaker in the auditorium. The sound from all the others—

---

① dais: *Noun* a low platform for a lectern or throne 低平台（可置讲经桌或王座）

② grotesque: *Adjective* comically or repulsively ugly or distorted 丑陋（而滑稽或令人厌恶）的；奇形怪状的（e. g. grotesque facial distortions 面部扭曲成的奇形怪状）

the music—would come from the speaker hidden among the chairs of the orchestra. When he had arranged the records in the concert order, he placed them on the machine but he didn't switch on at once. Instead he turned out all the lights in the room except one small one which lit up the conductor's dais and he sat down in the chair up on the stage, closed his eyes and allowed his thoughts to wander into the usual delicious regions; the great composer, nervous, impatient, waiting to present his latest masterpiece, the audience assembling, the murmur of their excited talk, and so on. Having dreamed himself right into the part, he stood up, picked up his baton and switched on the gramophone.

A tremendous wave of clapping filled the room. Mr. Botibol walked across the stage, mounted the dais, faced the audience and bowed. In the darkness he could just make out the faint outline of the seats on either side of the centre aisle, but he couldn't see the faces of the people. They were making enough noise. What an ovation[①]! Mr. Botibol turned and faced the orchestra. The applause behind him died down. The next record dropped. The symphony began.

This time it was more thrilling than ever, and during the performance he registered any number of prickly sensations around his solar plexus. Once, when it suddenly occurred to him that the music was being broadcast all over the world, a sort of shiver ran right down the length of his spine. But by far the most exciting part was the applause which came at the end. They cheered and clapped and stamped and shouted encore[②]! encore! encore! and he turned towards the darkened auditorium

---

① ovation: *Noun* a sustained and enthusiastic show of appreciation from an audience, especially by means of applause(听众或观众的)长时间热烈鼓掌;热烈欢迎

② encore: *Exclamation* called out by an audience at the end of a concert to request such a performance 再来一个

and bowed gravely to the left and right. Then he went off the stage, but they called him back. He bowed several more times and went off again, and again they, called him back. The audience had gone mad. They simply wouldn't let him go. It was terrific. It was truly a terrific ovation.

Later, when he was resting in his chair in the other room, he was still enjoying it. He closed his eyes because he didn't want anything to break the spell①. He lay there and he felt like he was floating. It was really a most marvellous floating feeling, and when he went upstairs and undressed and got into bed, it was still with him.

The following evening he conducted Beethoven's—or rather Botibol's—Second Symphony, and they were just as mad about that one as the first. The next few nights he played one symphony a night, and at the end of nine evenings he had worked through all nine of Beethoven's symphonies. It got more exciting every time because before each concert the audience kept saying, "He can't do it again, not another masterpiece. It's not humanly possible." But he did. They were all of them equally magnificent. The last symphony, the Ninth, was especially exciting because here the composer surprised and delighted everyone by suddenly providing a choral masterpiece. He had to conduct a huge choir as well as the orchestra itself, and Benjamino Gigli② had flown over from It-

---

① spell: *Noun* a short period 短时间;一段时间(e. g. I want to get away from racing for a spell. 我想暂时从比赛中离开一下。)

② Benjamino Gigli (1890—1957): Italian operatic tenor. He made his Milan debut with the conductor Toscanini in 1918, and retained his singing talents to a considerable age. 贝尼亚米诺·吉利(1890—1957),意大利歌剧男高音,1918 年与指挥家托斯卡尼尼首次在米兰登台,到年事很高时仍然保持着演唱水平。

aly to take the tenor[①] part. Enrico Pinza[②] sang bass[③]. At the end of it the audience shouted themselves hoarse. The whole musical world was on its feet cheering, and on all sides they were saying how you never could tell what wonderful things to expect next from this amazing person.

The composing, presenting and conducting of nine great symphonies in as many days is a fair achievement for any man, and it was not astonishing that it went a little to Mr. Botibol's head[④]. He decided now that he would once again surprise his public. He would compose a mass of marvellous piano music and he himself would give the recitals[⑤]. So early the next morning he set out for the show room of the people who sold

① tenor: *Noun* a singing voice between baritone and alto or counter-tenor, the highest of the ordinary adult male range 男高音

② Enrico Pinza (1892—1957): U. S. opera singer; born in Italy. A bass, he performed with the Metropolitan Opera from 1926 until 1948 and was responsible for the return of Mozart's operas to the Met repertory. In 1949, he branched out and appeared on Broadway in South Pacific. 恩里科·平扎(1892—1957),意大利出生的美国男低音,出生于意大利罗马。1926 年在大都会登场,在那里唱了 22 年(1926—1948)。1949 年,他在百老汇登场出演音乐剧,相当受欢迎。

③ bass: *Noun* the lowest adult male singing voice 男低音

④ go to someone's head: (of success) make someone conceited(成功)使某人冲昏头脑

⑤ recital: *Noun* a musical entertainment given usually by a single performer or by a performer and one or more accompanists 表演会(e. g. a piano recital 钢琴独奏会)

Bechsteins[1] and Steinways[2]. He felt so brisk and fit that he walked all the way, and as he walked he hummed little snatches[3] of new and lovely tunes for the piano. His head was full of them. All the time they kept coming to him and once, suddenly, he had the feeling the thousands of small notes, some white, some black, were cascading down a chute[4] into his head through a hole in his head, and that his brain, his amazing musical brain, was receiving them as fast as they could come and unscrambling them and arranging them neatly in a certain order so that they made wondrous melodies. There were Nocturnes[5], there were Etudes[6] and there were Waltzes[7], and soon, he told himself, soon he would give

---

① Bechstein: *Noun* a piano made by the German piano-builder Friedrich Wilhelm Carl Bechstein (1826—1900) or by the firm which he founded in 1856 贝希斯坦三角大钢琴(由德国钢琴制作家弗里德里希·威廉·卡尔·贝希斯坦(1826—1900)制作或由其1856年所创立的公司所制作

② Steinway (1797—1871): German piano-builder, resident in the US from 1849; born Heinrich Engelhard Steinweg. He founded his famous piano-making firm in New York in 1853 亨利·斯坦威(1797—1871),德国钢琴制造家,从1849年起定居美国,出生名:海因里希·恩格尔哈德·斯坦威,于1853年在纽约建立了自己著名的钢琴制造厂

③ snatch: *Noun* a fragment of song or talk(歌曲或谈话的)片段(e. g. picking up snatches of conversation 听到了对话的只言片语)

④ chute: *Noun* a sloping channel or slide for conveying things to a lower level 斜道;滑运道

⑤ nocturne: *Noun* (Music) a short composition of a romantic nature, typically for piano(音乐)(常由钢琴演奏的)夜曲

⑥ etude: *Noun* a musical composition, usually instrumental, intended mainly for the practice of some point of technique 练习曲

⑦ waltz: *Noun* a piece of music written for or in the style of a dance in triple time performed by a couple who as a pair turn rhythmically round and round as they progress around the dance floor 华尔兹舞曲

them all to a grateful and admiring world. When he arrived at the piano-shop, he pushed the door open and walked in with an air almost of confidence. He had changed much in the last few days. Some of his nervousness had left him and he was no longer wholly preoccupied with what others thought of his appearance. "I want," he said to the salesman, "a concert grand①, but you must arrange it so that when the notes are struck, no sound is produced."

The salesman leaned forward and raised his eyebrows②.

"Could that be arranged?" Mr. Botibol asked.

"Yes, sir, I think so, if you desire it. But might I inquire what you intend to use the instrument for?"

"If you want to know, I'm going to pretend I'm Chopin③. I'm going to sit and play while a gramophone makes the music. It gives me a kick④." It came out, just like that, and Mr. Botibol didn't know what had made him say it. But it was done now and he had said it and that

---

① concert grand: *Noun* the largest size of grand piano, up to 2.75 meter long, used for concerts(音乐会上用的)平台大钢琴

② raise one's eyebrows: show surprise, disbelief, or mild disapproval 抬眉；扬眉(表示吃惊、不信或轻度反对)

③ Chopin: *Noun* Frédéric Fransois Chopin (1810—1849), Polish-born French composer and pianist; Polish name Fryderyk Franciszek Szopen. Writing almost exclusively for the piano, he composed numerous mazurkas and polonaises inspired by Polish folk music, as well as nocturnes, preludes, and two piano concertos (1829; 1830). 弗雷德里克·弗朗索瓦·肖邦(1810—1849),波兰出生的法国作曲家、钢琴家;波兰语名,弗里德里克·弗朗齐歇克·索彭。作品大多为钢琴曲,受波兰民间音乐启发,写就众多玛祖卡舞曲和波洛涅兹舞曲,作品还包括夜曲、序曲和两部钢琴协奏曲。

④ kick: *Noun* a thrill of pleasurable, often reckless excitement 刺激;快感;极大的乐趣(e.g. Rich kids turn to crime just for kicks. 有钱的孩子犯罪只是为了寻求刺激。)

was that. In a way he felt relieved, because he had proved he didn't mind telling people what he was doing. The man would probably answer what a jolly[①] good idea. Or he might not. He might say well you ought to be locked up.

"So now you know," Mr. Botibol said.

The salesman laughed out loud. "Ha ha! Ha ha ha! That's very good, sir. Very good indeed. Serves me right for asking silly questions." He stopped suddenly in the middle of the laugh and looked hard at Mr. Botibol. "Of course, sir, you probably know that we sell a simple noiseless keyboard specially for silent practising."

"I want a concert grand," Mr. Botibol said. The salesman looked at him again.

Mr. Botibol chose his piano and got out of the shop as quickly as possible. He went on to the store that sold gramophone records and there he ordered a quantity of albums containing recordings of all Chopin's Nocturnes, Etudes and Waltzes, played by Arthur[②] Rubinstein[③].

"My goodness, you *are* going to have a lovely time!"

Mr. Botibol turned and saw standing beside him at the counter a squat, short-legged girl with a face as plain as a pudding.

"Yes," he answered. "Oh yes, I am." Normally he was strict a-

---

① jolly: *Adverb* [as sub-modifier] (Brit. informal) very; extremely(非正式英国英语表达)非常;很;极(e. g. That's a jolly good idea. 那是个非常好的主意。)

② Arthur: 这个名字的一般拼法为"Artur"。

③ Artur Rubinstein (1888—1982): Polish-born American pianist. He toured extensively in Europe and the US and among his many recordings are the complete works of Chopin 阿图尔·鲁宾斯坦(1888—1982),波兰出生的美国钢琴家;他在欧洲各地和美国做广泛的巡回演出,在他为数众多的唱片中有肖邦的全部作品。

bout not speaking to females in public places, but this one had taken him by surprise.

"I love Chopin," the girl said. She was holding a slim brown paper bag with string handles containing a single record she had just bought. "I like him better than any of the others."

It was comforting to hear the voice of this girl after the way the piano salesman had laughed. Mr. Botibol wanted to talk to her but he didn't know what to say.

The girl said, "I like the Nocturnes best, they're so soothing. Which are your favourites?"

Mr. Botibol said, "Well..." The girl looked up at him and she smiled pleasantly, trying to assist with his embarrassment. It was the smile that did it. He suddenly found himself saying, "Well now, perhaps, would you, I wonder... I mean I was wondering..." She smiled again; she couldn't help it this time. "What I mean is I would be glad if you would care to come along some time and listen to these records."

"Why how nice of you." She paused, wondering whether it was all right. "You really mean it?"

"Yes, I should be glad."

She had lived long enough in the city to discover that old men, if they are dirty old men, do not bother about trying to pick up a girl as unattractive as herself. Only twice in her life had she been accosted in public and each time the man had been drunk. But this one wasn't drunk. He was nervous and he was peculiar-looking, but he wasn't drunk. Come to think of it, it was she who had started the conversation in the first place. "It would be lovely," she said. "It really would. When could I come?"

Oh dear, Mr. Botibol thought. Oh dear, oh dear, oh dear, oh dear.

"I could come tomorrow," she went on. "It's my afternoon off."

“Well, yes, certainly,” he answered slowly. “Yes, of course. I'll give you my card. Here it is.”

“A. W. Botibol,” she read aloud. “What a funny name. Mine's Darlington. Miss L. Darlington. How d'you do, Mr. Botibol.” She put out her hand for him to shake. “Oh I *am* looking forward to this! What time shall I come?”

“Any time,” he said. “Please come any time.”

“Three o'clock?”

“Yes. Three o'clock.”

“Lovely! I'll be there.”

He watched her walk out of the shop, a squat, stumpy, thick-legged little person and my word①, he thought, what have I done! He was amazed at himself. But he was not displeased. Then at once he started to worry about whether or not he should let her see his concert-hall. He worried still more when he realized that it was the only place in the house where there was a gramophone.

That evening he had no concert. Instead he sat in his chair brooding about Miss Darlington and what he should do when she arrived. The next morning they brought the piano, a fine Bechstein in dark mahogany② which was carried in minus③ its legs and later assembled on the platform in the concert hall. It was an imposing④ instrument and when Mr. Boti-

① my word! (old-fashioned) used to express surprise (表示惊奇)哎呀;咦(e.g. My word! That was quick! 天呐!真快!)

② mahogany: *Noun* [mass noun] hard reddish-brown timber from a tropical tree, used for quality furniture 红木;桃花心木

③ minus: *Preposition* lacking or without(表示否定)没有;缺少;差(e.g. The statue survived through minus a leg. 雕像幸存了下来,缺了一条腿。)

④ imposing: *Adjective* grand and impressive in appearance 雄伟的;壮丽的(e.g. an imposing 17th-century manor house 雄伟的17世纪领主宅邸)

bol opened it and pressed a note with his finger, it made no sound at all. He had originally intended to astonish the world with a recital of his first piano compositions—a set of Etudes—as soon as the piano arrived, but it was no good now. He was too worried about Miss Darlington and three o'clock. At lunch-time his trepidation① had increased and he couldn't eat. "Mason," he said, "I'm, I'm expecting a young lady to call at three o'clock."

"A what, sir?" the butler said.

"A young lady, Mason."

"Very good, sir."

"Show her into the sitting-room."

"Yes, sir."

Precisely at three he heard the bell ring. A few moments later Mason was showing her into the room. She came in, smiling, and Mr. Botibol stood up and shook her hand. "My!" she exclaimed. "What a lovely house! I didn't know I was calling on a millionaire!"

She settled her small plump body into a large armchair and Mr. Botibol sat opposite. He didn't know what to say. He felt terrible. But almost at once she began to talk and she chattered away gaily about this and that for a long time without stopping. Mostly it was about his house and the furniture and the carpets and about how nice it was of him to invite her because she didn't have such an awful lot of excitement in her life. She worked hard all day and she shared a room with two other girls in a boarding-house and he could have no idea how thrilling it was for her to be here. Gradually Mr. Botibol began to feel better. He sat there listening to the girl, rather liking her, nodding his bald head slowly up and

---

① trepidation: *Noun* [mass noun] a feeling of fear or agitation about something that may happen(对可能发生的事的)惊恐;悸惧;不安(e. g. The men set off in fear and trepidation. 这些人战战兢兢地出发了。)

down, and the more she talked, the more he liked her. She was gay and chatty, but underneath all that any fool could see that she was a lonely tired little thing. Even Mr. Botibol could see that. He could see it very clearly indeed. It was at this point that he began to play with a daring and risky idea.

"Miss Darlington," he said. "I'd like to show you something." He led her out of the room straight to the little concert-hall. "Look," he said.

She stopped just inside the door. "My goodness! Just look at that! A theatre! A real little theatre!" Then she saw the piano on the platform and the conductor's dais with the brass rail running round it. "It's for concerts!" she cried. "Do you really have concerts here! Oh, Mr. Botibol, how exciting!"

"Do you like it?"

"Oh yes!"

"Come back into the other room and I'll tell you about it." Her enthusiasm had given him confidence and he wanted to get going. "Come back and listen while I tell you something funny." And when they were seated in the sitting-room again, he began at once to tell her his story. He told the whole thing, right from the beginning, how one day, listening to a symphony, he had imagined himself to be the composer, how he had stood up and started to conduct, how he had got an immense pleasure out of it, how he had done it again with similar results and how finally he had built himself the concert-hall where already he had conducted nine symphonies. But he cheated a little bit in the telling. He said that the only real reason he did it was in order to obtain the maximum appreciation from the music. There was only one way to listen to music, he told her, only one way to make yourself listen to every single note and chord. You had to do two things at once. You had to imagine that you had composed it, and at the same time you had to imagine that the public were hearing it for the first time. "Do you think," he said, "do you really think that any outsider has ever got half as great a thrill from a symphony as the composer himself when he first heard his work played by a full orchestra?"

"No," she answered timidly. "Of course not."

"Then become the composer! Steal his music! Take it away from him and give it to yourself!" He leaned back in his chair and for the first time she saw him smile. He had only just thought of this new complex explanation of his conduct, but to him it seemed a very good one and he smiled. "Well, what do you think, Miss Darlington?"

"I must say it's very very interesting." She was polite and puzzled but she was a long way away from him now.

"Would you like to try?"

"Oh no. Please."

"I wish you would."

"I'm afraid I don't think I should be able to feel the same way as you do about it, Mr. Botibol. I don't think I have a strong enough imagination."

She could see from his eyes he was disappointed. "But I'd love to sit in the audience and listen while you do it," she added.

Then he leapt up from his chair. "I've got it!" he cried. "A piano concerto[①]! You play the piano, I conduct. You the greatest pianist, the greatest in the world. First performance of my Piano Concerto No. 1. You playing, me conducting. The greatest pianist and the greatest composer together for the first time. A tremendous occasion! The audience will go mad! There'll be queueing all night outside the hall to get in. It'll

---

① concerto: *Noun* a musical composition for a solo instrument or instruments accompanied by an orchestra, especially one conceived on a relatively large scale(尤指规模较大的)协奏曲

be broadcast around the world. It'll, it'll..." Mr. Botibol stopped. He stood behind the chair with both hands resting on the back of the chair and suddenly he looked embarrassed and a trifle sheepish①. "I'm sorry," he said, "I get worked up. You see how it is. Even the thought of another performance gets me worked up." And then plaintively②, "Would you, Miss Darlington, would you play a piano concerto with me?"

"It's like children," she said, but she smiled.

"No one will know. No one but us will know anything about it."

"All right," she said at last. "I'll do it. I think I'm daft③ but just the same I'll do it. It'll be a bit of a lark④."

"Good!" Mr. Botibol cried. "When? Tonight?"

"Oh well, I don't..."

"Yes," he said eagerly. "Please. Make it tonight. Come back and have dinner here with me and we'll give the concert afterwards." Mr. Botibol was excited again now. "We must make a few plans. Which is your favourite piano concerto, Miss Darlington?"

"Oh well, I should say Beethoven's Emperor."

"The Emperor it shall be. You will play it tonight. Come to dinner at seven. Evening dress. You must have evening dress for the concert."

---

① sheepish: *Adjective* (of a person or expression) showing embarrassment from shame or a lack of self-confidence 窘迫的;局促不安的(e. g. a sheepish grin 局促不安的咧嘴一笑)

② plaintive: *Adjective* sounding sad and mournful 伤心的;哀伤的(e. g. a plaintive cry 悲号)

③ daft: *Adjective* (informal, chiefly Brit.) silly; foolish(主要为英国英语的非正式用法)傻的;愚蠢的

④ lark: *Noun* something done for fun, especially something mischievous or daring; an amusing adventure or escapade 嬉耍;玩笑;顽皮举动(e. g. I only went along for a lark. 我跟着去只是找点乐子。)

"I've got a dancing dress but I haven't worn it for years."

"You shall wear it tonight." He paused and looked at her in silence for a moment, then quite gently, he said, "You're not worried, Miss Darlington? Perhaps you would rather not do it. I'm afraid, I'm afraid I've let myself get rather carried away. I seem to have pushed you into this. And I know how stupid it must seem to you."

That's better, she thought. That's much better. Now I know it's all right. "Oh no," she said. "I'm really looking forward to it. But you frightened me a bit, taking it all so seriously."

When she had gone, he waited for five minutes, then went out into the town to the gramophone shop and bought the records of the Emperor Concerto, conductor, Toscanini[①]—soloist, Horowitz[②]. He returned at once, told his astonished butler that there would be a guest for dinner, then went upstairs and changed into his tails.

She arrived at seven. She was wearing a long sleeveless dress made of some shiny green material and to Mr. Botibol she did not look quite so plump or quite so plain as before. He took her straight in to dinner and

---

① Artaro Toscanini (1867—1957): Italian conductor. He was musical director at La Scala in Milan (1898—1903); 1906—1908) before becoming a conductor at the Metropolitan Opera, New York (1908—1921) 阿图罗·托斯卡尼尼(1867—1957),意大利指挥家,先后担任米兰斯卡拉歌剧院指挥(1898—1903;1906—1908),纽约大都会歌剧院指挥(1908—1921)

② Vladimir Horowitz (1904—1989): Russian pianist. He first toured the US in 1928, and settled there soon afterwards. A leading international virtuoso, he was best known for his performances of Scarlatti, Liszt, Scriabin, and Prokofiev 弗拉基米尔·霍罗维茨(1904—1989),俄罗斯钢琴家,1928年首次去美国巡回演出,后便在那儿定居;作为国际一流的钢琴演奏大师,他以演奏斯卡拉蒂、李斯特、斯克里亚宾和普罗科菲耶夫的作品而闻名于世。

in spite of the silent disapproving manner in which Mason prowled① around the table, the meal went well. She protested gaily when Mr. Botibol gave her a second glass of wine, but she didn't refuse it. She chattered away almost without a stop throughout the three courses and Mr. Botibol listened and nodded and kept refilling her glass as soon as it was half empty.

Afterwards, when they were seated in the living-room, Mr. Botibol said, "Now Miss Darlington, now we begin to fall into our parts." The wine, as usual, had made him happy, and the girl, who was even less used to it than the man, was not feeling so bad either. "You, Miss Darlington, are the great pianist. What is your first name, Miss Darlington?"

"Lucille," she said. "The great pianist Lucille Darlington. I am the composer Botibol. We must talk and act and think as though we are pianist and composer."

"What is your first name, Mr. Botibol? What does the A stand for?"

"Angel," he answered.

"Not Angel."

"Yes," he said irritably.

"Angel Botibol," she murmured and she began to giggle. But she checked herself and said, "I think it's a most unusual and distinguished name."

"Are you ready, Miss Darlington?"

"Yes."

Mr. Botibol stood up and began pacing nervously up and down the

---

① prowl: *Verb* (of a person or animal) move stealthily or restlessly as or like a hunter(人或动物)(偷偷而又不安地)徘徊(e. g. David had been prowling about in the garden, waiting for her car. 戴维一直在花园里徘徊,等着她的车出现。)

room. He looked at his watch. "It's nearly time to go on," he said. "They tell me the place is packed. Not an empty seat anywhere. I always get nervous before a concert. Do you get nervous, Miss Darlington?"

"Oh yes, I do, always. Especially playing with you."

"I think they'll like it. I put everything I've got into this concerto, Miss Darlington. It nearly killed me composing it. I was ill for weeks afterwards."

"Poor you," she said.

"It's time now," he said. "The orchestra are all in their places. Come on." He led her out and down the passage, then he made her wait outside the door of the concert-hall while he nipped[①] in, arranged the lighting and switched on the gramophone. He came back and fetched her and as they walked on to the stage, the applause broke out. They both stood and bowed towards the darkened auditorium and the applause was vigorous and it went on for a long time. Then Mr. Botibol mounted the dais and Miss Darlington took her seat at the piano. The applause died down. Mr. Botibol held up his baton. The next record dropped and the Emperor Concerto began.

It was an astonishing affair. The thin stalk-like Mr. Botibol, who had no shoulders, standing on the dais in his evening clothes waving his arms about in approximate time to the music; and the plump Miss Darlington in her shiny green dress seated at the keyboard of the enormous piano thumping the silent keys with both hands for all she was worth[②].

---

① nip: *Verb* (Chiefly British Slang) to leave stealthily; sneak away; flee (often followed by away)(主要为英国俚语)悄悄离开;溜走;快走(e.g. I'll nip out and buy a newspaper. 我赶紧出门买份报纸。)

② for all someone is worth: (informal) as energetically or enthusiastically as someone can 尽力;拼命(e.g. He thumps the drums for all he's worth. 他拼命击鼓。)

She recognized the passages where the piano was meant to be silent, and on these occasions she folded her hands primly① on her lap and stared straight ahead with a dreamy and enraptured expression on her face. Watching her, Mr. Botibol thought that she was particularly wonderful in the slow solo passages of the Second Movement. She allowed her hands to drift smoothly and gently up and down the keys and she inclined her head first to one side, then to the other, and once she closed her eyes for a long time while she played. During the exciting last movement, Mr. Botibol himself lost his balance and would have fallen off the platform had he not saved himself by clutching the brass rail. But in spite of everything, the concerto moved on majestically to its mighty conclusion. Then the real clapping came. Mr. Botibol walked over and took Miss Darlington by the hand and led her to the edge of the platform, and there they stood, the two of them, bowing, and bowing, and bowing again as the clapping and the shouting of 'encore' continued. Four times they left the stage and came back, and then, the fifth time, Mr. Botibol whispered, "It's you they want. You take this one alone."

"No," she said. "It's you. Please." But he pushed her forward and she took her call, and came back and said, "Now you. They want you. Can't you hear them shouting for you?" So Mr. Botibol walked alone on to the stage, bowed gravely to right, left and centre and came off just as the clapping stopped altogether.

He led her straight back to the living-room. He was breathing fast and the sweat was pouring down all over his face. She too was a little breathless, and her cheeks were shining red.

"A tremendous performance, Miss Darlington. Allow me to congrat-

① prim: *Adjective* stiffly formal and respectable; feeling or showing disapproval of anything regarded as improper 拘谨的;古板的;一本正经的

ulate you."

"But what a concerto, Mr. Botibol! What a superb concerto!"

"You played it perfectly, Miss Darlington. You have a real feeling for my music." He was wiping the sweat from his face with a handkerchief. "And tomorrow we perform my Second Concerto."

"Tomorrow?"

"Of course. Had you forgotten, Miss Darlington? We are booked to appear together for a whole week."

"Oh... oh yes... I'm afraid I had forgotten that."

"But it's all right, isn't it?" he asked anxiously. "After hearing you tonight I could not bear to have anyone else play my music."

"I think it's all right," she said. "Yes, I think that'll be all right." She looked at the clock on the mantelpiece. "My heavens, it's late! I must go! I'll never get up in the morning to get to work!"

"To work?" Mr. Botibol said. "To work?" Then slowly, reluctantly, he forced himself back to reality. "Ah yes, to work. Of course, you have to get to work."

"I certainly do."

"Where do you work, Miss Darlington?"

"Me? Well," and now she hesitated a moment, looking at Mr. Botibol. "As a matter of fact I work at the old Academy."

"I hope it is pleasant work," he said. "What Academy is that?"

"I teach the piano."

Mr. Botibol jumped as though someone had stuck him from behind with a hatpin[①]. His mouth opened very wide.

"It's quite all right," she said, smiling. "I've always wanted to be

---

① hatpin: *Noun* a long pin, typically with an ornamental head, that holds a woman's hat in position by securing it to her hair 帽针

Horowitz. And could I, do you think, could I please be Schnabel[①] tomorrow?"

三、翻译探索

这篇小说中,达尔向读者充分展示了一个小人物内心世界的"精彩"。同时,达尔本人也充分"卖弄"了一下自己在音乐方面的造诣,这在无形之中给翻译带来了障碍。因此,音乐方面词汇的适当表达——特别是音乐家及其作品的翻译——就成为本篇小说翻译的难点,需一丝不苟,一一查实,忠实表达。

音乐"大师"

博迪博尔先生推动饭店的旋转门,进入了大大的前厅。他摘下帽子,双手将帽子举到胸前,紧张兮兮地向前迈出几步,然后停下来向周围观瞧,在吃午餐的人群里搜寻一张张脸孔。有好几个人转过身,面露轻微吃惊之色,盯着他。他听见——或者说,他认为自己听见——至少一位女士的声音:"我亲爱的,一定得看看呐,刚刚进来的

① Artur Schnabel (1882—1951): He was an Austrian classical pianist, who also composed and taught. Schnabel was known for his intellectual seriousness as a musician, avoiding pure technical bravura. Among the 20th century's most respected and most important pianists, his playing displayed a vitality, profundity and spirituality in the Austro-German classics, particularly the works of Beethoven and Schubert. His performances of these compositions have often been hailed as models of interpretative penetration, and his best-known recordings are those of the Beethoven piano sonatas. Harold C. Schonberg referred to Schnabel as "the man who invented Beethoven". 阿图尔·施纳贝尔(1882—1951),他是奥地利古典钢琴家、作曲家和教师。作为音乐家,施纳贝尔以严谨的知识分子风范著称,对单纯的技巧炫耀不屑一顾。他是20世纪最受尊敬、最重要的钢琴家之一,擅长德奥作曲家(尤其是贝多芬和舒伯特)的经典曲目。施纳贝尔的演奏展现出活力、深度和精神性,他对上述德奥作曲家的作品的演绎深度被视为范本,其最有名的录音便是贝多芬的钢琴奏鸣曲。哈罗德·C·勋伯格称他为"发明了贝多芬的人"。

是什么啊!"

最终,他瞧见了克莱门茨先生,就坐在远处角落里一张小桌子旁边。于是,他急忙奔了过去。克莱门茨看见他走来,看着他在桌子和人群中谨小慎微地穿梭而行——踮起脚尖,双手在胸前攥紧帽子,一副温和顺从、谦逊有礼的样子。当时,克莱门茨想,谁看起来要是像这位博迪博尔那样引人注目、怪模怪样的话,那该多么可怜啊!他长得像一棵芦笋,而且像得程度无以复加。他那又长又细的茎秆上根本没有生出肩膀来,只是向上生长着,逐渐长成锥形,越往上越细、越往上越细,最终在顶部细成一个点,成为一个小小的秃脑袋。他将自己紧紧包裹在一件亮闪闪的、双排扣的蓝色外衣内。这一点,出于某种奇特的原因,加强了人们关于某种蔬菜的想象,这种想象达到了一种荒谬的程度。

克莱门茨站了起来,他们相互握手。还没等再坐下来,博迪博尔先生就立刻说道:"我已经决定,是的,我已经做出决定,接受你昨晚离开我办公室时向我提出的条件。"

这些日子以来,克莱门茨代表客户,一直交涉购买一家名为"博迪博尔公司"的事宜,而这家公司唯一的拥有者就是博迪博尔先生。前一个晚上,克莱门茨第一次提出了条件。那只是一个试探性的条件——出价过低,旨在向卖家发出一个信号:买家极其感兴趣。克莱门茨想,我的天啊,这个可怜的傻瓜竟然接受了。于是,他多次庄重地点了点头,力图掩盖自己的吃惊之情,说道:"好,好。听到这个消息,我十分高兴,博迪博尔先生。"然后,他示意男侍者,说道:"两大杯马提尼。"

"不,拜托!"博迪博尔伸出双手,惊恐地表示反对。

"来吧,"克莱门茨说。"时机正好。"

"我很少喝酒,中午的时候,从来都不,都不喝酒。"

可是现在,克莱门茨轻松愉快,根本没在意他的话,硬是点了马提尼酒。酒端上来后,在对方友好说辞的劝说下以及美好心情的影响下,博迪博尔先生迫不得已,把酒喝了,庆祝刚刚完成的交易。然后,克莱门茨简单谈了谈文件的起草和签订事宜。一切安排妥当后,他又点了两杯鸡尾酒。博迪博尔先生再次表示反对，但是，这次他不是那么强烈地表示反对了。克莱门茨点完酒，转过身，友好地微笑着，看着对方。“好了，博迪博尔先生，”他说，“既然一切都办妥当，我建议，我们俩一起愉快地吃个非商务性质的午餐。你觉得怎么样呢？我请客。”

“随你便，随你便，”博迪博尔先生毫无生气地回答。他的声音很小，有些忧郁的成分，而且，一字一顿慢慢地发出声音来，就好像在对着一个小孩子做出解释。

进入餐厅后，克莱门茨点了一瓶 1912 年的拉菲特，还点了两三只圆肥的烤山鹑做下酒菜。他已经在心里计算好能得到的佣金数额，而且，感觉良好。他开始欢快地交谈，从一个话题游刃有余地转到另一个话题，希望能触及某个或许令客人感兴趣的东西。但是，一点效果都没有。博迪博尔先生似乎一只耳朵听，另一只耳朵出，还不时地将自己的小秃脑袋往这边或者那边倾斜，说道：“的确。”酒上来的时候，克莱门茨就尽量往酒这个话题上谈。

“我敢肯定，酒是相当的棒，”博迪博尔先生说，“但是，请给我倒一丁点儿，就可以了。”

克莱门茨讲了个有趣儿的故事。讲完后，博迪博尔先生严肃地打量着他，打量了好一会儿，然后说：“多么有意思啊。”自那之后，克莱门茨就什么也不说了，跟他静静地吃了起来。博迪博尔先生喝着葡萄酒，东道主探过身，往他杯子里再次倒酒的时候，他似乎并没有反对的意思。吃完饭的时候，克莱门茨私底下估算了一下，发现这位客人至少喝掉了那瓶酒四分之三的量。

“抽雪茄吗，博迪博尔先生？”

“噢，不抽，谢谢。”

“来点儿白兰地？”

“不，真的不来了。不太习惯……”克莱门茨注意到，这位男子的面颊轻微有点发红，双眼也明亮起来，变得水汪汪的。他寻思着，不妨让这位老伙计彻底喝醉，我也差不多做到这一点了。于是，他冲着男侍者吩咐道：“两份白兰地。”

白兰地端上来的时候，博迪博尔先生用疑惑的眼光看了看自己那一大杯酒，看了好一会儿才端起酒杯，向鸟儿一样快速吸了一小口，然后又将杯子放下。“克莱门茨先生，”他突然发话，“我是多么羡慕你啊。”

“羡慕我？可是，为什么？”

“克莱门茨先生，我会说明的，要是我胆子够大的话，我会说明的。”他说话的声音里带着一种紧张不安，听起来怯生生的，使得他看起来似乎为自己的每一句话都要道歉一番。

“请跟我说说吧，”克莱门茨说。

“因为从我的角度来看，你的人生似乎获得了巨大的成功。”

克莱门茨想，他要醉了，开始发出忧郁的感慨啦。忧郁的人多得是，他只是其中之一，我可忍受不了。“成功，”他说，“在我身上，我看不出任何特别成功的影子。”

“噢，不，的确不像你说的样子。克莱门茨先生，你的一生——如果我可以这么说的话，看起来就是如此愉快、如此成功。”

“我是一个很普通的人，”克莱门茨说。他正试图估计一下，对方真正醉到什么程度。

“我相信，”博迪博尔先生说，说得很慢，谨慎地一个字、一个字往外蹦。“我相信，这酒有点上头了，可是……”他暂停下来，想着该用什么词儿。“……但是，我真的想问你一个问题，就一个问题。”他将盐倒出一些，倒到桌布上，然后用一个手指尖把盐弄成了一座小山的形状。

“克莱门茨先生，”他头也不抬地说道，“一个男人活到五十二岁，一生中所做的所有事情，没有一件获得过成功，哪怕是一个小小的成功，你认为这是可能的吗？”

“我亲爱的博迪博尔先生啊，”克莱门茨笑道，“不一定什么时候，人人都能获得小小的成功，不管那成功有多么渺小。”

“噢，不对，”博迪博尔先生轻柔地说。“你错了。拿我来说吧。我不记得，我一生中获得过一个成功，不管是什么类型的成功。”

“噢，得了吧！”克莱门茨一边说，一边微笑着。“你说得不可能是真的。嗨，今天早晨，你将自己的生意卖掉，卖了十万呢。我称之为天大的成功。"

"那生意是父亲留给我的。九年前他去世时，那生意值现价的四倍。在我的领导下，其价值失去了四分之三。为此，你无法说，那是成功啊。"

克莱门茨知道他说的不假。"是的，是的，好吧，"他说。"你说的或许属实，可是，不管怎么说，每一位活着的人都获得过一定数量小小的成功。这一点，你我都清楚。或许不是什么了不起的大成功，但是，总会有些小小的成功。真该死，我的意思是说，无论如何，甚至在学校进球得分，也是一个小小的成功，小小的胜利——就当时的情况而言。或者说，跑跑步、游游泳也算。只是不记得了，仅此而已。时间长了，就忘记啦。"

"我从未进球得过分，"博迪博尔先生说。"我从未学过游泳。"

克莱门茨两只手向上扬起，发出气恼的声音。"是，是，我知道，可是，难道你看不出，难道你看不出，有成千，甚至上万件其他方面的事情，如……哦……如抓到一条大鱼，或者修理汽车的引擎，或者送一份礼物让某人高兴，或者满意地种上一排菜豆，或者小赌一把赢了……或者……呀，见鬼，很多、很多，永远列不完的啊！"

"克莱门茨先生，或许*你*能做到，但是，就我所有知道的而言，那些事情我一件都没做过。这就是我要对你说的。"

克莱门茨放下白兰地杯子，盯着坐在对面的这位显眼的、没有肩膀的人，开始重新关注他了。克莱门茨感到恼怒，但是一点也没有产生同情之心。这家伙无法激起他人的同情，就是一个傻子，一定是一个傻子——傻得不得了，傻得很绝对。克莱门茨突然间产生了一种欲望，要使劲儿让他窘迫一下。"女人呢，博迪博尔先生？"他的语气里没有因为这个问题唐突而感到歉意。

"女人？"

"是的，女人。天底下，不管是什么样的男人，哪怕是最为悲惨、最为肮脏、最为穷困潦倒的流浪汉，总有某个时候会获得某种小小的、可怜的成功，成功地跟……"

"从未有过!"博迪博尔先生突然间来了精神,大声说道。"没有,尊贵的先生,从未有过!"

克莱门茨对自己说,我要对他大打出手了,我再也无法忍受了;要不是我行事谨慎,就会跳将起来,大打出手了。"你意思是说,你不喜欢她们?"他问道。

"噢,我的天啊,不,当然不,我喜欢她们。事实上,我很喜欢她们,确实喜欢得不得了。可是,我担心……噢,天呐……我不知道该如何表达……我担心,我似乎跟她们处不好关系。从未跟她们处好过关系,从来没有。你知道的,克莱门茨先生,我*模样*怪异,这一点,我也清楚。她们盯着我看,我经常看见她们冲着我发笑。随你怎么说,我跟她们之间的距离……噢,从来不是我能够得着的。说完,他的嘴边隐隐闪现出一丝微弱的笑容,一副极其忧伤的样子。

克莱门茨受够了。他嘟嘟囔囔地说,他肯定博迪博尔先生对自己的境况夸大其词,然后,瞥了眼腕表,叫人来结账。他说,他必须得回办公室了,很抱歉。

他们在饭店外面的大街上分头走开,博迪博尔先生打了辆出租车回到住处,开了正门,进入起居室,随即打开了收音机。然后,他坐进一把大大的皮革椅子里,身体向后一靠,闭上了眼睛。准确地说,他不觉得头晕,可是,两只耳朵嗡嗡作响,思考的速度也比以往更快了。那个律师给我喝的酒太多了,他自言自语地说。我得在这儿待一会,听听音乐,期望可以睡着。睡醒了,感觉会更好一些。

收音机里播放的是一首交响乐。博迪博尔先生经常随意听听交响音乐会广播,这足以让他辨别清楚,现在播放的是贝多芬的一首曲子。但是,仰躺在椅子里听着美妙音乐的同时,一个新想法开始在他泛起醉意的大脑里扩张。这不是梦中的事情,因为他还没睡着。这个想法能够很清晰地感觉得到:我就是这首音乐的作曲家——伟大的作曲家;这是我最新创作的交响曲,这是我的首场演奏。偌大的音乐厅挤满了人:有批评家,有音乐家,还有来自全国各地的音乐爱好者,而我就站在管弦乐队上方那儿,指挥演奏。

博迪博尔先生能够看到一切。他看见自己站在指挥台上,穿着

燕尾服，系着白色的领结。前方是管弦乐队，左侧集结了一组小提琴手，前面是中提琴手，右侧是大提琴手，大提琴手的后面是木管乐器手、巴松低音管手、鼓手以及击钹手。这些乐器手神情专注，近乎顶礼膜拜般看着他指挥棒做出的所有动作。在他身后，半明半暗的偌大音乐厅里，一排排狂喜的白色面孔仰起，朝他看来。大家越听越兴奋，还要听这位世界上前所未有的伟大作曲家的另一首新曲子。于是，这首新曲子就在他们眼前庄严地舒展开来。其中有些观众攥紧了拳头，手指甲深深嵌入手掌之中，因为音乐太美了，美得让他们忍受不了。这激动人心的一幕令博迪博尔先生忘乎所以，他开始摇摆起双臂，像指挥家那样随着音乐打起了节拍。他发现，这样做乐趣多多，于是就决定站起身，面朝收音机，好给自己腾出更大的自由移动的空间。

就这样，他这样一个瘦高的、没有肩膀的男子站在屋子中间那儿，还穿着他那身紧巴巴的、双排扣的蓝色外衣。随着手臂在空中舞动，他那只光秃的小脑袋，也从一边猛地摇向另一边。他十分熟悉这首交响曲，熟悉到偶尔还能预测到其速度和音量的变化。音量很大、速度很快的时候，他就在空中使劲儿打着节拍，差点把自己弄得人仰马翻。当音乐舒缓下来、声音趋于寂静的时候，他则身体前倾，伸出双手轻轻移动，示意乐手安静下来。无论何时，他都能感觉到身后大批观众的存在，感觉他们在全神贯注、一动不动地聆听着。最后，音乐强度加大，达到高潮、收尾之际，博迪博尔先生比方才更为痴狂起来，脸似乎一下子回转到一侧，使足了劲儿意欲让前方的管弦乐队在结尾强大的和音方面使出更大、更大的劲头来。

接着，一切结束了。播音员说了些什么，可是，博迪博尔先生迅速关掉了收音机，一下子跌进椅子，大口、大口喘着气。

“喔唷！”他大声说。“我的老天在上啊，我一*直在* 干些什么呢！”一小滴、一小滴汗珠从整个脸部和额头部位渗出，沿着脖子淌进衣领。他拽出一只手帕将汗水擦去，然后在那儿躺了一会儿，喘着气，精疲力竭，但是却愉悦到了极点。

“那么，我不得不说的就是，”他依然喘着气大声说，“这*很有* 意思。我以前从不知道,我的一生中还有如此这般乐趣。天呐,*很有* 意思。真的*很有* 意思啊!几乎与此同时,他又玩笑似地想再做一次。可是,他应该再做一次吗?他应该允许自己再做一次吗?现在,毋庸置疑的是,事后想想,对整个过程他觉得有点愧疚感。很快,他就想知道,这件事情本身是否存在某种完全不道德的成分。就让他那样去做吧!想象一下,他是个天才!这样不对。他敢肯定,其他人不会这样做。要是梅森半道进来,看见他做的事,那该怎么办啊!那会是很糟糕的事情!

他伸手够来报纸,假装阅读,但是,读着,读着,他就开始偷偷摸摸地在收音节目栏里搜寻晚上的节目,手指指向这样一行字的下面:"8:30——交响音乐会,勃拉姆斯2号交响曲"。他在这行字上盯了好长时间。盯着,盯着,"勃拉姆斯"这四个字开始模糊起来,逐渐退去,一点点儿消失不见,最后被这四个大字代替:"博迪博尔"。结果,那行字变成了"博迪博尔2号交响曲",而且印刷得十分清楚。此时,他正在阅读那行字。"是的,是的,"他低声说。"第一场演出。世人都在等着听呢。大家都在问,这部作品会跟他早期作品一样伟大吗?或者,更加伟大吗?有人说服作曲家本人亲自指挥,但他很腼腆、很疲乏,几乎很少在公共场合露面。可是,在这种情况下,他已经被人说服要……"

博迪博尔在椅子里倚身向前。按响了壁炉边的那个铃。随后,管家梅森——家中除他之外唯一一个外人——出现在门口。梅森上了年纪,个头矮小,一脸严肃相。

"哦……梅森,家里有什么葡萄酒吗?"

"先生,葡萄酒吗?"

"是的,葡萄酒。"

"噢,没有,先生。十五六年以来,我们一直没买过葡萄酒。先生,你的父亲……"

"我知道,梅森,我知道。可是,拜托你买些回来。吃晚饭时,我想喝上一瓶。"

管家很是震惊。"很好,先生。买什么样的呢?

"红葡萄酒吧,梅森。挑最好的买。买一盒,告诉他们立刻送过来。"

又剩下他一个人的时候,顷刻之间,他惊骇不已,只是因为刚才做出决定的那种方式。吃晚饭时,喝瓶葡萄酒!就是那个样子!那么,对,为什么不能那样?现在,仔细那么一想,为什么不能那样呢?他是自己的主人。不管怎么说,他喝些酒是绝对必要的。看起来效果不错,的确相当不错。他需要酒,而且,酒就要买回来了。梅森怎么说,才不管呢。

那天下午余下的时间里,他都在休息。七点半,梅森宣布开饭。那瓶酒摆在桌子上,于是,他开始喝了起来。他再次往杯子里倒酒的时候,梅森看着他,但他毫不在乎。他往杯子里重新倒了三次酒。喝完后,他离开餐桌,交代说不要进来打扰,就回到了起居室。要等上十五分钟,节目才能开始。现在,除了即将开始的音乐会,他脑子里什么都没想。他仰卧在椅子里,任由思绪美滋滋地漫游到八点三十分。他是一位伟大的作曲家,正在音乐会大厅的化妆间里急切地等待着。远处,人们纷纷落座,他听到人群中有人兴奋地低声耳语。他清楚他们相互间说的是什么,类似于报纸几个月来一直报道的内容:博迪博尔是个天才,贝多芬、巴赫、勃拉姆斯、莫扎特等人有一个算一个,比他们谁都伟大,而且伟大得多。他的每一部新作品都比上一部更辉煌壮丽。下一部作品会怎样呢?我们要聆听,都等不及了!噢,是的,他清楚大家正在说的是什么。他站起身来,开始在屋子里踱步。现在,时间差不多要到了。他从桌子上抓起一支铅笔,当做指挥棒,然后打开了收音机。播音员刚刚做完铺垫性介绍,突然之间,一阵掌声响起,那就意味着,指挥正向台上走来。下午的那场音乐会是录制到唱片上播放的,但是,今晚这次是真正的现场演出。博迪博尔先生转过身来,面朝壁炉,弯下腰优雅地鞠了一躬。接着,他转身面向收音机,举起了指挥棒。掌声停止了,片刻的宁静,观众中有人咳嗽了一声。博迪博尔先生等待着,交响乐随即响起。

开始指挥时,他又一次能够清晰看到前方整个管弦乐队,以及乐手张张面孔,甚至还能看清他们脸上的表情。其中,有三名小提琴手长着灰色的头发,有一名大提琴手很胖,另一名则戴了副厚重的棕色镶边眼镜,还有就是,第二排有一名吹号的男子,其脸部一侧的肌肉抽动了一下。不管怎么说,这些乐手都很卓越,音乐也很卓越。在某些令人赞叹的段落中,博迪博尔先生情绪激昂,欢快地大叫起来。第三乐章进行期间,有一次,一丝狂喜的震颤不由自主地从他的腹腔神经丛辐射开来,如针刺一般沿着腹部皮肤表面向下传递。但是,最为辉煌的莫过于音乐结束时传来的雷鸣般掌声和欢呼声。他慢慢转向壁炉,鞠躬。掌声不断,他继续鞠躬,直到最后,声音渐渐消失为止。突然间,播音员的声音猛地将他的思绪拉回到起居室中。他关掉收音机,跌进椅子,感到精疲力竭,但却十分开心。

他仰卧在椅子里,脸上露出喜悦的微笑。他擦了擦湿漉漉的脸,上气不接下气地喘息着,同时做好了下次表演的各种打算。可是,为什么不把表演做得彻底些呢?为什么不把其中一个房间改造成音乐厅,里面造一座舞台,摆上一排椅子,彻底表演一番呢?买一台留声机,想什么时候表演,就什么时候表演,而无须依靠收音机的节目。哇,天呐,他会办到的啊!

第二天早晨,博迪博尔先生跟一家装修公司约定好,将家中最大的一个房间改造成一个小型音乐厅:一端筑起一个抬高的舞台,地面其余地方放置一排排红色的长毛绒座椅。"我要在这里举行一些小型音乐会,"他对装修公司的那名男子说。那名男子点了点头,说那样很不错。与此同时,他吩咐一家收音机商店,为他安装一部自动换唱片的留声机,配上两个扩音器,一个放在舞台上,另一个放在观众席后面。这一切做完后,他出去买回贝多芬九部交响曲所有的唱片。从一家专门从事音响录制的地方,他购买了几张热情观众拍手鼓掌的唱片。最后,他为自己买了一支指挥棒,是一根象牙做的细棍,放置在一个内衬着蓝色丝绸的盒子里。

用了八天的时间,屋子改造完成。一切都很完美:有红色的椅子,有沿着观众席中央向前伸展的通道,舞台上甚至还有一个低矮的小台子,台子周边还为指挥家设置了黄铜扶手。博迪博尔先生决定当天晚饭过后就进行第一场音乐会的表演。

七点,他上楼进了卧室,换上燕尾服和白色的领结,感觉棒极了。看着镜子中的自己,对自己那副没有肩膀奇形怪状的模样,他一点也不感到烦恼了。他微笑地想,一名伟大的作曲家喜欢自己是什么样子,就是什么样子,人们*期望*他独特怪异。不管怎么说,他希望头上长出些头发来,而且很想让头发长得长长的。他下楼吃晚饭,迅速吃完,喝了半瓶酒,仍然感觉良好。“不要为我担心,梅森,”他说。“我没有疯,我只是自享其乐。”

“好的,先生。”

“这里不再需要你了,烦请不要前来打扰。”博迪博尔先生从餐厅走进了小型音乐厅。他拿出贝多芬第一交响曲的唱片,但是在放入留声机前,他又放入另外两张,其中一张要先播放,唱片的标签上写着:“加长型热情洋溢的掌声”,另外一张要在音乐会结束时播放,标签写着:“持久型掌声、拍手声、欢呼声,以及‘再来一个’的喊叫声”。唱片制造商通过换片器上的一个简单的机械装置,让第一张和最后一张唱片——掌声部分——只通过观众席上的扩音器播放出来,而让其他唱片上的声音——音乐部分——通过乐手椅子中间隐藏的喇叭释放出来。他按照音乐会的次序将唱片排好,放置到留声机上,但并没有立即打开开关,而是将屋子里所有的灯熄灭,但照亮指挥家台子的那盏小灯除外。他在舞台椅子上坐下来,闭上双眼,任由思绪向着总是令人愉悦的领域漫游:伟大的音乐家很紧张,急切等待着要将自己最新的杰作呈献给观众;观众集结而来,兴奋地低声交谈,以及诸如此类的情景。梦想着自己进入角色后,他站起身来,拿起指挥棒,打开了留声机。

顿时,房间里充满了响亮的拍手声。博迪博尔先生穿过舞台,登上了指挥台,面朝观众鞠躬。黑暗中,他能够辨清中央过道两侧座位的轮廓,但是,他看不清观众的脸。他们掌声足够强烈,多么热烈的掌声啊！博迪博尔先生转过身,面朝管弦乐队。身后的掌声渐渐平息,下一张唱片落下,交响乐开始演奏。

这一次比以往任何一次都令人兴奋难抑。表演期间,腹腔神经丛周围多次流露出针刺般的感觉。其中有一次,他突发奇想,认为音乐会正向全世界广播，于是，一种震颤感沿着整条脊柱往下传去。但是，到目前为止，最令人兴奋的部分就是最后阶段的掌声了。大家欢呼、拍手、跺脚，同时大喊："再来一个！再来一个！再来一个！"他转身朝向黑暗中的观众席，庄重地左右鞠躬，然后走下舞台。但是，观众将他叫回，他频频鞠躬，又走开了。于是，观众又将他叫回。观众疯狂了，就是不肯让他走开。棒极了。热烈的掌声经久不息，棒极了。

后来，坐在另一个房间椅子上休息的时候，他依然沉浸其中。他闭上了双眼，不想让任何事情打断这段美妙的时光。他仰卧在那儿，如同漂浮一般——真是一种极其美妙的漂浮般感觉。上楼换下衣服、上床躺下之际，这种感觉犹在。

接下来那天晚上，他指挥演奏的是贝多芬的第二交响曲，倒不如说是博迪博尔的第二交响曲。观众对这一首就像对第一首那样疯狂。余下的几天晚上，每天晚上他指挥演奏一首。到了第九天晚上结束的时候，他将贝多芬的九首交响曲都指挥、演奏完毕。每一次都比上一次更加令人兴奋不已，因为每次演奏前，观众都说："他再也不可能做到的，不会再有杰作产生了。人能力所限，不可能做到的。"但是，他做到了，所有作品都一样的壮丽、辉煌。最后一首——第九交响曲，特别令人兴奋叫绝，因为在这首曲子里，作曲家突然加入了人声合唱部分，堪称杰作，令大家惊奇不已、赏心悦目。其间，他必须同时指挥一个大型的合唱团和一个管弦乐队。贝尼亚米诺·吉利从意大利飞过来，演唱男高音部分，而恩里科·平扎演唱的是男低音部分。最后，观众嗓子都喊哑了。整个音乐界都起立欢呼，四面八方传来他们的声音：你永远都无法预料，这个令人惊叹之人下一步会做出什么非凡之举。

这么多天以来，对于任何一个人而言，九部伟大交响乐作品的谱曲、演奏、指挥都算是一个相当大的成就了。博迪博尔的头脑被稍微冲昏了一点，这也不是什么令人惊愕的事情。现在，他决定要再让公众吃惊一次。他要谱一大批美妙的钢琴曲，自己独奏表演。因此，第二天很早的时候，他就出发了，去那些人的陈列室，那里出售贝希斯坦三角大钢琴及斯坦威钢琴。他感到轻松愉快、能力十足,一路走了过去。边走边哼唱着新谱的美妙钢琴曲片段。他满脑子全是钢琴曲,而且还源源不断地一个劲儿往脑袋里涌。有一次,突然之间,他感觉有数千只小小的音符——有些是白色的,有些是黑色的——沿着一条滑道,穿过他脑袋上的一个孔,倾泻而入。这样,他的大脑——令人惊奇的音乐大脑,就以最快的速度将它们接收下来,再把它们恢复原貌,以一定的顺序将它们整齐排列好,完美无瑕的曲调就产生了:有小夜曲,有练习曲,还有华尔兹舞曲。他对自己说,用不了多久,他很快就会将这些曲子奉献给那些对他表示感激和钦佩的世人。

到达钢琴商店,他推开门,几乎带着自信的神态走了进去。过去那几天时间里,他变了很多,身上的一些紧张不安的感觉已经消失殆尽,外表也不再是其他人想的那个样子了。"我想,"他对销售员说,"买一台举办音乐会用的平台大钢琴,但是,你必须得给它改造一下,按下琴键,却不发出声响。"

销售员倚身向前,扬起了眉毛。

"能改造吗?"博迪博尔先生问道。

"能的,先生。如果你希望如此,我想可以。但是,可否问一问,你打算用这样的乐器来干什么呢?"

"要是你想知道,我就告诉你。我要假装我是肖邦,留声机播放音乐,我坐下来演奏,这样能给我带来极大的快乐。"话就这样说出了口,连博迪博尔先生也不知道怎么会这样说。可是,话已经说出来了,而且已经说完,就是这个样子。从某个方面来说,他感到解脱,因为他已经向人证明:自己要做什么,就能说出来,却不会介意。对方或许会回答:哇,你的主意真棒啊!或者,对方不会这样回答。对方或许会说:噢,应该将你关押起来。

"所以嘛,现在你知道了,"博迪博尔先生说。

销售员大声笑了出来。"哈,哈哈!哈哈哈!很不错,先生。的确很好。问此类愚蠢的问题,算我多嘴了。"笑着,笑着,他突然半道儿停了下来,盯向博迪博尔先生,说:"当然啦,先生,你或许知道,我们这里出售一种简单的无声键盘，特地供弹奏练习时不发出声音用的。"

"我要买的是一台音乐会用的平台大钢琴，"博迪博尔先生说。销售员又一次看了看他。

博迪博尔先生选好钢琴，就尽可能快地走出来。接着，他去了家卖唱片的商店，订了大量唱片专辑，包括肖邦所有的小夜曲、练习曲、华尔兹舞曲，这些曲子都是阿图尔·鲁宾斯坦演奏的。

"我的天呐，你将会度过一段快乐的时光！"

博迪博尔先生循声转过身，看见他身旁的柜台边站着一个女孩子，女孩子又矮又胖，两只腿很短，一张脸普普通通、圆胖呆板。

"是的，"他回答。"噢，会的，我会的。"通常情况下，他严格遵循公共场合不跟女性说话的原则，但是，眼前这个女孩子令他感到措手不及。

"我酷爱肖邦，"女孩说。她拎着一只薄薄的棕色纸袋，纸袋的提手是用细绳做成的，里面就装了一张她刚买的唱片。"我喜欢肖邦，胜过喜欢其他人。"

听完钢琴销售员大笑的声音后，这个女孩的声音颇具安慰感。博迪博尔先生想跟她交谈，但又不知该说些什么好。

女孩说："我最喜欢的是他的小夜曲，听了让人心平气和。你最喜欢的是哪一曲？"

博迪博尔先生回答："这个嘛……"女孩子抬头看了看他，欢快地微笑着，意欲打消一点他的窘迫感。她的微笑起了作用。他感觉自己突然之间开口说道："这个啊，噢，或许，你可否，我纳闷……我的意思是，我想知道……"她再次微笑起来，这次微笑情不自禁。"我的意思是说，你要是愿意找个时间能到家里来，听听这些唱片，我会十分高兴的。"

"哇，你真好啊。"她暂停一下，合计着这件事儿是否合适。"你说话当真吗？"

"是的，我会很高兴的。"

她在这个城市里生活了这么长时间，结果却发现，老男人——即便是脏兮兮的老男人，对于像她这样没有魅力的女孩子，也是不屑一顾的。一生之中，只有两次有人跟她搭讪，而每一次跟她搭讪的都是喝醉酒的男子。但是，眼前这位男子没有喝醉。他紧张兮兮，模样怪异，但没有喝醉。回过头仔细想想，倒是她首先开始说话的。"太好了，"她说。"真的太好了。我什么时候能来？"

噢，天啊，博迪博尔先生想。噢，天啊，噢，天啊，噢，天啊，噢，天啊。

"明天我能来，"她继续说。"我下午休息。"

"噢，可以，当然，"他慢慢回答。"好的，当然。这是我的名片，给你。"

"A·W·博迪博尔，"她大声念道。"名字真有意思。我的名字是达林顿，称呼我L·达林顿小姐吧。你好，博迪博尔先生。"她伸出一只手要他来握。"哦，我*盼待着*这一刻！我什么时间来呢？"

"随时，"他回答。"随时欢迎。"

"三点钟？"

"好的，三点钟。"

"太好了！我会到的。"

他看着她——一个又矮又胖、又短又粗、两腿粗粗的小人——走出商店。好家伙，他想，我都做了些什么呢！他对自己的所作所为感到大吃一惊，但并没有不高兴的意思。接着，他开始担心起来：该不该让她看到自己的音乐厅呢？意识到家中唯一的一个有留声机的地方就在音乐厅时，他更加担心起来。

那天晚上，他没有进行音乐会表演，却坐在椅子上考虑着达林顿的事儿，想着她要是来了该怎么办。第二天早晨，钢琴送来了，是一架漂亮的贝希斯坦三角大钢琴，用暗色红木制作。搬进来时没有安装支腿，搬进来后在音乐厅的舞台上组装完毕。这是一件摆样子用的乐器，博迪博尔先生将其打开，用手指按下一个键，根本就没有声音发出来。钢琴一安装到位，他本来打算让世人震惊一下，先独奏自己第一组曲子，是一套练习曲，但现在看来，实现不了了。他太担心达林顿小姐了，担心三点钟的到来。午餐的时候，他的惶恐感增加了,饭也吃不下去了。“梅森,”他说,“我要,我要迎接一位年轻女士来访,三点钟。”

“一位什么,先生?”管家问。

“一位年轻女士,梅森。”

“很好,先生。”

“把她领进起居室。”

“好的,先生。”

三点整,他听到门铃响。不一会儿,梅森将她领进起居室。她微笑着走进来,博迪博尔先生站起来,握了握她的手。“天啊!”她惊叹道。“房子太漂亮了!到一位百万富翁家拜访,我竟然不知道啊!”

她那矮小、粗胖的身体落入一把大大的扶手椅里,博迪博尔先生坐到她对面,不知道该说些什么,感觉糟透了。可是,几乎与此同时,她开始说了起来,欢快地说个不停,一会儿说这儿,一会儿说那儿,说了很长时间。她说的大多数内容是关于他的房子、家具、地毯,还有他多么多么好,邀请她来做客,因为她的人生没有那么多令人兴奋的事情发生。她说,她整天辛苦地工作,跟其他两个女孩子在一所寄宿公寓合住一个房间。他无法想象,她来到这儿是多么激动和兴奋。经她这么一说,博迪博尔先生渐渐感觉好了起来。他坐在那儿,听着女孩子说话,对她有了几分喜欢。他一边听,一边上下点着自己那光秃的脑袋。她说得越多,他越喜欢她。她兴高采烈、轻松活泼,可是,抛开外表看本质,什么样的傻子都能看得出,她这个小矮人很孤独、很疲倦。这一点,就连博迪博尔先生也看出来了,而且还看得真真切切。就在这一刻,他开始有了一个顽皮的想法,这个想法很大胆、很冒险。

“达林顿小姐,”他说。“我很想让你看点儿东西。”他带着她走出房间,直接进入那间小音乐厅。“瞧,”他说。

她刚跨进门,就停住了。“我的天呐!看看呐!一座剧院!真的是一座小小的剧院啊!”接着,她看到了舞台上那架钢琴,还有四周安装了扶手的指挥台。“这是用来开音乐会啊!”她叫道。“你真的在此举行音乐会啊!噢,博迪博尔先生,多么令人兴奋啊!”

“你喜欢吗?”

“噢,喜欢!”

“再到刚才的房间来,我跟你说说这事儿。”她的热情让他信心十足,想继续进行下去。“回来,听我跟你讲讲有趣儿的事情吧。”他俩再次坐到起居室的时候,他就立刻对她讲了自己的经历。他将一切都讲了一遍,从最开始讲到某一天他听一曲交响乐的时候,他想象着自己就是那位作曲家,于是就站起来开始指挥,从指挥中他获得了极大的乐趣。他还讲到取得相似效果的另一次指挥。最后,他讲到改造这座音乐厅的全过程,并在那儿指挥了九首交响乐作品。可是,讲述过程中,有个地方没有照实说。他说,他这样做唯一的、真正的原因,就是最大程度欣赏音乐。他对她说,听音乐只有一种方式,听每一个音符及和音只有一种方式,那就是,你必须同时做两样事情:你必须得想象曲子是你谱写的,同时,你必须得想象观众是首次听你的曲子。“你是否认为,”他说,“你是否真的认为,从一首交响乐中,一个外行之人第一次听到完整的管弦乐队演奏这首曲子,会获得作曲家本人所能获得的震撼感的一半呢?”

“不会,”她怯生生地回答。“当然不会。”

“那么,就成为作曲家吧!偷走他的音乐!从他那里拿走音乐,变成你自己的!”他在椅子里将身体向后靠了靠,微笑起来。这是她第一次看见他微笑。他只是刚刚才想到,他对自己行为新做出的解释有多么复杂,但是对他而言,这种解释很棒,因而他微笑起来。“那么,达林顿小姐,你的想法呢?”

“我必须要说的是,这一切非常、非常有趣儿。”她很客气,也很迷惑。现在,毕竟她跟他之间隔着很长的距离。

“你愿意试试吗?”

“哦,不啦,谢谢。”

“我希望你试试。”

“我担心,对这事儿我想,我不能达到跟你相同的感受,博迪博尔先生。我想,我的想象力不够强大。”

从他的眼神中,她看得出来,他很失望。“可是,你演奏的时候,我喜欢坐在观众席上聆听，”她补充道。

紧接着，他从椅子上跳了起来。“我知道啦！”他叫道。“来首钢琴协奏曲！你弹钢琴，我指挥。你，最伟大的钢琴家——世界上最伟大的。我的第一钢琴协奏曲的首场演出，你弹，我指挥。最伟大的钢琴家与最伟大的作曲家第一次合作。多么绝妙的场景！观众会疯狂起来！音乐厅外面，整个晚上会排起长队，等待入场。现场会向全世界直播。这会，这会……”博迪博尔先生停了下来。他站在椅子后面，双手放在椅背上，整个人突然间感到尴尬起来，有点不好意思了。“我有些激动，”他说，“很抱歉。你明白了整个过程。即使是想到要进行另一场表演，我就会激动不已。”接着，他低沉下来，说道：“你愿意吗，达林顿小姐。你愿意跟我一起演奏钢琴协奏曲吗？”

“像孩子一样，”她说，但却微笑起来。

“没人会知道。关于这件事儿，没人会知道，就我俩知道。”

“好吧，”她最终说。“我愿意做。我想呢，我有点傻气，但不管怎么说，我会做的。这事儿有点顽皮的味道。”

“好！”博迪博尔先生叫道。“什么时间？今晚？”

“哦，那么，我认为我不……”

“是的，”他急切地说。“拜托，就今晚吧。回这儿来，跟我一起吃晚饭，然后，我们一起开音乐会。”现在，博迪博尔先生又激动起来。“我们必须得做出几项计划出来。达林顿小姐，你最喜欢的钢琴协奏曲是哪一首？”

“哦，那么，我应该说，是贝多芬的《皇帝协奏曲》。”

“那就《皇帝协奏曲》啦。今晚你演奏。七点来吃晚饭，穿上晚礼服，音乐会必须得穿晚礼服。”

“我有件舞蹈服，但是，多年没有穿过了。”

“那你今晚应该穿一穿，”他暂停下来，默不作声看了她一会儿，然后，他用相当轻柔的声音说道：“达林顿小姐，你不是在担心吧？或许，你更愿意不去做这件事情。我想呢，我想我放纵自己、忘乎所以了。我似乎将你硬推到这一步。我知道，在你看来，这一切有多么愚蠢。”

她想，他那样说，感觉好多了。那样说，要好得多；现在，我知道，一切都很妥当。“噢，不，”她说。“我真的期待做这件事儿，可是，你那么一本正经地看待这件事情，让我有点恐惧。”

她走后，他等了五分钟。然后，他出门进城，去那家唱片店，买了《皇帝协奏曲》的唱片——指挥：托斯卡尼尼，钢琴独奏：霍罗维茨。买完后立刻返回，对大吃一惊的管家说，今晚有一位客人要来吃饭。随即上楼，换上了燕尾服。

客人七点到来。她穿着一件长长的无袖连衣裙，是用某种绿色的发光材料做成的。在博迪博尔看来，她看起来不再那么圆胖，也不像先前那样平淡无奇了。他直接带她进屋吃晚饭。晚饭吃得很好，尽管在吃饭期间默不作声的梅森绕着餐桌忙来忙去，时而流露出不以为然的神情。博迪博尔先生给她倒第二杯酒的时候，她面露喜色加以反对，却没有拒绝。在吃晚餐的三道菜过程中，她谈这说那，几乎没有停歇过。博迪博尔先生则一边听着，一边点着头，还不断往她喝完一半的杯子里倒酒。

晚餐过后，他俩来到起居室坐下。博迪博尔先生说：“现在，达林顿小姐，现在我们开始进入各自的角色。”跟往常一样，葡萄酒令他开心。尽管跟他比起来，女孩子不太习惯喝酒，但她的感觉也不是很糟糕。“你——达林顿小姐，就是伟大的钢琴家。达林顿小姐，你的名字叫什么呢？”

“露西尔，”她回答。

“伟大的钢琴演奏家露西尔·达林顿，我是作曲家博迪博尔。我们说话、做事、思考一定要像钢琴家和作曲家那样。”

“博迪博尔先生，你的名字叫什么呢？你名字的首字母‘A’代表什么呢？”

“安杰尔——‘使者’的意思，”他回答。

“不会是安杰尔吧！”

“是的，”他说，有点急躁、恼怒。

“安杰尔·博迪博尔，”她小声说完，就开始咯咯笑了起来，但却克制住自己，说道：“我想，这是一个非同寻常的、声望卓著的名字。”

"准备好了吗,达林顿小姐?"

"是的。"

博迪博尔先生站了起来,开始在屋子里紧张不安地来回踱步。他看了看腕表。"几乎到上台的时间了,"他说。"他们告诉我说,这地方挤满了人,一个空座都没有了。音乐会开始前,我总是紧张不安。你也是吗,达林顿小姐?"

"噢,是的,我也总是这样,特别是跟你一起演奏。"

"我想他们会喜欢的。达林顿小姐,我将一切都投入到这首协奏曲上了。谱写这首曲子几乎要了我的命。写完后,我病倒了,病了好几个星期。"

"你真可怜"她说。

"现在,时间到了,"他说。"管弦乐队成员都已就位,快啊。"他带着她走出屋子,沿着过道走过去,让她在音乐厅门外等候,他自己则快速走进去,安排好灯光,打开了留声机。妥当之后,他出来,接她一起走了进去。他俩走上舞台之际,掌声响起。他们都站在那儿,向黑暗中的观众席鞠躬。于是,掌声热烈起来,持续了很长时间。接着,博迪博尔先生登上了指挥台,达林顿小姐在钢琴前坐好。掌声逐渐平息下来,博迪博尔举起了指挥棒。第二张唱片落下,《皇帝协奏曲》开始播放。

这个场景令人印象深刻。博迪博尔先生没有肩膀,身体如茎秆般瘦弱,穿着晚礼服,站在指挥台上,上下左右挥舞着手臂,随着音乐大致接近地打着节拍。圆胖的达林顿小姐穿着亮闪闪的绿色连衣裙坐在一只巨大钢琴前靠近琴键的地方,使出全身力气,双手猛力弹奏着并不发出声响的琴键。她意识到有些段落不需要弹奏钢琴,于是,她就双手合拢、十指交叉握住,拘谨地放到大腿部位,眼睛盯着正前方,脸上露出梦幻般喜滋滋的表情。博迪博尔先生看着她,心里想:第二乐章的慢板独奏段落,她表现相当出色。她任由自己的双手流畅地滑移,轻柔地在键盘上下移动,头先偏向一侧,再偏向另一侧。有一次弹奏时,她闭上了双眼,闭了很长时间。在表演令人兴奋的最后一个乐章期间,博迪博尔先生自己失去了平衡,要不是当时他紧紧抓住了黄铜扶手自救的话,就会从指挥台上跌落下去了。但是,无论如何,协奏曲还是雄伟地进行下去,进行到了强劲的尾声。接着,传来强烈的鼓掌声。博迪博尔先生走过去,抓起达林顿小姐的一只手,领着她走到舞台边缘。他俩站在那儿,鞠躬,再鞠躬。掌声持续不断,"再来一个"的喊声此起彼伏,他俩又鞠了一躬。他俩曾四次离开舞台,每次又都返回。到了第五次的时候,博迪博尔小声说:"他们要的是你。这一次,你单独回去谢幕。""不是的,"她说。"他们要的是你,请吧。"可是,他向前推她,她响应了观众的召唤。回来后,她说:"现在轮到你啦,他们喊你。难道你没有听见他们喊着要你吗?"因此,博迪博尔单独走上舞台,严肃地向左、向右、向中间鞠躬。就在掌声完全停息之际,他走了下来。

他领着她直接回到了起居室。他呼吸急促,汗水顺着他的脸流淌。她也有点上气不接下气,两只脸颊泛着红光。

"一次非凡的表演,达林顿小姐。请允许我向你表示祝贺。"

"可是,博迪博尔先生,协奏曲多棒啊! 多么一流的协奏曲啊!"

"你演奏得很完美,达林顿小姐。对于我的音乐,你颇有真情实感。"他用一只手绢擦拭着脸上的汗水。"明天,我们表演我的第二首协奏曲。"

"明天?"

"当然啦。难道你忘记了吗,达林顿小姐? 我们的票都预定出去了。整整一周时间,我们要联袂出演。"

"哦……哦,是的……我想,我恐怕是忘记了。"

"可是,没有什么问题,是吧?"他急切地问道。"今晚听了你的演奏后,要是再让他人演奏我的音乐,我就无法忍受。"

"我想,没有什么问题,"她说。"是的,我想,应该没有什么问题。"她看了看壁炉架上的时钟。"我的天呐,太晚了! 我必须得走啦! 照这样,我早晨永远都不会及时起来去工作了!"

"去工作?"博迪博尔问。"去工作?"随后,他很不情愿地强迫自己慢慢地回到了现实。"啊,是的,去工作。当然,你必须得去工作。"

"我当然得工作。"

“你在哪儿工作呢，达林顿小姐？”

“我？哦。”现在，她看了看博迪博尔先生，犹豫了一会儿。“事实上，我在那座老学院工作。”

“我希望工作会令你愉快，”他说。“什么工作呢？”

“我教人弹钢琴。”

博迪博尔先生一下子跳了起来，好似有人用一根帽针从背后戳了他一下。他的嘴张得大大的。

“一点关系都没有，”她微笑着说。“我总是想成为霍罗维茨。你认为，我可否，明天我可否成为施纳贝尔呢？”

第二节 《品酒“大师”》*Taste*

罗尔德·达尔的《品酒“大师”》（*Taste*）首次发表在美国的一本文学性刊物《纽约客》（*The New Yorker*）杂志1951年12月号上，也发表在知名成人杂志《花花公子》（*Playboy*）杂志1956年4月号上。后来，这篇小说收录到《罗尔德·达尔短篇故事集锦》（*The Collected Short Stories of Roald Dahl*）、《罗尔德·达尔小说精品集》（*The Best of Roald Dahl*）、《完全出人意料故事集》（*Completely Unexpected Tales*）、《五部畅销书集》（*5 Bestsellers*）、《如你之人》（*Someone like You*）、《罗尔德·达尔选集》（*The Roald Dahl Omnibus*）以及《<卖伞男子>及其他故事集》（*The Umbrella Man and Other Stories*）等书中，可见这部小说的受欢迎程度。

另外，这部小说还被改编成电视系列剧中的一集——1980年4月12日播映的《出乎意料的故事集》（*Tales of the Unexpected*）第二部中的第7集（Episode 2.7），还被改变成歌剧，题为《味觉之疑》（*A Question of Taste*）。

一、原作导读

这个故事发生在股票经纪人迈克·斯科菲尔德先生位于伦敦的

家中。这篇小说是以第一人称"我"(姓名未知)的视角展开的,但叙述者"我"是"隐身"的——地位是无足轻重的,起到了"纽带"或者"桥梁"的作用,可以看成作家罗尔德·达尔本人的化身。主要涉及以下几个人物:迈克、迈克的妻子、迈克的女儿、"我"以及"我"的妻子,还有理查德·普拉特以及迈克家的女仆。

男主人迈克·斯科菲尔德先生邀请几位客人到家中共进晚餐。受邀的几个人中,有一位叫理查德·普拉特的先生,是位出了名美食家,喜欢炫耀自己对美酒和佳肴方面的渊博知识。但是,在"我"看来,他不是一个令人感到愉悦的人。前两次到斯科菲尔德先生家聚餐饮酒时,他都受邀而来,但是每次都跟男主人赌上一把,赌的内容都是一样的,都令人感到奇怪:斯科菲尔德先生赌普拉特辨别不出当晚拿来招待客人的是什么样的葡萄酒。但是,普拉特先生每次都能辨别出来,每次都赢了。

正因如此,今晚这次宴会,斯科菲尔德先生做足了准备,想最终赢这位美食家一把。开胃菜吃完、开胃酒喝完后,斯科菲尔德先生宣布说,该喝晚宴主打红酒了,说完就要取酒去。这时,"我"禁不住问道:

"你取酒去吗,迈克?"我问道。"到哪儿取呢?"

"到我书房取,塞子已经拔出来了——酒正在吸收新鲜空气呢。"

"为什么放书房啊?"

"当然是要酒达到室温。在那儿放了二十四小时了。"

"可是,为什么非放到书房不可?"

"书房是家里最好的地方。上次聚会时,理查德帮我选的地方。"

"You go and fetch it, Mike?" I said. "Where is it?"

"In my study, with the cork out—breathing."

"Why the study?"

"Acquiring room temperature, of course. It's been there twenty-four hours."

"But why the study?"

"It's the best place in the house. Richard helped me choose it last time he was here."

原来,斯科菲尔德先生从法国一家规模很小的酒庄买了一种十分罕见红葡萄酒,并在宴会上大肆宣扬,说普拉特先生永远都不会辨别不出这是一种什么样的葡萄酒,包括其品牌、年份和产地。像前两次一样,他要跟普拉特先生赌一赌。在这之前,心不在焉的普拉特先生一直跟男主人斯科菲尔德先生那芳龄十八的漂亮女儿路易丝小姐谈得火热。看到男主人拿出那瓶酒,普拉特先生随口就应承下来,说可以赌一赌,但却出人意料地要抬高赌注的价码——拿出自己的两处房子做赌注,赌赢了,让斯科菲尔德先生把女儿嫁给他。斯科菲尔德太太和女儿路易丝当时都提出了反对意见,但是斯科菲尔德先生硬是设法说服了母女俩,因为他认为普拉特先生这次毫无胜算。母女俩勉强答应下来。

接下来,普拉特先生开始像模像样、架势十足地品尝起葡萄酒来了。经过一系列的推敲和判断,他逐渐缩小了那瓶葡萄酒的产地范围,并最终说对了产地的名字,令越来越坐卧不安的斯科菲尔德先生惊恐不已,意欲赖账。见此情景,普拉特先生恼怒起来,随时准备动粗了。就在此时,斯科菲尔德先生家中那位一直默默无闻、忙来忙去的女仆站到理查德·普拉特身旁,伸出手来,手拿着一副眼镜,递给了普拉特先生。

"这幅眼镜,您落在斯科菲尔德先生的书房里了,"她说。这话说得很不自然,彬彬有礼的口气是故意装出来的。"先生,那是在吃饭前,你自己恰巧溜达着走进书房,眼镜就落在那个绿色的文件柜顶上了。"

"You left them in Mr. Schofield's study," she said. Her voice was unnaturally, deliberately polite. "On top of the green filing cabinet in his study, sir, when you happened to go in there by yourself before dinner."

二、原作释读

在这部小说中，罗尔德·达尔提到了很多葡萄酒方面的术语，有些还是法语词，增加了阅读理解的难度。另外，还要注意通过阅读作家对人物动作、神态的刻画，来理解人物的性格特点。

Taste①

There were six of us to dinner that night at Mike Schofield's house in London: Mike and his wife and daughter, and my wife and I, and a man called Richard Pratt.

Richard Pratt was a famous gourmet②. He was president of a small society known as the Epicures③, and each month he circulated privately to its members a pamphlet on food and wines. He organized dinners where sumptuous④ dishes and rare wines were served. He refused to smoke for fear of harming his palate⑤, and when discussing a wine, he

---

① 本部小说原文出自"DAHL, R. *The Best of Roald Dahl*. London: Penguin Books Ltd., 2006"。

② gourmet: *Noun* a person devoted to refined sensuous enjoyment (especially good food and drink) 讲究吃喝的人；美食家

③ epicure: *Noun* a person devoted to refined sensuous enjoyment (especially good food and drink) 讲究饮食的人

本篇小说中，这个词首字母大写，指的是一个美食家协会，"翻译探索"中采取近似音译的方法来处理。

④ sumptuous: *Adjective* rich and superior in quality 豪华的；奢侈的(e. g. The banquet was a sumptuous and luxurious meal. 这宴会是一次豪华、奢侈的聚餐。)

⑤ palate: *Noun* the upper surface of the mouth that separates the oral and nasal cavities 味觉；品味的能力

had a curious, rather droll[①] habit of referring to it as though it were a living being. "A prudent wine," he would say, "rather diffident[②] and evasive[③], but quite prudent." Or, "A good-humoured wine, benevolent[④] and cheerful—slightly obscene[⑤], perhaps, but none the less good-humoured."

I had been to dinner at Mike's twice before when Richard Pratt was there, and on each occasion Mike and his wife had gone out of their way to produce a special meal for the famous gourmet. And this one, clearly, was to be no exception. The moment we entered the dining-room, I could see that the table was laid for a feast. The tall candles, the yellow roses, the quantity of shining silver, the three wineglasses to each person, and above all, the faint scent of roasting meat from the kitchen brought the first warm oozings[⑥] of saliva[⑦] to my mouth.

As we sat down, I remembered that on both Richard Pratt's previous visits Mike had played a little betting game with him over the claret[⑧],

---

① droll: *Adjective* comical in an odd or whimsical manner 离奇古怪的;滑稽的(e. g. His unique brand of droll self-mockery. 他别具一格的奇趣自嘲。)

② diffident: *Adjective* lacking self-confidence; showing modest reserve 缺乏自信的;露出怯态的(e. g He has a politely diffident manner. 他的态度是客气中带有羞怯。)

③ evasive: *Adjective* directed towards avoidance or escape 躲避的;逃避的;规避的(e. g. They decided to take evasive action. 他们决定采取回避行动。)

④ benevolent: *Adjective* doing or producing good 好心肠的;与人为善的

⑤ obscene: *Adjective* designed to incite to indecency or lust 淫秽的;下流的;猥亵的

⑥ oozing: *Noun* the process of seeping 漏出;渗透

⑦ saliva: *Noun* a clear liquid secreted into the mouth by the salivary glands and mucous glands of the mouth 唾液;口水

⑧ claret: *Noun* a dark purplish red 红葡萄酒

challenging him to name its breed and its vintage[1]. Pratt had replied that that should not be too difficult provided it was one of the great years. Mike had then bet him a case of the wine in question that he could not do it. Pratt had accepted, and had won both times. Tonight I felt sure that the little game would be played over again, for Mike was quite willing to lose the bet in order to prove that his wine was good enough to be recognized, and Pratt, for his part, seemed to take a grave, restrained pleasure in displaying his knowledge.

The meal began with a plate of whitebait[2], fried very crisp in butter, and to go with it there was a Moselle[3]. Mike got up and poured the wine himself, and when he sat down again, I could see that he was watching Richard Pratt. He had set the bottle in front of me so that I could read the label. It said, "Geierslay Ohligsberg, 1945". He leaned over and whispered to me that Geierslay was a tiny village in the Moselle, almost unknown outside Germany. He said that this wine we were drinking was something unusual, that the output of the vineyard was so small that it was almost impossible for a stranger to get any of it. He had visited Geierslay personally the previous summer in order to obtain the few bottles that they had finally allowed him to have.

"I doubt whether anyone else in the country has any of it at the moment," he said. I saw him glance again at Richard Pratt. "Great thing about Moselle," he continued, raising his voice, "it's the perfect wine to serve before a claret. A lot of people serve a Rhine wine instead, but

---

① vintage: *Noun* the year or place in which wine, especially wine of high quality, was produced(尤指优质葡萄酒)生产年份;生产地区

② whitebait: *Noun* [mass noun] the small silvery-white young of herrings, sprats, and similar marine fish, eaten in numbers as food 银鱼;小鲱鱼

③ Moselle: *Noun* [mass noun] a light medium-dry white wine produced in the valley of the River Moselle 摩泽尔白葡萄酒

that's because they don't know any better. A Rhine[1] wine will kill a delicate claret, you know that? It's barbaric to serve a Rhine before a claret. But a Moselle—ah! —a Moselle is exactly right."

Mike Schofield was an amiable, middle-aged man, but he was a stockbroker. To be precise, he was a jobber[2] in the stock market, and like a number of his kind, he seemed to be somewhat embarrassed, almost ashamed to find that he had made so much money with so slight a talent. In his heart he knew that he was not really much more than a book*m*aker[3]—an unctuous[4], infinitely respectable, secretly unscrupulous[5] book*m*aker—and he knew that his friends knew it, too. So he was seeking now to become a man of culture, to cultivate a literary and aesthetic taste, to collect paintings, music, books, and all the rest of it.

---

① Rhine: *Noun* a river in western Europe which rises in the Swiss Alps and flows for 1,320 *km* (820 miles) to the North Sea, forming the German-Swiss border, before flowing through Germany and the Netherlands. German name Rhein; French name Rhin 莱茵河(欧洲西部河流,源于瑞士阿尔卑斯山,全长1,320公里,即820英里,形成德国和瑞士两国边界,然后流经德国和荷兰注入北海。德语名"Rhein",法语名"Rhin"。)

本文中,这个词指的是"Rhine wine"(莱茵白葡萄酒)。

② jobber: *Noun* (historical) (in the UK) a principal or wholesaler who dealt only on the Stock Exchange with brokers, not directly with the public(历史上的用法)(英国)股票自营商

③ book*m*aker: *Noun* a gambler who accepts and pays off bets (especially on horse races)(赛马)赌注登记经纪人

④ unctuous: *Adjective* (of a person) excessively or ingratiatingly flattering; oily(人)甜言蜜语的;油腔滑调的;过度谄媚的(e. g. He seemed anxious to please but not in an unctuous way. 他似乎很想让人高兴,但并不是讨好巴结。)

⑤ unscrupulous: *Adjective* having or showing no moral principles; not honest or fair 无道理原则的;无耻的;肆无忌惮的(e. g. It was unscrupulous of their lawyer to withhold evidence. 他们的律师隐瞒证据是不道德的。)

His little sermon about Rhine wine and Moselle was a part of this thing, this culture that he sought.

"A charming little wine, don't you think?" he said. He was still watching Richard Pratt. I could see him give a rapid furtive① glance down the table each time he dropped his head to take a mouthful of whitebait. I could almost feel him waiting for the moment when Pratt would take his first sip, and look up from his glass with a smile of pleasure, of astonishment, perhaps even of wonder, and then there would be a discussion and Mike would tell him about the village of Geierslay.

But Richard Pratt did not taste his wine. He was completely engrossed in conversation with Mike's eighteen-year-old daughter, Louise. He was half turned towards her, smiling at her, telling her, so far as I could gather②, some story about a chef in a Paris restaurant. As he spoke, he leaned closer and closer to her, seeming in his eagerness almost to impinge upon③ her, and the poor girl leaned as far as she could away from him nodding politely, rather desperately, and looking not at his face but at the topmost button of his dinner jacket.

We finished our fish, and the maid came round removing the plates. When she came to Pratt, she saw that he had not yet touched his food, so

---

① furtive: *Adjective* attempting to avoid notice or attention, typically because of guilt or a belief that discovery would lead to trouble; secretive 偷偷摸摸的;鬼鬼祟祟的;秘密的;遮遮掩掩的(e. g. They spent a furtive day together. 他们在一起偷偷摸摸地过了一天。)

② gather: *Verb* [with obj.] infer; understand 推断;猜测;以为(e. g. You're still with Anthea, I gather. 我猜,你还是和安西娅在一起。)

③ impinge on sb/sth (also impinge upon sb/sth—more formal): to have a strong effect on sb/sth, especially a bad one 对……有重大(或严重)影响(e. g. She didn't allow her personal problems to impinge on her work. 她没有让个人问题妨碍自己工作。)

she hesitated, and Pratt noticed her. He waved her away, broke off his conversation, and quickly began to eat, popping the little crisp brown fish quickly into his mouth with rapid jabbing movements of his fork. Then, when he had finished, he reached for his glass, and in two short swallows he tipped the wine down his throat and turned immediately to resume his conversation with Louise Schofield.

Mike saw it all. I was conscious of him sitting there, very still, containing himself, looking at his guest. His round jovial① face seemed to loosen slightly and to sag②, but he contained himself and was still and said nothing.

Soon the maid came forward with the second course. This was a large roast beef. She placed it on the table in front of Mike who stood up and carved it, cutting the slices very thin, laying them gently on the plates for the maid to take around. When he had served everyone, including himself, he put down the carving knife and leaned forward with both hands on the edge of the table.

"Now," he said, speaking to all of us but looking at Richard Pratt. "Now for the claret. I must go and fetch the claret, if you'll excuse me."

"You go and fetch it, Mike?" I said. "Where is it?"

"In my study, with the cork out—breathing."

"Why the study?"

"Acquiring room temperature, of course. It's been there twenty-four hours."

"But why the study?"

"It's the best place in the house. Richard helped me choose it last time he was here."

---

① jovial: *Adjective* cheerful and friendly 友善快活的;愉快的

② sag: *Verb* droop, sink, or settle from or as if from pressure or loss of tautness 向下凹或中间下陷

At the sound of his name, Pratt looked round.

"That's right, isn't it?" Mike said.

"Yes," Pratt answered, nodding gravely. "That's right."

"On top of the green filing cabinet[①] in my study," Mike said. "That's the place we chose. A good draught-free spot in a room with an even temperature. Excuse me now, will you, while I fetch it."

The thought of another wine to play with had restored his humour, and he hurried out of the door, to return a minute later more slowly, walking softly, holding in both hands a wine basket in which a dark bottle lay. The label was out of sight, facing downwards. "Now!" he cried as he came towards the table. "What about this one, Richard? You'll never name this one!"

Richard Pratt turned slowly and looked up at Mike, then his eyes travelled down to the bottle nestling in its small wicker[②] basket, and he raised his eyebrows; a slight supercilious[③] arching of the brows, and with it a pushing outward of the wet lower lip, suddenly imperious[④] and ugly.

"You'll never get it," Mike said. "Not in a hundred years."

---

① filing cabinet: *Noun* a large piece of office furniture, typically made of metal, with deep drawers for storing documents 文件柜

② wicker: *Noun* slender flexible branches or twigs (especially of willow or some canes); used for wickerwork(编结篮、筐或家具用的)树枝或藤条

③ supercilious: *Adjective* behaving or looking as though one thinks one is superior to others 傲慢的;目空一切的(e.g. a supercilious lady's maid 一位傲慢贵妇人的女仆。)

④ imperious: *Adjective* assuming power or authority without justification; arrogant and domineering 专横的;傲慢的;盛气凌人的(e.g. his imperious demands 他专横的要求。)

"A claret?" Richard Pratt asked, condescending[①].

"Of course."

"I assume, then, that it's from one of the smaller vineyards?"

"Maybe it is, Richard. And then again, maybe it isn't."

"But it's a good year? One of the great years?"

"Yes, I guarantee that."

"Then it shouldn't be too difficult," Richard Pratt said, drawling his words, looking exceedingly bored. Except that, to me, there was something strange about his drawling[②] and his boredom: between the eyes a shadow of something evil, and in his bearing an intentness that gave me a faint sense of uneasiness as I watched him.

"This one is really rather difficult," Mike said. "I won't force you to bet on this one."

"Indeed. And why not?" Again the slow arching of the brows, the cool, intent look.

"Because it's difficult."

"That's not very complimentary to me, you know."

"My dear man," Mike said, "I'll bet you with pleasure, if that's what you wish."

"It shouldn't be too hard to name it."

"You mean you want to bet?"

"I'm perfectly willing to bet," Richard Pratt said.

"All right, then, we'll have the usual. A case of the wine itself."

---

① condescending: *Adjective* acting in a way that betrays a feeling of patronizing superiority towards someone 有优越感的(e. g. She thought the teachers were arrogant and condescending. 她认为教师们傲慢自大且居高临下。)

② drawl: *Verb* [no obj.] speak in a slow, lazy way with prolonged vowel sounds 慢吞吞说话;拉长调子讲话(e. g. 'Suits me fine,' he drawled. "很适合我,"他慢吞吞地说。)

"You don't think I'll be able to name it, do you?"

"As a matter of fact, and with all due respect, I don't," Mike said. He was making some effort to remain polite, but Pratt was not bothering overmuch to conceal his contempt for the whole proceeding. And yet, curiously, his next question seemed to betray a certain interest.

"You like to increase the bet?"

"No, Richard. A case is plenty."

"Would you like to bet fifty cases?"

"That would be silly."

Mike stood very still behind his chair at the head of the table, carefully holding the bottle in its ridiculous wicker basket. There was a trace of whiteness around his nostrils now, and his mouth was shut very tight.

Pratt was lolling[①] back in his chair, looking up at him, the eyebrows raised, the eyes half closed, a little smile touching the corners of his lips. And again I saw, or thought I saw, something distinctly disturbing about the man's face, that shadow of intentness between the eyes, and in the eyes themselves, right in their centres where it was black, a small slow spark of shrewdness, hiding.

"So you don't want to increase the bet?"

"As far as I'm concerned, old man, I don't give a damn," Mike said. "I'll bet you anything you like."

The three women and I sat quietly, watching the two men. Mike's wife was becoming annoyed; her mouth had gone sour and I felt that at any moment she was going to interrupt. Our roast beef lay before us on our plates, slowly steaming.

"So you'll bet me anything I like?"

---

① loll: *Verb* [no obj., with adverbial] sit, lie, or stand in a lazy, relaxed way 懒洋洋地坐(或躺、站)(e.g. The two girls lolled in their chairs. 两个女孩懒洋洋地坐在椅子上。)

"That's what I told you. I'll bet you anything you damn well please, if you want to make an issue out of it."

"Even ten thousand pounds?"

"Certainly I will, if that's the way you want it." Mike was more confident now. He knew quite well that he could call any sum Pratt cared to mention.

"So you say I can name the bet?" Pratt asked again.

"That's what I said."

There was a pause while Pratt looked slowly around the table, first at me, then at the three women, each in turn. He appeared to be reminding us that we were witness to the offer.

"Mike!" Mrs. Schofield said. "Mike, why don't we stop this nonsense and eat our food. It's getting cold."

"But it isn't nonsense," Pratt told her evenly. "We're making a little bet."

I noticed the maid standing in the background holding a dish of vegetables, wondering whether to come forward with them or not.

"All right then," Pratt said. "I'll tell you what I want you to bet."

"Come on, then," Mike said, rather reckless. "I don't give a damn what it is—you're on."

Pratt nodded, and again the little smile moved the corners of his lips, and then, quite slowly, looking at Mike all the time, he said, "I want you to bet me the hand of your daughter in marriage."

Louise Schofield gave a jump. "Hey!" she cried. "No! That's not funny! Look here, Daddy, that's not funny at all."

"No, dear," her mother said. "They're only joking."

"I'm not joking," Richard Pratt said.

"It's ridiculous," Mike said. He was off balance again now.

"You said you'd bet anything I liked."

"I meant money."

“You didn’t *say* money.”

“That’s what I meant.”

“Then it’s a pity you didn’t say it. But anyway, if you wish to go back on your offer, that’s quite all right with me.”

“It’s not a question of going back on my offer, old man. It’s a no-bet any way, because you can’t match the stake. You yourself don’t happen to have a daughter to put up against mine in case you lose. And if you had, I wouldn’t want to marry her.”

“I’m glad of that, dear,” his wife said.

“I’ll put up anything you like,” Pratt announced. “My house, for example. How about my house?”

“Which one?” Mike asked, joking now.

“The country one.”

“Why not the other one as well?”

“All right then, if you wish it. Both my houses.”

At that point I saw Mike pause. He took a step forward and placed the bottle in its basket gently down on the table. He moved the saltcellar[①] to one side, then the pepper, and then he picked up his knife, studied the blade thoughtfully for a moment, and put it down again. His daughter, too, had seen him pause.

“Now, Daddy!” she cried. “Don’t be *absurd*! It’s *too* silly for words. I refuse to be betted on like this.”

“Quite right, dear,” her mother said. “Stop it at once, Mike, and sit down and eat your food.”

Mike ignored her. He looked over at his daughter and he smiled, a slow, fatherly, protective smile. But in his eyes, suddenly, there glimmered a little triumph. “You know,” he said, smiling as he spoke.

① saltcellar: *Noun* a small container for holding salt at the dining table 盐瓶

"You know, Louise, we ought to think about this a bit."

"Now, stop it, Daddy! I refuse even to listen to you! Why, I've never heard anything so ridiculous in my life!"

"No, seriously, my dear. Just wait a moment and hear what I have to say."

"But I don't *want* to hear it."

"Louise! Please! It's like this. Richard, here, has offered us a serious bet. He is the one who wants to make it, not me. And if he loses, he will have to hand over a considerable amount of property. Now, wait a minute, my dear, don't interrupt. The point is this. *He cannot possibly win.*"

"He seems to think he can."

"Now listen to me, because I know what I'm talking about. The expert, when tasting a claret—so long as it is not one of the famous great wines like Lafite① or Latour—can only get a certain way towards naming the vineyard. He can, of course, tell you the Bordeaux district from which the wine comes, whether it is from St Emilion, Pomerol, Graves, or Medoc. But then each district has several communes, little counties, and each county has many, many small vineyards. It is impossible for a man to differentiate between them all by taste and smell alone. I don't mind telling you that this one I've got here is a wine from a small vineyard that is surrounded by many other small vineyards, and he'll never get it. It's impossible."

"You can't be sure of that," his daughter said.

"I'm telling you I can. Though I say it myself, I understand quite a bit about this wine business, you know. And anyway, heavens alive,

---

① 此处的"Lafite"以及本段中出现的"Latour""Bordeaux""St Emilion""Pomerol""Graves""Medoc"都是法国的葡萄酒产区或酒庄名字,以及相应的葡萄酒品牌。

girl, I'm your father and you don't think I'd let you in for—for something you didn't want, do you? I'm trying to make you some money."

"Mike!" his wife said sharply. "Stop it now, Mike, please!"

Again he ignored her. "If you will take this bet," he said to his daughter, "in ten minutes you will be the owner of two large houses."

"But I don't want two large houses, Daddy."

"Then sell them. Sell them back to him on the spot. I'll arrange all that for you. And then, just think of it, my dear, you'll be rich! You'll be independent for the rest of your life!"

"Oh, Daddy, I don't like it. I think it's silly."

"So do I," the mother said. She jerked① her head briskly up and down as she spoke, like a hen. "You ought to be ashamed of yourself, Michael, even suggesting such a thing! Your own daughter, too!"

Mike didn't even look at her. "Take it!" he said eagerly, staring hard at the girl. "Take it, quick! I'll guarantee you won't lose."

"But I don't like it, Daddy."

"Come on, girl. Take it!"

Mike was pushing her hard. He was leaning towards her, fixing her with two hard bright eyes, and it was not easy for the daughter to resist him.

"But what if I lose?"

"I keep telling you, you can't lose. I'll guarantee it."

"Oh, Daddy must I?"

"I'm making you a fortune. So come on now. What do you say, Louise? All right?"

For the last time, she hesitated. Then she gave a helpless little

---

① jerk: *Verb* [with obj. and adverbial] make (something) move with a jerk 使猝然一动(e. g. She jerked her chin up. 她突然抬起下巴。)

shrug of the shoulders and said, "Oh, all right, then. Just so long as you swear there's no danger of losing."

"Good!" Mike cried. "That's fine! Then it's a bet!"

"Yes," Richard Pratt said, looking at the girl. "It's a bet."

Immediately, Mike picked up the wine, tipped the first thimbleful① into his own glass, then skipped excitedly around the table filling up the others. Now everyone was watching Richard Pratt, watching his face as he reached slowly for his glass with his right hand and lifted it to his nose. The man was about fifty years old and he did not have a pleasant face. Somehow, it was all mouth—mouth and lips—the full, wet lips of the professional gourmet, the lower lip hanging downward in the centre, a pendulous, permanently open taster's lip, shaped open to receive the rim of a glass or a morsel② of food. Like a keyhole, I thought, watching it; his mouth is like a large wet keyhole.

Slowly he lifted the glass to his nose. The point of the nose entered the glass and moved over the surface of the wine, delicately sniffing. He swirled the wine gently around in the glass to receive the bouquet③. His concentration was intense. He had closed his eyes, and now the whole top half of his body, the head and neck and chest, seemed to become a kind of huge sensitive smelling-machine, receiving, filtering, analysing the message from the sniffing nose.

---

① thimbleful: *Noun* as much as a thimble will hold(酒等的)极少量

② morsel: *Noun* a small piece or amount of food; a mouthful(食物)一小份;一小口(e. g. Juliet pushed a last morsel of toast into her mouth. 朱丽叶把最后一小口烤面包放进了嘴里。)

③ bouquet: *Noun* the characteristic scent of a wine or perfume(酒或香水的)香味;芬芳(e. g. The aperitif has a faint bouquet of almonds. 开胃酒有一股淡淡的杏仁香味。)

Mike, I noticed, was lounging[1] in his chair, apparently unconcerned, but he was watching every move. Mrs. Schofield, the wife, sat prim and upright at the other end of the table, looking straight ahead, her face tight with disapproval. The daughter, Louise, had shifted her chair away a little, and sidewise, facing the gourmet, and she, like her father, was watching closely.

For at least a minute, the smelling process continued; then, without opening his eyes or moving his head, Pratt lowered the glass to his mouth and tipped in almost half the contents. He paused, his mouth full of wine, getting the first taste; then, he permitted some of it to trickle[2] down his throat and I saw his Adam's apple move as it passed by. But most of it he retained in his mouth. And now, without swallowing again, he drew in through the lips a thin breath of air which mingled with the fumes of the wine in the mouth and passed on down into his lungs. He held the breath, blew it out through his nose, and finally began to roll the wine around under the tongue, and chewed it, actually chewed it with his teeth as though it were bread.

It was a solemn, impressive performance, and I must say he did it well.

"Um," he said, putting down the glass, running a pink tongue over his lips, "Um—yes. A very interesting little wine gentle and gracious, almost feminine in the after-taste."

There was an excess of saliva in his mouth, and as he spoke he spat

---

① lounge: *Verb* [no obj., with adverbial of place] lie, sit, or stand in relaxed or lazy way 懒洋洋地躺(或坐、站)着(e. g. Several students were lounging about reading papers. 几个学生懒洋洋地在那里看报。)

② trickle: *Verb* [no obj., with adverbial of direction] (of a liquid) flow in a small stream(液体)滴;淌(e. g. A solitary tear trickled down her cheek. 一颗泪珠滑下她的脸颊。)

an occasional bright speck of it on to the table.

"Now we can start to eliminate," he said. "You will pardon me for doing this carefully, but there is much at stake. Normally I would perhaps take a bit of a chance, leaping forward quickly and landing right in the middle of the vineyard of my choice. But this time—I must move cautiously this time, must I not?" He looked up at Mike and he smiled, a thick-lipped, wet-lipped smile. Mike did not smile back.

"First, then, which district in Bordeaux does this wine come from? That's not too difficult to guess. It is far too light in the body to be from either St Emilion or Graves. It is obviously a Medoc. There's no doubt about that.

"Now—from which commune in Medco does it come? That also, by elimination, should not be too difficult to decide. Margaux? No. It cannot be Margaux. It has not the violent bouquet of a Margaux. Pauillac? It cannot be Pauillac, either. It is too tender, too gentle and wistful for Pauillac. The wine of Pauillac has a character that is almost imperious in its taste. And also, to me, a Pauillac contains just a little pith①, a curious dusty, pithy flavour that the grape acquires from the soil of the district. No, no. This—this is a very gentle wine, demure② and bashful③ in the first taste, emerging shyly but quite graciously in the second. A little

---

① pith: *Noun* (Botany) the spongy cellular tissue in the stems and branches of many higher plants(植物学)(高等植物的)(木)髓;树心

② demure: *Adjective* (of a woman or her behaviour) reserved, modest, and shy(女子或其举止)端庄娴静的;谦逊而羞怯的(e.g. demure little wife who sits at home minding the house 待在家里料理家务的娴静小媳妇)

③ bashful: *Adjective* reluctant to draw attention to oneself; shy 羞怯的;忸怩的

arch[①], perhaps, in the second taste, and a little naughty also, teasing the tongue with a trace, just a trace of tannin[②]. Then, in the after-taste, delightful—consoling and feminine, with a certain blithely[③] generous quality that one associates only with the wines of the commune of St Julien. Unmistakably this is a St Julien."

He leaned back in his chair, held his hands up level with his chest, and placed the fingertips carefully together. He was becoming ridiculously pompous[④], but I thought that some of it was deliberate, simply to mock his host. I found myself waiting rather tensely for him to go on. The girl Louise was lighting a cigarette. Pratt heard the match strike and

---

① arch: *Adjective* deliberately or affectedly playful and teasing 故意(或假装)调皮逗弄的(e. g. a somewhat arch tone of voice 带一点调皮的声调)

② tannin: *Noun* any of various complex phenolic substances of plant origin; used in tanning and in medicine 鞣酸;丹宁酸;单宁

注:单宁是葡萄酒的基本成分之一,是酒的结构、酒的口味和酒的陈化潜力的决定因素之一。只有红葡萄酒拥有单宁,因为单宁是从葡萄皮里的红色素(花色素)转换而来的。单宁不足的红酒要尽快喝掉,因为它经不起储藏,酒香会很快消散。单宁也使红酒具有了预防心脏病的特质。含单宁丰富的酒通常涩度高,我们说其具"收敛"性。如果一瓶红酒涩度过高,那通常是因为它年岁太小,最好等过了几年让酒体充分展开后再喝。单宁在窖藏过程中会转换成酒香。

③ blithely: *Adverb* in a joyous manner 欢乐地;快活地;无挂虑地(e. g. They blithely carried on chatting, ignoring the customers who were waiting to be served. 他们继续开心地聊天,将等着购物的顾客们置于一边。)

④ pompous: *Adjective* affectedly and irritatingly grand, solemn, or self-important 炫耀的;自负的(e. g. a pompous ass who pretends he knows everything 以为自己什么都知道的自负的傻瓜。)

he turned on her, flaring[①] suddenly with real anger. "Please!" he said. "Please don't do that! It's a disgusting habit, to smoke at table!"

She looked up at him, still holding the burning match in one hand, the big slow eyes settling on his face, resting there a moment, moving away again, slow and contemptuous. She bent her head and blew out the match, but continued to hold the unlighted cigarette in her fingers.

"I'm sorry, my dear," Pratt said, "but I simply cannot have smoking at table."

She didn't look at him again.

"Now, let me see—where were we?" he said. "Ah, yes. This wine is from Bordeaux, from the commune of St Julien, in the district of Medoc. So far, so good. But now we come to the more difficult part—the name of the vineyard itself. For in St Julien there are many vineyards, and as our host so rightly remarked earlier on, there is often not much difference between the wine of one and wine of another. But we shall see."

He paused again, closing his eyes. "I am trying to establish the 'growth'," he said. "If I can do that, it will be half the battle. Now, let me see. This wine is obviously not from a first-growth vineyard nor even a second. It is not a great wine. The quality, the—the—what do you call it? —the radiance, the power, is lacking. But a third growth—that it could be. And yet I doubt it. We know it is a good year—our host has said so—and this is probably flattering it a little bit. I must be careful. I must be very careful here."

He picked up his glass and took another small sip.

"Yes," he said, sucking his lips, "I was right. It is a fourth

---

① flare: *Verb* (of an emotion) suddenly become manifest in someone or their expression(情感)突发;突现(e. g. Alarm flared in her eyes. 她双眼突然现出了恐慌神情。)

growth. Now I am sure of it. A fourth growth from a very good year from a great year, in fact. And that's what made it taste for a moment like a third—or even a second-growth wine. Good! That's better! Now we are closing in! What are the fourth-growth vineyards in the commune of St Julien?"

Again he paused, took up his glass, and held the rim against that sagging, pendulous lower lip of his. Then I saw the tongue shoot out, pink and narrow, the tip of it dipping into the wine, withdrawing swiftly again—a repulsive sight. When he lowered the glass, his eyes remained closed, the face concentrated, only the lips moving, sliding over each other like two pieces of wet, spongy rubber.

"There it is again!" he cried. "Tannin in the middle taste, and the quick astringent[①] squeeze upon the tongue. Yes, yes, of course! Now I have it! The wine comes from one of those small vineyards around Beychevelle. I remember now. The Beychevelle district, and the river and the little harbour that has silted[②] up so the wine ships can no longer use it. Beychevelle... could it actually be a Beychevelle itself? No, I don't think so. Not quite. But it is somewhere very close. Chateau Talbot? Could it be Talbot? Yes, it could. Wait one moment."

He sipped the wine again, and out of the side of my eye I noticed Mike Schofield and how he was leaning farther and farther forward over the table, his mouth slightly open, his small eyes fixed upon Richard Pratt.

"No. I was wrong. It is not a Talbot. A Talbot comes forward to you

---

① astringent: *Noun* a substance that causes the contraction of body tissues, typically used to protect the skin and to reduce bleeding from minor abrasions(导致身体组织收缩的)收敛剂

② silt: *Verb* [no obj.] become filled or blocked with silt 淤塞(e. g. The river's mouth had silted up. 河口淤塞了。)

just a little quicker than this one; the fruit is nearer the surface. If it is a '34, which I believe it is, then it couldn't be Talbot. Well, well. Let me think. It is not a Beychevelle and it is not a Talbot, and yet—yet it is so close to both of them, so close, that the vineyard must be almost in between. Now, which could that be?"

He hesitated, and we waited, watching his face. Everyone, even Mike's wife, was watching him now. I heard the maid put down the dish of vegetables on the sideboard behind me, gently, so as not to disturb the silence.

"Ah!" he cried. "I have it! Yes, I think I have it!"

For the last time, he sipped the wine. Then, still holding the glass up near his mouth, he turned to Mike and he smiled, a slow, silky smile, and he said, "You know what this is? This is the little Chateau Branaire-Ducru."

Mike sat tight, not moving.

"And the year, 1934."

We all looked at Mike, waiting for him to turn the bottle around in its basket and show the label.

"Is that your final answer?" Mike said.

"Yes, I think so."

"Well, is it or isn't it?"

"Yes, it is."

"What was the name again?"

"Chateau Branaire-Ducru. Pretty little vineyard. Lovely old chateau. Know it quite well. Can't think why I didn't recognize it at once."

"Come on, Daddy," the girl said. "Turn it round and let's have a peek. I want my two houses."

"Just a minute," Mike said. "Wait just a minute." He was sitting very quiet, bewildered-looking, and his face was becoming puffy[1] and pale, as though all the force was draining slowly out of him.

"Michael!" his wife called sharply from the other end of the table. "What's the matter?"

"Keep out of this, Margaret, will you please."

Richard Pratt was looking at Mike, smiling with his mouth, his eyes small and bright. Mike was not looking at anyone.

"Daddy!" the daughter cried, agonized. "But, Daddy, you don't mean to say he guessed it right!"

"Now, stop worrying, my dear," Mike said. "There's nothing to worry about."

I think it was more to get away from his family than anything else that Mike then turned to Richard Pratt and said, "I'll tell you what, Richard. I think you and I better slip off into the next room and have a little chat."

"I don't want a little chat," Pratt said. "All I want is to see the label on that bottle." He knew he was a winner now; he had the bearing[2], the quiet arrogance of a winner, and I could see that he was prepared to become thoroughly nasty if there was any trouble. "What are you waiting for?" he said to Mike. "Go on and turn it round."

Then this happened: the maid, the tiny, erect figure of the maid in her white-and-black uniform, was standing beside Richard Pratt, holding something out in her hand. "I believe these are yours, sir," she said.

---

① puffy: *Adjective* (especially of part of the body) unusually swollen and soft (尤指身体部位)膨胀的;浮肿的(e. g. Her eyes were puffy and full of tears. 她双眼浮肿噙满泪水。)

② bearing: *Noun* the way a person behaves or conducts themselves 举止;风度;仪态(e. g. She has the bearing of a First Lady. 她具有第一夫人的仪态。)

Pratt glanced around, saw the pair of thin horn-rimmed[①] spectacles that she held out to him, and for a moment he hesitated. "Are they? Perhaps they are, I don't know."

"Yes, sir, they're yours." The maid was an elderly woman—nearer seventy than sixty—a faithful family retainer of many years' standing. She put the spectacles down on the table beside him.

Without thanking her, Pratt took them up and slipped them into his top pocket, behind the white handkerchief.

But the maid didn't go away. She remained standing beside and slightly behind Richard Pratt, and there was something so unusual in her manner and in the way she stood there, small, motionless and erect, that I for one found myself watching her with a sudden apprehension. Her old grey face had a frosty, determined look, the lips were compressed, the little chin was out, and the hands were clasped together tight before her. The curious cap on her head and the flash of white down the front of her uniform made her seem like some tiny, ruffled[②], white-breasted bird.

"You left them in Mr. Schofield's study," she said. Her voice was unnaturally, deliberately polite. "On top of the green filing cabinet in his study, sir, when you happened to go in there by yourself before dinner."

---

① horn-rimmed: *Adjective* having the frame made of horn or tortoise shell or plastic that simulates either 角质架的(眼镜)

② ruffle: *Verb* (of a bird) erect (its feathers) in anger or display(鸟发怒或炫耀时)竖起(羽毛)(e. g. They warbled incessantly, their throat feathers ruffled. 它们不停地啭鸣,喉部的羽毛竖了起来。)

"ruffled"这里可以看作形容词,理解为"羽毛蓬乱的""羽毛蓬松的"的意思。

It took a few moments for the full meaning of her words to penetrate[①], and in the silence that followed I became aware of Mike and how he was slowly drawing himself up in his chair, and the colour coming to his face, and the eyes opening wide, and the curl of the mouth, and the dangerous little patch of whiteness beginning to spread around the area of the nostrils.

"Now, Michael!" his wife said. "Keep calm now, Michael dear! Keep calm!"

三、翻译探索

跟在小说中喜欢炫耀的品酒"大师"普拉特先生一样，作家罗尔德·达尔在这里也着实"炫耀"了一下自己在葡萄酒方面的专业知识，无形中构成了翻译的难点，弄不好就会在翻译中"说外行话"。另外，对普拉特先生品酒神态细腻而生动的描述，在翻译中做好风格上的再现，也绝非易事，有待进一步探索。

品酒"大师"

那天夜晚，我们一共有六个人在迈克·斯科菲尔德家吃饭：迈克、迈克的妻子及女儿、我和我妻子，还有一个叫理查德·普拉特的男子。迈克家在伦敦。

理查德·普拉特是位出了名的美食家。他是一家小型协会的会长，协会的名字叫"伊璧鸠鲁美食协会"。每个月他都私下里给会员传阅某本有关吃喝方面的小册子，还一次次组织聚餐活动，吃的是奢华的佳肴，喝的是稀有的美酒。吃的时候，他拒绝吸烟，怕殃及味觉；谈酒时，他有一个奇特的，甚至是滑稽的习惯，就是把酒说成一个有生命的人。"谨慎之酒，"他会这样说，"相当缺乏自信、缩手缩脚，但

① penetrate: *Verb* [no obj.] be fully understood or realized by someone 被某人完全理解(或意识到)(e. g. As his words penetrated, she saw a mental picture of him with Dawn. 由于理解了他的话，她和道恩明白他在想什么了。)

却十分谨慎”,或者这样说:“幽默风趣之酒,乐善好施、欢天喜地,或许会有那么一点儿低级淫秽,但仍不失幽默风趣之感。”

我以前到迈克家吃晚饭,且理查德·普拉特也在场,总共有两次。每次,迈克和妻子都绞尽脑汁为这位名声在外的美食家烹饪点特殊的。很明显,这一次也不会例外。一进餐厅,我就看到餐桌摆好、盛宴上场了。有高高的蜡烛、黄黄的玫瑰、闪闪的银器,还有高脚玻璃杯,每人一套共三只。但是,最值得一提的是,厨房隐隐飘来烤肉的香气,我的嘴立马就缓缓渗出一层暖暖的口水。

刚一落座,我就记起来:前两次聚餐理查德·普拉特在场的时候,主人迈克都跟他就红葡萄酒玩一个小小的打赌游戏,跟他赌酒的品牌、年份和产地。普拉特当时说,只要酒是大丰收之年出的,猜出答案应该不是什么难事。然后,迈克就用一盒待猜的红酒做赌注,赌他猜不中。普拉特表示同意,而且两次都赢了。今晚嘛,我有把握地感觉到,这个小游戏会再次上演,因为迈克十分愿意输掉赌注,目的就是证明他的葡萄酒品质上乘,很好辨别。而普拉特本人呢,似乎很乐意展示自己的才识,态度严肃,却有所克制。

最先上的是一盘银鱼,裹上奶油炸得很脆。跟银鱼相配,喝的酒是一瓶摩泽尔白葡萄酒。迈克起身,给自己倒了杯。他再次坐下时,我看得出,他眼睛看着理查德·普拉特。他把瓶子放到我面前,标签冲着我,上写着“奥里克斯堡盖尔斯莱,1945 年”的字样。他倾斜着身体小声告诉我说,盖尔斯莱是摩泽尔河谷一个再小不过的村落——出了德国,就没人知道这个村落。他还对我说,这种酒非比寻常,因为这个酒庄的产量极少,外人要想买到,几乎不可能。他还说,他去年夏天亲自去过盖尔斯莱,就是为了要买到那种少得可怜的酒。最后,软磨硬泡之下,人家总算答应卖给他几瓶。

“我不相信,此时此刻,我们国家还有谁手头上有这种酒,哪怕是一瓶半瓶的,”他说。我注意到,他又看了一眼理查德·普拉特。“摩泽尔酒的了不起之处在于,”他继续说,嗓门也提高了,“某种红酒没上之前,喝它算是尽善尽美了。但是,很多人在红酒之前喝的是莱茵白葡萄酒,那是因为他们还不知道有更好的酒可以喝。莱茵酒会把红酒的清香一笔勾销,你们大家知道吗?红酒没上之前喝莱茵酒,那是未开化的野蛮行径。但,摩泽尔酒嘛——啊哈,一瓶摩泽尔酒恰到好处,正合适。”

迈克·斯科菲尔德已到中年,人很亲切温和。可他却是个股票经纪人,准确地说,他在股票交易市场做批销生意。他与很多跟他做同样买卖的人一样,学浅才疏,却大钱赚到手,所以有点难为情,几乎感到惭愧。在内心深处,他清楚,他比赌马经纪人强不到哪儿去——那些人油滑得很,相当正派体面,背地里却不择手段。他清楚,他的朋友也清楚这一点。所以嘛,他现在竭尽所能,摇身一变想成为一个文化人——陶冶文学修养,培育审美情趣,也收集绘画、音乐、书籍以及诸如此类的东西。刚才一番关于莱茵酒和摩泽尔酒的小小铺垫,只是一个开场白,是他寻求的文化因素。

“这是一种迷人的小酒,难道你们不这样认为吗?”他说,仍旧看着理查德·普拉特。我看到,他每次低头吃一口炸银鱼时,都会快速地、偷偷地瞄一眼桌底。我几乎能感觉到,他正等待这一时刻的到来:普拉特会喝下第一小口酒,端着杯子抬起头来,脸上露出一丝愉悦的微笑——吃惊的微笑,或许甚至是一丝惊奇的微笑。紧接着,议论一番,最后,迈克就会告诉他有关那个叫盖尔斯莱的小村落的故事。

但问题是,理查德·普拉特并没有品尝,正跟迈克那芳龄十八的女儿路易丝谈得不亦乐乎,而且完全沉浸其中。他一半身体转向她,边冲她微笑,边讲着什么。就我尽可能听到的内容来推断,他正跟她讲巴黎一家饭店的一个大厨的故事。讲的时候,他身体一点点地向她越靠越近,看起来一副急切的样子,几乎要把她压在身下了。可怜的女孩儿,尽可能移开身体,离他远些。她边听边点头,以示礼貌,却相当无可奈何;边听边看着他那件非正式晚礼服最上排的纽扣,而不是他的脸。

鱼吃完,女仆进来,走一圈,收盘子。走到普拉特跟前时,她发现他盘子里的食物原封未动,就犹豫起来,而普拉特也注意到她的这一点。他手一挥,示意她走开。然后,不再交谈,快速吃了起来:快速挥舞起叉子,猛劲儿飞快地往嘴里戳炸成棕褐色的松脆小银鱼。吃完就伸手拿起酒杯,快速"咕噜"两口,就把酒倒进嗓子眼,随即立马转身,继续跟路易丝·斯科菲尔德交谈。

这一切,迈克都看在眼里。他知趣儿地坐在原位,一动不动。他打量着客人,控制住自己。他那张圆圆的、快活的脸似乎慢慢松弛下来,甚至开始下垂,但是,他还是控制着自己,一动不动地坐着,一言不发。

很快,女仆过来上第二道菜,是一大块烤牛肉。她把烤肉放到迈克面前的桌子上,迈克随即起身,切割起来。他把肉片切得薄薄的,轻轻地放入一个个盘子里,让女仆端给客人。大家都拿到烤肉后——当然,他自己也拿了一份,身子向前倚着桌子,双手把住桌边。

"现在,"他开口对我们大家说,眼睛却看着理查德·普拉特。"现在该喝红葡萄酒了。我必须得取酒去了,失陪一会,请原谅。"

"你取酒去吗,迈克?"我问道。"到哪儿取呢?"

"到我书房取,塞子已经拔出来了——酒正在吸收新鲜空气呢。"

"为什么放书房啊?"

"当然是要酒达到室温。在那儿放了二十四小时了。"

"可是,为什么非放到书房不可?"

"书房是家里最好的地方。上次聚会时,理查德帮我选的地方。"

普拉特听到有人提到自己的名字,回过身来。

"是个好地方,对不对?"迈克问。

"对的,"普拉特回答,郑重其事地点了点头。"没错。"

"放在我书房的绿色文件柜顶上,"迈克说。"那是我俩选的地方,是屋子里的一快好地方,温度均衡,空气不流通,保湿性很好。我去取一下,失陪一会,请原谅。"

一想到还有一瓶酒可以显摆,他的幽默劲又上来了。他匆忙走出餐厅,一分钟后返回,速度慢多了——轻轻迈步,双手捧着一只装酒的篮子,里面放了一只深色瓶子,标签冲下,看不到写的是什么。"现在,"他走到餐桌前喊道。"这瓶酒怎样呢,理查德?你永远也猜不出名字的。"

理查德·普拉特慢慢转过身来,抬头看着迈克,然后顺势向下看了眼躺在藤条编制的小篮子里那瓶酒。此时,他眉毛挑起,稍微一弯,显示出不屑的样子。与此同时,他湿乎乎的下嘴唇向外一撇,突然有点盛气凌人,却有点丑陋难看。

“你永远都不会猜出来的,”迈克说。“一百年,你也不会猜出来。”

“是一瓶红葡萄酒吗?”理查德·普拉特问,一副居高临下的架势。

“当然啦。”

“那么,我猜猜,是出自一个较小的葡萄庄园吗?”

“理查德,也许是的。再者说,也许不是的。”

“可是,是丰年出的吗?是大丰收之年出的吗?”

“是的。这点我保证。”

“那样的话,猜起来就不应该太难,”理查德·普拉特说,说起话来慢慢吞吞的,看起来十分倦怠的样子。在我看来,除此之外,他的慢吞吞和倦怠有点令人感到奇怪:两眼之间隐隐显露某种邪恶的东西,举手投足之间流露某种专注,而且据我观察,这种专注让我感觉到一点点不安。

“这种酒真的是相当难猜的,”迈克说。“我可不逼你赌这种酒啊。”

“确实如此。为何不赌呢?”他的眉毛又慢慢弯起,露出镇定、专注的神情。

“就因为难猜。”

“你知道,对我来说,那算不上什么成就感。”

“我的老伙计啊。”迈克说,“如你所愿,我很乐意跟你赌。”

“猜出答案,不应该太难。”

“你的意思是,你愿意赌吗?”

“我万分情愿来赌,”理查德·普拉特回答。

“好的。那么,还是老规矩,赌一盒这种酒。”

“你认为我无法猜出答案,是吧?”

“很明显啦。尽管我对你恭敬有加,回答还是否定的,”迈克说。尽管他竭力做到彬彬有礼,但普拉特不以为然,自始至终毫无掩饰自己不屑一顾的神情。然而,令人奇怪得很,他提的下一个问题似乎与人们眼下的兴趣无关。

“赌注你想加码吗?”

“不,理查德。一盒足矣。”

“赌五十盒,你愿意吗?”

“那很荒唐。”

迈克一动不动站在那儿,站在椅子后面,手小心地把住那瓶酒,酒瓶还没有从藤条篮子里拿出来。他的样子有点滑稽可笑。他两只鼻孔周围稍微变白,嘴紧紧地合拢到一起。

普拉特将身体懒洋洋地向后靠到了椅子上,抬头看了看他,两只眉毛挑起,双眼半睁半闭,嘴角掠过一丝微笑。我又看见,或者说,我想,我又看见,这个男子脸上明显有点不安,两眼间的专注隐隐显露,而且就在他眼睛中间的黑眼球部分,慢慢地闪现出一点点狡黠的光芒,当然是藏而不露的。

“那么说,赌注你不想加码了?”

“就我而言,老伙计啊,我无所谓啦,”迈克说,“你喜欢赌什么,我就赌什么。”

我,还有那三个女士坐在那儿,一言未发,看着这两位男士你来我往的。迈克的妻子有些恼火,她嘴不饶人,而且我感到,她随时准备横插一杠。烤牛肉就摆在我们面前的盘子里,缓缓冒着热气。

“这么说,我喜欢什么,你就赌什么了?”

“那是我说的。你愿意下什么该死的注,我都奉陪到底,要是你非得弄出个什么子午卯酉的话。”

“甚至赌一万英镑也可以吗?”

“当然啦,如果你想那样的话,我赌。”迈克现在信心更足了。他十分清楚,普拉特喜欢赌多少,他就能跟多少。

“你是说,赌注随我下了?”普拉特又问道。

“那是我说的。”

暂时消停了一会。这当儿，普拉特慢慢地环视桌子四周，然后挨个看了看三个女士。看他的样子，他是想提醒她们作证人，为他要下的注作证。

“迈克!”斯科菲尔德夫人喊道。“迈克，我们大家不要瞎闹了，开吃吧。都要凉了。”

“可，这不是瞎闹啊，”普拉特心平气和地说。“我们只是小赌一把。”

我注意到，那个女仆站在后面，端着一盘蔬菜，不知道是该端上来呢，还是该端回去。

“那么，好吧，”普拉特说。“我告诉你我要你赌什么吧。”

“有屁就放呗，”迈克说，语气相当地粗鲁。“我才不在乎你下的——是什么鬼注呢。”

普拉特点了点头，嘴角又掠过一丝微笑。接着，他直盯着迈克，十分缓慢地说：“我想让你赌：我把你女儿娶到手。”

路易丝·斯科菲尔德“嘭”地跳了起来。“嘿!”她叫道。“不。那可不好玩儿。爸爸，你看看，那根本就不是什么好玩儿的事情。”

“不会的，宝贝儿，”她母亲说。“他们只不过是在开玩笑。”

“我不是开玩笑的，”理查德·普拉特回应道。

“这是扯淡，”迈克说。现在，他又有些失衡了。

“你说过的，我喜欢赌什么，你就赌什么。”

“我是指钱啊。”

“你也没说，*光*赌钱啊。”

“我的意思就是赌钱。”

“好吧。没说就没说，太遗憾了。但不管怎样，如果你要食言，我倒没什么。”

“老伙计，这不是食言不食言的问题。不管怎么讲，你提出的都不算是什么赌注，因为咱俩的赌注不匹配。你倒是好，万一输掉，正好没有女儿押给我。就算你有女儿可押，我还不愿意娶呢。”

“亲爱的，你那样说，我很高兴，”他妻子说道。

“你喜欢我押什么，我就押什么，”普拉特宣布。“比如说，押我的房子。我把房子押上,怎样?”

“押哪一座呢?”迈克问道,现在有点玩笑的性质了。

“乡下的那一座。”

“为什么不把另一座也押上呢?”

“那么,好吧。既然你喜欢,那我把两座都押上。”

就在那一刻,我看到迈克停顿了一下。他向前跨一步,把还没有从篮子里拿出来的那瓶酒连同篮子轻轻放到桌子上,随后把桌上的盐瓶移到一边,又把胡椒瓶移走,然后拿起餐刀,若有所思地打量了一会刀刃,最后又放了下来。他女儿也看到他停顿了这么一会儿。

“好了,爸爸!”她叫道。“别做*荒唐事*。这事儿*愚蠢* 得说不出口。像这样给人拿来做赌注,我拒绝接受。”

“说得很对,宝贝儿,”她母亲说道。“迈克,立刻打住。坐下,吃你的东西。”

迈克没有搭理她。他看了看自己的女儿,慢慢地微微一笑,那一笑饱含父亲的慈爱和袒护。可突然间,他那双眼睛闪现出一丝胜利的喜悦之光。“要知道,”他边说边微笑,“路易丝啊,要知道,我们应该稍加考虑的。”

“打住,爸爸,就现在!我甚至不愿意听你说话!想知道为什么吗?我一生中从来没有听到如此荒唐可笑的事情。”

“我的宝贝,说正经的,不可笑。就给我一会儿时间,听我跟你说道说道。”

“但我*真的* 不想听。”

“路易丝,求你了!是这样的。在这儿,是理查德主动下的注,他是当真的。是他想这样赌,而不是我。况且,要是他输了,他也必将交出数量相当可观的财产。现在,给我一分钟,不要插嘴。问题的关键是,他*不可能,也没有可能赢* 。”

“他似乎认为自己能赢。”

“现在,听我说,因为我不糊涂,清楚自己在说什么。红葡萄酒,只要不是像拉菲特酒庄,或者拉杜尔酒庄出产的名酒,鉴别起来,专家也只能把产地酒庄的名字说个大概。当然,专家能说出酒是否出自波尔多地区，或者是否出自圣艾美利安、波美侯、格拉夫或者梅多克什么的。可问题是，每个这样的地区又有好多个城镇，好多个小县城，而每个县城还有许多、许多的小酒庄。单靠口感和味道，一个人要是对产地细加分辨的话，那是不可能的。我不妨告诉你吧，我这儿放的这瓶酒出自一个小酒庄，而那个小酒庄周围还有许多其他的小酒庄。他永远猜不到的，猜到是不可能的事。"

"你不可能那么肯定的，"他女儿说。

"我对你说，我能肯定的。要知道，尽管我自己这样说，我还是多少懂得一点葡萄酒这一行的。女儿啊，不管怎么说，老天在上，我是你父亲，你认为我会设套让你往里钻——去做你不愿意做的事情吗？我在努力为你赚些银子呢。"

"迈克！"他妻子尖声喊道。"就此打住，迈克。求你了！"

他还是没有搭理她。"要是你愿意接受这个赌注，"他对女儿说，"不到十分钟的工夫，你就拥有两座大房子啦。"

"可是，爸爸，我不想要两座什么大房子。"

"那就卖掉，当场卖给他。这一切都交给我，我会为你安排得好好的。那么，我的宝贝，你就想想吧，你要有钱了，后半辈子你就不用靠谁了！"

"噢，爸爸，我不喜欢这样。我想，这样做很是荒唐可笑。"

"我也是这么认为的，"母亲发话了。说话时，她猛地上下快速点着头，就像一只啄食的母鸡。"迈克尔，提议这样的事，你应该感到羞耻！也对不起你自己的女儿！"她开始喊起他的大名了。

迈克连看都没看她一眼。"应承下来吧！"他急切地说，使劲盯着女儿。"答应啊，快！我保证，你输不了的。"

"但是，爸爸，我不喜欢这样。"

迈克紧逼女儿不放。他靠近她，一双铮亮的眼睛使劲盯着她。他女儿想不屈从，也是不容易的。

"可是，万一输了怎么办呢？"

"跟你说过多少遍了，你输不了。我打包票。"

"噢，爸爸，我别无选择吗？"

"我要让你发财啦。所以,现在就答应吧。你还要说什么呢,路易丝? 好不好?"

她最后一次犹豫起来。接着,她轻轻一耸双肩,无助地说道:"哦,那好吧,只要你信誓旦旦地说没有什么危险,不会输掉。"

"好极了,"迈克喊道。"太好了。那么,赌了。"

"好的,"理查德·普拉特边说,边看了眼女孩。"赌了。"

迈克立即拿起酒,先给自己的杯子倒了一点点,然后兴奋地围着桌子活蹦乱跳地把其他人的杯子也倒上。至此,大家都看着理查德·普拉特,看着他的脸。只见他慢慢用右手端起酒杯,举到鼻子跟前。这家伙约有五十岁,脸看起来不很友善。可不知道为什么,感觉他满脸就剩那张大嘴了——还有上下嘴唇,那是一副厚厚的、湿乎乎的、专门品尝美食的嘴唇,下嘴唇从中间部位向下耷拉着。他的双唇悬吊着,从没有闭合过,仿佛随时要品尝什么东西。那嘴压根儿就是张着的,正好能放进酒杯的圆弧边缘或者一小口食物。我看着那张嘴,心想:他的嘴怎么那么像锁眼——大大的、湿乎乎的锁眼。

他慢慢地把杯子举到鼻子跟前,鼻尖伸进酒杯,在酒的表面一边移动,一边娴熟地嗅闻着。他轻轻地摇动杯子,让酒在里面打着旋儿,以便释放出芳香。他闭着眼睛,神情专注。现在,他整个上半部身体,包括头、脖子还有胸部,似乎变成一种大型的、敏锐的味道探测机器,正在接收、过滤、分析通过鼻子吸进的气息。

我注意到,迈克懒洋洋地坐在椅子上,看起来毫不在意,但实际上没有漏掉一举一动。他的妻子斯科菲尔德夫人坐在桌子的另一端,腰板挺直、规规矩矩、目视前方。由于不赞同这种做法,她的脸绷得紧紧的。女儿路易丝把椅子向侧面挪了挪,正对着这位品酒的。她跟她父亲一样,仔仔细细观看着。

普拉特在那儿嗅来闻去,至少有一分钟。接着,头不动,眼不睁,压低杯子,把几乎一半的酒倒进嘴里。他嘴里含满酒停顿了一下,感觉着第一口酒的味道。然后,让一部分酒慢慢流进喉咙。我看到,随着酒往下流去,他的喉结也一动一动的,但多数酒还是含在嘴里。现在,他不再往下吞,而是嘴唇微张,稍微吸入一点空气跟嘴里酒的气味混合到一起，然后把空气吸进肺部。他屏住呼吸，再把空气通过鼻子呼出来。最后，把压在舌头底部的酒翻转几下，咀嚼着。实际上，他是用牙齿嚼，好像把酒当成了面包。

这一举止很是郑重其事，令人印象深刻。我不得不说的是，他做得很到位。

“呃，”他放下杯子，粉红色的舌头舔了一圈嘴唇说。“呃——有了。很有意思的一种小酒——既温柔又雅致，余味颇具女性的阴柔感。”

他嘴里还残留些多余的口水。讲话的同时，偶尔会往桌子上喷溅一点亮晶晶的口水斑点。

“现在，我要开始逐一排除，”他说。“我做得这么细微，还请原谅，毕竟赌注不匪。正常情况下，我只要稍微尝试一下，三下五除二，冒点儿险，就对备选的产地酒庄猜得八九不离十了。可是，这次呢——这次我必须谨慎行事，我说得对吧？”他抬头看着迈克，微笑一下，那是厚厚的、湿乎乎的嘴唇发出的微笑。迈克并没有以微笑回应。

“那么，首先，这种酒出自波尔多的哪个地区呢？答案不是太难猜出的。这种酒本身重量太轻了，不可能出自圣艾美利安或格拉夫。很明显，是梅多克的酒，这一点，毫无疑问。”

“现在嘛，出自梅多克的哪个城镇呢？通过排除法，答案也不是太难确定的。是玛尔戈吗？不，不可能是玛尔戈的。这种酒没有玛尔戈红酒那种浓烈的芳香。是波亚克的吗？可不可能是波亚克的？这种酒太脆嫩、太温柔、太想入非非了，而波亚克的红酒没有这个特点。波亚克酒特点是，味道近乎于盛气凌人。况且对我来说，波亚克酒只不过带点儿木髓味，那味有点古怪，带有泥土气息，是葡萄从生长地区的土壤里获得的。不，不是的。这种酒嘛，第一口品尝的时候，很温柔、很矜持、很腼腆，而品尝第二口时，味道就羞答答地，却十分优雅地散发出来了。尝第二口时，这种酒或许有一点儿故意逗弄的架势，也有一点儿顽皮的样子，会用一点点的——就一点点的——单宁戏弄舌头一下。可是，其余的味很是讨人喜欢的，带有安慰性和女性的阴柔感，具有某种无忧无虑、慷慨大方的品质。这些特点使人自然而然联想到圣祖利安出产的红葡萄酒。不会有错的,这种就是圣祖利安的。”

他坐在椅子上向后一靠,双手举起,与胸部平齐,指尖很小心地并拢到一起。他的举止浮夸,有些滑稽可笑,可我认为他的某些动作是故意做出来的,只不过是想嘲弄一下这屋子的主人。我自己竟然还绷紧神经等待他继续讲下去。这时,路易丝正要点烟。普拉特听到火柴摩擦发出“哧”的一声,立刻转向女孩,愤怒之情也“哧”地燃起,真的生气了。“拜托!”他说。“拜托你,不要抽烟。这个习惯令人作呕,特别是就餐的时候。”

她抬头看了他一眼,一只手仍然擎着燃烧的火柴,两只大大的眼睛缓缓移到他的脸上,停留了一会,又慢慢地移开了,满不在乎的蔑视之情溢于言表。她头一低,吹灭了火柴,但手指还夹着那支没有点着的香烟。

“亲爱的,我很抱歉,”普拉特说,“可我就是无法容忍餐桌上抽烟。”

她再也不看他了。

“现在,让我想想——刚才说到哪儿了?”他问。“啊,想起来了。这种酒出自波尔多的圣祖利安,是梅多克地区的。猜到这儿,还算顺利。往下要猜的话,就更难了——酒庄的名字。因为在圣祖利安,酒庄很多,况且我们的房主人开始的时候说过,每个酒庄产的酒本身差别甚微。可是,我们倒要看看。”

他又暂停一会,闭上双眼。“我想就‘种植等级’说道说道,”他说。“要是我能把等级确定下来,这瓶酒一半的秘密就显现了。现在,容我想想。这种酒很显然不是出自一级种植园的,也不是二级的,因为这酒没有那么棒。这酒的品……品……品质,叫什么来着?对,光鲜度,光鲜的程度不足。要说是三级种植园的嘛,还差不多,但我还是持怀疑态度。我们大家知道,这是丰年出的酒——我们的房主人开始就这样说过。说是丰年的,或许有一点点夸奖的成分。我一定要当心这点。猜到这儿,我必须十分当心。”

他端起杯子,又喝了一小口。

“对，”他吧唧吧唧嘴唇说。“我刚才的怀疑是对的。这酒出自四级种植园。现在，这点我是肯定了。丰收年景中的一个四级种植园——实际上，是个大丰收年。这也就说明，为什么刚才有那么一小会儿，它品尝起来像是出自三级——甚至二级种植园的酒。好，好多啦！现在，就要揭底了！是圣祖利安哪一个四级种植园的酒庄出产的呢？”

他又暂停一下，拿起了杯子，杯子圆弧边缘抵到他那个凹陷的、悬吊着的下嘴唇。接下来，我看见他那狭窄的粉红色舌头“倏”地弹射出来，舌尖浸入酒中，又“嗖”地收拢回去，看着直叫人恶心。他放下杯子的时候，眼睛还没有睁开，一脸专注的神情，只有上下嘴唇抿来抿去的，就像两块湿乎乎的、软绵绵的橡皮蹭来蹭去。

“又有了！”他喊道。“尝到一半就遇到单宁的涩味，舌头很快就被其收敛性绷紧。是的，是的，没跑了！现在，我想到了。这种酒出自龙船周边的某个小型葡萄园。我现在想起来了，是龙船地区，那儿有一条河，还有一个小港口，由于港口淤泥充塞，过往运酒的船只也就不再停靠。是出自龙船地区——会正好是龙船酒庄本身吗？不会的，我想不会的。不会这么巧的。可是，会是很近的某个地方。大宝城堡吗？会是大宝酒庄吗？是的，有可能。可是，且慢。”

普拉特又小口品尝了一下。从眼睛的余光中，我看到了旁边的迈克·斯科菲尔德，也看到他俯身桌子上方，身体不断地向前倾斜，越倾越厉害。他的嘴稍微张开，两只小小的眼睛死死地盯着理查德·普拉特。

“不，我说错了，不是大宝酒庄的。大宝酒扑鼻而来的速度比这种酒要快一点儿，且葡萄味更靠近酒的表面。如果这种酒的年份是1934年的——我相信是的，那么，就不可能是大宝酒。那么，好吧，我再想想。不是龙船的，也不是大宝的，却离它们这么近。从近的程度看，这种酒的产地庄园一定介于它们之间。现在看看，可能是它们之间的哪一个呢？”

他犹豫不决，我们大伙儿就等待着，看着他的脸。现在，大伙儿的目光，包括迈克妻子的目光，都集中到他一个人身上了。我听到女仆往我身后餐具柜上放菜盘的声音,她轻拿轻放,生怕打破目前的寂静。

“啊,”他叫道。“想到了!是的,我想,我知道了!”

他最后一次小口品尝了一下。随后,仍然举着酒杯放在靠嘴边很近的地方,转向迈克,微微一笑,那是一种慢腾腾的、滑溜溜的微笑。他说:“你知道这酒的产地吗?你这酒出自小小的班尼城堡。”

迈克坐在那里,一动不动。

“至于年份嘛,1934年的。”

我们大家目光“唰”地集中到迈克身上,等着他把放在篮子里的酒瓶翻过来,露出标签。

“那是你最终的答案吗?”迈克问。

“是的,我想是的。”

“那么,到底是,还是不是?”

“是,是的。”

“再说一下,叫什么名字来着?”

“班尼城堡酒庄,特别小的一个葡萄庄园,一座可爱的老城堡酒庄。我对它相当熟悉。真不知道怎么搞的,一开始竟没有品尝出来。”

“得啦,别问了,爸爸,”他女儿说道。“瓶子转过来,让我瞧一眼。我想要那两座大房子。”

“就等一小会儿,”迈克说。“就等那么一小会儿。”他坐在那儿沉默不语,露出迷惑的表情。他的脸胀鼓鼓的,脸色苍白,就好像浑身的力气一点点耗尽了。

“迈克尔!”他妻子从桌子另一端尖声喊着他的大名。“你怎么回事啊?”

“玛格丽特,不要插一杠子了,拜托。”

理查德·普拉特看着迈克,嘴在笑,小小的、发亮的眼睛也在笑,而迈克却谁都不看。

“爸爸!”女儿喊道,变得极其紧张。“可是,爸爸,你不要告诉我,他猜对了啊。”

“我的宝贝，现在别瞎担心，”迈克说。“没什么可担心的。”

我想，我宁愿转身离开他家，也不愿意随后看到迈克转向理查德·普拉特，听到他说道：“理查德，听我说。我想，我和你去隔壁房间，私下谈谈如何？”

“我不想私下谈谈，”普拉特回答。“我就想看看那瓶子上的标签。”他知道，他现在赢定了。看他那举止，一副赢家的高傲姿态，不说也看得出来。我能够看得出，要是有谁节外生枝、招惹麻烦的话，他随时准备撕破脸皮、动起粗来的。“你还等什么呢？”他对迈克说。“去把瓶子翻过来啊。”

随后，出现了这么一幕：那个女仆，那个长得瘦小、腰板挺直的女仆，穿着黑白相间的制服，站到理查德·普拉特身旁，伸出手来，手拿着什么东西，说道：“先生，我想，这东西是你的吧。”

普拉特转身一看，看到她伸出手，手里拿的是一副薄薄的、角质架的眼镜。他一愣，不知道是接好呢，还是不接好呢。“是我的吗？或许是吧。我不清楚。”

“是的，先生，是你的。”女仆年纪不小了，没有七十，也六十好几了。她在这家干了好多年了，兢兢业业、忠心耿耿。她把眼镜放到他身边的桌子上。

普拉特连一声“谢谢”都没有说，随手拾起眼镜，顺势塞进上衣顶部兜子的那个白手帕后面。

但是，女仆并没有走开。她仍然站在一边，站在稍微靠近理查德·普拉特后面的位置上。她的行为举止和站立方式，太不同寻常了：矮矮的个头，一动不动站着，腰板笔挺。看到她那副样子，顿时让人心生畏惧。她那张苍老的、灰白的脸饱经风霜，表情坚毅，双唇紧紧闭合在一起，小小的下巴向前伸出，两手紧紧扣在一起放到身前。她头戴的帽子看起来古里古怪的，胸前制服的白色部分，一闪一闪发着光，这就使她整个人看起来像某种鸟——体型瘦小、羽毛蓬乱、胸部白白。

“这幅眼镜，您落在斯科菲尔德先生的书房里了，”她说。这话说得很不自然，彬彬有礼的口气是故意装出来的。“先生，那是在吃饭前,你自己恰巧溜达着走进书房,眼镜就落在那个绿色的文件柜顶上了。”

过了好一会儿,她说的话的全部意思才得以领会。就在沉默的当儿,我注意到迈克的变化:他坐在椅子上,慢慢地直起身子,脸上颜色也恢复了,两只眼睛睁得圆圆的,撅起的嘴舒展开了,两只鼻孔周围看起来吓人的小白斑块也开始均匀地扩散开来。

“噢,迈克尔!”他妻子又称呼起他的大名说道。“现在要冷静啊,迈克尔,亲爱的!冷静!”

第二章 意识之流

“意识流”这个词可谓形象生动——意识如河流，不断流淌。其实，这应该是译自英语“stream of consciousness”的一个词。“stream of consciousness”是美国机能主义心理学派的先驱威廉·詹姆斯（William James，1842—1910）创造并提出的，用来表示意识的流动特性，即意识的内容是不断变化的，从来不会静止不动。美国《心灵》（Mind）杂志1884年第9期上发表了威廉·詹姆斯的论文《论内省心理学所忽略的几个问题》（On some omissions of introspective psychology），文中威廉·詹姆斯提到了“意识流”或“思想流”（stream of thought）这类问题，后来这篇论文收入他1890年出版的心理学专著《心理学原理》（Principles of Psychology）一书中①。

接下来，这个词被引入文学界，成为现代主义文学的一个分支——意识流文学。在文学上，“作为一种文学流派，它主要指流行于20世纪20至40年代的英、法、美诸国的一种小说流派”（曾艳兵，2004）。有人认为，“较早发表意识流文学理论观点的是威廉·詹姆斯的弟弟——亨利·詹姆斯，他要求作家‘退出小说’，主张表现人物

① 参见“屈光．中国古典诗词中的意识流［J］．中国社会科学，2000（5）：155”，括号内的英文为著者所加。

复杂的心理活动,认为小说中的人物心理是‘一个随时准备容纳痛苦的器皿,一只深深的瓷器小杯,可以在其中混合各种辛辣的酸性液体’”(屈光,2000);也有人认为,“首次将‘意识流’这一术语引入文学批评中的是英国小说家梅·辛克莱(May Sinclair,1879—1946)。据库麦(Shiv K. Kumar)考证,辛克莱在1918年4月号的《个人主义者》杂志上发表评论英国作家多萝西·理查森的小说《人生历程》(又译作《朝圣》)的文章时最早将意识流这一概念引入文学界”(曾艳兵,2004);还有的人认为,“意识流文学源于从古希腊文学中便已出现文学的内心独白,和欧洲文学传统有着紧密的联系,如《哈姆莱特》中的大段内心独白”(刘卫东,2009)。“意识流”在西方文学界兴起后不久,就被引进中国文学。“‘意识流’最早流入中国文坛具体时段……大概要圈定于郑振铎所撰著,上海商务印书馆于1927年4月出版的《文学大纲》(下册)。该‘大纲’对法国意识流代表作家普鲁斯特略有提及,认为:‘普鲁斯特是很值得读的’”(吴锡民,2002)。但是,“‘意识流’最初流入中国现代文坛的形式和规模,均无法与20世纪30、40年代中国文坛对它的吸收和接纳相比”(吴锡民,2002)。

具体来说,在文学中,“意识流手法”是“一种模糊了理性与非理性、逻辑与非逻辑的特定心理状态,也许是最纯粹的自我表现形式。意识流进入小说创作视野,使现代小说进入新的领域。意识流小说借用跳跃、倒叙、平行等手法,直接模仿意识的运动。在运用这种新语言的小说里,作者也不必站在一旁评点人物,也不必直接告诉读者人物在想什么,而是让读者进入人物思维”(刘卫东,2009)。

源于西方的“意识流”手法当然会对英国作家罗尔德·达尔产生一定的影响,“意识之流”当然也会在他的一些作品中流淌。但是,本章不对“意识流手法”做纯文学意义上的专业性探讨,而是选取罗尔德·达尔两篇“流淌”出意识之流的短篇小说,权作对“意识流”的一种“观照”。这里有士兵母亲与儿子在意识上的交流,还有空战中意识之流的流淌。

在达尔的意识之流中,“仅此而已”远非如此洒脱,“老手之死”也许出人意料。

第一节 《仅此而已》Only This

罗尔德·达尔的《仅此而已》(Only This)收录在《罗尔德·达尔短篇故事集锦》(*The Collected Short Stories of Roald Dahl*)、《向你飞跃》(*Over to You*)以及《五部畅销书集》(5 *Bestsellers*)等书中。

一、原作导读

月光透过打开的窗户,泻入英国一座乡村小屋的卧室。卧室里,一位老妇人已经进入了梦乡。卧室的"梳妆台上放了一把发刷、一封信,还有一张大幅照片,照片上有一名年轻的男子,身穿军人制服,紧身短上衣左侧佩戴了一对飞行胸章"(On the dressing-table there was a hairbrush, a letter and a large photograph of a young boy in uniform who wore a pair of wings on the left side of his tunic),那是她参军儿子的照片。

突然之间,远方传来隆隆的声响,惊醒了睡梦中的老妇人。她清楚,轰炸机要飞往战场、投入战斗了,也许其中就有自己儿子驾驶的战机。她起身下床,站到了窗户跟前,祈祷上帝保佑儿子平安无事——那可是她唯一的孩子啊。要是失去了儿子,她也就失去生活下去的意义。

老妇人干脆临窗而坐,思念起自己的儿子。她似乎看见了儿子,听见儿子跟她说话。于是,她闭上眼睛,眼前出现了儿子驾驶的战机。意念之中,她站到了驾驶舱中儿子的身旁。儿子冲着她微微一笑,她感到开心无比。飞机靠近战场了,透过驾驶舱的玻璃罩她看到一束束探照灯光,还有一闪一闪的防空火力。她眼睁睁看着儿子的飞机被火力击中,引擎冒起了火焰,担心极了。但是,儿子还是冲着她微笑,若无其事地继续飞行。一声巨响过后,座舱烟雾弥漫,她害怕极了。机组成员跳伞逃生,儿子却在奋力控制着已经失控的飞机。惊惧之余,她用力要把儿子从座椅上拉下来,但儿子失去了知觉,任凭她怎么拉都拉不动，也解不开各种扣子。绝望之中，她扑到儿子身上，失声痛哭起来。飞机旋转着不断下降，最终坠毁。

英国一座乡村小屋的卧室里，这位老妇人仰靠在椅子里，身上盖着毯子，闭上了双眼。这时，隆隆声再次响起，那预示着幸存下来的战机正往回飞，飞往英军空军基地，“但是，这位坐在窗户边的妇人却再也没有动弹一下。她已经死去好长一段时间了”（But the woman who sat by the window never moved. She had been dead for some time）。

二、原作释读

本篇小说线索相对单一，将母亲对投入战斗的儿子的思念化作一股意识之流，流淌到儿子驾驶的飞机上，从一个侧面揭示了战争的残酷和失去亲人的痛苦。

Only This[①]

That night the frost was very heavy. It covered the hedges and whitened the grass in the fields so that it seemed almost as though it had been snowing. But the night was clear and beautiful and bright with stars, and the moon was nearly full.

The cottage stood alone in a corner of the big field. There was a path from the front door which led across the field to a stile[②] and on over the next field to a gate which opened on to the lane about three miles from the village. There were no other houses in sight and the country around was open and flat and many of the fields were under the plough because of the war.

---

① 本部小说原文出自“DAHL，R. *The Collected Short Stories of Roald Dahl* [M]. London：Penguin Books Ltd.，1992”。

② stile：*Noun* an arrangement of steps that allows people but not animals to climb over a fence or wall（篱或墙）两边的阶梯（供人越过用）

The light of the moon shone upon the cottage. It shone through the open window into the bedroom where the woman was asleep. She slept lying on her back, with her face upturned to the ceiling, with her long hair spread out around her on the pillow, and although she was asleep, her face was not the face of someone who is resting. Once she had been beautiful, but now there were thin furrows running across her forehead and there was a tightness about the way in which her skin was stretched over the cheekbones. But her mouth was still gentle, and as she slept, she did not close her lips.

The bedroom was small, with a low ceiling, and for furniture there was a dressing-table[①] and an armchair. The clothes of the woman lay over the back of the armchair where she had put them when she undressed. Her black shoes were on the floor beside the chair. On the dressing-table there was a hairbrush, a letter and a large photograph of a young boy in uniform who wore a pair of wings[②] on the left side of his tunic[③]. It was a smiling photograph, the kind that one likes to send to one's mother and it had a thin, black frame made of wood. The moon shone through the open window and the woman slept her restless sleep. There was no noise anywhere save for the soft, regular noise of her breathing and the rustle of the bedclothes as she stirred in her sleep.

Then, from far away, there came a deep, gentle rumble which grew

---

① dressing table or dressing-table: *Noun* a table with a mirror and drawers for cosmetics, etc., used while dressing or applying make-up 梳妆台

② wing: *Noun* (wings) a pilot's certificate of ability to fly a plane, indicated by a badge representing a pair of wings 飞行胸章(一种以双翼为图案,证明佩带者能驾机飞行的徽章)(e. g. Michael earned his wings as a commercial pilot. 迈克尔被授予合格商业飞行员胸章。)

③ tunic: *Noun* a close-fitting short coat as part of a uniform, especially a police or military uniform(尤指警察、军人的)紧身短上衣

and grew and became louder and louder until soon the whole sky seemed to be filled with a great noise which throbbed① and throbbed and kept on throbbing and did not stop.

Right at the beginning, even before it came close, the woman had heard the noise. In her sleep she had been waiting for it, listening for the noise and dreading the moment when it would come. When she heard it, she opened her eyes and for a while she lay quite still, listening. Then she sat up, pushed the bedclothes aside and got out of bed. She went over to the window and placing her hands on the window sill, she leaned out, looking up into the sky; and her long hair fell down over her shoulders, over the thin cotton nightdress which she wore.

For many minutes she stood there in the cold, leaning out of the window, hearing the noise, looking up and searching the sky; but she saw only the bright moon and the stars.

"God keep you," she said aloud. "Oh dear God keep you safe."

Then she turned and went quickly over to the bed, pulled the blankets away and wrapped them round her shoulders like a shawl②. She slipped her bare feet into the black shoes and walked over to the armchair and pushed it forward so that it was right up in front of the window. Then she sat down.

The noise and the throbbing overhead was very great. For a long time it continued as the huge procession of bombers moved towards the

---

① throb: *Verb* [no obj.] beat or sound with a strong, regular rhythm; pulsate steadily 有节奏地震动(或跳动、搏动);有规律地颤动(e. g. The crowded streets throbbed with life. 拥挤的街道上生机勃勃。)

② shawl: *Noun* a piece of fabric worn by women over the shoulders or head or wrapped round a baby(妇女戴的)披肩(或披巾);(裹婴儿的)包巾

south. All the while the woman sat huddled[①] in her blankets, looking out of the window into the sky.

Then it was over. Once more the night became silent. The frost lay heavy on the field and on the hedges and it seemed as though the whole countryside was holding its breath. An army was marching in the sky. All along the route people had heard the noise and knew what it was; they knew that soon, even before they had gone to sleep, there would be a battle. Men drinking beer in the pubs had stopped their talking in order to listen. Families in their houses had turned off the radio and gone out into their gardens, where they stood looking up into the sky. Soldiers arguing in their tents had stopped their shouting, and men and women walking home at night from the factories had stood still on the road, listening to the noise.

It is always the same. As the bombers move south across the country at night, the people who hear them become strangely silent. For those women whose men are with the planes, the moment is not an easy one to bear.

Now they had gone, and the woman lay back in the armchair and closed her eyes, but she did not sleep. Her face was white and the skin seemed to have been drawn tightly over her cheeks and gathered up in wrinkles around her eyes. Her lips were parted and it was as though she were listening to someone talking. Almost she could hear the sound of his voice as he used to call to her from outside the window when he came back from working in the fields. She could hear him saying he was hungry and asking what there was for supper, and then when he came in he would put his arm around her shoulder and talk to her about what he had

① huddle: *Verb* curl one's body into a small space(身子)缩成一团(e. g. She huddled up close to him. 她紧紧偎依着他。)

been doing all day. She would bring in the supper and he would sit down and start to eat and always he would say, why don't you have some and she never knew what to answer except that she wasn't hungry. She would sit and watch him and pour out his tea, and after a while she would take his plate and go out into the kitchen to get him some more.

It was not easy having only one child. The emptiness when he was not there and the knowing all the time that something might happen; the deep conscious knowing that there was nothing else to live for except this; that if something did happen, then you too would be dead. There would be no use in sweeping the floor or washing the dishes or cleaning the house; there would be no use in gathering wood for the fire or in feeding the hens; there would be no use in living.

Now, as she sat there by the open window she did not feel the cold; she felt only a great loneliness and a great fear. The fear took hold of her and grew upon her so that she could not bear it, and she got up from the chair and leaned out of the window again, looking up into the sky. And as she looked the night was no longer beautiful; it was cold and clear and immensely dangerous. She did not see the fields or the hedges or the carpet of frost upon the countryside; she saw only the depths of the sky and the danger that was there.

Slowly she turned and sank down again into her chair. Now the fear was great. She could think of nothing at all except that she must see him and be with him, that she must see him now because tomorrow would be too late. She let her head rest against the back of the chair and when she closed her eyes she saw the aircraft; she saw it clearly in the moonlight, moving forward through the night like a great, black bird. She was so close to it and she could see the way in which the nose of the machine reached out far ahead of everything, as though the bird was craning[①] its neck in the eagerness of its passage. She could see the markings on the wings and on the body and she knew that he was inside. Twice she called to him, but there was no answer; then the fear and the longing welled[②] up within her so that she could stand it no longer and it carried her forward through the night and on and on until she was with him, beside him, so close that she could have touched him had she put out her hand.

He was sitting at the controls with gloves on his hands, dressed in a great bulky[③] flying-suit which made his body look huge and shapeless and twice its normal size. He was looking straight ahead at the instruments on the panel, concentrating upon what he was doing and thinking of nothing except flying the machine.

Now she called to him again and he heard her. He looked around and when he saw her, he smiled and stretched out a hand and touched her shoulder, and then all the fear and the loneliness and the longing went out of her and she was happy.

For a long time she stood beside him watching him as he flew the machine. Every now and then he would look around and smile at her, and once he said something, but she could not hear what it was because of the noise of the engines. Suddenly he pointed ahead through the glass

---

① crane: *Verb* [no obj., with adverbial of direction] stretch out one's body or neck in order to see something 伸长脖子(看)(e. g. She craned forward to look more clearly. 她伸长脖子以看得清楚些。)

② well: *Verb* [no obj., with adverbial] (of a liquid) rise up to the surface and spill or be about to spill(液体)涌上;冒出(e. g. Tears were beginning to well in her eyes. 眼泪开始涌上她的眼眶。)

③ bulky: *Adjective* taking up much space, typically inconveniently; large and unwieldy 大的;容量大的;体积大的(e. g. a bulky carrier bag 一只容量很大的提包。)

windshield of the aeroplane and she saw that the sky was full of searchlights. There were many hundreds of them; long white fingers of light travelling lazily across the sky, swaying this way and that, working in unison[①] so that sometimes several of them would come together and meet in the same spot and after a while they would separate and meet again somewhere else, all the time searching the night for the bombers which were moving in on the target.

Behind the searchlights she saw the flak[②]. It was coming up from the town in a thick many-coloured curtain, and the flash of the shells as they burst in the sky lit up the inside of the bomber.

He was looking straight ahead now, concentrating upon the flying, weaving through the searchlights and going directly into this curtain of flak, and she watched and waited and did not dare to move or to speak lest she distract him from his task.

She knew that they had been hit when she saw the flames from the nearest engine on the left side. She watched them through the glass of the side panel, licking against the surface of the wing as the wind blew them backwards, and she watched them take hold of the wing and come dancing over the black surface until they were right up under the cockpit itself. At first she was not frightened. She could see him sitting there, very cool, glancing continually to one side, watching the flames and flying the machine, and once he looked quickly around and smiled at her and she knew then that there was no danger. All around she saw the search-

---

① in unison: If people or organizations are working in unison, they are working together, because they agree with each other 一致地;协调地(e.g. I am pleased to report that the various committees are now working in unison to thoroughly investigate this matter. 我很高兴地告诉大家,各委员会正在一致行动,彻底调查这件事。)

② flak: *Noun* (also as "flack") [mass noun] anti-aircraft fire 高射炮火

lights and the flak and the explosions of the flak and the colours of the tracer①, and the sky was not a sky but just a small confined space which was so full of lights and explosions that it did not seem possible that one could fly through it.

But the flames were brighter now on the left wing. They had spread over the whole surface. They were alive and active, feeding on the fabric②, leaning backwards in the wind which fanned them and encouraged them and gave them no chance of going out.

Then came the explosion. There was a blinding white flash and a hollow *crumph* as though someone had burst a blown-up paper bag; then there was nothing but flames and thick whitish-grey smoke. The flames were coming up through the floor and through the sides of the cockpit; the smoke was so thick that it was difficult to see and almost impossible to breathe. She became terrified and panicky because he was still sitting there at the controls, flying the machine, fighting to keep it on an even keel③, turning the wheel first to one side, then to the other, and suddenly there was a blast of cold air and she had a vague impression of urgent crouching figures scrambling past her and throwing themselves away from the burning aircraft.

Now the whole thing was a mass of flames and through the smoke she could see him still sitting there, fighting with the wheel while the crew got out, and as he did so he held one arm up over his face because the heat was so great. She rushed forward and took him by the shoulders and shook him and shouted, "Come on, quickly, you must get out,

---

① tracer: *Noun* a bullet or shell whose course is made visible in flight by a trail of flames or smoke, used to assist in aiming 曳光弹

② fabric: *Noun* the body of a car or aircraft 车身;飞机机身

③ on an even keel: regular and well-balanced and not likely to change suddenly 平稳地;稳定的

quickly, quickly."

Then she saw that his head had fallen forward upon his chest and that he was limp[①] and unconscious. Frantically she tried to pull him out of the seat and towards the door, but he was too limp and heavy. The smoke was filling her lungs and her throat so that she began to retch[②] and gasp for breath. She was hysterical now, fighting against death and against everything and she managed to get her hands under his arms and drag him a little way towards the door. But it was impossible to get him farther. His legs were tangled[③] around the wheel and there was a buckle somewhere which she could not undo. She knew then that it was impossible, that there was no hope because of the smoke and the fire and because there was no time; and suddenly all the strength drained out of her body. She fell down on top of him and began to cry as she had never cried before.

Then came the spin and the fierce rushing drive downwards and she was thrown forward into the fire so that the last she knew was the bright yellow of the flames and the smell of the burning.

Her eyes were closed and her head was resting against the back of the chair. Her hands were clutching the edges of the blankets as though she were trying to pull them tighter around her body and her long hair fell down over her shoulders.

Outside the moon was low in the sky. The frost lay heavier than ever

---

① limp: *Adjective* lacking internal strength or structure; not stiff or firm 无力的;不坚挺的;松弛的(e. g. She let her whole body go limp. 她让自己的整个身体松弛下来。)

② retch: *Verb* [no obj.] make the sound and movement of vomiting 干呕

③ tangle: *Verb* [with obj.] (often as "be tangled") twist together into a confused mass 缠绕;纠结(e. g. The broom somehow got tangled up in my long skirt. 扫帚不知怎么和我的长裙缠在一起了。)

on the fields and on the hedges and there was no noise anywhere. Then from far away in the south came a deep gentle rumble which grew and grew and became louder and louder until soon the whole sky was filled with the noise and the singing of those who were coming back.

But the woman who sat by the window never moved. She had been dead for some time.

三、翻译探索

这篇小说虽然将现实与意识的流动完美的结合起来,翻译起来难度不是很大,但需把握好译文的整体风格,力争做到真实而形象的再现。

仅此而已

那天晚上,霜降得很浓,盖住了树篱,染白了田野中的绿草,几乎相当于下了一场雪。但是,那天晚上却清澈、美丽,星星隐约闪烁,月亮也几乎圆了。

在一大块田地的一角,一座乡村小屋孤零零地立在那儿。屋子的前门伸出一条小道,小道穿越田地通向围墙边的一个阶梯,越过阶梯就来到另一块田地之上。这块田地通向一个栅栏门,打开这道栅栏门就走进一个小巷,小巷离村子有不到五公里的距离。视野所见,再也没有其他房屋了,周围的乡野很是开阔、平坦。由于战争的缘故,很多的田地还没有犁过。

月光照在乡村小屋上,并通过开启的窗户射进小屋的卧室。卧室里,一位妇人已入梦乡。这位妇人仰卧着,脸冲着天花板,长发在她枕头的周围散落开来。尽管她人已经睡着,但是,她的脸却与安睡中的人的脸不一样。她曾经美丽过,但如今,一道道细细的皱纹已经爬上了额头,面颊骨表面的皮肤紧巴巴的。她那张嘴温柔如初,睡觉时,双唇并没有紧闭。

卧室很小,天花板很矮。至于家具摆设,屋子里有一张梳妆台,还有一把扶手椅。睡前脱衣时,妇人将衣物搭到了扶手椅的椅背上,只是那双黑鞋放在椅子旁边的地板上。梳妆台上放了一把发刷、一封信,还有一张大幅照片,照片上有一名年轻的男子,身穿军人制服,紧身短上衣左侧佩戴了一对飞行胸章。照片镶在一个很薄的黑色木相框内,照片上的男子面带微笑。孩子喜欢邮寄给母亲看的正是这样的照片。月光透过开启的窗户照射进来,妇人进入了梦乡,但是,睡得并不安稳。除了妇人轻柔的、有规律的呼吸声,还有睡梦中翻身时铺盖发出的窸窣声音之外,周围的一切都静悄悄的。

接着,从很远的地方传来隆隆的声音,声音低沉而轻微,但音量却渐渐扩大,越来越响、越来越响。转眼间,整个天空似乎都充满了这样一种巨大的噪音。这种噪音剧烈地震荡着、震荡着,不停地震荡着,没有停歇。

就在这种声音刚刚升起、还没有传过来的时候,这位妇人就已经听到了。在她的睡梦之中,她一直等待着这种声音,时刻在听着这种声音,而这种声音真正传来那一刻,她又惊恐起来。听到这种声音,她睁开了双眼,一动不动地躺在那儿,听了好一会儿。紧接着,她坐了起来,将铺盖推到一边,下了床。她走到窗户跟前,双手放在窗台上,倚身窗外,眼睛向天空观望。她的长发垂到双肩上,垂在她那单薄的棉睡袍上面。就这样,在寒冷之中,她在那儿站了不知多少分钟——倚身窗外,听着这种声音,抬起头搜寻着天空,但眼睛所见却只有明亮的月亮,还有稀疏隐约的星星。

"上帝保佑你,"她大声说。"哦,亲爱的孩子,上帝保佑你安然无恙。"

然后,她转身,快速走回床边,把毯子从床上扯下来,当成披肩缠绕到肩上,再将光着的两只脚伸进黑鞋里,走到扶手椅那儿,将椅子推到窗户前,坐了下来。

头顶上的噪音以及噪音带来的震荡感很是剧烈。一大长串轰炸机向南飞去,发出的噪音持续了很长时间。其间,这位妇人蜷缩在毯子里坐在那儿,向窗外的天空看去。

接着,一切都结束了。夜晚再次寂静起来,霜浓浓地覆盖着田地和树篱,而就在刚才,整个乡村似乎屏住了呼吸。一支军队在天空行进,沿途的人们听到了其行进的声音,心里清楚是怎么回事,于是,这些人甚至在没有入睡前就知道,一场战斗很快就会开始。各个酒吧里,喝着啤酒的男子也不再彼此交谈,而是停下来听着这种声音。各家各户的人也都关掉收音机,走进各自的花园中,站在那儿,仰望天空。营地帐篷里争论不休的士兵也不再大喊大叫了。夜晚工厂里干完活往家走的男男女女也都停下了脚步,一动不动地站在路上,听着这种声音。

每次情况都是一样的。夜晚,轰炸机穿过乡村的天空向南飞去,人们听到了飞机的声音都安静了下来。对于丈夫也在其中驾机战斗的妻子而言,这一时刻可不是那么好过的。

现在,这些飞机已经飞远,声音消失了。这位妇人躺到扶手椅子上,闭上了双眼,但并没有入睡。她的脸色苍白,面颊表面的皮肤似乎绷得更紧了,都聚到了眼睛周围,形成了道道皱纹。她的双唇没有合上,好似听着什么人说话,似乎听到了他从窗户外面朝着她喊叫的声音——他从田地里劳作回来经常这样喊叫。她能够听得见他的喊叫,说他饿了,问晚饭要吃什么。进屋后,他就用一只胳膊搂着她的肩膀,告诉她这一整天他在外面都干了些什么活儿。然后,她端来晚饭,于是,他就坐下来,吃了起来。每次吃的时候,他总会问,你为什么不一起吃点儿啊。每每此时,她就不知道如何回答,只是说她不饿。接着,她就坐下来,看着他吃,然后给他倒茶。再过一会儿,她就会端起他的盘子,走进厨房,再给他盛一些端回来。

只生一个孩子的日子不好过。孩子不在家,房子空空如也;总是提心吊胆:孩子或许会遭遇什么不幸;深深地意识到,没有了孩子,人生就没有了奔头。孩子果真有什么三长两短,做母亲的就不如一死了之,活着也就没有什么意义了:打扫地板没有什么意义,洗盘洗碗没有什么意义,清理房间没有什么意义,搜集木柴生火没有什么意义,喂养母鸡没有什么意义。

现在,她坐在开启的窗户前,并不感到寒冷,只是感觉无比孤寂、非常恐惧。这种恐惧感占据了她的全身,蔓延开来,令她无法忍受。于是,她又一次倚身窗外,向夜空张望。可这次,她眼中的夜晚不再那么美丽，而是变得寒冷、清澈，危机四伏。她眼中所见，并没有田地、树篱、乡下浓密的凝霜，只有深邃的夜空，还有夜空里藏匿的危险。

她慢慢地转回身，一屁股又坐到椅子上。现在，这种恐惧感更强烈了。除了想一定要见到他、跟他在一起之外，她什么都不想。现在，她等不及了，必须得见到他，明天太晚了。她将头靠到椅子的后背上休息，但一闭上眼睛，眼前就出现了那架飞机。月光里，那架飞机看得清清楚楚，像一只巨大的黑鸟，穿过夜空向前飞行。她离飞机太近了，能够看见机头单独凸了出来、向前远远伸出，就像鸟儿伸长了脖子、急切往前飞去，甚至还能看到机翼上、机身上的标识。于是，她知道，他就在这架飞机上。她冲着他喊了两次，但是，他没有回应。接着，恐惧感和渴望感从她的内心喷涌而出，令她再也无法忍受，任由飞机载着她穿过夜空一直向前，不停地向前飞呀，飞呀。最终，她跟他在一起了，站到了他的身旁，跟他挨得很近，几乎伸出一只手，就能够触摸到他。

他坐在那儿，双手戴着手套，周围尽是些控制装置。他身穿大大的、笨重的飞行服，看不出什么体形来，身体显得臃肿不堪，甚至达到正常身体大小的两倍。他的眼睛笔直盯着前面控制面板上的各种仪表，精神高度集中，除了驾驶飞机，他心无旁骛。

现在，她又冲着他喊了一声。这次，他听到了，只见他向周围看了看，看见了她，然后他微微一笑，伸出一只手，触摸一下她的肩膀。就在那时，她所有的恐惧感、孤寂感、渴望感都消失不见，她感到十分开心。

她在他身旁站了很长时间，看着他驾驶着飞机。他不时地转过来，冲着她微笑。有一次，他还说了句什么，但是，她没有听见他说的是什么，因为引擎发出的噪音太大了。突然，通过驾驶舱的玻璃罩，他用手指指向前方。她一眼看过去，发现前方的天空里出现了一束束探照灯的光柱。光柱有成百上千束之多，犹如长长的白色手指，懒洋洋地在天空里划来闪去、移来扭去。这些光束步调一致，甚至有的时候，其中有好几束会相遇，聚集到相同的地点。相聚一会儿后，分开,然后又在别的地点相遇、聚齐。这些探照灯,无时无刻不在搜寻着夜晚的天空。一旦搜寻到轰炸机,就朝其开火。

透过束束光柱,她看到高射炮发出的炮火,炮火从城镇那儿涌起,形成一道稠密而多彩的帘幕。炮弹在夜空爆炸闪出的光芒照亮了轰炸机的驾驶舱。

现在,他笔直盯着前方,集中精力驾驶着,迂回地穿过束束光柱,径直飞进高射炮火的帘幕之中。她观看着、等待着,不敢移动,也不敢说话,唯恐分散了他的注意力,耽误他执行任务。

她看到左翼最近处的一个引擎冒烟起火了,于是,她知道,飞机给击中了。她通过侧板的玻璃看着火焰,风将火焰贴着机翼的表面向后吹去。她看着火焰弥漫了整个机翼,在机翼黑色的表面跳跃,最后消失到驾驶舱底下。一开始的时候,她并不害怕,因为她能够看见他坐在那儿,很是镇定,不断瞅着一侧,看着火焰,继续驾驶着飞机。有那么一次,他快速转了过来,冲着她微笑了一下,于是,她知道,那时候没有任何危险存在。她看到周围尽是探照灯的光柱、高射炮火、炮弹爆炸的闪光、闪光的色彩。那时,天空已不再是天空,而只是一小片受限的空间,布满了光柱,弥漫着爆炸的闪光,似乎不可能从其中飞过。

可是,飞机左翼的火焰越来越明亮起来,已经波及整个飞机表面。火焰生机勃勃、活蹦乱跳,撕咬着机身。风扇动着火焰,从后面推动着火焰,激励着火焰继续燃烧,根本不给火焰熄灭的机会。

接着,传来了爆炸声,只见耀眼的白光一闪,听到低沉的“咔嚓”一声响,就好像有人将吹涨的纸袋弄爆一般。紧接着,就只能看见火焰,还有灰中稍带点白色的浓烟。火焰透过驾驶舱的地板和四周窜了出来,随即产生浓烈的烟雾,很难看清东西,几乎不可能呼吸。她恐惧害怕、惊慌失措,因为他依然坐在控制装置前驾驶着飞机,奋力使飞机保持平稳状态,先向一边转向,再向另一边转向。突然之间,一股冷空气扑面而来,她模糊感觉有人急速下蹲,从她身旁快速爬过,然后纵身跃出燃烧着的飞机。

现在,整个飞机都成了一大团火焰。通过烟雾,她能够看到他依然坐在那儿,奋力控制着方向,而机组人员都跳了出去。他一边控制着方向,一边举起一只胳膊,挡在脸上,因为火焰发出了巨大的热量。于是,她冲上前,抓住他的双肩,边摇晃边喊道:“快跳,快。你必须跳了,快,快。”

接着,她看到他的头向胸前倒去,整个人也没有了力气,失去了知觉。她疯一般尽力将他拉下座位,要拖向舱门。可是,他整个人软绵绵的,沉重得拖拉不动。烟雾呛进了她的肺部和嗓子,呛得她干呕起来,上气不接下气。现在,她歇斯底里起来,要与死亡抗争,要与一切抗争。只见她将双手插到他的胳膊下,要一点一点将他拽向舱门,但是,不可能将他拽出多远。他的双腿缠绕到方向舵上,也不知道什么地方还有一个带扣,她无法解开。她知道,解开是不可能的,也没有什么希望了,因为浓烟滚滚,火焰炽烈,也没有时间了。突然之间,她耗尽了浑身的气力,跌倒在他的身上,开始大哭起来。以前,她从来没有这样哭过。

接下来,飞机旋转起来,猛烈向下俯冲,她也被向前甩去,被甩入火焰。她最后记得的是火焰那明亮的黄色,还有燃烧的气味。

她的双眼紧闭,头靠在椅子背上,长发垂到了双肩,双手攥住毯子边缘,就好像她要将毯子更紧地缠绕到身体上似的。

外面,月亮在天空低垂下来,田地里、树篱上的霜变得更浓了,四周静悄悄的一片。接着,从南方很远的地方传来低沉、轻微的隆隆声,音量却渐渐扩大,越来越响、越来越响。转眼间,整个天空都充满了这样一种巨大的噪音,还伴随着返回飞行员的歌声。

但是,这位坐在窗户边的妇人却再也没有动弹一下。她已经死去好长一段时间了。

第二节 《老手之死》*Beath of an Old Old Man*

罗尔德·达尔的《老手之死》(Death of an Old Old Man)首次发表在《女士家庭杂志》(*Ladies' Home Journal*)1945 年 9 月号上。后

来，这篇小说又收录到《向你飞跃》(*Over to You*)、《罗尔德·达尔短篇故事集锦》(*The Collected Short Stories of Roald Dahl*)、《五部畅销书集》(*5 Bestsellers*)以及《〈女士家庭杂志〉珍品集》(*The Ladies' Home Journal Treasury*)等书中。

一、原作导读

达尔的这篇小说分为三个部分，第一部分是以第一人称视角的"意识流"状态来写的，第二部分则转向第三人称的角度——叙述的是一场空战的惨烈，第三部分是故事的结尾，作者又将视角转向了第一人称"我"的"意识流"状态。

"我"是飞行员查利，刚刚接到了上级的指令。一接到指令，"我"就知道"我"要起飞作战了，要冒着枪林弹雨驾机作战了，不由得感叹："噢，天呐，我是多么恐惧害怕啊"(Oh God, how I am frightened)，但"我"却装出一副不以为然的样子，就好像早就知道这道指令的内容似的。可是，今非昔比，现在接到这道指令的心情跟以前大不相同了。不管怎么说，"我"不是胆小鬼，不会打退堂鼓，要勇往直前，奋勇杀敌。

飞行员查利笔直地坐在驾驶舱里，双手、双眼、双脚灵敏地操作和运动，时刻警惕着前方可能出现的敌机。突然，他看到了"一架福克沃尔夫战斗机，机翼上都装备了加农机关炮，驾驶舱里坐的则是一名活生生的德国飞行员"(a life-size German pilot sitting in a Focke Wulf which had cannon in its wings)。空中鏖战开始了。他跟那个福克沃尔夫战斗机驾驶员势均力敌，旗鼓相当，不分胜负，但最终双方险些迎面相撞。双方驾驶员分别弹射跳伞，落向地面。查利知道，那个德军驾驶员会紧随自己落地。不幸的是，查利落到了一个池塘里，被降落伞绳索缠住，无法立即脱身。落入池塘之中的查利意识到那个德军飞行员已经落地，将他往水下摁去，他开始渐渐失去了知觉……

"我"不想再去挣扎，挣扎没有任何意义。

看看吧，天空是多么明媚，这块田野是多么美丽，上面有一头头奶牛、小小的池塘，还有绿绿的树篱，中间生长着黄色的报春花。

See how sunny it is and what a beautiful field this is, with the cows and the little pond and the green hedges with primroses growing in the hedges.

那个德军飞行员似乎从池塘里将一个沉沉的东西拖了上来，拽到草地上。噢，原来他拖的是一具男子的尸体——“事实上，我想，他拖的就是我”(As a matter of fact, I think it's me)。

现在，他跪了下来，在我的衣兜里翻来翻去，将我的钱和身份证件掏了出来，他还找到我的烟斗以及一封信，那封信是我今天早晨收到的，是母亲写给我的。他将我的手表也摘了下来。现在，他站起身，要走开。

Now he's kneeling down, searching in my pockets, taking out my money and my identification card. He's found my pipe and the letter I got this morning from my mother. He's taking off my watch. Now he's getting up. He's going away.

“我”想，他应该向“我”一样学会放松，于是，“我”提醒他说：“你为什么不放松一下呢？”(Why don't you relax a bit?)。听到这句话，他吓坏了，撒腿就跑，不停地奔跑，头也不回。

我想，我要在这儿待一会，然后沿着树篱走走，采摘一些报春花。要是运气好的话，或许我会找到几朵白色的紫罗兰。接着，我就开始睡觉，在太阳底下暖洋洋地睡觉。

I think I'll stay here for a bit. I think I'll go along the hedges and find some primroses, and if I am lucky I may find some white violets. Then I will go to sleep. I will go to sleep in the sun.

二、原作释读

这部作品是作家罗尔德·达尔从英国皇家空军退役后不久写的另一篇"二战"题材的短篇小说，角度的切换以及现实与意识的转换有些不那么自然，但仍不失为一篇扣人心弦的作品，值得一读。

Death of an Old Old Man[①]

Oh God, how I am frightened.

Now that I am alone I don't have to hide it; I don't have to hide anything any longer. I can let my face go because no one can see me; because there's twenty-one thousand feet between me and them and because now that it's happening again I couldn't pretend any more even if I wanted to. Now I don't have to press my teeth together and tighten the muscles of my jaw as I did during lunch when the corporal[②] brought in the message; when he handed it to Tinker and Tinker looked up at me and said, "Charlie, it's your turn. You're next up." As if I didn't know that. As if I didn't know that I was next up. As if I didn't know it last night when I went to bed, and at midnight when I was still awake and all the way through the night, at one in the morning and at two and three and four and five and six and at seven o'clock when I got up. As if I didn't know it while I was dressing and while I was having breakfast and while I was

① 本部小说原文出自"DAHL, R. *The Collected Short Stories of Roald Dahl*, London: Penguin Books Ltd., 1992"。

② corporal: *Noun* a rank of non-commissioned officer in the army, above lance corporal or private first class and below sergeant 下士

reading the magazines in the mess, playing shove-halfpenny[1] in the mess, reading the notices in the mess, playing billiards in the mess. I knew it then and I knew it when we went in to lunch, while we were eating that mutton for lunch. And when the corporal came into the room with the message it wasn't anything at all. It wasn't anything more than when it begins to rain because there is a black cloud in the sky. When he handed the paper to Tinker I knew what Tinker was going to say before he had opened his mouth. I knew exactly what he was going to say.

So that wasn't anything either.

But when he folded the message up and put it in his pocket and said, "Finish your pudding. You've got plenty of time," that was when it got worse, because I knew for certain then that it was going to happen again, that within half an hour I would be strapping myself in and testing the engine and signalling to the airmen to pull away the chocks[2]. The others were all sitting around eating their pudding; mine was still on my plate in front of me, and I couldn't take another mouthful. But it was fine when I tightened my jaw muscles and said, "Thank God for that. I'm tired of sitting around here picking my nose." It was certainly fine when I said that. It must have sounded like any of the others just before they started off. And when I got up to leave the table and said, "See you at tea time," that must have sounded all right too.

But now I don't have to do any of that. Thank Christ I don't have to

---

① shove-halfpenny: *Noun* [mass noun] a game in which coins are struck so that they slide across a marked board on a table 打硬币游戏(将放在桌面上的硬币打入标线区)

② chock: *Noun* a wedge or block placed against a wheel or rounded object, to prevent it from moving(轮子或圆形物下防滚动的)楔子;垫木

do that now. I can just loosen up[①] and let myself go. I can do or say anything I want so long as I fly this aeroplane properly. It didn't use to be like this. Four years ago it was wonderful. I loved doing it because it was exciting, because the waiting on the aerodrome was nothing more than the waiting before a football game or before going in to bat; and three years ago it was all right too. But then always the three months of resting and the going back again and the resting and the going back; always going back and always getting away with it, everyone saying what a fine pilot, no one knowing what a near thing it was that time near Brussels[②] and how lucky it was that time over Dieppe[③] and how bad it was that other time over Dieppe and how lucky and bad and scared I've been every minute of every trip every week this year. No one knows that. They all say, "Charlie's a great pilot,"

"Charlie's a born flyer,"

"Charlie's terrific."

I think he was once, but not any longer.

---

① loosen up: *Verb* make or become relaxed (loosen someone up)(使)放松(e. g. They taught me to have fun at work and loosen up. 他们教我上班时开心点儿,要学会放松。)

② Brussels: *Noun* the capital of Belgium and in the Belgian province of Brabant; pop. 954,000 (1991). The headquarters of the European Commission is located there. 布鲁塞尔(比利时首都,在布拉班特省;1991 年人口 954,000,欧洲委员会总部设在此地。)

③ Dieppe: *Noun* a channel port in northern France, from which ferries run to Newhaven and elsewhere; pop. 36,600 (1990). In August 1942 it was the scene of an unsuccessful amphibious raid by a joint force of British and Canadian troops to destroy the German-held port and airfield. 迪耶普(位于法国北部的一个海峡港口,有渡船通往纽黑文和其他地方,1990 年人口 36,600;1942 年 8 月,英国和加拿大联军对该地发动两栖攻击,试图摧毁德军控制的港口和机场,但遭失败。)

Each time now it gets worse. At first it begins to grow upon you slowly, coming upon you slowly, creeping up on you from behind, making no noise, so that you do not turn round and see it coming. If you saw it coming, perhaps you could stop it, but there is no warning. It creeps closer and closer, like a cat creeps closer stalking[①] a sparrow, and then when it is right behind you, it doesn't spring like the cat would spring; it just leans forward and whispers in your ear. It touches you gently on the shoulder and whispers to you that you are young, that you have a million things to do and a million things to say, that if you are not careful you will buy it[②], that you are almost certain to buy it sooner or later, and that when you do you will not be anything any longer; you will just be a charred corpse. It whispers to you about how your corpse will look when it is charred, how black it will be and how it will be twisted and brittle[③], with the face and the fingers black and the shoes off the feet because the shoes always come off the feet when you die like that. At first it whispers to you only at night, when you are lying awake in bed at night. Then it whispers to you at odd moments during the day, when you are doing your teeth or drinking a beer or when you are walking down the passage; and in the end it becomes so that you hear it all day and all night all the time.

---

① stalk: *Verb* [with obj.] pursue or approach stealthily 悄悄地追踪(或靠近)(e. g. a cat stalking a bird 一只悄悄靠近鸟儿的猫)

② buy it: (Slang) to be killed(俚语)被杀;被枪杀

③ brittle: *Adjective* hard but liable to break or shatter easily 脆的;易碎的(e. g. Her bones became fragile and brittle. 她的骨头变得脆而易碎。)

There's Ijmuiden[①]. Just the same as ever, with the little knob[②] sticking out just beside it. There are the Frisians, Texel, Vlieland, Terschelling, Ameland, Juist and Norderney. I know them all. They look like bacteria under a microscope. There's the Zuider Zee, there's Holland, there's the North Sea[③], there's Belgium, and there's the world; there's the whole bloody world right there, with all the people who aren't going to get killed and all the houses and the towns and the sea with all the fish. The fish aren't going to get killed either. I'm the only one that's going to get killed. I don't want to die. Oh God, I don't want to die. I don't want to die today anyway. And it isn't the pain. Really it isn't the pain. I don't mind having my leg mashed or my arm burnt off; I swear to you that I don't mind that. But I don't want to die. Four years ago I didn't mind. I remember distinctly not minding about it four years ago. I didn't mind about it three years ago either. It was all fine and exciting; it always is when it looks as though you may be going to lose, as it did then. It is always fine to fight when you are going to lose everything anyway, and that was how it was four years ago. But now we're going to win. It is so different when you are going to win. If I die now I lose fifty years of life, and I don't want to lose that. I'll lose anything except that because that would be all the things I want to do and all the things I want to see; all the things like going on sleeping with Joey. Like going home

---

① 这里的"Ijmuiden",以及本段提到的"Frisians""Texel""Vlieland""Terschelling""Ameland""Juist""Norderney""Zuider Zee",都是欧洲一些国家(特别是荷兰和德国)的地名,主要为岛屿名称。

② knob: *Noun* (chiefly N. Amer.) a prominent round hill(主要为北美英语用法)圆形小山

③ North Sea: *Noun* an arm of the Atlantic Ocean lying between the mainland of Europe and the coast of Britain, important for its oil and gas deposits. 北海(大西洋位于欧洲大陆和不列颠岛海岸之间的部分,为产石油及天然气的重要地区。)

sometimes. Like walking through a wood. Like pouring out a drink from a bottle. Like looking forward to week ends and like being alive every hour every day every year for fifty years. If I die now I will miss all that, and I will miss everything else. I will miss the things that I don't know about. I think those are really the things I am frightened of missing. I think the reason I do not want to die is because of the things I hope will happen. Yes, that's right. I'm sure that's right. Point a revolver at a tramp, at a wet shivering tramp on the side of the road and say, "I'm going to shoot you," and he will cry, "Don't shoot. Please don't shoot." The tramp clings to life because of the things he hopes will happen. I am clinging to it for the same reason; but I have clung for so long now that I cannot hold on much longer. Soon I will have to let go. It is like hanging over the edge of a cliff, that's what it is like; and I've been hanging on too long now, holding on to the top of the cliff with my fingers, not being able to pull myself back up, with my fingers getting more and more tired, beginning to hurt and to ache, so that I know that sooner or later I will have to let go. I dare not cry out for help; that is one thing that I dare not do; so I go on hanging over the side of this cliff, and as I hang I keep kicking a little with my feet against the side of the cliff, trying desperately to find a foothold[①], but it is steep and smooth like the side of a ship, and there isn't any foothold. I am kicking now, that's what I am doing. I am kicking against the smooth side of the cliff, and there isn't any foothold. Soon I shall have to let go. The longer I hang on the more certain I am of that, and so each hour, each day, each night, each week, I become more and more frightened. Four years ago I wasn't hanging over the edge like this. I was running about in the field above, and although I

---

① foothold: *Noun* a place where a person's foot can be lodged to support them securely, especially while climbing(尤指攀登时踩脚的)立足处

knew that there was a cliff somewhere and that I might fall over it, I did not mind. Three years ago it was the same, but now it is different.

I know that I am not a coward. I am certain of that. I will always keep going. Here I am today, at two o'clock in the afternoon, sitting here flying a course of one hundred and thirty-five at three hundred and sixty miles an hour and flying well; and although I am so frightened that I can hardly think, yet I am going on to do this thing. There was never any question of not going or of turning back. I would rather die than turn back, Turning back never enters into it. It would be easier if it did. I would prefer to have to fight that than to have to fight this fear.

There's Wassalt①. Little camouflaged② group of buildings and great big camouflaged aerodrome, probably full of one-o-nines and one-nineties. Holland looks wonderful. It must be a lovely place in the summer. I expect they are haymaking down there now. I expect the German soldiers are watching the Dutch girls haymaking. Bastards. Watching them haymaking, then making them come home with them afterwards. I would like to be haymaking now. I would like to be haymaking and drinking cider③.

The pilot was sitting upright in the cockpit. His face was nearly hid-

① "Wassalt"这个地名,要么是作家达尔虚构的,要么就是拼写有误,无从查找。

② camouflage: *Verb* [with obj.] (often as "be camouflaged") hide or disguise the presence of (a person, animal, or object) by means of camouflage 伪装;掩饰;遮掩(人、动物或物体)(e. g. The caravan was camouflaged with netting and branches from trees. 运输车队用网和树枝来作掩护。)

③ cider: *Noun* [mass noun] (Brit.) an alcoholic drink made from fermented apple juice(英国英语)苹果酒

den by his goggles[1] and by his oxygen mask. His right hand was resting lightly upon the stick, and his left hand was forward on the throttle[2]. All the time he was looking around him into the sky. From force of habit his head never ceased to move from one side to the other, slowly, mechanically, like clockwork, so that each moment almost, he searched every part of the blue sky, above, below and all around. But it was into the light of the sun itself that he looked twice as long as he looked anywhere else; for that is the place where the enemy hides and waits before he jumps upon you. There are only two places in which you can hide yourself when you are up in the sky. One is in cloud and the other is in the light of the sun.

He flew on; and although his mind was working upon many things and although his brain was the brain of a frightened man, yet his instinct was the instinct of a pilot who is in the sky of the enemy. With a quick glance, without stopping the movement of his head, he looked down and checked his instruments.

The glance took no more than a second, and like a camera can record a dozen things at once with the opening of a shutter[3], so he at a glance recorded with his eyes his oil pressure, his petrol, his oxygen, his rev counter, boost and his air-speed, and in the same instant almost he was looking up again into the sky. He looked at the sun, and as he looked, as he screwed up his eyes and searched into the dazzling brightness of the sun, he thought that he saw something. Yes, there it was; a

---

① goggle: *Noun* (goggles) close-fitting glasses with side shields, for protecting the eyes from glare, dust, water, etc. (用以挡光、防尘、防水等的)护目镜

② throttle: *Noun* a device controlling the flow of fuel or power to an engine 油门杆

③ shutter: *Noun* (Photography) a device that opens and closes to expose the film in a camera(摄影)快门

small black speck moving slowly across the bright surface of the sun, and to him the speck was not a speck but a life-size German pilot sitting in a Focke Wulf① which had cannon② in its wings.

He knew that he had been seen. He was certain that the one above was watching him, taking his time, sure of being hidden in the brightness of the sun, watching the Spitfire③ and waiting to pounce. The man in the Spitfire did not take his eye away from the small speck of black. His head was quite still now. He was watching the enemy, and as he watched, his left hand came away from the throttle and began to move delicately around the cockpit. It moved quickly and surely, touching this thing and that, switching on his reflector sight, turning his trigger button from "safe" over to "fire" and pressing gently with his thumb upon a lever④ which increased, ever so slightly, the pitch of the airscrew⑤.

There was no thought in his head now save for the thought of battle. He was no longer frightened or thinking of being frightened. All that was a dream, and as a sleeper who opens his eyes in the morning and forgets his dream, so this man had seen the enemy and had forgotten that he was frightened. It was always the same. It had happened a hundred times before, and now it was happening again. Suddenly, in an instant he had become cool and precise, and as he prepared himself, as he made ready

---

① 这里的"Focke Wulf",指的是德国福克沃尔夫战机,为单座位、单引擎战斗机,被视为"二战"期间最优秀的战斗机之一。

② cannon: *Noun* an automatic heavy gun that fires shells from an aircraft or tank(飞机或坦克上的)机关炮

③ 这里的"Spitfire",指的是"二战"时期英国的斯比特喷火战机。

④ lever: *Noun* a projecting arm or handle that is moved to operate a mechanism(机械装置的)操作手柄;控制杆;操纵杆(e. g. She pulled a lever at the base of the cage. 她拉了一下机器罩壳底座上的一根控制杆。)

⑤ airscrew: *Noun* (Brit.) an aircraft propeller(英国英语)螺旋桨

his cockpit, he watched the German, waiting to see what he would do.

This man was a great pilot. He was great because when the time came, whenever the moment arrived, his coolness was great and his courage was great, and more than anything else his instinct was great, greater by far than his coolness or his courage or his experience. Now he eased open the throttle and pulled the stick gently backwards, trying to gain height, trying to gain a little of the five-thousand-feet advantage which the German had over him. But there was not much time. The Focke Wulf came out of the sun with its nose down and it came fast. The pilot saw it coming and he kept going straight on, pretending that he had not seen it, and all the time he was looking over his shoulder, watching the German, waiting for the moment to turn. If he turned too soon, the German would turn with him, and he would be duck soup[①]. If he turned too late, the German would get him anyway provided that he could shoot straight, and he would be duck soup then too. So he watched and waited, turning his head and looking over his shoulder, judging his distance; and as the German came within range, as he was about to press his thumb upon the trigger button, the pilot swerved. He yanked[②] the stick hard back and over to the left, he kicked hard with his left foot upon the rudder-bar, and like a leaf which is caught up and carried away by a gust of wind, the Spitfire flipped over on to its side and changed direction. The pilot blacked out[③].

---

① duck soup: *Noun* [mass noun] (N. Amer. informal) an easy task, or someone easy to overcome(北美英语非正式用法)易如反掌的事;容易对付的人(e. g. We had some great battles, but against me he was duck soup. 我们之间有过几番重大的较量,但他远非我的对手。)

② yank: *Verb* [with obj.] pull with a jerk 用力猛拉

③ black out: (of a person) undergo a sudden and temporary loss of consciousness(人)突然失去知觉;晕眩

As his sight came back, as the blood drained away from his head and from his eyes, he looked up and saw the German fighter way ahead, turning with him, banking hard, trying to turn tighter and tighter in order to get back on the tail of the Spitfire. The fight was on. "Here we go," he said to himself. "Here we go again," and he smiled once, quickly, because he was confident and because he had done this so many times before and because each time he had won.

The man was a beautiful pilot. But the German was good too, and when the Spitfire applied a little flap in order to turn in tighter circles, the Focke Wulf appeared to do the same, and they turned together. When the Spitfire throttled back suddenly and got on his tail, the Focke Wulf half-rolled and dived out and under and was away, pulling up again in a loop and rolling off the top, so that he came in again from behind. The Spitfire half-rolled and dived away, but the Focke Wulf anticipated him, and half-rolled and dived with him, behind him on his tail, and here he took a quick shot at the Spitfire, but he missed. For at least fifteen minutes the two small aircraft rolled and dived around each other in the sky. Sometimes they would separate, wheeling around and around in tight turns, watching one another, circling and watching like two boxers circling each other in the ring, waiting for an opening or for the dropping of a guard; then there would be a stall-turn① and one would attack the other, and the diving and the rolling and the zooming would start all over again.

All the time the pilot of the Spitfire sat upright in his cockpit, and he flew his aircraft not with his hands but with the tips of his fingers, and the Spitfire was not a Spitfire but a part of his own body; the muscles of

---

① stall turn or stall turn: *Noun* an aerobatic manoeuvre in which the aircraft climbs vertically before being stalled, when it turns on one wing into a dive(特技飞行中的)失速转弯;跃升失速倒转

his arms and legs were in the wings and in the tail of the machine so that when he banked and turned and dived and climbed he was not moving his hands and his legs, but only the wings and the tail and the body of the aeroplane; for the body of the Spitfire was the body of the pilot, and there was no difference between the one and the other.

So it went on, and all the while, as they fought and as they flew, they lost height, coming down nearer and nearer to the fields of Holland, so that soon they were fighting only three thousand feet above the ground, and one could see the hedges and the small trees and shadows which the small trees made upon the grass.

Once the German tried a long shot, from a thousand yards, and the pilot of the Spitfire saw the tracer streaming past in front of the nose of his machine. Once, when they flew close past each other, he saw, for a moment, the head and shoulders of the German under the glass roof of his cockpit, the head turned towards him, with the brown helmet, the goggles, the nose and the white scarf. Once when he blacked out from a quick pull-out[①], the black-out lasted longer than usual. It lasted maybe five seconds, and when his sight came back, he looked quickly around for the Focke Wulf and saw it half a mile away, flying straight at him on the beam[②], a thin inch-long black line which grew quickly, so that almost at once it was no longer an inch, but an inch and a half, then two inches, then six and then a foot. There was hardly any time. There was a second or perhaps two at the most, but it was enough because he did not have to think or to wonder what to do; he had only to allow his instinct to control his arms and his legs and the wings and the body of the aeroplane. There was only one thing to do, and the Spitfire did it. It banked

① pull-out or pullout: *Noun* change from a dive to level flight(飞机的)改出动作(俯冲后恢复水平飞行的动作)

② on the beam: (informal) on the right track(非正式)方向正确

steeply and turned at right-angles towards the Focke Wulf, facing it and flying straight towards it for a head-on attack.

The two machines flew fast towards each other. The pilot of the Spitfire sat upright in his cockpit, and now, more than ever, the aircraft was a pan of his body. His eye was upon the reflector sight, the small yellow electric-light dot which was projected up in front of the windshield, and it was upon the thinness of the Focke Wulf beyond. Quickly, precisely, he moved his aircraft a little this way and that, and the yellow dot, which moved with the aircraft, danced and jerked this way and that, and then suddenly it was upon the thin line of the Focke Wuif and there it stayed. His right thumb in the leather glove felt for the firing-button; he squeezed it gently, as a rifleman① squeezes a trigger, his guns fired, and at the same time, he saw the small spurts② of flame from the cannon in the nose of the Focke Wulf. The whole thing, from beginning to end, took perhaps as long as it would take you to light a cigarette. The German pilot came straight on at him and he had a sudden, vivid, colourless view of the round nose and the thin outstretched wings of the Focke Wulf. Then there was a crack as their wing-tips met, and there was a splintering③ as the port wing of the Spitfire came away from the body of the machine.

The Spitfire was dead. It fell like a dead bird falls, fluttering a little as it died; continuing in the direction of its flight as it fell. The hands of the pilot, almost in a single movement, undid his straps, tore off his helmet and slid back the hood of the cockpit; then they grasped the edges of

---

① rifleman: *Noun* a soldier armed with a rifle, especially a private in a rifle regiment 步枪手;步兵(尤指步兵团的列兵)

② spurt: *Noun* a sudden gushing stream 喷射流(e. g. a sudden spurt of blood gushed into her eyes 一股血喷进她的眼里。)

③ splinter: *Verb* break or cause to break into small sharp fragments(使)裂成碎片

the cockpit and he was out and away, falling, reaching for the ripcord[①], grasping it with his right hand, pulling on it so that his parachute billowed out and opened and the straps jerked him hard between the fork of his legs.

All of a sudden the silence was great. The wind was blowing on his face and in his hair and he reached up a hand and brushed the hair away from his eyes. He was about a thousand feet up, and he looked down and saw flat green country with fields and hedges and no trees. He could see some cows in the field below him. Then he looked up, and as he looked, he said "Good God," and his right hand moved quickly to his right hip, feeling for his revolver which he had not brought with him. For there, not more than five hundred yards away, parachuting down at the same time and at the same height, was another man, and he knew when he saw him that it could be only the German pilot. Obviously his plane had been damaged at the same time as the Spitfire in the collision. He must have got out quickly too; and now here they were, both of them parachuting down so close to each other that they might even land in the same field.

He looked again at the German, hanging there in his straps with his legs apart, his hands above his head grasping the cords of the parachute. He seemed to be a small man, thickly built and by no means young. The German was looking at him too. He kept looking, and when his body swung around the other way, he turned his head, looking over his shoulder.

So they went on down. Both men were watching each other, thinking about what would happen soon, and the German was the king because he was landing in his own territory. The pilot of the Spitfire was coming

① ripcord: *Noun* a cord that is pulled to open a parachute(降落伞的)开伞索

down in enemy country; he would be taken prisoner, or he would be killed, or he would kill the German, and if he did that, he would escape. I will escape anyway, he thought. I'm sure I can run faster than the German. He does not look as though he could run very fast. I will race him across the fields and get away.

The ground was close now. There were not many seconds to go. He saw that the German would almost certainly land in the same field as he, the field with the cows. He looked down to see what the field was like and whether the hedges were thick and whether there was a gate in the hedge, and as he looked, he saw below him in the field a small pond, and there was a small stream running through the pond. It was a cow-drinking pond, muddy round the edges and muddy in the water. The pond was right below him. He was no more than the height of a horse above it and he was dropping fast; he was dropping right into the middle of the pond. Quickly he grasped the cords above his head and tried to spill the parachute to one side so that he would change direction, but he was too late; it wasn't any good. All at once something brushed the surface of his brain and the top of his stomach, and the fear which he had forgotten in the fighting was upon him again. He saw the pond and the black surface of the water of the pond, and the pond was not a pond, and the water was not water; it was a small black hole in the surface of the earth which went on down and down for miles and miles, with steep smooth sides like the sides of a ship, and it was so deep that when you fell into it, you went on falling and falling and you fell for ever. He saw the mouth of the hole and the deepness of it, and he was only a small brown pebble which someone had picked up and thrown into the air so that it would fall into the hole. He was a pebble which someone had picked up in the grass of the field. That was all he was and now he was falling and the hole was below him.

Splash[①]. He hit the water. He went through the water and his feet hit the bottom of the pond. They sank into the mud on the bottom and his head went under the water, but it came up again and he was standing with the water up to his shoulders. The parachute was on top of him; his head was tangled in a mass of cords and white silk and he pulled at them with his hands, first this way and then that, but it only got worse, and the fear got worse because the white silk was covering his head so that he could see nothing but a mass of white cloth and a tangle of cords. Then he tried to move towards the bank, but his feet were stuck in the mud; he had sunk up to his knees in the mud. So he fought the parachute and the tangled cords of the parachute, pulling at them with his hands and trying to get them clear of his head; and as he did so he heard the sound of footsteps running on the grass. He heard the noise of the footsteps coming closer and the German must have jumped, because there was a splash and he was knocked over by the weight of a man's body.

He was under the water, and instinctively he began to struggle. But his feet were still stuck in the mud, the man was on top of him and there were hands around his neck holding him under and squeezing his neck with strong fingers. He opened his eyes and saw brown water. He noticed the bubbles in the water, small bright bubbles rising slowly upward in the brown water. There was no noise or shouting or anything else, but only the bright bubbles moving upward in the water, and suddenly, as he watched them, his mind became clear and calm like a sunny day. I won't struggle, he thought. There is no point in struggling, for when there is a black cloud in the sky, it is bound to rain.

He relaxed his body and all the muscles in his body because he had

---

① splash: *Noun* a sound made by something striking or falling into liquid 物体击打(或落入)液体时发出的声音;啪啪声;泼溅声(e.g. We hit the water with a mighty splash. 我们用力拍水发出很大的响声。)

no further wish to struggle. How nice it is not to struggle, he thought. There is no point in struggling. I was a fool to have struggled so much and for so long; I was a fool to have prayed for the sun when there was a black cloud in the sky. I should have prayed for rain; I should have shouted for rain. I should have shouted, Let it rain, let it rain in solid sheets and I will not care. Then it would have been easy. It would have been so easy then. I have struggled for five years and now I don't have to do it any more. This is so much better; this is ever so much better, because there is a wood somewhere that I wish to walk through, and you cannot walk struggling through a wood. There is a girl somewhere that I wish to sleep with, and you cannot sleep struggling with a girl. You cannot do anything struggling; especially you cannot live struggling, and so now I am going to do all the things that I want to do, and there will be no more struggling.

See how calm and lovely it is like this. See how sunny it is and what a beautiful field this is, with the cows and the little pond and the green hedges with primroses① growing in the hedges. Nothing will worry me any more now, nothing nothing nothing; not even that man splashing in the water of the pond over there. He seems very puffed② and out of breath. He seems to be dragging something out of the pond, something heavy. Now he's got it to the side and he's pulling it up on to the grass. How funny; it's a body. It's a body of a man. As a matter of fact, I think it's me. Yes, it is me. I know it is because of that smudge③ of yellow paint

---

① primrose: *Noun* a European plant of woodland and hedgerows, which produces pale yellow flowers in the early spring 报春花;樱草

② puff: *Verb* [no obj.] breathe in repeated short gasps 喘;喘气(e.g. Exercises make you puff. 锻炼让你气喘吁吁的。)

③ smudge: *Noun* a blurred or smeared mark on the surface of something 污迹(e.g. a smudge of blood on the floor 地板上的一块血迹。)

on the front of my flying suit. Now he's kneeling down, searching in my pockets, taking out my money and my identification card. He's found my pipe and the letter I got this morning from my mother. He's taking off my watch. Now he's getting up. He's going away. He's going to leave my body behind, lying on the grass beside the pond. He's walking quickly away across the field towards the gate. How wet and excited he looks. He ought to relax a bit. He ought to relax like me. He can't be enjoying himself that way. I think I will tell him.

"Why don't you relax a bit?"

Goodness, how he jumped when I spoke to him. And his face; just look at his face. I've never seen a man look as frightened as that. He's starting to run. He keeps looking back over his shoulder, but he keeps on running. But just look at his face; just look how unhappy and frightened he is. I do not want to go with him. I think I'll leave him. I think I'll stay here for a bit. I think I'll go along the hedges and find some primroses, and if I am lucky I may find some white violets[①]. Then I will go to sleep. I will go to sleep in the sun.

三、翻译探索

在这篇小说中，作家罗尔德·达尔提及一些地名，翻译时需一一落实。无从查找时，可依据读音进行音译。第一部分里的大段内心独白式的"意识流"，在翻译时需谨慎处理，避免误解。

老手之死

噢，天呐，我是多么恐惧害怕啊。

既然现在剩下我孤零零一个人，我也不必隐藏这种状态了，我也

① violet: *Noun* a herbaceous plant of temperate regions, typically having purple, blue, or white five-petalled flowers, one petal of which forms a landing pad for pollinating insects 堇菜；紫罗兰

没有必要再去隐藏什么了。我可以不要脸面，因为没有谁能够看到我，因为我和他们之间远隔六千三百米，因为既然这种事情再一次发生，我就是想装，也不能再装下去了。现在，我的上下牙齿不必再紧紧咬到一起，也不必将颌部肌肉绷得紧紧的，但午饭期间，下士带来那个便条的时候，我却咬紧牙关、绷紧肌肉。当时，下士把便条递给廷克，廷克抬头看了看我，说道："查利，轮到你了，你下一个起飞升空。"他那口气，好像我一无所知似的，就好像我不知道下一个起飞的就是我；他那口气，就好像昨晚上床睡觉时、半夜醒来时我不知道这个消息似的，就好像后半夜一点、两点、三点、四点、五点、六点、七点起来的时候，我不知道这个消息似的；他那口气，就好像穿衣服时、吃早饭时我不知道这个消息似的；他那口气，就好像在军人食堂看杂志时、玩打硬币游戏时、读告示时、打台球时我不知道这个消息似的。那时候，我就知道了。走进去吃午饭时我就知道了，午饭吃的是羊肉。所以嘛，那名下士带着那张便条走进屋子时，这个消息根本就算不上什么事儿了。当时，这个消息根本算不上什么事儿了，就如同天空有一块乌云就会下起雨来一样。下士将便条递给廷克时，即使廷克还没有张开嘴说话，我就知道他要说什么了。我知道他要说什么的，分毫不差地知道。

所以，他要说什么也就不是什么事儿啦。

他将纸条折起来，揣进衣兜，说："把布丁吃完，你有的是时间。"可就在此时，这种事情就变得更为糟糕起来，因为当时我肯定地知道，这种事情又来了。那就意味着，半个小时之内，我就得系好安全带，测试好引擎，然后示意空勤人员将固定轮子的支架抽走。但此时，其他人都坐成一圈吃着布丁，而我的布丁仍然放在面前的盘子里，却一口也吃不下。但是，当我绷紧颌部肌肉说："为了那事儿，我感谢上帝。围坐在这儿，抠着鼻孔，我开始感到厌倦了。"说完，我感觉好了起来。说完那话之后，我的感觉当然是不错了。我那语气听起来一定很像其他所有人起飞前说话的语气。站起身离开餐桌时，我说："下午茶点时间见。"那话听起来也一定轻松、自然。

但是现在，那样的事情我一件都不用做了。感谢基督耶稣，现在我不用去做那样的事情了。我仅仅需要放松些,然后出发。只要我驾驶好这架飞机,我想做什么就可以做什么,想说什么就可以说什么,但是,以前的情况可不是这个样子。四年前,情况很美好。那时,我酷爱开飞机,因为飞机开起来很令人兴奋,在小型机场的等待如同足球赛前的等待,或者类似于击球前的等待。三年前,情况也还算可以,但是接下来,情况就总是这样的:回来休息三个月,再返回,接着再休息,再返回;总是返回,然后侥幸成功,安然无恙。人人都说,当飞行员如何、如何好,但是,没有人知道,那一次在靠近布鲁塞尔时,险象环生,我却侥幸脱险。没有人知道,那一次在迪耶普上空时,我的运气是多么好,而另一次也是在迪耶普上空,情况又是多么糟糕。没有人知道,今年每一周每一次飞行当中的每一分钟,我是多么幸运,又是多么糟糕,又是多么害怕。没人知道这一切。大家都说"查利飞得真棒""查利天生就是个飞行员的料"以及"查利真是了不起"等话语。

我想,他曾经是这样的,但现在,不再如此了。

现在,每飞行一次,情况就变得更为糟糕。起先,糟糕的情况慢慢地降临,慢慢地靠近,从身后蹑手蹑脚地接近,一点声响也没有发出来,结果就是,你没有转身,也没有看到它靠近。要是你看到它靠近,或许你就会阻止它的出现,可问题是,一点危险的前兆都没有。它蹑手蹑脚地靠近,再靠近,就像一只猫蹑手蹑脚、悄无声息地靠近一只麻雀。接下来,它到了你的身后,却并不像那只猫那样"嗖"的一下跳出来、扑上前,它只是倾斜一下,俯身在你的耳朵上,跟你低声耳语。它轻柔地碰一下你的肩膀,压低声音对你说,你还年轻,你有多如牛毛的事情要做,有多如牛毛的话要说,你要是不加小心的话,你就得自负后果,而且几乎可以肯定的是,你迟早会自负后果的。它还说,你要是自负后果的话,你就什么都不是了,你就仅仅是一具烧焦的尸体了。它就会继续压低声音对你说,你的尸体烧焦后会是什么样子,尸体的颜色会多么黑,尸体会多么扭曲变形、软弱易碎——脸和手指都黑黑的,鞋也从脚上脱落,因为像那样死去,鞋总是会从脚上脱落的。刚开始的时候,只有在夜晚,它才压低声音对你说这样的话，趁夜间你在床上醒来的时候对你说。接着，它就会在白天见缝插针，压低声音对你说这样的话，趁着你咬紧牙关、喝啤酒、沿着过道行走的时候对你说。到了最后，不管是白天还是黑夜，你都会听到它无时无刻不对你说这样的话了。

艾默伊登这个地方，跟以往一样，旁边凸起一座圆形小山。弗里西亚群岛、泰瑟尔岛、弗利兰岛、泰尔斯海灵岛、阿默兰岛、于斯特岛和诺德奈岛，这些我都熟悉，它们看起来就像在显微镜下观察到的细菌。有须得海湾、荷兰、北海、比利时，还有整个世界，整个世界就在那儿——整个世界上的人都不该送命，整个世界上所有的房子和城镇都不该被摧毁，整个世界上所有的海洋连同海洋里所有的鱼都不该灭亡。所有的鱼都不该死掉，唯一该死掉的就是我，但我不愿意死去。噢，上帝啊，我不想死去。不管怎么说，我不想今天就死去。我不想死，不是因为疼痛。说真的，不是因为什么疼痛。腿被砸烂，胳膊被烧掉，我不介意——我向你发誓，我不介意。可是，我不想死去。四年前，对于死亡，我不介意。我清清楚楚地记得，四年前我对死亡毫不介意。三年前，对于死亡，我也不介意。当时，干什么都行，且令人兴奋不已；看起来你好像或许会失败的时候——当时的情形的确如此，情况总是如此：干什么都行，且令人兴奋不已。无论如何，在你行将失去所有的时候，总是会奋不顾身、英勇作战，但那是四年以前的情况。现在的情况是，我们要赢了，要赢的时候，情况迥然不同。要是现在我死了，五十年的生命我就丢掉了，这五十年我还想好好活着呢。我将失去所有，所有想做的事情我都做不成，所有想看的东西我都看不到。我将失去所有人生乐趣，包括跟乔伊共枕同眠、偶尔回家看看、穿越树林散步、从瓶子里倒出一杯酒、盼望周末的到来，以及五十年里的每一年、每一年里的每一天、每一天里的每一小时，都时时刻刻处于活着的状态，等等。现在，要是我死了，我将失去所有这一切，失去所有其他方面的东西。我将失去我所不知道的东西。我想，这些东西真的是我害怕会失去的东西。我想，我不想死去是因为有些事情我希望会发生的。是的，没错，我敢肯定没错。用左轮手枪指着流浪汉——站在路边的一个湿漉漉的、浑身颤抖的流浪汉，说：

"我要毙了你。"此时,他会大哭:"不要杀我,请不要杀我。"流浪汉求生,是因为有些事情他希望会发生的。可是,时至今日,我求生的时间拖得太长,无法拖得更久了。很快,我就将起飞出发,如同悬挂到了悬崖边缘的上方,目前就是这么一个情况——命悬一线。何况现在,我悬挂的时间太长了,手指紧紧抓住悬崖的顶部,却没有气力将自己拉上去,而且我的手指越来越疲乏,受了伤,开始疼痛起来,因此我知道,迟早我不得不松手、落下。我不敢大喊救命,喊救命是我不敢去做的一件事情。所以,我只能继续在悬崖边悬挂着,悬挂的同时,我不断用脚踢悬崖的侧面,拼命想找到一个落脚点,可是,崖边太陡峭、太光滑,什么落脚点也踢不出来,就如同轮船的侧面。现在,我不断踢着崖边,那就是我现在的所作所为。我不断地踢向光滑的悬崖边缘,可是一个立脚点也踢不出来。很快,我将不得不放手、下落。这一点,抓的时间越长,我越敢肯定。所以,随着时间一个小时接着一个小时、一个白天接着一个白天、一个夜晚接着一个夜晚、一个星期接着一个星期的流逝,我越发恐惧不已。四年前,我可不是像这样悬挂在悬崖的边缘,我是在悬崖顶端的田野里四处奔跑。尽管我知道某处有悬崖,我或许会掉下去,但是,我不介意。三年前,也是一样的,但是现在,情况迥然不同。

我知道,我不是一个胆小鬼,对此我十分肯定。我始终如一,勇往直前。此时此地,下午两点钟,我坐在这里,以每小时近五百八十公里的航速,飞越近二百二十公里的航程,而且飞行状况良好。尽管我恐惧害怕到了几乎无法思考的程度,我还是要勇往直前去完成任务。从来没有考虑过畏缩不前而打退堂鼓,我宁愿一命呜呼,而不会打退堂鼓。打退堂鼓的念头从来没有产生过,但话说回来,打退堂鼓容易得很。我宁愿勇往直前与敌厮杀,也不愿意因为恐惧而思前想后。

在瓦斯索尔特,有一小排伪装起来的房子和一大片伪装起来的飞机场,或许停满了109型或者190型战机。荷兰看起来美极了,那里的夏季一定是个可爱的地方。我期望那里的天空下,人们正在晾晒干草。我期望,德国兵在那儿看着荷兰女孩晾晒干草。这些狗杂种。他们看着她们晾晒干草,然后迫使她们跟他们一起回家。现在,我很想晾晒干草。我很想晾晒干草,喝着苹果酒。

这位飞行员笔直坐在驾驶舱里,护目镜和氧气罩几乎将他的脸遮挡起来了。他的右手轻轻放在操纵杆上,左手向前推动油门杆。他的眼睛始终扫视着周围的天空,他的脑袋已经习惯成自然,从未停止过转动——慢慢地机械式转动,从一侧转到另一侧,如同时钟一般。这样的话,几乎每时每刻,他都在搜寻着蓝天的每一个角落:上面、下面以及周围的方方面面,但是,要是进入阳光照射下耀眼的区域,他搜寻的时间是其他区域的两倍长,因为这样的区域往往是敌人隐藏起来的区域,敌人就是从这样的区域向你扑来。飞到空中后,只有两个区域你可以躲藏,一个是云彩里的区域,另一个就是阳光照射下耀眼的区域。

他继续飞行。尽管他在心里思考着很多事情,尽管他的大脑仍然是一个恐惧害怕之士的大脑,但是,他的直觉却是一位飞入敌人上空的飞行员的直觉。他的脑袋不停地移动,眼睛飞速转动,审视下方,查看各种仪表。他的眼睛扫过一遍的时间不超过一秒钟,就像一台照相机一次开启快门能同时记录下多种事物一样,他眼睛的每一次扫视就能够查看到油压、油量、氧气量、引擎转数、提升量、空速,而且几乎在同一时刻,他还会抬头看一看上空。他看向太阳,在阳光的刺激下,他收紧了眼部肌肉,在太阳炫目的光亮里搜寻着。就这样,一眼看过去,他想,他看到了什么东西了。是的,那里是有某个东西,一粒小小的黑斑慢慢地穿过太阳的表面移动着。对于他来说,那可不是一般的斑点,而是一架福克沃尔夫战斗机,机翼上都装备了加农机关炮,驾驶舱里坐的则是一名活生生的德国飞行员。

他知道自己已经暴露了,他敢肯定,上方那个家伙正观察着他,但却并不着忙。那个家伙认为自己藏在太阳的光芒里万无一失,因此,他只是看着下方的斯比特喷火战机,等待时机猛冲出来。现在,下方坐在斯比特喷火战机的这位男子的脑袋一动不动的,眼睛始终盯着那个小小的黑斑——他的敌人,与此同时,他的左手从油门杆上移开,开始在驾驶舱里面灵巧地摸了起来。他的那只手摸来摸去,很是迅速,对摸到的每一样东西都把握十足。随后,那只手打开反射瞄准镜,将扳机开关从“保险”位置推向“开火”位置,大拇指轻轻地压到一个操纵杆上,这样会增加爬行的高度,但是,增加的幅度很是轻微。

现在,他的大脑中除了投入战斗的想法,其他任何想法都没有了。他不再恐惧害怕,也不再去想恐惧害怕这件事情了。所有的恐惧都是一场梦,早晨梦醒后睁开双眼,梦中的一切统统都忘掉。因此,这名男子看到了敌人,恐惧害怕这件事情早就抛到九霄云外了。这样的过程都是一样的,以前出现过一百次了,而现在又一次出现了。突然,就在一闪念之间,他镇定下来,一切变得有条不紊了。他开始做准备,在驾驶舱里做好了战斗的准备,同时他看到,那个德国兵正等待着,看看对方会有什么样的举动。

这名男子是一位了不起的飞行员。他之所以了不起,就是因为时机一到,也不管什么时候事到临头,他的镇定和勇气都是了不起的,尤其了不起的是他的直觉。到目前为止,他的直觉比他的镇定、勇气,抑或他的经验,都要更加的了不起。现在,他不再加大油门,而是将油门杆轻轻地往后拉,尽力要提升高度,尽力要拉近一点儿,跟上方那个德国飞行员之间保持一千五百米的差距,但是,没有多少时间了。福克沃尔夫战机机头朝下,从太阳的光芒里窜了出来,而且速度很快。下方这位飞行员看到它俯冲过来,但是,还是笔直上升,假装没有看见它。他自始至终从肩膀上方看过去,看着那个德国兵,等待着时机的成熟。要是他过早转弯,德国兵也会跟着转弯,那么,他就成了对方的盘中餐了。要是转弯太迟,德国飞行员只要能够笔直射击的话,也能击中他,他也会成为对方的盘中餐。所以,他只能观察、等待,并回头从肩膀上方看过去,同时判断着与对方之间的距离。上方的德国飞行员进入了有效射程、就要在扳机按钮上将大拇指按下的时候,下方的飞行员却突然改变了方向,只见他用力向后猛拉操纵杆,跃向左侧,然后用左脚使劲踹了下橡胶套杆。紧接着,斯比特喷火战机向一侧翻转过去,改变了方向,就像一片叶子被一股劲风顶住、又刮跑一样。于是,斯比特喷火战机的飞行员眩晕起来。

视觉再次恢复的时候,他的大脑和双眼已不再充血。他抬头看了看,发现德国战斗机在前方很远的地方,正往他这边转弯,机身侧倾得很厉害,弯转得越来越急、越来越急,目的是想飞回到斯比特喷火战机的尾部。激战在所难免了。"我们开始吧,"他自言自语。"我们又碰面啦,"说完,他笑了一下,飞快地笑了一下,因为对此他信心十足,这样的事情以前经历过很多次了,而且每次他都能旗开得胜。

这位飞行员干得十分漂亮,但是,那位德国飞行员同样身手敏捷。斯比特喷火战机轻微侧翻了一下,意欲急转几个圈子,而福克沃尔夫战机看起来也在鹦鹉学舌,于是,它们一起旋转起来。斯比特喷火战机调整油门突然间减慢了速度,飞到了福克沃尔夫战机的尾部,而福克沃尔夫战机则半翻转一下,下降了高度,从底部溜走,一个回环之后又提升了高度,从顶部横滚下来,这样,它就又从尾部上来了。于是,斯比特喷火战机半翻转一下,往下一潜就溜走了,但是,福克沃尔夫战机预料到这一点,也跟着它一起半翻转、下潜,紧紧尾随着。就在此刻,福克沃尔夫战机里的飞行员飞快地朝斯比特喷火战机射击一下,但是没有命中。在足足十五分钟的时间里,这两架小战机在天空里翻滚着,一会儿你潜到我下面,一会儿我潜到你下面,僵持不下。有的时候,它们彼此分开,在周围绕来绕去,急速转着圈子,观察着对方。它们就像两名拳击选手一样,在场地里彼此绕来绕去,等待着要打开缺口,或者等待对方放松警惕。一旦逮着机会,双方就会在跃升失速的倒转过程中相互射击,然后再下潜、翻转,接着又开始了新的一轮陡直上升的过程。

自始至终,驾驶斯比特喷火战机的这位飞行员都是笔直坐在驾驶舱里,他不是用双手驾驶飞机,而是用手指尖操作。这样的话,斯比特喷火战机就不是一架战机了,而是成了他身体的一部分。他的胳膊和腿部的肌肉溶进了机翼和飞机的尾部,这样,要是他侧倾、转弯、下潜、爬升的时候,他就不用移动手和腿,而只是移动机翼和机身就可以啦,因为斯比特喷火战机的身体就是他的身体,战机跟他的身体融合到一起,没有任何区别了。

就这样,这种情况持续着。他们且飞且战,然后失去高度,离荷兰的地面越来越近、越来越近,很快,他们就搏击在距离地面九百米的天空之上,能够看到地面上的树篱、小树,还有小树在草地上投下的影子。

有一次,德国飞行员远距离射击,距离约摸有九百多米,斯比特喷火战机的飞行员看见了曳光弹从飞机前部流过的轨迹。有一次,他们贴得很近,擦肩飞过,有那么一小会儿的时间,他看到了对方战机驾驶舱玻璃罩下面那名德国飞行员的脑袋和肩膀,脑袋戴着棕色的头盔向他这边转过来,他还看到对方的护目镜、鼻子,以及白色的围巾。有一次,一个俯冲过后,再将飞机拉直飞行时,他眩晕过去,这次眩晕比往常持续时间要长些,持续时间或许有五秒钟吧。视觉再次恢复后,他快速向四周观瞧,找寻福克沃尔夫战机,发现它在一里半以远的地方,正朝他笔直地飞来,一点误差都没有。起先,它看起来只是一条两厘米半长的线条,但长度迅速增加,几乎就在一瞬间,它不再是两厘米半长了,而是将近四厘米长了,紧接着变成五厘米长、十五厘米长,最后竟然达到三十厘米长。几乎没有什么时间了,只剩下一秒钟,或许至多两秒钟,但那也足矣,因为他不必去思考,也不必去算计该如何去做。他唯有凭借自己的直觉来控制胳膊和腿,控制机翼和机身。只有一件事情可做,而斯比特喷火战机做到了。只见它急剧侧身,呈直角转向福克沃尔夫战机,面对面飞向它,径直飞过去要来个迎头痛击。

两架战机急速向彼此飞去。斯比特喷火战机的飞行员笔直坐在驾驶舱里,他的飞机从来没有像现在这样,已经完全成了他身体的一部分。他的一只眼睛盯着反射瞄准镜,盯着那上面的一个小小的黄色电子光点,光点定位到下方那架福克沃尔夫战机映射成的弱小影像上,同时,那个光点也被映射到面前的挡风玻璃上面。他驾驶着自己的战机一会儿向这边挪一下,一会儿向那边移一点,身手敏捷、移位准确。那个小黄点,也随着机身的移动而移动,只见它一边跳跃着,一边向这、向那猛烈晃动起来。突然之间,它定位到福克沃尔夫战机细长的影像轮廓上面，凝固不动了。他那只戴着皮革手套的右手的大拇指触摸到了开火按钮，并轻轻按压一下，如同一位步枪手轻扣扳机一样。枪声随即响起，与此同时，他看见福克沃尔夫战机前部的加农机关炮里喷射出一股股发出微光的火焰。整个过程，从最开始的时候算起，到最后结束，持续的时间也就是点燃一支香烟所用的时间。那名德国飞行员径直向他迎头奔来，突然之间，他看到了无色的福克沃尔夫战机的前部，还有其向外伸展开来的细细的翅膀，那画面近在眼前、栩栩如生。紧接着，听到"咔嚓"一声响，两架飞机的翅膀尖相碰，然后，"哗啦"一下，斯比特喷火战机的左舷机翼碎裂，与机身分裂开来。

斯比特喷火战机完蛋了，只见它像一只死鸟一般掉落，边掉落边扑棱着翅膀，边掉落边沿着原来的方向继续飞行。紧接着，飞行员的双手几乎是一气呵成所有的动作：解开安全带，扯掉头盔，掀开驾驶舱盖，然后抓住驾驶舱边缘，整个人出舱、下落，下落的同时伸出右手去够伞索，够到后紧紧抓住，然后一拉，这样降落伞就迎风鼓胀起来，整只伞打开，伞绳从他两腿之间的分叉处将他猛地一下拖住。

突然间，一切都变得静谧起来。风吹向他的脸，吹进他的头发，他抬起一只手，将头发从眼前轻轻拂去。他现在悬浮在约三百米的空中，向下看了看，看到了平坦的绿色乡村，那里有田野、树篱，但是没有树木，他还能够看到身下的田野里有一些奶牛。然后，他抬头看去，边看边说："老天啊。"随即，他快速伸出右手，向右屁股摸去，要摸自己的左轮手枪，但是，他忘记随身携带了。在他的上方约四百五十米以远的地方，还有一个男子跟他在同一时间、同一高度跳伞下落。一看到那个人，他就清楚，那个人不能是别人，只能是那名德国飞行员。很明显，在跟斯比特喷火战机碰撞的同时，他的战机也毁掉了，他当时一定也是快速出舱。所以呢，天空中现在有了他们两个人，他们两个人都跳伞下落，而且他们彼此离得很近，或许会在同一地点落地。

他又看了看那个德国人，只见他双腿岔开，由伞带牵引着下落，双手举过头顶，紧紧地抓住伞的绳索。那个德国人看起来个头矮小，但身体粗壮,肯定不年轻了。德国人也正看着他,一直看个不停,即使身体被风吹向另一侧,还是转过头,从肩膀上方看过来。

就这样,他们两个继续下降,边下降,边彼此观察着,都在琢磨马上会出现什么样的情况。德国伞兵是大王,因为他是在自己的国家降落,而斯比特喷火战机的伞兵则是在敌国的领地降落,他就是囚徒。不是他被德国兵杀死,就是他杀死德国兵。如果杀死了德国兵,他就得逃跑。他想,无论如何,我要跑掉,我肯定,我跑得比德国兵快,那个德国兵看起来不像是能跑得很快的人,我要和他比赛穿过田野,然后跑掉。

现在接近地面了,用不了几秒的时间就到达地面了。他看到,那个德国兵几乎可以肯定会跟他降落到同一块田野里,也就是有很多奶牛的那块田野。他向下看去,要看看那块田野是什么样子,树篱是否很厚实,树篱是否有栅栏门。看着看着,他看到下方的田野里有一小块池塘,一条小溪穿越池塘流淌。那块池塘是供牛饮水用的,池塘里外都很泥泞。池塘就在他下方,他离池塘的距离不足一匹马的高度,而且他下落的速度很快,正好就要落到池塘的中间。于是,他快速抓住头顶的伞绳,欲将伞体偏向一侧,以便改变下落方向,但是已经太晚了,一点用处都没有。突然之间,某种东西一下子擦过他的大脑皮层,拂过他的肚子表皮。此时,激战中被他抛到九霄云外的恐惧害怕再度降临。他看到了池塘,看到了池塘黑色的水面。顿时,池塘也不再是池塘,池水也不再是池水了。池塘变成了地球表面上的一个小小的黑色洞穴,这个洞穴往下延伸了一公里又一公里,其陡峭、光滑的边缘如同轮船的侧面,而且深不见底,以至于你一旦跌入其中,你就一直不停地下落、下落,永远下落不止。他看到了洞口,也看到了它深不可测。他仅仅是一块小小的、棕色的圆石头,被人拾起,抛入空中,就要落入洞穴。他就是一块被某个人从草地的泥土中拾起来的小圆石头。他就是这个样子。现在,他就要落下,洞穴就在他身下。

“啪嗒”一声,他的身体拍击到水面。他落入水中,双脚碰到了池塘的底部,陷入底部淤泥之中,脑袋也没入水中,但又伸了出来,整个人站在水里,水面跟肩膀齐平。降落伞落在他的上面,他的脑袋被一团绳索和白色的丝质伞布缠住,他用双手拉扯着绳索和伞布,向这边拉拉,再往那面拽拽,但是,情况越来越糟,拉扯不开。同时,恐惧害怕感也越来越强烈,因为白色的丝质伞布遮住了他的脑袋,他看到的除了一大片白布和一团乱糟糟的绳索之外,什么都没有。接下来,他试图向岸边挪动,但是,他的双脚陷进烂泥中,陷到了膝盖的部位。就这样,他撕扯着降落伞,拉扯着乱糟糟缠绕成一团的伞绳,双手奋力撕拉,欲将脑袋挣脱开来。忙碌之中,他听到草地上有人奔跑的脚步声,嘈杂的脚步声越来越近,那个德国人一定是跳进了池塘,只听得"啪嗒"一声水响,他被一名男子的体重的力量击倒。

他落入水中,本能地开始挣脱,但是,双脚仍然陷在烂泥之中,况且,还有那个家伙在他的上方。两只手扼住了他的脖子往下压,手指使劲掐住了他的脖子。他睁开双眼,看到了棕色的池水,还注意到串串气泡——明亮的、小小的气泡——在棕色的水中慢慢地升腾。没有噪音,没有喊叫,什么都没有,只有明亮的气泡在水中往上冒。他看着串串气泡,突然之间,内心清澈、平静起来,如同阳光明媚的天气一样。他想,我不再挣扎了,挣扎一点用处也没有,正所谓,天上黑云密布,必将有雨降落。

他放松身体,松弛身上所有的肌肉,因为他不想再挣扎。他想,不去挣扎感觉多放松啊。挣扎没有任何意义。刚才竟然奋力挣扎了这么久,我有多傻啊。天空中乌云一片,却祈求太阳露面,我有多傻啊。我应该祈求下雨才对,我应该放声大叫,求雨降落。我应该大喊:让雨降落吧,让雨大片、大片地落下,我会笑哈哈。那么,事情就容易了,到那时一切都迎刃而解。我已经挣扎了五年,现在,我不必再挣扎了。这样的感觉好多了,从来没有这么好过,因为某处有一片树林,我希望步行穿过,而挣扎之中你是无法步行穿越一片树林的。某处有一个女孩子,我希望与她同枕共眠,而挣扎之中你是无法与一个女孩子共枕缠绵的。挣扎之中,你是无法做成任何事情的,特别值得一提的是,你无法挣扎着生活。所以现在,我要做我喜欢做的所有事情,不再挣扎来、挣扎去的啦。

看看吧，像这样有多么平静和美好啊。看看吧，天空是多么明媚，这块田野是多么美丽，上面有一头头奶牛、小小的池塘，还有绿绿的树篱，中间生长着黄色的报春花。现在，没有什么可令我牵挂了，没有什么、没有什么、没有什么可让我担心了，就连那边"啪嗒"一声跳进池塘的那个家伙都算上。那个家伙似乎在一阵阵地喷着水、吐着气，气喘吁吁。他似乎从池塘里把什么东西拖了上来，那东西还挺沉的。现在，他已经将那东西拖到了岸边，拽到草地上了。太有意思啦，他拖的是一具尸体，是一具男子的尸体。事实上，我想，他拖的就是我。没错，是我。我知道，那就是我，因为我飞行服的前面有一块黄色油漆留下的污迹。现在，他跪了下来，在我的衣兜里翻来翻去，将我的钱和身份证件掏了出来，他还找到我的烟斗以及一封信，那封信是我今天早晨收到的，是母亲写给我的。他将我的手表也摘了下来。现在，他站起身，要走开。他要把我的尸体丢下，任其躺在池塘边的草地上。他穿过这片田野，快速走开，走向栅栏门。他看起来浑身湿漉漉的，而且无比兴奋。他真应该放松一下，就像我一样放松下来。不放松的话，他什么乐趣都享受不到。我想，我应该让他知道这一点。

"你为什么不放松一下呢？"

天呐，我一跟他说话，他就吓得大跳起来。他的脸，就看看他的脸吧，我从来没有看到谁的脸像他的脸那样，露出恐惧害怕的神情。他开始奔跑，边跑边从肩膀上方向后看，但始终不停地奔跑。就看看他那张脸吧，看看他是多么闷闷不乐、恐惧害怕吧。我可不想跟他一起奔跑，我想，让他自己狂奔吧。我想，我要在这儿待一会，然后沿着树篱走走，采摘一些报春花。要是运气好的话，或许我会找到几朵白色的紫罗兰。接着，我就开始睡觉，在太阳底下暖洋洋地睡觉。

第三章 科幻色彩

“科幻”(SF 或 Sci-Fi)是“科学幻想”或“科幻小说”(Science Fiction)的简称,对其定义多种多样,大家莫衷一是。网络版不列颠大百科全书(Encyclopaedia Britannica Online[①])有这样的描述:“(It is) a form of fiction that deals principally with the impact of actual or imagined science upon society or individuals”(主要以真实或想象的科学对社会和个人的影响为基础的一种文学形式);就“科幻小说”这一词条,《辞海》的定义是:“依据科学技术上的新发现、新成就以及在这些基础上可能达到的预见,用幻想的方式描述人类利用这些新成果完成某些奇迹的新型小说。”不管定义如何,人们普遍认为,只要作品中含有“超现实”的因素,便可算作科幻作品。

自诞生之日起,科幻作品就呈现出“百花齐放,百家争鸣”的局面,划分范畴不一,类型颇多,有预言类、抒情类、荒诞类、探险类、幽默类、社会类、机关类、恐怖类等等。但是,一般的观点认为,正统的科幻作品应将科学和幻想统一起来,两者缺一不可。要是科幻作品里没有任何科学根据,那只能称其为奇幻、魔幻、玄幻等超现实作品。另外,只有科学写实、而无超现实幻想的作品,也称不上科幻作品,那

① 网址为:http://global.britannica.com/。

充其量只能算是一个科学写实故事。

如此看来,本章所选罗尔德·达尔的这两篇小说就具有了科幻色彩,幻想的内容还颇为奇特,还具有幽默、讽刺等风格元素。可以这样说,达尔的这两部作品具有科幻色彩,但又不仅仅是为了"科幻"而去"科幻",而是借助一些"超现实"因素来达到一定的"现实"目的。

在《器官实验》中,医生将身患绝症而死去的威廉的大脑和一只眼球"供养"起来,使威廉得以"部分复活",这让受不了威廉生前"折磨"的妻子玛丽看到了一线"生机"——感到丈夫死后自己的生活似乎会"美好"起来;在《探声机器》中,耳朵患病的主人公克劳斯纳别出心裁,发明了一台能探测到人耳听不见的声音的机器,并用这台机器听到了植物发出的无以言表的声音,还打电话让他的主治医生来来见证,可医生的到来却令场面变得无法收拾。

走进罗尔德·达尔的科幻世界,去听听"器官实验"背后的故事,去看看"探声机器"最后的模样吧。

第一节 《器官实验》*William and Mary*

罗尔德·达尔的《器官实验》(*William and Mary*)收录在《罗尔德·达尔短篇故事集锦》(*The Collected Short Stories of Roald Dahl*)、《罗尔德·达尔小说精品集》(*The Best of Roald Dahl*)、《五部畅销书集》(*5 Bestsellers*)、《吻了又吻》(*Kiss Kiss*)、《罗尔德·达尔选集》(*The Roald Dahl Omnibus*)以及《完全出人意料故事集》(*Completely Unexpected Tales*)等书中。这部小说还被改编成电视系列剧中的一集——1979 年4 月7 日播映的《出乎意料的故事集》(*Tales of the Unexpected*)第一部中的第 3 集(*Episode* 1.3),具有一定的影响力。另外,达尔的这部小说还被改编成其他电视剧版本,并多次改编成喜剧,搬上了舞台。

据说达尔在创作这部小说前，作了大量的神经外科学（neurosurgery[①]）方面的研究，以确保小说里所描述的器官实验尽可能接近医学现实。另一个有意思的方面是，本篇小说的主人公威廉（William）和玛丽（Mary）这两个名字，在达尔后来创作的儿童文学作品《女巫》（*The Witches*）中，则变成了两只白老鼠的名字。这也从一个侧面说明，达尔很“贪材”——充分甚至反复利用已有的素材[②]。横向来看，中国第一位诺贝尔文学奖得主莫言，也具备这方面的“天赋”。

一、原作导读

威廉·珀尔死后没有给他的妻子玛丽·珀尔留下什么丰厚的遗产。威廉死去一周后，珀尔太太去律师那儿听律师宣读遗嘱，律师随后将威廉生前写的一封信转交给了珀尔太太。

玛丽回到家中，点上一支香烟，欢喜地打量着自己新买的电视机，准备看信。她心里合计起来：横挑鼻子竖挑眼的丈夫在信中能跟自己说些什么呢？或许他最终良心发现，感激自己三十年以来对他的奉献和伺候。令她意想不到的是，丈夫在长达二十页的信中说的几乎都是牛津大学一位名叫兰迪的同事如何说服他，让他自愿配合做一个科学实验方面的事情！威廉身患癌症去世后，他的大脑被那个同事从脑壳中取出，放入一个盛满林格溶液的特制盆子里，然后将大脑跟一个人工心脏机器连接起来，机器不断为大脑泵送含氧的血液，“供养”大脑，这样他的大脑就能够存活下来。医术高明的兰迪甚至还设法将威廉的一只眼球保留了下来。那只眼球被装在一个塑料盒中，通过视觉神经跟大脑相连，漂浮在林格溶液上面。在信中，威廉要她不要感到恶心和恐惧，要勇敢地到兰迪医生那里看看实验进行得怎么样了。在信的附言栏，威廉一再向她强调：不要喝鸡尾酒、

---

① neurosurgery：*Noun* ［mass noun］ surgery performed on the nervous system，especially the brain and spinal cord（尤指大脑和脊髓部的）神经外科学

② 这一点在《罗尔德·达尔短篇故事品读及汉译探索（第 1 卷）》第一章第二节也有所涉及。

不要浪费钱、不要抽烟、不要买电视机,等等。

玛丽得知丈夫会“部分复活”并继续对自己发号施令,惊骇不已,但是,一种由来已久的义务感还是迫使她走向实验室去见兰迪医生,看看情况如何。兰迪医生带她看了丈夫那个被放在盆子里、处于存活状态的大脑,还有漂浮在溶液上方的那只眼球。不知怎么的,她吃惊地发现,对于丈夫的这种状态,她内心产生了一种爱恋之意。

“医生,”她说。“我确信,突然之间,我对他产生了极其强烈的爱恋之情。那听起来奇怪吗?”

“我想,那是相当可以理解的。”

“他躺在那儿,就在那只小盆子里,就躺在水的下面,一个人静悄悄的,显得多么孤立无助啊。”

“是的,我知道。”

“他像是一个婴儿。对,就像是一个婴儿。真的,他酷似一个小小的婴儿。”

兰迪站在她身后,一动不动地观察着。

“那么,”她看着盆子,轻柔地说。“从现在起,玛丽要亲自照料你,这个世界上你也没有什么可担心的。医生,我什么时候能把他带回家?”

“Doctor,” she said. “I do believe I'm suddenly getting to feel the most enormous affection for him. Does that sound queer?”

“I think it's quite understandable.”

“He looks so helpless and silent lying there under the water in his little basin.”

“Yes, I know.

“He's like a baby, that's what he's like. He's exactly like a little baby.”

Landy stood still behind her, watching.

“There,” she said softly, peering into the basin. “From now on Mary's going to look after you *all* by herself and you've nothing to worry about in the world. When can I have him back home, Doctor?"

闻听此言,兰迪大吃一惊,设法劝说她放弃这样的念头,但她仍然固执己见。她俯身丈夫那只眼球上方,双唇夹起烟,打算吸一口。这时,"……她看到一个微小的、但却耀眼的光点;瞳孔收缩成一个极其微小的黑色小点,绝对是怒火高涨的样子"(... she saw a tiny but brilliant flash of light, and the pupil contracted into a minute black pin-point of absolute fury.)。正所谓"三十年河东,三十年河西",玛丽现在有了掌控权。

"威廉,不要如此恼羞成怒啊,"她轻轻地说。"恼怒发火可是没有任何好处的。"

兰迪转过头,要看看她在干什么。

"你不能再那样了,"她低声耳语。"因为从现在起,我的宠物啊,玛丽要你做什么,你就得分毫不差地做什么。你明白吗?"

"Don't look so cross, William," she said softly. "It isn't any good looking cross."

Landy turned his head to see what she was doing.

"Not any more it isn't," she whispered. "Because from now on, my pet, you're going to do just exactly what Mary tells you. Do you understand that?"

兰迪拽着她,要将她拽出房间。她不情愿地跟着兰迪一边往外走,一边说:

"难道他不可爱吗?我就是要把他弄回家去,迫不及待了。"

"Isn't he darling? I just can't wait to get him home."

二、原作释读

在这篇具有科幻色彩的小说中,达尔提到了很多医学方面的表达，特别是神经外科学方面的词汇，这恐怕是阅读中的一大障碍了。

William and Mary[①]

William Pearl did not leave a great deal of money when he died, and his will was a simple one. With the exception of a few small bequests[②] to relatives, he left all his property to his wife.

The solicitor and Mrs. Pearl went over[③] it together in the solicitor's[④] office, and when the business was completed, the widow got up to leave. At that point, the solicitor took a sealed envelope from the folder on his desk and held it out to his client.

"I have been instructed to give you this," he said. "Your husband sent it to us shortly before he passed away." The solicitor was pale and prim, and out of respect for a widow he kept his head on one side as he spoke, looking downward. "It appears that it might be something personal, Mrs. Pearl. No doubt you'd like to take it home with you and read it in privacy."

Mrs. Pearl accepted the envelope and went out into the street. She

---

① 本部小说原文出自"DAHL, R. *The Best of Roald Dahl*. London: Penguin Books Ltd., 2006"。

② bequest: *Noun* a legacy 遗产；遗物（e. g. a bequest of over £ 300,000 一笔价值超过30万英镑的遗产）

③ go over: *Verb* examine, consider, or check the details of (something) 检查；考虑；仔细核查（e. g. I want to go over these plans with you again. 我想和你一起再检查一下这些计划。）

④ solicitor: *Noun* (Brit.) a member of the legal profession qualified to deal with conveyancing, the drawing up of wills, and other legal matters. A solicitor may also advise clients, instruct barristers, and represent clients in some courts（英国英语）（处理产权转让、起草遗嘱和处理其他法律事务的）初级律师；诉状律师

paused on the pavement, feeling the thing with her fingers. A letter of farewell from William? Probably, yes. A formal letter. It was bound to be formal—stiff and formal. The man was incapable of acting otherwise. He had never done anything informal in his life.

My dear Mary, I trust that you will not permit my departure from this world to upset you too much, but that you will continue to observe those precepts[①] which have guided you so well during our partnership together. Be diligent and dignified in all things. Be thrifty with your money. Be very careful that you do not... et cetera, et cetera.

A typical William letter.

Or was it possible that he might have broken down at the last moment and written her something beautiful? Maybe this was a beautiful tender message, a sort of love letter, a lovely warm note of thanks to her for giving him thirty years of her life and for ironing a million shirts and cooking a million meals and making a million beds, something that she could read over and over again, once a day at least, and she would keep it for ever in the box on the dressing-table together with her brooches[②].

There is no knowing what people will do when they are about to die, Mrs. Pearl told herself, and she tucked the envelope under her arm and hurried home.

She let herself in the front door and went straight to the living-room and sat down on the sofa without removing her hat or coat. Then she

---

① precept: *Noun* a general rule intended to regulate behaviour or thought 规诫；戒律；箴言(e. g. the legal precept of being innocent until proven guilty 被证明有罪之前作无罪推定这一法律规定)

② brooch: *Noun* an ornament fastened to clothing with a hinged pin and catch 胸针；领针

opened the envelope and drew out the contents. These consisted, she saw, of some fifteen or twenty sheets of lined white paper, folded over once and held together at the top left-hand corner by a clip. Each sheet was covered with the small, neat, forward-sloping writing that she knew so well, but when she noticed how much of it there was, and in what a neat businesslike manner it was written, and how the first page didn't even begin in the nice way a letter should, she began to get suspicious.

She looked away. She lit herself a cigarette. She took one puff① and laid the cigarette in the ashtray.

If this is about what I am beginning to suspect it is about, she told herself, then I don't want to read it.

Can one refuse to read a letter from the dead?

Yes.

Well...

She glanced over at William's empty chair on the other side of the fireplace. It was a big brown leather armchair, and there was a depression② on the seat of it, made by his buttocks over the years. Higher up, on the backrest③, there was a dark oval stain on the leather where his head had rested. He used to sit reading in that chair and she would be opposite him on the sofa, sewing on buttons or mending socks or putting a patch on the elbow of one of his jackets, and every now and then a pair of eyes would glance up from the book and settle on her, watchful, but strangely impersonal, as if calculating something. She had never liked

---

① puff: *Noun* an act of drawing quickly on a pipe, cigarette, or cigar 猛吸(烟斗、香烟或雪茄)(e.g. He took a puff of his cigar. 他猛吸了一口雪茄烟。)

② depression: *Noun* [count noun] a sunken place or hollow on a surface 凹面;低凹处(e.g. The original shallow depressions were slowly converted to creeks. 原来的浅浅的低凹处慢慢变成了小溪。)

③ backrest: *Noun* a support for a person's back when they are seated 靠背

those eyes. They were ice blue, cold, small, and rather close together, with two deep vertical lines of disapproval dividing them. All her life they had been watching her. And even now, after a week alone in the house, she sometimes had an uneasy feeling that they were still there, following her around, staring at her from doorways, from empty chairs, through a window at night.

Slowly she reached into her handbag and took out her spectacles and put them on. Then, holding the pages up high in front of her so that they caught the late afternoon light from the window behind, she started to read:

This note, my dear Mary, is entirely for you, and will be given you shortly after I am gone.

Do not be alarmed by the sight of all this writing. It is nothing but an attempt on my part to explain to you precisely what Landy is going to do to me, and why I have agreed that he should do it, and what are his theories and his hopes. You are my wife and you have a right to know these things. In fact you *must* know them. During the past few days, I have tried very hard to speak with you about Landy, but you have steadfastly refused to give me a hearing. This, as I have already told you, is a very foolish attitude to take, and I find it not entirely an unselfish one either. It stems mostly from ignorance, and I am absolutely convinced that if only you were made aware of all the facts, you would immediately change your view. That is why I am hoping that when I am no longer with you, and your mind is less distracted, you will consent to listen to me more carefully through these pages. I swear to you that when you have read my story, your sense of antipathy[①] will vanish, and enthusiasm will take its place. I even dare to hope that you will become a little proud of what I have done.

As you read on, you must forgive me, if you will, for the coolness of my style, but this is the only way I know of getting my message over to you clearly. You see, as my time draws near, it is natural that I begin to brim with every kind of sentimentality[②] under the sun. Each day I grow more extravagantly wistful, especially in the evenings, and unless I watch myself closely my emotions will be overflowing on to these pages.

I have a wish, for example, to write something about you and what a satisfactory wife you have been to me through the years and I am promising myself that if there is time, and I still have the strength, I shall do that next.

I have a yearning also to speak about this Oxford of mine where I have been living and teaching for the past seventeen years, to tell something about the glory of the place and to explain, if I can, a little of what it has meant to have been allowed to work in its midst. All the things and places that I loved so well keep crowding in on me now in this gloomy bedroom. They are bright and beautiful as they always were, and today, for some reason, I can see them more clearly than ever. The path around

---

① antipathy: *Noun* [mass noun] a deep-seated feeling of aversion 根深蒂固的反感;厌恶(e. g. his fundamental antipathy to capitalism 他对资本主义根深蒂固的强烈反感)

② sentimentality: *Noun* [mass noun] excessive tenderness, sadness, or nostalgia 多愁善感;伤感癖(e. g. There are passages which verge on sentimentality. 有几篇近乎多愁善感的文章。)

the lake in the gardens of Worcester① College, where Lovelace② used to walk. The gateway③ at Pembroke④. The view westward over the town from Magdalen Tower. The great hail at Christchurch. The little rockery⑤ at St John's where I have counted more than a dozen varieties of campanula⑥, including the rare and dainty⑦ *C. Waldsteiniana*. But there, you see! I haven't even begun and already I'm falling into the trap. So let me

---

① Worcester: *Noun* a cathedral city in western England, on the River Severn, the administrative centre of Worcestershire; pop. 81,000 (1991). It was the scene in 1651, during the English Civil War, of a battle in which Oliver Cromwell defeated a Scottish army under Charles II. It has been a centre of porcelain manufacture since 1751. 武斯特(英国西部教区总教堂所在城市,位于塞汶河畔,武斯特郡首府,1991 年人口 81,000;是 1651 年英国内战中奥利弗·克伦威打败查尔斯二世领导下的苏格兰军队的战场,自 1751 年起一直为瓷器制造中心。)

② Lovelace: *Noun* Richard Lovelace (1618—1657), English poet. A Royalist, he was imprisoned in 1642, when he probably wrote his famous poem "*To Althea, from Prison*". 理查德·洛夫莱斯(1618—1657,英国诗人,保王党成员;于 1642 年被投入监狱,并可能在狱中写下了著名的《在狱中致阿西娅》。)

③ gateway: *Noun* an opening that can be closed by a gate 门口;门道;出入口;通道(e. g. We turned into a gateway leading to a small cottage. 我们进入一条通往一间小屋的通道。)

④ Pembroke: *Noun* a port in SW Wales, in Pembrokeshire; pop. 15,600 (1981). It was a Norman stronghold from the 11th century. 彭布罗克(威尔士西南部港口,位于彭布鲁克郡,1981 年人口 15,600,从 11 世纪开始就是诺曼人的一个堡垒。)

⑤ rockery: *Noun* a heaped arrangement of rough stones with soil between them, planted with rock plants, especially alpines 假山;岩石园;假山园

⑥ campanula: *Noun* another term for bellflower 同"bellflower";风铃草属植物

⑦ dainty: *Adjective* delicately small and pretty 精致的;娇俏的;优雅的;美味的(e. g. The little girl wore a dainty dress. 小姑娘穿着一件漂亮的连衣裙。)

get started now; and let you read it slowly, my dear, without any of that sense of sorrow or disapproval that might otherwise embarrass your understanding. Promise me now that you will read it slowly, and that you will put yourself in a cool and patient frame of mind before you begin.

The details of the illness that struck me down so suddenly in my middle life are known to you. I need not waste time upon them—except to admit at once how foolish I was not to have gone earlier to my doctor. Cancer is one of the few remaining diseases that these modern drugs cannot cure. A surgeon can operate if it has not spread too far; but with me, not only did I leave it too late, but the thing had the effrontery① to attack me in the pancreas②, making both surgery and survival equally impossible.

So here I was with somewhere between one and six months left to live, growing more melancholy every hour—and then, all of a sudden, in comes Landy.

That was six weeks ago, on a Tuesday morning, very early, long before your visiting time, and the moment he entered I knew there was some sort of madness in the wind.

He didn't creep in on his toes, sheepish and embarrassed, not knowing what to say, like all my other visitors. He came in strong and smiling, and he strode up to the bed and stood there looking down at me with a wild bright glimmer in his eyes, and he said, "William, my boy, this is perfect. You're just the one I want!"

---

① effrontery: *Noun* [mass noun] insolent or impertinent behaviour 厚颜无耻的行为;放肆(e. g. One juror had the effrontery to challenge the coroner's decision. 一位陪审员竟无礼地对验尸官的结论提出质疑。)

② pancreas: *Noun* a large gland behind the stomach which secretes digestive enzymes into the duodenum. Embedded in the pancreas are the islets of Langerhans, which secrete into the blood the hormones insulin and glucagon 胰腺

Perhaps I should explain to you here that although John Landy has never been to our house, and you have seldom if ever met him, I myself have been friendly with him for at least nine years. I am, of course, primarily a teacher of philosophy, but as you know I've lately been dabbling① a good deal in psychology as well. Landy's interests and mine have therefore slightly overlapped. He is a magnificent neuro-surgeon②, one of the finest, and recently he has been kind enough to let me study the results of some of his work, especially the varying effects of prefrontal③ lobotomies④ upon different types of psychopath⑤. So you can see that when he suddenly burst in on me that Tuesday morning, we were by no means strangers to one another.

"Look," he said, pulling up a chair beside the bed. "In a few weeks you're going to be dead. Correct?"

Coming from Landy, the question didn't seem especially unkind. In

① dabble: *Verb* [no obj.] (figurative) take part in an activity in a casual or superficial way(喻)涉猎(e. g. He dabbled in left-wing politics. 他参与左翼政治。)

② neurosurgeon or neuro-surgeon: *Noun* a doctor who performs operations involving the brain or nerves 神经外科医生(e. g. "The doctors' sense was that the girls fared well, but it remained to be determined whether they suffered any brain damage," said Dr. John Frazee, another neurosurgeon. 而另一位神经外科医生约翰·弗雷齐博士却说,"医生的感觉是,虽然目前这对姐妹的情况很好,但还不能确保她们的脑部没有受到损伤。")

③ prefrontal: *Adjective* [attrib.] (Anatomy) in or relating to the foremost part of the frontal lobe of the brain(解剖学)额叶前部的;前额的(e. g. the prefrontal cortex 额叶前皮层)

④ lobotomy: *Noun* a surgical operation involving incision into the prefrontal lobe of the brain, formerly used to treat mental illness 脑白质切断术

⑤ psychopath: *Noun* a person suffering from chronic mental disorder with abnormal or violent social behaviour 精神变态者;精神病患者;变态人格者

a way it was refreshing to have a visitor brave enough to touch upon the forbidden subject.

"You're going to expire① right here in this room, and then they'll take you out and cremate② you."

"Bury me," I said.

"That's even worse. And then what? Do you believe you'll go to heaven?"

"I doubt it," I said, "though it would be comforting to think so."

"Or hell, perhaps?"

"I don't really see why they should send me there."

"You never know, my dear William."

"What's all this about?" I asked.

"Well," he said, and I could see him watching me carefully, "personally, I don't believe that after you're dead you'll ever hear of yourself again—unless..." and here he paused and smiled and leaned closer "...unless, of course, you have the sense to put yourself into my hands. Would you care to consider a proposition?"

The way he was staring at me, and studying me, and appraising me with a queer kind of hungriness, I might have been a piece of prime beef on the counter and he had bought it and was waiting for them to wrap it up.

"I'm really serious about it, William. Would you care to consider a proposition?"

"I don't know what you're talking about."

"Then listen and I'll tell you. Will you listen to me?"

"Go on then, if you like. I doubt I've got very much to lose by

① expire: *Verb* (of a person) die(人)死亡;断气

② cremate: *Verb* [with obj.] (usu. as "be cremated") dispose of (a dead person's body) by burning it to ashes, typically after a funeral ceremony 火化;火葬

hearing it."

"On the contrary, you have a great deal to gain—especially *after you're dead*."

I am sure he was expecting me to jump when he said this, but for some reason I was ready for t. I lay quite still, watching his face and that slow white smile of his that always revealed the gold clasp on an upper denture① curled around the canine② on the left side of his mouth.

"This is a thing, William, that I've been working on quietly for some years. One or two others here at the hospital have been helping me especially Morrison, and we've completed a number of fairly successful trials with laboratory animals. I'm at the stage now where I'm ready to have a go with a man. It's a big idea, and it may sound a bit far-fetched at first, but from a surgical point of view there doesn't seem to be any reason why it shouldn't be more or less practicable."

Landy leaned forward and placed both hands on the edge of my bed. He has a good face, handsome in a bony sort of way, with none of the usual doctor's look about it. You know that look, most of them have it. It glimmers at you out of their eyeballs like a dull electric sign and it reads ONLY I CAN SAVE YOU. But John Landy's eyes were wide and bright and little sparks of excitement were dancing in the centres of them.

"Quite a long time ago," he said, "I saw a short medical film that

---

① dentures: *Noun* false teeth fixed to a small piece of plastic or similar material, which fits inside the mouth of someone who does not have their own teeth(一副)假牙(e. g. Do you wear dentures? 你戴假牙吗?)

② canine: *Noun* (Also as "canine tooth") a pointed tooth between the incisors and premolars of a mammal, often greatly enlarged in carnivores(哺乳动物的)犬齿;犬牙

had been brought over from Russia. It was a rather gruesome[①] thing, but interesting. It showed a dog's head completely severed[②] from the body, but with the normal blood supply being maintained through the arteries[③] and veins[④] by means of an artificial heart. Now the thing is this: that dog's head, sitting there all alone on a sort of tray, was *alive*. The brain was functioning. They proved it by several tests. For example, when food was smeared[⑤] on the dog's lips, the tongue would come out and lick it away: and the eyes would follow a person moving across the room.

"It seemed reasonable to conclude from this that the head and the brain did not need to be attached to the rest of the body in order to remain alive provided, of course, that a supply of properly oxygenated blood could be maintained.

"Now then. My own thought, which grew out of seeing this film, was to remove the brain from the skull of a human and keep it alive and functioning as an independent unit for an unlimited period after he is dead. *Your* brain, for example, after *you* are dead."

---

① gruesome: *Adjective* causing repulsion or horror; grisly 令人厌恶的;可怕的;恐怖的(e. g. the most gruesome murder 最恐怖的谋杀。)

② sever: *Verb* [with obj.] divide by cutting or slicing, especially suddenly and forcibly(尤指突然或用力)切断;切割(e. g. The head was severed from the body. 头从身体上被砍下。)

③ artery: *Noun* any of the muscular-walled tubes forming part of the circulation system by which blood (mainly that which has been oxygenated) is conveyed from the heart to all parts of the body 动脉

④ vein: *Noun* any of the tubes forming part of the blood circulation system of the body, carrying mainly oxygen-depleted blood towards the heart 静脉

⑤ smear: *Verb* [with obj. and adverbial] spread (a greasy or sticky substance) over something(在某物上)涂抹(油脂或黏性物质)(e. g. She smeared sun tan lotion all over herself. 她在全身涂满防晒油。)

"I don't like that," I said.

"Don't interrupt, William. Let me finish. So far as I can tell from subsequent experiments, the brain is a peculiarly self-supporting object. It manufactures its own cerebrospinal fluid①. The magic processes of thought and memory which go on inside it are manifestly not impaired by the absence of limbs or trunk or even of skull, provided, as I say, that you keep pumping in the right kind of oxygenated blood under the proper conditions.

"My dear William, just think for a moment of your own brain. It is in perfect shape. It is crammed full of a lifetime of learning. It has taken you years of work to make it what it is. It is just beginning to give out some first-rate original ideas. Yet soon it is going to have to die along with the rest of your body simply because your silly little pancreas is riddled with cancer."

"No thank you," I said to him. "You can stop there. It's a repulsive idea, and even if you could do it, which I doubt, it would be quite pointless. What possible use is there in keeping my brain alive if I couldn't talk or see or hear or feel? Personally, I can think of nothing more unpleasant."

"I believe that you *would* be able to communicate with us," Landy said. "And we might even succeed in giving you a certain amount of vision. But let's take this slowly. I'll come to all that later on. The fact remains that you're going to die fairly soon whatever happens; and my plans would not involve touching you at all until *after* you are dead. Come now, William. No true philosopher could object to lending his dead body to the cause of science."

---

① cerebrospinal fluid: *Noun* [mass noun] (Anatomy) clear watery fluid which fills the space between the arachnoid membrane and the pia mater(解剖学)脑脊髓液

"That's not putting it quite straight," I answered. "It seems to me there'd be some doubts as to whether I were dead or alive by the time you'd finished with me."

"Well," he said, smiling a little, "I suppose you're right about that. But I don't think you ought to turn me down quite so quickly, before you know a bit more about it."

"I said I don't want to hear it."

"Have a cigarette," he said, holding out his case.

"I don't smoke, you know that."

He took one himself and lit it with a tiny silver lighter that was no bigger than a shilling[①] piece. "A present from the people who make my instruments," he said. "Ingenious[②], isn't it?"

I examined the lighter, then handed it back.

"May I go on?" he asked.

"I'd rather you didn't."

"Just lie still and listen. I think you'll find it quite interesting."

There were some blue grapes on a plate beside my bed. I put the plate on my chest and began eating the grapes.

"At the very moment of death," Landy said, "I should have to be standing by so that I could step in immediately and try to keep your brain alive."

"You mean leaving it in the head?"

"To start with, yes. I'd have to."

"And where would you put it after that?"

---

① shilling: *Noun* a former British coin and monetary unit equal to one twentieth of a pound or twelve pence 先令(原英国货币单位,等于1/20镑或12便士。)

② ingenious: *Adjective* (of a person) clever, original, and inventive(人)机灵的;有独创性的;具创造力的(e. g. He was ingenious enough to overcome the limited budget. 他足智多谋,足以克服预算有限的困难。)

"If you want to know, in a sort of basin."

"Are you really serious about this?"

"Certainly I'm serious."

"All right. Go on."

"I suppose you know that when the heart stops and the brain is deprived of fresh blood and oxygen, its tissues die very rapidly. Anything from four to six minutes and the whole thing's dead. Even after three minutes you may get a certain amount of damage. So I should have to work rapidly to prevent this from happening. But with the help of the machine, it should all be quite simple."

"What machine?"

"The artificial heart. We've got a nice adaptation here of the one originally devised by Alexis Carrel[①] and Lindbergh. It oxygenates the blood, keeps it at the right temperature, pumps it in at the right pressure, and does a number of other little necessary things. It's really not at all complicated."

"Tell me what you would do at the moment of death," I said. "What is the first thing you would do?"

"Do you know anything about the vascular[②] and venous[③] arrangement of the brain?"

---

① Carrel: *Noun* Alexis Carrel (1873—1944), French surgeon and biologist. He developed improved techniques for suturing arteries and veins, and carried out some of the first organ transplants. Nobel Prize for Physiology or Medicine (1912) 亚历克西·卡雷尔(1873—1944,法国外科医生、生物学家,改进了动静脉缝合技术,并进行了首批器官移植,1912 年获诺贝尔生理医学奖。)

② vascular: *Adjective* (Anatomy, Zoology, & Medicine) of, relating to, affecting, or consisting of a vessel or vessels, especially those which carry blood(解剖学、动物学和医学)管(尤指脉管)的;血管的(e. g. vascular disease 血管疾病。)

③ venous: *Adjective* of or relating to a vein or the veins 静脉的

"No.

"Then listen. It's not difficult. The blood supply to the brain is derived from two main sources, the internal carotid[①] arteries and the vertebral[②] arteries. There are two of each, making four arteries in all. Got that?"

"Yes."

"And the return system is even simpler. The blood is drained away by only two large veins, the internal jugulars[③]. So you have four arteries going up—they go up the neck of course and two veins coming down. Around the brain itself they naturally branch out into other channels, but those don't concern us. We never touch them."

"All right," I said. "Imagine that I've just died. Now what would you do?"

"I should immediately open your neck and locate the four arteries, the carotids and the vertebrals. I should then perfuse[④] them, which means that I'd stick a large hollow needle into each. These four needles would be connected by tubes to the artificial heart.

"Then, working quickly, I would dissect out both the left and right jugular veins and hitch these also to the heart machine to complete the circuit. Now switch on the machine, which is already primed with the

---

① carotid: *Adjective* of, relating to, or denoting the two main arteries which carry blood to the head and neck, and their two main branches(与)颈动脉(有关)的

② vertebral: *Adjective* relating to the vertebra or spine 脊椎的;有脊椎的

③ jugular: *Adjective* of the neck or throat 颈的;喉的

Noun short for jugular vein "jugular vein""颈静脉"的简称

④ perfuse: *Verb* (Medicine) supply (an organ, tissue, or body) with a fluid, typically treated blood or a blood substitute, by circulating it through blood vessels or other natural channels(医学)灌注;灌流(器官、组织或身体)

right type of blood and there you are. The circulation through your brain would be restored."

"I'd be like that Russian dog."

"I don't think you would. For one thing, you'd certainly lose consciousness when you died, and I very much doubt whether you would come to again for quite a long time—if indeed you came to at all. But, conscious or not, you'd be in a rather interesting position, wouldn't you? You'd have a cold dead body and a living brain."

Landy paused to savour this delightful prospect. The man was so entranced and bemused by the whole idea that he evidently found it impossible to believe I might not be feeling the same way.

"We could now afford to take our time," he said. "And believe me, we'd need it. The first thing we'd do would be to wheel you to the operating-room, accompanied of course by the machine, which must never stop pumping. The next problem..."

"All right," I said. "That's enough. I don't have to hear the details."

"Oh but you must," he said. "It is important that you should know precisely what is going to happen to you all the way through. You see, afterwards, when you regain consciousness, it will be much more satisfactory from your point of view if you are able to remember exactly where you are and how you came to be there. If only for your own peace of mind you should know that. You agree?"

I lay still on the bed, watching him.

"So the next problem would be to remove your brain, intact and undamaged, from your dead body. The body is useless. In fact it has already started to decay. The skull and the face are also useless. They are both encumbrances[①] and I don't want them around. All I want is the brain, the clean beautiful brain, alive and perfect. So when I get you on the table I will take a saw, a small oscillating[②] saw, and with this I shall proceed to remove the whole vault of your skull. You'd still be unconscious at that point so I wouldn't have to bother with anaesthetic[③]."

"Like hell, you wouldn't," I said.

"You'd be out cold, I promise you that, William. Don't forget you died just a few minutes before."

"Nobody's sawing off the top of my skull without an anaesthetic," I said.

Landy shrugged his shoulders. "It makes no difference to me," he said. "I'll be glad to give you a little procaine[④] if you want it. If it will make you any happier I'll infiltrate[⑤] the whole scalp with procaine, the whole head, from the neck up."

"Thanks very much," I said.

"You know," he went on, "it's extraordinary what sometimes happens. Only last week a man was brought in unconscious, and I opened his head without any anaesthetic at all and removed a small blood clot. I

① encumbrance: *Noun* a burden or impediment 负担;累赘;障碍物

② oscillate: *Verb* [no obj.] move or swing back and forth at a regular speed 摆动(e. g. It oscillates in a plane at right angles to the cam axis. 它在和凸轮轴正交的平面上摆动。)

③ anaesthetic or anesthetic: *Noun* a substance that induces insensitivity to pain 麻醉剂

④ procaine: *Noun* [mass noun] a synthetic compound derived from benzoic acid, used as a local anaesthetic, especially in dentistry 普鲁卡因(局部麻醉药,尤用于牙科)

⑤ infiltrate: *Verb* introduce (a liquid) into something in this way 使(液体)渗入(e. g. Lignocaine was infiltrated into the wound. 让利多卡因渗入伤口。)

was still working inside the skull when he woke up and began talking.

"'Where am I?'" he asked.

"'You're in hospital.'"

"'Well,'" he said. "'Fancy that.'"

"'Tell me,'" I asked him, "'is this bothering you, what I'm doing?'"

"'No,'" he answered. "'Not at all. What *are* you doing?'"

"'I'm just removing a blood clot from your brain.'"

"'You are?'"

"'Just lie still. Don't move, I'm nearly finished.'"

"'So that's the bastard who's been giving me all those headaches,' the man said."

Landy paused and smiled, remembering the occasion. "That's word for word what the man said," he went on, "although the next day he couldn't even recollect the incident. It's a funny thing, the brain."

"I'll have the procaine," I said.

"As you wish, William. And now, as I say, I'd take a small oscillating saw and carefully remove your complete calvarium[①]—the whole vault of the skull. This would expose the top half of the brain, or rather the outer covering in which it is wrapped. You may or may not know that there are three separate coverings around the brain itself the outer one

---

① calvarium: *Noun* The upper domelike portion of the skull without the lower jaw or the lower jaw and the facial parts 颅盖

called the dura mater① or dura, the middle one called the arachnoid②, and the inner one called the pia mater③ or pia. Most laymen seem to have the idea that the brain is a naked thing floating around in fluid in your head. But it isn't. It's wrapped up neatly in these three strong coverings, and the cerebrospinal fluid actually flows within the little gap between the two coverings, known as the subarachnoid space. As I told you before, this fluid is manufactured by the brain and it drains off into the venous system by osmosis④.

"I myself would leave all three coverings—don't they have lovely names, the dura, the arachnoid, and the pia? —I'd leave them all intact. There are many reasons for this, not least among them being the fact that within the dura run the venous channels that drain the blood from the brain into the jugular.

"Now," he went on, "we've got the upper half of your skull off so that the top of the brain, wrapped in its outer covering, is exposed. The next step is the really tricky one: to release the whole package so that it

---

① dura (mater): *Noun* The tough fibrous membrane covering the brain and the spinal cord and lining the inner surface of the skull. It is the outermost of the three meninges that surround the brain and spinal cord 硬脑(脊)膜

② arachnoid: *Noun* (Also as "arachnoid membrane") (Anatomy) a fine, delicate membrane, the middle one of the three membranes or meninges that surround the brain and spinal cord, situated between the dura mater and the pia mater(解剖学)蛛网膜

③ pia (mater): *Noun* the fine vascular membrane that closely envelops the brain and spinal cord under the arachnoid and the dura mater 软膜;软脑脊膜

④ osmosis: *Noun* [mass noun] (Biology & Chemistry) a process by which molecules of a solvent tend to pass through a semipermeable membrane from a less concentrated solution into a more concentrated one(生物和化学)渗透(作用)

can be lifted cleanly away, leaving the stubs[①] of the four supply arteries and the two veins hanging underneath ready to be re-connected to the machine. This is an immensely lengthy and complicated business involving the delicate chipping away of much bone, the severing of many nerves, and the cutting and tying of numerous blood vessels. The only way I could do it with any hope of success would be by taking a rongeur[②] and slowly biting off the rest of your skull, peeling it off downward like an orange until the sides and underneath of the brain covering are fully exposed. The problems involved are highly technical and I won't go into them but I feel fairly sure that the work can be done. It's simply a question of surgical skill and patience. And don't forget that I'd have plenty of time, as much as I wanted, because the artificial heart would be continually pumping away alongside the operating-table, keeping the brain alive.

"Now, let's assume that I've succeeded in peeling off your skull and removing everything else that surrounds the sides of the brain. That leaves it connected to the body only at the base, mainly by the spinal column and by the two large veins and the four arteries that are supplying it with blood. So what next?

"I would sever the spinal column just above the first cervical vertebra[③], taking great care not to harm the two vertebral arteries which are in that area. But you must remember that the dura or outer covering is open at this place to receive the spinal column, so I'd have to close this open-

① stub: *Noun* the truncated remnant of a pencil, cigarette, or similar-shaped object after use 残端;残余部分;铅笔头;烟蒂;烟屁股

② rongeur: *Noun* an instrument for removing small rough portions of bone 咬骨钳;咬割坚硬组织(尤其是骨)的器械

③ cervical vertebra: *Noun* one of 7 vertebrae in the human spine located in the neck region 颈骨;颈椎骨的统称

ing by sewing the edges of the dura together. There'd be no problem there.

"At this point, I would be ready for the final move. To one side, on a table, I'd have a basin of a special shape, and this would be filled with what we call Ringer's Solution①.

That is a special kind of fluid we use for irrigation in neurosurgery. I would now cut the brain completely loose by severing the supply arteries and the veins. Then I would simply pick it up in my hands and transfer it to the basin. This would be the only other time during the whole proceeding when the blood flow would be cut off; but once it was in the basin, it wouldn't take a moment to re-connect the stubs of the arteries and veins to the artificial heart.

"So there you are," Landy said. "Your brain is now in the basin, and still alive, and there isn't any reason why it shouldn't stay alive for a very long time, years and years perhaps, provided we looked after the blood and the machine."

"But would it *function*?"

"My dear William, how should I know? I can't even tell you whether it would regain consciousness."

"And if it did?"

"There now! That would be fascinating!"

"Would it?" I said, and I must admit I had my doubts.

"Of course it would! Lying there with all your thinking processes working beautifully, and your memory as well..." And not being able to see or feel or smell or hear or talk," I said.

"Ah!" he cried. "I knew I'd forgotten something! I never told you

---

① Ringer's solution: *Noun* [mass noun] (Biology) a physiological saline solution that typically contains, in addition to sodium chloride, salts of potassium and calcium（生物学）林格（溶）液

about the eye. Listen. I am going to try to leave one of your optic nerves[①] intact, as well as the eye itself.

The optic nerve is a little thing about the thickness of a clinical thermometer[②] and about two inches in length as it stretches between the brain and the eye. The beauty of it is that it's not really a nerve at all. It's an outpouching[③] of the brain itself, and the dura or brain covering extends along it and is attached to the eyeball. The back of the eye is therefore in very close contact with the brain, and cerebrospinal fluid flows right up to it.

"All this suits my purpose very well, and makes it reasonable to suppose that I could succeed in preserving one of your eyes. I've already constructed a small plastic case to contain the eyeball, instead of your own socket, and when the brain is in the basin, submerged in Ringer's Solution, the eyeball in its case will float on the surface of the liquid."

"Staring at the ceiling," I said.

"I suppose so, yes. I'm afraid there wouldn't be any muscles there to move it around. But it might be sort of fun to lie there so quietly and comfortably peering out at the world from your basin."

"Hilarious[④]," I said. "How about leaving me an ear as well?"

---

① optic nerve: *Noun* (Anatomy) each of the second pair of cranial nerves, transmitting impulses to the brain from the retina at the back of the eye(解剖学)视神经

② clinical thermometer: *Noun* a small medical thermometer with a short but finely calibrated range, for taking a person's temperature 医用温度计;体温表

③ outpouching: *Noun* a part or structure that is produced by evagination 外翻(一层或一部分组织突出,形成一个囊袋)

④ hilarious: *Adjective* extremely amusing 十分有趣的;非常滑稽的;欢闹的(e. g. The party got quite hilarious after they brought more wine. 在他们又拿来更多的酒之后,派对变得更加热闹起来。)

"I'd rather not try an ear this time."

"I want an ear," I said. "I insist upon an ear."

"No."

"I want to listen to Bach."

"You don't understand how difficult it would be," Landy said gently. "The hearing apparatus—the cochlea①, as it's called is a far more delicate mechanism than the eye. What's more, it is encased in bone. So is a part of the auditory nerve that connects it with the brain. I couldn't possibly chisel② the whole thing out intact."

"Couldn't you leave it encased in the bone and bring the bone to the basin?"

"No," he said firmly. "This thing is complicated enough already. And anyway, if the eye works, it doesn't matter all that much about your hearing. We can always hold up messages for you to read. You really must leave me to decide what is possible and what isn't."

"I haven't yet said that I'm going to do it."

"I know, William, I know."

"I'm not sure I fancy the idea very much."

"Would you rather be dead altogether?"

"Perhaps I would. I don't know yet. I wouldn't be able to talk, would I?"

"Of course not."

"Then how would I communicate with you? How would you know that I'm conscious?"

"It would be easy for us to know whether or not you regain con-

---

① cochlea: *Noun* the spiral cavity of the inner ear containing the organ of Corti, which produces nerve impulses in response to sound vibrations 耳蜗

② chisel: *Verb* cut or shape (something) with a chisel 凿;镌;雕(e. g. Carefully chisel a recess inside the pencil line. 仔细在铅笔线以内凿一道凹槽。)

sciousness," Landy said. "The ordinary electro-encephalograph[①] could tell us that. We'd attach the electrodes directly to the frontal lobes of your brain, there in the basin."

"And you could actually tell?"

"Oh, definitely. Any hospital could do that pan of it."

"But *I* couldn't communicate with *you*."

"As a matter of fact," Landy said, "I believe you could. There's a man up in London called Wertheimer who's doing some interesting work on the subject of thought communication, and I've been in touch with him. You know, don't you, that the thinking brain throws off electrical and chemical discharges? And that these discharges go out in the form of waves, rather like radio waves?"

"I know a bit about it," I said.

"Well, Wertheimer has constructed an apparatus somewhat similar to the encephalograph[②], though far more sensitive, and he maintains that within certain narrow limits it can help him to interpret the actual things that a brain is thinking. It produces a kind of graph which is apparently decipherable[③] into words or thoughts. Would you like me to ask Wertheimer to come and see you?"

"No," I said. Landy was already taking it for granted that I was going to go through with this business, and I resented his attitude. "Go away now and leave me alone," I told him. "You won't get anywhere by

---

① electroencephalograph or electro-encephalograph: *Noun* a machine used for electroencephalography 脑电图仪;脑电描记器

② encephalograph = encephalogram: *Noun* (Medicine) an image, trace, or other record of the structure or electrical activity of the brain(医学)脑 X 射线(照)片;脑造影照片;气脑图

③ decipher: *Verb* [with obj.] convert (a text written in code, or a coded signal) into normal language 破译(密码);译解(电码)

trying to rush me."

He stood up at once and crossed to the door.

"One question," I said.

He paused with a hand on the doorknob. "Yes, William?"

"Simply this. Do you yourself honestly believe that when my brain is in that basin, my mind will be able to function exactly as it is doing at present? Do you believe that I will be able to think and reason as I can now? And will the power of memory remain?"

"I don't see why not," he answered. "It's the same brain. It's alive. It's undamaged. In fact, it's completely untouched. We haven't even opened the dura. The big difference, of course, would be that we've severed every single nerve that leads into it—except for the one optic nerve—and this means that your thinking would no longer be influenced by your senses. You'd be living in an extraordinary pure and detached world. Nothing to bother you at all, not even pain. You couldn't possibly feel pain because there wouldn't be any nerves to feel it with. In a way, it would be an almost perfect situation. No worries or fears or pains or hunger or thirst. Not even any desires. Just your memories and your thoughts and if the remaining eye happened to function, then you could read books as well. It all sounds rather pleasant to me."

"It does, does it?"

"Yes, William, it does. And particularly for a Doctor of Philosophy[①]. It would be a tremendous experience. You'd be able to reflect upon the ways of the world with a detachment and a serenity[②] that no man

---

① Doctor of Philosophy: *Noun* a doctorate in any faculty except law, medicine, or sometimes theology(除法律、医学或有时神学之外的)博士学位

② serenity: *Noun* [mass noun] the state of being calm, peaceful, and untroubled 平静;宁静(e. g. an oasis of serenity amidst the bustling city 繁忙的城市中宁静的绿洲。)

had ever attained before. And who knows what might not happen then! Great thoughts and solutions might come to you, great ideas that could revolutionize our way of life! Try to imagine, if you can, the degree of concentration that you'd be able to achieve!"

"And the frustration," I said.

"Nonsense. There couldn't be any frustration. You can't have frustration without desire, and you couldn't possibly have any desire. Not physical desire, anyway."

"I should certainly be capable of remembering my previous life in the world, and I might desire to return to it."

"What, to this mess! Out of your comfortable basin and back into this madhouse[①]!"

"Answer one more question," I said. "How long do you believe you could keep it alive?"

"The brain? Who knows? Possibly for years and years. The conditions would be ideal. Most of the factors that cause deterioration would be absent, thanks to the artificial heart. The blood-pressure would remain constant at all times, an impossible condition in real life. The temperature would also be constant. The chemical composition of the blood would be near perfect. There would be no impurities in it, or virus, no bacteria, nothing. Of course it's foolish to guess, but I believe that a brain might live for two or three hundred years in circumstances like these. Goodbye for now," he said. "I'll drop in and see you tomorrow." He went out quickly, leaving me, as you might guess, in a fairly disturbed state of mind.

My immediate reaction after he had gone was one of revulsion to-

① madhouse: *Noun* [in sing.] a scene of extreme confusion or uproar 喧闹的情景;混乱的地方(e.g. This place is a madhouse. 这个地方很吵。)

wards the whole business. Somehow, it wasn't at all nice. There was something basically repulsive about the idea that I myself, with all my mental faculties intact, should be reduced to a small slimy① blob② lying in a pool of water. It was monstrous, obscene, unholy. Another thing that bothered me was the feeling of helplessness that I was bound to experience once Landy had got me into the basin. There could be no going back after that, no way of protesting or explaining. I would be committed for as long as they could keep me alive.

And what, for example, if I could not stand it? What if it turned out to be terribly painful? What if I became hysterical?

No legs to run away on. No voice to scream with. Nothing. I'd just have to grin and bear it for the next two centuries.

No mouth to grin with either.

At this point, a curious thought struck me, and it was this: Does not a man who has had a leg amputated③ often suffer from the delusion that the leg is still there? Does he not tell the nurse that the toes he doesn't have any more are itching like mad, and so on and so forth? I seemed to have heard something to that effect quite recently.

Very well. On the same premise, was it not possible that my brain, lying there alone in that basin, might not suffer from a similar delusion in regard to my body? In which case, all my usual aches and pains could

---

① slimy: *Adjective* covered by or having the feel or consistency of slime 满是黏泥的;分泌黏液的;黏糊糊的(e. g. The walls were slimy with lichen. 墙上布满黏湿的苔藓。)

② blob: *Noun* an indeterminate roundish mass or shape 形状不易确定的一团(e. g. A big pink blob of a face was at the window. 窗口出现了一张肉团团的粉红色大脸。)

③ amputate: *Verb* [with obj.] cut off (a limb) by surgical operation 截(肢)(e. g. Surgeons had to amputate her left hand. 外科医生不得不截掉她的左手。)

come flooding over me and I wouldn't even be able to take an aspirin to relieve them. One moment I might be imagining that I had the most excruciating[①] cramp[②] in my leg, or a violent indigestion, and a few minutes later, I might easily get the feeling that my poor bladder—you know me was so full that if I didn't get to emptying it soon it would burst.

Heaven forbid.

I lay there for a long time thinking these horrid thoughts. Then quite suddenly, round about midday, my mood began to change. I became less concerned with the unpleasant aspect of the affair and found myself able to examine Landy's proposals in a more reasonable light. Was there not, after all, I asked myself, something a bit comforting in the thought that my brain might not necessarily have to die and disappear in a few weeks' time? There was indeed. I am rather proud of my brain. It is a sensitive, lucid, and uberous[③] organ. It contains a prodigious[④] store of information, and it is still capable of producing imaginative and original theories. As brains go, it is a damn good one, though I say it myself. Whereas my body, my poor old body, the thing that Landy wants to throw away—well, even you, my dear Mary, will have to agree with me that there is really nothing about that which is worth preserving any more.

---

① excruciating: *Adjective* intensely painful 极痛苦的；难以忍受的（e. g. excruciating back pain 难以忍受的背痛。）

② cramp: *Noun* [mass noun] painful involuntary contraction of a muscle or muscles, typically caused by fatigue or strain（多指疲倦或过度劳累导致的）痉挛；抽筋（e. g. an attack of cramp 一阵痉挛）

③ uberous: *Adjective* fruitful; copious; abundant; plentiful 多产的；多育的；繁殖的

④ prodigious: *Adjective* remarkably or impressively great in extent, size, or degree（范围、规模或程度）巨大的；庞大的（e. g. The stove consumed a prodigious amount of fuel. 这种炉子消耗大量燃料。）

I was lying on my back eating a grape. Delicious it was, and there were three little seeds in it which I took out of my mouth and placed on the edge of the plate.

"I'm going to do it," I said quietly. "Yes, by God, I'm going to do it. When Landy comes back to see me tomorrow I shall tell him straight out that I'm going to do it."

It was as quick as that. And from then on, I began to feel very much better. I surprised everyone by gobbling[①] an enormous lunch, and shortly after that you came in to visit me as usual.

But how well I looked, you told me. How bright and well and chirpy[②]. Had anything happened? Was there some good news?

Yes, I said there was. And then, if you remember, I bade you sit down and make yourself comfortable and I began immediately to explain to you as gently as I could what was in the wind[③].

Alas, you would have none of it. I had hardly begun telling you the barest details when you flew into a fury and said that the thing was revolting, disgusting, horrible, unthinkable, and when I tried to go on, you marched out of the room.

Well, Mary, as you know, I have tried to discuss this subject with you many times since then, but you have consistently refused to give me a hearing. Hence this note, and I can only hope that you will have the good sense to permit yourself to read it. It has taken me a long time to write. Two weeks have gone since I started to scribble the first sentence,

---

① gobble: *Verb* [with obj.] eat (something) hurriedly and noisily 狼吞虎咽;大口吞食(e.g. One man gobbled up a kipper. 一个男人大口猛吃腌鱼。)

② chirpy: *Adjective* (informal) cheerful and lively(非正式)兴高采烈的;活泼的

③ in the wind: about to happen soon, although you do not know exactly when 即将发生;在酝中(e.g. I can see some changes in the wind. 我看情况要起变化。)

and I'm now a good deal weaker than I was then. I doubt whether I have the strength to say much more. Certainly I won't say good-bye, because there's a chance, just a tiny chance, that if Landy succeeds in his work I may actually see you again later, that is if you bring yourself to come and visit me.

I am giving orders that these pages shall not be delivered to you until a week after I am gone. By now, therefore, as you sit reading them, seven days have already elapsed since Landy did the deed. You yourself may even know what the outcome has been. If you don't, if you have purposely kept yourself apart and have refused to have anything to do with it—which I suspect may be the case—please change your mind now and give Landy a call to see how things went with me. That is the least you can do. I have told him that he may expect to hear from you on the seventh day.

Your faithful husband

William

P.S. Be good when I am gone, and always remember that it is harder to be a widow than a wife. Do not drink cocktails. Do not waste money. Do not smoke cigarettes. Do not eat pastry. Do not use lipstick. Do not buy a television apparatus. Keep my rose beds and my rockery well weeded in the summers. And incidentally I suggest that you have the telephone disconnected now that I shall have no further use for it.

W.

Mrs. Pearl laid the last page of the manuscript slowly down on the sofa beside her. Her little mouth was pursed① up tight and there was a whiteness around her nostrils.

But really! You would think a widow was entitled to a bit of peace after all these years.

The whole thing was just too awful to think about. Beastly and awful. It gave her the shudders.

She reached for her bag and found herself another cigarette. She lit it, inhaling the smoke deeply and blowing it out in clouds all over the room. Through the smoke she could see her lovely television set, brand new lustrous②, huge, crouching defiantly③ but also a little self-consciously on top of what used to be William's worktable.

What would he say, she wondered, if he could see that now?

She paused, to remember the last time he had caught her smoking a cigarette. That was about a year ago, and she was sitting in the kitchen by the open window having a quick one before he came home from work. She'd had the radio on loud playing dance music and she had turned round to pour herself another cup of coffee and there he was standing in the doorway, huge and grim, staring down at her with those awful eyes, a little black dot of fury blazing in the centre of each.

For four weeks after that, he had paid the housekeeping bills himself and given her no money at all, but of course he wasn't to know that she

---

① purse: *Verb* (with reference to the lips) pucker or contract, typically to express disapproval or irritation(嘴唇)皱起;缩拢;噘起(多表示不赞成、恼怒)(e.g. Marianne took a glance at her reflection and pursed her lips disgustedly. 玛丽安娜瞥了一眼自己的倒影,厌烦地噘起嘴。)

② lustrous: *Adjective* having lustre; shining 有光泽的;光亮的(e.g. large, lustrous eyes 明亮的大眼睛)

③ defiant: *Adjective* showing defiance 挑衅的;蔑视的(e.g. She was in defiant mood. 她是在寻衅。)

had over six pounds salted away in a soap-flake carton in the cupboard under the sink.

"What is it?" she had said to him once during supper. "Are you worried about me getting lung cancer?"

"I am not," he had answered.

"Then why can't I smoke?"

"Because I disapprove, that's why."

He had also disapproved of children, and as a result they had never had any of them either.

Where was he now, this William of hers, the great disapprover?

Landy would be expecting her to call up. Did she have to call Landy?

Well, not really, no.

She finished her cigarette, then lit another one immediately from the old stub. She looked at the telephone that was sitting on the worktable beside the television set. William had asked her to call. He had specifically requested that she telephone Landy as soon as she had read the letter. She hesitated, fighting hard now against that old ingrained① sense of duty that she didn't quite yet dare to shake off. Then, slowly, she got to her feet and crossed over to the phone on the worktable. She found a number in the book, dialled it, and waited.

"I want to speak to Mr. Landy, please."

"Who is calling?"

"Mrs. Pearl. Mrs. William Pearl."

"One moment, please."

Almost at once, Landy was on the other end of the wire.

---

① ingrain or engrain: *Verb* [with obj.] firmly fix or establish (a habit, belief, or attitude) in a person 使(习惯、信仰或态度)根深蒂固

"Mrs. Pearl?"

"This is Mrs. Pearl."

There was a slight pause.

"I am so glad you called at last, Mrs. Pearl. You are quite well, I hope?" The voice was quiet, unemotional, courteous. "I wonder if you would care to come over to the hospital? Then we can have a little chat. I expect you are very eager to know how it all came out."

She didn't answer.

"I can tell you now that everything went pretty smoothly, one way and another. Far better, in fact, than I was entitled to hope. It is not only alive, Mrs. Pearl, it is conscious. It recovered consciousness on the second day. Isn't that interesting?"

She waited for him to go on.

"And the eye is seeing. We are sure of that because we get an immediate change in the deflections[①] on the encephalograph when we hold something up in front of it. And now we're giving it the newspaper to read every day."

"Which newspaper?" Mrs. Pearl asked sharply.

"*The Daily Mirror*. The headlines are larger."

"He hates the *Mirror*. Give him *The Times*."

There was a pause, then the doctor said, "Very well, Mrs. Pearl. We'll give it *The Times*. We naturally want to do all we can to keep it happy."

"*Him*," she said. "Not *it*. *Him*!"

"Him," the doctor said. "Yes, I beg your pardon. To keep him happy. That's one reason why I suggested you should come along here as

---

① deflection or deflexion: *Noun* [count noun] the amount by which something is deflected 偏离量;偏度(e. g. an 11-mile deflection of the river 河流偏离 11 英里)

soon as possible. I think it would be good for him to see you. You could indicate how delighted you were to be with him again—smile at him and blow him a kiss and all that sort of thing. It's bound to be a comfort to him to know that you are standing by."

There was a long pause.

"Well," Mrs. Pearl said at last, her voice suddenly very meek and tired. "I suppose I had better come on over and see how he is."

"Good. I knew you would. I'll wait here for you. Come straight up to my office on the second floor. Good-bye."

Half an hour later, Mrs. Pearl was at the hospital.

"You mustn't be surprised by what he looks like," Landy said as he walked beside her down a corridor.

"No, I won't."

"It's bound to be a bit of a shock to you at first. He's not very prepossessing① in his present state, I'm afraid."

"I didn't marry him for his looks, Doctor."

Landy turned and stared at her. What a queer little woman this was, he thought with her large eyes and her sullen, resentful air. Her features, which must have been quite pleasant once, had now gone completely. The mouth was slack, the cheeks loose and flabby②, and the whole face gave the impression of having slowly but surely sagged to pieces through years and years of joyless married life. They walked on for a while in silence.

---

① prepossessing: *Adjective* [often with negative] attractive or appealing in appearance(外貌)给人好感的;打动人的;有吸引力的(e.g. He was not a prepossessing sight. 他外表没什么吸引人之处。)

② flabby: *Adjective* (of a part of a person's body) soft, loose, and fleshy(人体某一部位)松弛的;冗赘的(e.g. This exercise helps to flatten a flabby stomach. 这种锻炼能促使松弛的腹部变得平坦。)

"Take your time when you get inside," Landy said. "He won't know you're in there until you place your face directly above his eye. The eye is always open, but he can't move it at all, so the field of vision is very narrow. At present we have it looking up at the ceiling. And of course he can't hear anything. We can talk together as much as we like. It's in here."

Landy opened a door and ushered her into a small square room.

"I wouldn't go too close yet," he said, putting a hand on her arm. "Stay back here a moment with me until you get used to it all."

There was a biggish white enamel[①] bowl about the size of a washbasin standing on a high white table in the centre of the room, and there were half a dozen thin plastic tubes coming out of it. These tubes were connected with a whole lot of glass piping in which you could see the blood flowing to and from the heart machine. The machine itself made a soft rhythmic pulsing sound.

"He's in there," Landy said, pointing to the basin, which was too high for her to see into. "Come just a little closer. Not too near."

He led her two paces forward.

By stretching her neck, Mrs. Pearl could now see the surface of the liquid inside the basin. It was clear and still, and on it there floated a small oval capsule, about the size of a pigeon's egg.

"That's the eye in there," Landy said. "Can you see it?"

"Yes."

"So far as we can tell, it is still in perfect condition. It's his right eye, and the plastic container has a lens on it similar to the one he used in his own spectacles. At this moment he's probably seeing quite as well

① enamel: *Noun* [mass noun] an opaque or semi-transparent glassy substance applied to metallic or other hard surfaces for ornament or as a protective coating 搪瓷;珐琅

as he did before."

"The ceiling isn't much to look at," Mrs. Pearl said.

"Don't worry about that. We're in the process of working out a whole programme to keep him amused, but we don't want to go too quickly at first."

"Give him a good book."

"We will, we will. Are you feeling all right, Mrs. Pearl?"

"Yes."

"Then we'll go forward a little more, shall we, and you'll be able to see the whole thing."

He led her forward until they were standing only a couple of yards from the table and now she could see right down into the basin.

"There you are," Landy said. "That's William."

He was far larger than she had imagined he would be, and darker in colour. With all the ridges and creases running over his surface, he reminded her of nothing so much as an enormous pickled walnut. She could see the stubs of the four big arteries and the two veins coming out from the base of him and the neat way in which they were joined to the plastic tubes; and with each throb of the heart machine, all the tubes gave a little jerk in unison as the blood was pushed through them.

"You'll have to lean over," Landy said, "and put your pretty face right above the eye. He'll see you then, and you can smile at him and blow him a kiss. If I were you I'd say a few nice things as well. He won't actually hear them, but I'm sure he'll get the general idea."

"He hates people blowing kisses at him," Mrs. Pearl said. "I'll do it my own way if you don't mind." She stepped up to the edge of the table, leaned forward until her face was directly over the basin, and looked straight down in William's eye.

"Hallo, dear," she whispered. "It's me Mary."

The eye, bright as ever, stared back at her with a peculiar, fixed intensity.

"How are you, dear?" she said.

The plastic capsule was transparent all the way round so that the whole of the eyeball was visible. The optic nerve connecting the underside of it to the brain looked a short length of grey spaghetti①.

"Are you feeling all right, William?"

It was a queer sensation peering into her husband's eye when there was no face to go with it. All she had to look at was the eye, and she kept staring at it, and gradually it grew bigger and bigger, and in the end it was the only thing that she could see—a sort of face in itself. There was a network of tiny red veins running over the white surface of the eyeball, and in the ice-blue of the iris there were three or four rather pretty darkish streaks② radiating from the pupil in the centre. The pupil was large and black, with a little spark of light reflecting from one side of it.

"I got your letter, dear, and came over at once to see how you were. Dr. Landy says you are doing wonderfully well. Perhaps if I talk slowly you can understand a little of what I am saying by reading my lips."

There was no doubt that the eye was watching her.

"They are doing everything possible to take care of you, dear. This marvellous machine thing here is pumping away all the time and I'm sure it's a lot better than those silly old hearts all the rest of us have. Ours are liable to break down at any moment, but yours will go on for ever."

She was studying the eye closely, trying to discover what there was about it that gave it such an unusual appearance.

---

① spaghetti: *Noun* (plural noun) pasta made in solid strings, between macaroni and vermicelli in thickness 意大利式细面条

② streak: *Noun* a long, thin line or mark of a different substance or colour from its surroundings 条纹;条痕;色带

"You seem fine, dear, simply fine. Really you do."

It looked ever so much nicer, this eye, than either of his eyes used to look, she told herself. There was a softness about it somewhere, a calm, kindly quality that she had never seen before. Maybe it had to do with the dot in the very centre, the pupil. William's pupils used always to be tiny black pinheads. They used to glint① at you, stabbing into your brain, seeing right through you, and they always knew at once what you were up to and even what you were thinking. But this one she was looking at now was large and soft and gentle, almost cowlike.

"Are you quite sure he's conscious?" she asked, not looking up.

"Oh yes, completely," Landy said.

"And he *can* see me?"

"Perfectly."

"Isn't that marvellous? I expect he's wondering what happened."

"Not at all. He knows perfectly well where he is and why he's there. He can't possibly have forgotten that."

"You mean he *knows* he's in this basin?"

"Of course. And if only he had the power of speech, he would probably be able to carry on a perfectly normal conversation with you this very minute. So far as I can see, there should be absolutely no difference mentally between this William here and the one you used to know back home."

"Good *gracious* me," Mrs. Pearl said, and she paused to consider this intriguing aspect.

You know what, she told herself, looking behind the eye now and

① glint: *Verb* (of a person's eyes) shine with a particular emotion(眼睛表达某种情感时)闪光(e.g. His eyes glinted angrily. 他的眼睛闪着愤怒的光芒。)

staring hard at the great grey pulpy[①] walnut that lay so placidly under the water, I'm not at all sure that I don't prefer him as he is at present. In fact, I believe that I could live very comfortably with this kind of a William. I could cope with this one.

"Quiet, isn't he?" she said.

"Naturally he's quiet."

No arguments and criticisms, she thought, no constant admonitions[②], no rules to obey, no ban on smoking cigarettes, no pair of cold disapproving eyes watching me over the top of a book in the evenings, no shirts to wash and iron, no meals to cook nothing but the throb of the heart machine, which was rather a soothing sound anyway and certainly not loud enough to interfere with television.

"Doctor," she said. "I do believe I'm suddenly getting to feel the most enormous affection for him. Does that sound queer?"

"I think it's quite understandable."

"He looks so helpless and silent lying there under the water in his little basin."

"Yes, I know.

"He's like a baby, that's what he's like. He's exactly like a little baby."

Landy stood still behind her, watching.

"There," she said softly, peering into the basin. "From now on Mary's going to look after you *all* by herself and you've nothing to worry about in the world. When can I have him back home, Doctor?"

---

① pulpy: *Adjective* like a pulp or overripe; not having stiffness 果肉状的;多汁的;柔软的

② admonition: *Adjective* mild, kind, yet earnest reproof; cautionary advice or warning(温和的)责备;告诫;劝告;忠告(e. g. He admonished his friend not to be late for work. 他规劝他的朋友上班不要迟到。)

"I beg your pardon?"

"I said when can I have him back—back in my own house?"

"You're joking," Landy said.

She turned her head slowly around and looked directly at him. "Why should I joke?" she asked. Her face was bright, her eyes round and bright as two diamonds.

"He couldn't possibly be moved."

"I don't see why not."

"This is an experiment, Mrs. Pearl."

"It's my husband, Dr. Landy."

A funny little nervous half-smile appeared on Landy's mouth. "Well..." he said.

"It *is* my husband, you know." There was no anger in her voice. She spoke quietly, as though merely reminding him of a simple fact.

"That's rather a tricky point," Landy said, wetting his lips. "You're a widow now, Mrs. Pearl. I think you must resign yourself to that fact."

She turned away suddenly from the table and crossed over to the window. "I mean it," she said, fishing in her bag for a cigarette. "I want him back."

Landy watched her as she put the cigarette between her lips and lit it. Unless he were very much mistaken, there was something a bit odd about this woman, he thought. She seemed almost pleased to have her husband over there in the basin.

He tried to imagine what his own feelings would be if it were *his* wife's brain lying there and *her* eye staring at him out of that capsule.

He wouldn't like it.

"Shall we go back to my room now?" he said.

She was standing by the window, apparently quite calm and relaxed, puffing her cigarette.

"Yes, all right."

On her way past the table she stopped and leaned over the basin once more. "Mary's leaving now, sweetheart," she said. "And don't you worry about a single thing, you understand? We're going to get you right back home where we can look after you properly just as soon as we possibly can. And listen dear..." At this point she paused and carried the cigarette to her lips, intending to take a puff.

Instantly the eye flashed.

She was looking straight into it at the time and right in the centre of it she saw a tiny but brilliant flash of light, and the pupil contracted into a minute black pinpoint① of absolute fury.

At first she didn't move. She stood bending over the basin, holding the cigarette up to her mouth, watching the eye.

Then very slowly, deliberately, she put the cigarette between her lips and took a long suck. She inhaled deeply, and she held the smoke inside her lungs for three or four seconds; then suddenly, whoosh②, out it came through her nostrils in two thin jets which struck the water in the basin, and billowed③ out over the surface in a thick blue cloud, enveloping the eye.

Landy was over by the door, with his back to her, waiting. "Come on, Mrs. Pearl," he called.

"Don't look so cross, William," she said softly. "It isn't any good

---

① pinpoint: *Noun* a tiny dot or point 小点

② whoosh or woosh: *Verb* [no obj., with adverbial of direction] move quickly or suddenly with a rushing sound 嗖嗖地(或呼呼地)迅速移动(e.g. A train whooshed by. 火车嗖地飞速驶过。)

③ billow: *Verb* (of smoke, cloud, or steam) move or flow outward with an undulating motion(烟、云或蒸汽)翻腾;汹涌(e.g. Smoke was billowing from the chimney-mouth. 烟雾从烟囱口涌出来。)

looking cross."

Landy turned his head to see what she was doing.

"Not any more it isn't," she whispered. "Because from now on, my pet, you're going to do just exactly what Mary tells you. Do you understand that?"

"Mrs. Pearl," Landy said, moving towards her.

"So don't be a naughty boy again, will you, my precious," she said, taking another pull at the cigarette. "Naughty boys are liable to get punished most severely nowadays, you ought to know that."

Landy was beside her now, and he took her by the arm and began drawing her firmly but gently away from the table.

"Good-bye, darling," she called. "I'll be back soon."

"That's enough, Mrs. Pearl."

"Isn't he sweet?" she cried, looking up at Landy with big bright eyes. "Isn't he darling? I just can't wait to get him home."

三、翻译探索

这篇小说的题目很简单，就是男女主人公的名字——威廉和玛丽，但为求四字格的总体翻译效果，实际翻译时，将题目做了"写实"性转换。翻译这篇小说的主要障碍恐怕是一些医学方面的表达，要力求准确，但个别地方还需根据上下文在"动态对等"的基础上加以变通。

器官实验

威廉·珀尔死后，并没有留下大笔金钱。他的遗嘱也很简单：除了几笔小规模的遗产留给了一些亲戚之外，其他所有财产都归他妻子所有。

律师办公室里，珀尔太太跟律师仔细核对了丈夫留给她的遗产清单。核对完之后，这位遗孀起身就要离开。就在这当儿，律师从桌上一个文件夹中抽出一封信，递给了当事人。信封是密封好了的。

"受你丈夫生前委托，把这个转交给你，"他说。"他去世前不久，把这个寄给了我们。"这名律师脸色苍白、表情严肃，出于对一个刚刚失去丈夫的女性的尊重，说话时把头偏向一边，眼睛朝下看去。"珀尔太太，这封信似乎是个人信件，你完全可以带回家，私下里阅读。"

珀尔太太接过信，出了门，走上大街。走到人行道上的时候，她暂停下来，用手摸了摸信件。是威廉写给她的告别信吗？或许是吧。是一封正式信函吧，一定是很庄重的那种信函：内容拘谨、行文严肃。她的丈夫没有别的能力，做起事来除了庄重，就是严肃。他一生中，从未做过什么不拘礼节的事情。

我亲爱的玛丽：你不要因为我离开了这个世界而心慌意乱，我相信你不会这样的。我也相信，你会遵循我们婚姻生活中的那些清规戒律，毕竟它们给你以指导，让你生活得很好。做什么事情，都要勤勉，都要有尊严，用钱要节俭。要十分谨慎，不要……等等，等等。

这就是威廉写信的典型风格。

他能否一反常态，在生命的最后时刻，别出心裁地为她写出一些漂亮、雅致的话语？或许，这封信就是这般漂亮的，传达的是柔情蜜意，就是类似于情书的那种信函——表达爱意，暖意融融，且心存感激。感激她三十年以来对他的奉献：熨烫了无数件衬衫、烹饪了无数顿饭菜、整理过无数次床铺。信里或许会写上某些类似的事情，令她读完一遍又一遍，一天至少读一遍。这样的一封信，她会爱不释手的，永远保存在梳妆台上那个小盒子里，跟她的胸针放到一起。

珀尔太太对自己说，人要死的时候会做些什么，无法得知。她把信封夹到胳膊底下，匆匆忙忙往家走去。

从正门直接进屋后，她就直奔起居室。外衣没脱，帽子没摘，就一屁股坐到沙发上。随后，打开信封，抽出信纸。信纸是一些带有横线的白纸，没有二十张，起码也有十五张；这些信纸叠成一个折，折合处的左角那儿别了一枚回形针。每一页纸上都整整齐齐写满了小小的字母,字体向前倾斜,这种笔体她太熟悉了。写了很多,写得密密麻麻、整整齐齐、一丝不苟,而且第一页甚至没有像普通信件那样有一个像样的开头。至此,她开始心生疑虑了。

她把目光从信纸上移开,点燃一支香烟,猛吸一口,随手把烟放到烟灰缸里。

她对自己说:如果信的内容像我开始怀疑的那样严肃、庄重,那么,我就不想看了。

人都死了,写的信能拒绝阅读吗?

能的。

那么……

她眼睛向壁炉的另一侧瞥了过去,那儿有一把空椅子,是威廉坐过的。那把椅子个头很大,是用皮革做的,是一把棕色的扶手椅。座位上有一处凹痕,是他的屁股这么多年坐出来的。再往椅子的上方瞧,靠背的皮革上面有一块黑黑的椭圆形斑痕,那是他头部长期倚靠的结果。他过去经常坐在那把椅子上看书,而她就坐在他对面的沙发上,或者缝扣子,或者补袜子,或者给他的一件夹克衫的胳膊肘那个地方打补丁。他那两只眼睛时不时地从书后溜出来,落到她的脸上,但是颇为奇怪的是,那双眼睛虽然转来转去看着她,却毫无神情可言,就好像在对什么东西进行估算。她从来就没有喜欢过那双眼睛——冰蓝色的、小小的,显得冷漠无情;紧紧地靠在一起,但中间却由两条深深的垂直线条分隔着,显示出事事都不以为然的样子。在她的一生中,那双眼睛就这么一直看着她,甚至到了现在他死去一周的时间里,她独处家中,有时候还会有一种心神不安的感觉,感觉那两只眼睛还在那儿,随着她转来转去,从门口那儿、空椅子上盯着她,甚至夜晚睡觉时还透过窗户挤进来看。

她慢慢地把手伸进手提包,掏出眼镜戴上。然后,把信纸高高举到眼前,借助身后窗户透进来的、午后落日前的光线,开始阅读起来:

我亲爱的玛丽,这封短信纯粹是为你写的,在我离世后不久会转交到你手中。

看到我写的东西，你切莫惊慌失措。其实，就我而言，写这封信也没有什么大不了的事情，只不过想试着向你准确解释一下，兰迪要对我做些什么，为什么我同意他那样做，以及他的理论是什么、希望是什么。你是我妻子，有权知道这些事情。事实上，你*必须*得知道。在过去那几天里，我一直很努力要跟你谈谈兰迪的事，你却坚决不肯听我说。就像我早先对你说过的那样，你的这种做法源于你所采取的一种很愚蠢的态度。我发现，你的这种态度也不是完完全全没有私心的。你采取这种态度，主要是出于无知，而我绝对相信，你要是知道了所有的实情，你就会立马改变看法的。这也就是我希望你阅读这封信的原因：我离你远去之后，你就不会心烦意乱、注意力不集中了，你就会同意仔仔细细听我说话了——通过这封信向你述说。我敢向你保证，读完我给你写的，你那由来已久的厌恶感就会烟消云散，转而热情洋溢。我甚至敢怀有这样的希望：你会为我的所作所为感到一点点的骄傲。

如果可以的话，你越往下读，你就越要原谅我，原谅我这种冷漠的写作风格。但我知道，要让你清清楚楚地领会我的意思，我只能采用这种风格。你知道的，随着我活着的时间一天天减少，这个世界上任何一件多愁善感之事都会充斥我的大脑，这是自然而然的。每过一天，我就变得更加依依不舍，特别是到了晚上，只要不是独自发呆的话，我的情感就会翻涌上来，宣泄到这些信纸上。

比方说吧，我有一个心愿，就是要写写你，写写这么多年以来，你对我来说，是一位多么令人满意的妻子。我对自己许下诺言，如果有时间、还有气力的话，就开始写。

我还有一个渴望，说说我心目中的牛津，因为过去的十七年时间里，我一直在那儿生活、教学；说说那儿带给我的荣耀感；要是可以的话，稍微解释一下，有幸在那儿工作具有什么样的意义。现在，在这个压抑阴沉的卧室里，我曾经热爱的所有东西和地方，都接二连三地涌上心头。这些东西和地方始终都是那么的明亮和美丽。时至今天，出于某种原因，它们看起来比以前更加清晰：有武斯特学院花园里的那条环湖小路，洛夫莱斯以前经常在那条小路上散步；有出入彭布罗克港的通道；有从马格达伦塔楼上西望整个城镇上空的景色；有克赖斯特教堂里那个大大的厅堂；有圣约翰大教堂那儿小小的假山园，在那里我数出了十多个品种的风铃草属植物，包括稀有而俏丽的林石草。你看看啊！我甚至还没开始跟你说正事，就已经刹不住闸了。好吧，现在就让我进入正题吧。我亲爱的，你也慢慢地读下去，不要有任何的悲伤和不以为然。否则，就会妨碍你的理解力。现在答应我，你要慢慢地阅读下去。阅读前答应我，你会抱着冷静、忍耐的心态阅读下去。

在我人生的中点，这种疾病突然之间把我击垮，其细节你是知道的，就用不着我浪费时间详述了。但是，有一点我立刻会承认的，就是我太愚蠢，没有能够早一些去看医生。剩下的几种疾病中，现代药品没有办法根治，癌症便是其中之一。癌细胞要是没有扩散开来，外科医生可以做手术来治疗。可是就我而言，不仅病情我关注得太晚，而且这东西竟然放肆得很，打入我的胰腺内部。这样的话，不管是做外科手术，还是继续存活，都是不可能的事情。

所以，结果就是，我只有一到六个月的活头了，而且每过一个小时，我就愈加忧郁沮丧。紧接着，兰迪就猛地一下子冒了出来。

那是六周以前的事情了，是一个星期二的早晨。当时是早晨很早的时候，远在你探视之前，他就来了。他一进来，我就知道，他走路带的那股风里就有某种疯狂的成分。他并没有像所有其他来看我的人那样，大脚趾着地，轻手轻脚地走进来，谨小慎微、局促不安，不知道该说些什么。相反的，他面带微笑，风风火火走进来，大步流星走到病床前，站在那儿，低头看着我，眼神狂放、眼睛发亮。他说："好家伙，威廉，这真是十全十美。你正是我要找的人啊！"

至此，我或许应该向你解释一下，尽管约翰·兰迪从来没有到过我们家，你也几乎没有遇到过他，但是我本人跟他交往至少有九年的时光了。当然，我主要是教哲学，但你是知道的，近来我也大量涉猎心理学。因此，我和兰迪的兴趣点就稍微具有交叉之处。他是一位卓越的神经外科医生，也可以说，是其中最优秀的一位。最近，他大发慈悲，让我看了些他的研究成果，特别是脑前额叶切除术的研究成果，说的是这种切除术对不同类型精神变态者所产生的各种影响。所以，你就明白星期二早晨他突然闯进来那件事了。当时，我们彼此并不陌生，而是相当熟悉的。

“看啊，”他边说，边拉过来一把椅子坐到床边。“再过几周，你就要死了，是不是呢？”

由于这话出自兰迪之口，这问题似乎也就没什么不妥之处。从某种角度来说，有人来访，大胆触及禁忌话题，倒令我精神为之一振。

“就在这儿，就是这间屋子里，你的生命将终止。接着，有人就会把你推出去，化成灰。”

“就埋掉，”我说。

“甚至更糟。你知道接下来会怎样吗？你相信你会升入天堂吗？”

“我不敢肯定是否能，”我回答，“尽管一想到自己能升入天堂，就会得到些安慰。”

“没准儿，还下地狱呢？”

“我真的不明白，有什么理由让我下地狱。”

“我亲爱的威廉，你永远不会弄明白的。”

“问这些干什么？”我说。

“噢，”他说。我看见，他仔仔细细地打量着我。“从个人角度来说，我相信，你死后，你将再也听不到关于你自己的事情了，除非……”说到这，他暂停下来，微笑着，身体向前靠得更近了。“……当然啦，除非你愿意把你自己交由我处置。你愿意考虑我的一个提议吗？”

说来古怪得很，他有些饥饿的样子。他盯着我，仔细地端详，对我进行估量，那架势让我感觉，我自己好似一块被他买下的上等牛肉，放在柜台上，等待店家打包完毕，他就拿起带走。

“威廉，我很认真的。你愿意考虑我的一个提议吗？”

“我不明白你在说些什么。”

“那就听着，我给你讲。愿意听我说吗？”

“愿意讲，就继续吧。我不相信，听你说几句，就会损失惨重的。”

“正相反,你将受益匪浅,特别是*在你死后* 。”

我敢肯定,他一定期待着,我听到这句话会跳起来的,但是不知怎么的,我有所防备,反而一动不动地继续躺着。我看着他那张白白的脸,还有脸上那抹慢慢浮现的微笑。他这么一笑,口腔上部那颗假牙的金扣子就露出来了,那金扣子是绕着他嘴里左边那颗犬齿缠上去的。

“威廉,这么多年以来,这件事我一直默默地潜心研究着。这家医院有那么一两个人一直帮我忙,特别是莫里森这个人。我们一起在实验室用动物做实验,很多次尝试都相当的成功。现在,到了这样的阶段:准备用人实验。这个想法很大胆,乍听起来或许有点不合情理,但是从外科手术的角度来看,似乎没有任何理由证明,这一想法在一定程度上不可行的。”

兰迪身体前倾,双手支撑到我那张病床的边上。他长了一张和善的脸,脸上骨架凸显、棱角分明而显得英俊,但一点也没有当医生的容貌。你知道当医生的容貌是什么样子,多数医生都有的:看你的时候,眼睛微微放出光彩,眼球犹如单调的电光标志,脸上的表情似乎在说:“只有我能救你的命。”但是,约翰·兰迪的眼睛就不一样了:圆圆的、亮亮的,中间还有兴奋的小火花跳跃着。

“好久以前,”他说,“我看到一个医学短片,是有人从俄罗斯带回来的。其内容虽然很倒胃口,却也很有意思:一只狗的头部与其身体完完全全分割开来,用人工心脏的动脉和静脉系统维持头部的正常血液供给。现在,我要说的是这样的:那只狗头虽然是孤零零地放在某种托盘上,却是*活着* 的生命体,大脑还在发挥作用。短片里有好几个测试都证明了这一点。比如说,把食物涂抹到狗的唇部,它的舌头就会伸出来舔净。还有,要是有人穿过房间,它的眼睛就跟着移动。

“要维持存活的状态,头部和大脑并不必要与身体的其他部位相连。得出这样的结论,似乎是合情合理的。当然啦,这是有条件的,那就是,含氧量适当的血液供给系统要维持好。”

“那么,现在呢,看完这部短片,我自己产生了一个想法,就是一个人死后,把其大脑从颅骨里取出,供养起来,作为一个独立体而发挥作用。而且,要它活多长时间,它就会活多长时间。比如说,*你*死后,*你的*大脑就可以这样。”

“我不喜欢那样,”我说。

“威廉,让我说完,不要插嘴。我从随后所做实验的结果得知,大脑很独特,是一个具有自我供给能力的物体,能自我制造脑脊髓液供自身使用。很显然,在没有四肢或躯干,甚至没有颅骨的情况下,大脑内部进行的魔法般的思维和记忆过程不会受到妨碍。但是,就像我说过的,那是有条件的,就是要在合适的情况下,为大脑泵入配型正确的含氧血液。”

“我亲爱的威廉,想一想你的大脑吧,就想一小会儿。其形状完美,里面满满地装着你一生的学识和才华。你是花费多年的辛劳,才让它变成现在这般模样,它刚刚开始把你的那些一流的原创思想释放出来。但是,过不了多久,它就会随着你身体上的其他部位一起死去,只是因为你那小小的胰腺布满了癌细胞。这很荒唐,很不值得。”

“不,谢谢你。”我对他说。“你可以就此打住,你的提议令人作呕。就算你能做到——对此我还持怀疑态度,一点意义也没有。让我的大脑活下来,而我说不出、看不见、听不到、摸不着,那又有什么用处?就我个人而言,我想不出有什么事情比那更令人不愉快的啦。”

“我相信,你*能够*跟我们交流的,”兰迪说。“我们甚至可能做到的是,为你提供一定程度的视觉能力。但是,这个我们需要慢慢来,以后我再跟你详细交代。目前的事实是,不管发生什么情况,用不了多久你就会死去。按照我的计划,在你死*之前*,不会碰你半下的。答应吧,威廉。真正的哲学家,要是把遗体用于科学事业,没有一个会提出反对意见的。”

“你那话说的不是很到位,”我回答。“你对我做完这一切的时候,我是死了呢,还是活着,我似乎有些怀疑。”

“这样啊,”他边说边微微笑了一下。“我认为你说的没错。可问题是,你还没有深入一点儿了解这件事情的原委呢。这样的话,我想,你不应该这么快就拒绝我的提议。”

“我说过了,我不想听。”

“抽支烟吧,”他说。随即把烟盒递了过来。

“我不抽烟,你是知道的。”

他自己抽出一支,点上了。他点烟用的是一把微型银白色打火机,比一先令硬币大不了多少。“一件礼物,是为我制造实验仪器的人送我的,”他说。“设计得很精巧,不是吗?”

我仔细看了看火机,然后递还给他。

“我可以继续说吗?”他问。

“你最好别说了。”

“你只要静静躺着听就行。我想,你会发现我要说的是相当有意思的。”

我床边的一个盘子里放了一些蓝色的葡萄,我就把盘子放到胸前,开始吃葡萄。

“就在死亡的那一刻,”兰迪说,“我应该守在近旁,准备一下子跨进来,尽力把你大脑维持在存活状态。”

“你的意思是说,让大脑存活在脑袋里吗?”

“我必须说的是,开始的时候,是的。”

“然后呢,会把大脑放哪儿?”

“如果你想知道的话,告诉你吧,放到某种类型的盆子里。”

“你说的可当真?”

“当然啦,当真的。”

“好吧,继续说。”

“我想你是知道的,心脏停止跳动、不给大脑供给新鲜血液和氧气,脑组织就会迅速死亡。只需四到六分钟的时间,整个大脑就死掉了。即使过去三分钟,脑部也会有一定程度的损伤。因此,我必须手脚麻利,迅速行动,防止这样的事情发生。但是,有了机器的帮助,一切都相当简单了。”

“什么机器?”

“就是人工心脏。我们这里就有这样一款在适应性方面做了改造的产品，其原始产品是亚历克西·卡雷尔和林德伯格设计的。这个人工心脏的作用是往血液里溶氧，使血液保持正确的温度，用正确的压力给大脑泵入血液，还做其他一些必须要做的小事情。其实，这机器一点也不复杂。”

“告诉我，死亡那一刻你要做些什么，”我说。“首先，你要做什么？”

“你知道大脑的动脉血管和静脉血管排列这回事吗？”

“不知道。”

“那就听着，不难的。大脑的血液供给有两个主要来源：颈内动脉和椎动脉。每种动脉各有两条，加起来共有四条动脉。明白了吗？”

“是的。”

“回流系统甚至更简单。血液只通过两条静脉血管从大脑内排走，那两条血管被称为颈内静脉。总结一下，大脑供血系统有四条上行动脉——当然，沿着脖子上去，还有两条下行静脉。这些血管在大脑周围自然分叉，形成其他类型的管路，但是，与我们无关，我们从来不碰这些管路的。”

“随你怎么说吧，”我说。“设想一下，我刚刚死去。现在，你会怎么做呢？”

“我就应该立即切开你的脖子，找到那四条动脉，也就是两条颈内动脉和两条椎动脉。然后，就应该给它们灌注，也就是说，要往每条动脉里插一根大个头的针，针的中间是空的。然后，再把每根针同人工心脏的管路连接起来。”

“接着，动作就要快速、麻利。我会剖开那两条颈内静脉——左右各一条，再分别跟机器搭接。这样，血液循环这一程序就算完成。要知道，机器里已经装入配型无误的血液。现在，只需打开机器开关，一切就搞定。你大脑的血液循环系统就得以恢复。”

“我就会像短片里那只俄罗斯狗那样。”

“我认为，你不会像那样的。原因之一，死后你就必然会失去意识。倘若你的意识真的能恢复，或者相当长一段时间后，还是否能够恢复过来，我很是怀疑。话说回来了，不管你有无意识，你的处境将是相当有意思的，你说是吧？你的身体死去，很是冰冷，而你的大脑还活着。"

兰迪暂停一会，品味着这一可能出现的景象，感觉很得意。他为自己这一整套想法欣喜、着迷。很显然，我的想法要是跟他的不一样的话，他认为那是难以置信的。

"现在，我们就可以慢慢来了，"他说。"相信我，我们需要慢慢来。现在，我们首先要做的就是把你推进手术室。当然，陪伴你的还有那台机器，它的泵入的动作永远也不会停止。下一个问题是……"

"好啦，"我说。"不用再说了，我没有必要听细节。"

"哦，可是，你必须听，"他说。"整个过程中，在你身上会发生什么情况，你应该准确了解到，这很重要。你知道的，以后倘若你意识恢复，从你的角度来看，你能够准确记得你在哪里，以及你如何到达那里，将令你十分心平气和。要是你了解这些的话，你的心境就会安稳。你同意吗？"

我躺在床上一动不动地看着他。

"所以嘛，下一个问题就是，把你的大脑从你的尸体上移走，而且要原封不动、完好无损地移走。之后，你的躯体就没有什么用处，而实际上，它已经开始腐烂。颅骨和脸部也没有什么用处，因为它们都成了累赘的东西，也不是我想要的。我想要的就是大脑——活着的、完美的、干净的、漂亮的大脑。因此，把你安置到手术台上之后，我就用一把锯把你颅骨中整个穹窿移走。那不是一把普通的锯，而是一把小小的专用摆锯。锯的时候，也用不着给你麻醉，因为你那时依然没有意识。"

"天啊，你怎么能忍心不用麻醉剂呢，"我说。

"威廉，我向你保证，你那时没有知觉的，身体冰冷。不要忘记，几分钟前，你已经死去。"

"不给麻醉，谁都休想锯走我颅顶，"我说。

兰迪耸耸肩。"对我而言，麻醉不麻醉，毫无区别，"他说。"要是你需要，我很乐意给你用上一点普鲁卡因，那是一种局部麻醉药。

如果那样令你更开心的话,我将用普鲁卡因把整个头皮部分浸透,甚至整个头部浸一下,从脖子往上的部分。"

"十分感谢,"我说。

"要知道,"他继续说,"有时候发生的事情很是匪夷所思。就在上一周,一名男子被送了进来,但是,已经没有了知觉。我根本没有给他注射任何麻醉剂,就打开他的头部,从中取出一小块血液凝块。我正在他颅骨内操作的时候,他突然苏醒过来,开始说话了。"

"'我在哪里?'他问。"

"'在医院里。'"

"'哦,'他说。'我就知道是在这儿。'"

"'告诉我,'我问,'我正在做的事情,令你感到不安了吗?'"

"'没有,'他回答。'一点也没有。你*正在*做什么呢?'"

"'我刚从你的大脑里取出一个血液凝块。'"

"'是吗?'"

"'静静躺着,不要动弹,就要完成了。'"

"'如此说来,我头痛不止,就是那个混蛋玩意造成的啦,'那人说道。"

兰迪暂停下来,微微一笑,回过神来。"那男子就这样说的,我一字不差照录下来,说给你听,"他继续说。"但是,第二天他甚至记不得那段小插曲了。大脑啊,真是一个有趣儿的东西。"

"给我用普鲁卡因,"我说。

"威廉,如你所愿。现在,就像我说的那样,我要用一把小小的摆锯,仔仔细细地移走你整个颅盖,也就是你颅骨里整个穹窿那部分。这样,你大脑顶部的一半就会露出来。或者确切地说,包裹大脑外表层那部分就会露出来。不管你知道与否,大脑周围由三个彼此独立皮层包裹着。外面那一层被称作硬膜,或者脑脊膜;中间那层被称为蛛网膜;内层被称为软膜,或者软脊膜。外行的人似乎大都认为,大脑是一个在头部液体里漂浮着的一个裸露的东西。但事实上,不是这样的。大脑被那三个结实的皮层完好地包裹着。脑脊液实际上是在里面两个皮层窄窄的间隙里循环流动的,这个间隙就是人们所知的蛛网膜下隙。就像我前面对你讲过的那样，这种液体是大脑制造出来的，然后通过渗透作用进入静脉系统排走。”

“我本人是不会去动那三个皮层的，即脑脊膜、蛛网膜、软脊膜，这三个名称难道不可爱吗？这三个皮层，我会保护得完好如初。这样做的原因有很多，其中最不值得一提的就是，在脑脊膜那一层分布着静脉管路，静脉管路负责把血液排入颈部静脉。”

“现在，”他继续说，“我们已经剖开了你脑颅的上半部分。这样，包裹着外皮层的脑顶就露出来了。下一步嘛，还真是一个技术活：把完整的脑部剥离，以便把这部分整个利利索索地提起来，同时，要让四条供血动脉和两条回流静脉的残端保持下垂状态，随时准备与机器对接。这项工作繁重耗时、复杂无比，要把多数骨质部分巧妙地拆除，要把很多神经切掉，还要把数不清的血管切断并结扎好。这项工作要是有希望完成的话，我唯一能做的就是，使用一把咬骨钳，慢慢地把你颅骨的其余部分咬割掉，像剥桔子皮一样往下剥离，直到大脑的侧面和底部皮层完全露出来为止。所涉及的问题高度技术化，我不想详细阐述。但是，我相当有把握地认为，这项工作能完成，只不过是一个外科技术和耐性的问题。不要忘记，我有的是时间，要多少有多少，因为手术台旁边的人工心脏会连续不断地工作，泵送血液以维持大脑的存活状态。”

“现在，让我们设想一下，我成功地把大脑跟颅骨剥离开来，也把围绕大脑侧面所有组织都移除。这样，大脑与躯体相连的部分只剩下底部的脊柱、两条大静脉和四条动脉，动脉是为大脑供血用的。那么，下一步要做什么呢？”

“我就会切开脊柱，脊柱就在第一根脊椎骨的上方。这时，我会十分小心的，万万不可危及那个区域里的椎动脉。但此时，必须记住的是，这个区域里的脑硬膜，也就是外皮层部分，为了能容纳脊柱，是打开着的。所以，我必须把这个开口沿着硬膜边缘缝合起来。这很容易做到，不应当有任何问题的。”

“就在这一关口，我就要准备进行最后一步了。旁边的一张桌子上，我放好了一个形状特殊的盆子，里面盛满了我们称作林格溶液的一种液体。这种液体很特殊,神经外科学中我们用来做冲洗剂。现在,我就切断供血动脉以及回流静脉,把大脑完完全全剥离开来。然后,两手端起大脑,移到盆子里。在整个操作过程中,这个间隔是血液循环被切断唯一的一小段时间。放到盆子里后,动脉和静脉的残端转瞬之间就会与人工心脏对接完毕。"

"这样,一切妥当啦,"兰迪说。"现在,你的大脑放置在盆中,仍然活着,有充分的理由可以活很长、很长的时间。一年又一年过去了,仍然活着,前提是,我们要照顾好机器及其泵入的血液。"

"但是,它会*发挥机能*吗?"

"我亲爱的威廉,我怎么会知道呢? 我甚至无法对你肯定,它是否能恢复意识。"

"要是能行使机能,会怎样?"

"又来了你! 那可就了不得啦!"

"是吗?"我说。必须承认,我是疑心重重的。

"当然是啊! 想想啊,待在那儿,思维过程完好无损,而且记忆力也……"

"可就是看不见、摸不到、嗅不了、听不到,也说不了话呀,"我说。

"哎呀!"他喊道。"我就说嘛,我忘点什么事儿啦! 我从没有跟你提起眼睛的事情。听着,我要力争做到把你的视觉神经连同一只眼睛保存完好。视觉神经是个小东西,最厚处相当于医用体温计的厚度;在大脑和眼睛之间伸展开来时,其长度有五厘米多一点。它的美就在于,它根本算不上一根真正的神经,而是大脑本身的一个外翻部分。硬膜,也就是大脑外皮层,沿着它伸展,最后粘附到眼球上。因此,眼睛的后部与大脑接触紧密,脑脊液正好也流到那儿。"

"所有这一切都与我的目的十分吻合。这样,要保留好你的一只眼睛的设想就变得合情合理了。我已经做好了一个小塑料盒,取代你原来的眼窝,用来装你那只眼球。大脑装入盆里、浸入林格溶液后,装在盒里的眼球就会在溶液表面漂浮。"

"瞪着天花板看,"我说。

"是的,我想是这样的。恐怕没有任何肌肉来帮助眼球转动。但是,安安静静地待在那儿,舒舒服服地从盆子里看着这个世界,或许也是一种乐趣。"

"十分滑稽可笑,"我说。"给我留下一只耳朵,如何?"

"这次,我就不做这个尝试了。"

"我想要一只耳朵,"我说。"我想,我一定要保留一只耳朵。"

"不行。"

"我喜欢听巴赫的曲子。"

"你不明白,那样做难度会有多大,"兰迪轻柔地说。"听觉器官被称作耳蜗,这个机制比眼睛要精细、复杂得多。更何况,它是封存于骨质组织中的。听觉神经的一部分也是这样的,然后再与大脑相连。用楔形工具完好无损地把耳蜗整个移出来,我是不可能做到的。"

"你就不能让它封存于骨质组织中,然后整个放入盆子里吗?"

"不能,"他坚决地说。"这东西已经够复杂的了。不管怎么说,要是眼睛能发挥作用,听不听就无所谓啦。我们会始终把想说的写出来,举到你眼前,让你阅读。说真的,你必须让我自己决定,什么有可能保留,什么不可能保留。"

"我没说,我要答应你做这件事情。"

"我知道,威廉。我知道的。"

"我还不能肯定地说,我很喜欢你的想法。"

"但最后,你总归要死的吧?"

"或许会吧,我还不知道呢。我没有办法说话,对吧?"

"当然说不了。"

"那么,我怎么跟你交流?你又怎么能知道我有知觉呢?"

"你是否恢复意识,我们很容易得知,"兰迪说。"用一台普通的脑电描记器就可以做到。我们把这种仪器的电极直接连接到盆子里你大脑的额叶部分。"

"能把实际的意识情况显示出来?"

"噢,当然。任何一家医院都能做到这一点。"

"但是,*我*还是不能跟*你*交流。"

“事实上，”兰迪说，“我相信你能的。伦敦繁华区有一个人名叫韦特海默。他正在进行思想交流方面的一个有趣的研究，我已经跟他联系上了。你知道，大脑若是在思考的话，就会释放出电流和化学物质，而且这些电流和物质会以波的形式释放出来。确切点说，像无线电波。这些你难道不知道吗？”

“我知道一点儿，”我说。

“好的。韦特海默已经制造出一种仪器，有点类似于脑电描记器，但更敏感一些。他坚持认为，在有限的范围内，这台仪器能帮助他解释出大脑思考的实际内容，因为它能够画出某种图表，而图表似乎能翻译成文字或思想内容。我要求韦特海默来看看你，你愿意吗？”

“不愿意，”我回答。兰迪已经想当然地认为，我会赞同这件事情的，而对他这种态度，我感到不愉快。“你立马走人，让我一个人待着，”我告诉他。“任凭你怎么催我，也不会有什么结果的。”

他立刻起身，穿过房间，走到了门口。

“问个问题，”我说。

他一只手放在门把手上，停住了。“什么问题，威廉？“

“很简单。实话实说，我的大脑放到那个盆子里后，我的思维就会像现在这样起作用，你本人相信吗？你相信我能像现在这样思考和推理吗？记忆力会维持原状吗？”

“我看不出，为什么不会这样，”他回答。“一样的大脑，照常活着，一切都没有改变。实际上，它完好如初，我们甚至连硬膜都没有打开过。当然，大的区别就在于，我们切断了通向它的每一根神经，那根视觉神经除外。这就意味着，你的思维能力不再受到你的那些感觉器官的影响——你将生活在一个超常纯洁和独立超然的世界之中，没有什么会让你烦恼、不安，甚至痛苦也与你无关。你是不可能感觉到痛苦的，因为没有任何一根神经会让你去感知痛苦。从某种意义上来说，这是一种近乎十全十美的境界：没有担心、没有恐惧、没有痛苦、没有饥饿，甚至没有任何欲望，有的只是你的记忆和思想。要是碰巧那只保留下来的眼睛起作用的话，你也能看书。对我而言，这一切听起来相当地令我心旷神怡。”

“的确如此，对吧？”

“是的，威廉，的确如此，特别是对于一个哲学博士来说，读书很重要。那将是一次非凡的经历。你将会超然洒脱、安详宁静地对这个世界进行思考，这种思考方式以前从没有人使用过，又有谁会预料得到还会有什么情况因此而发生呢？伟大的思想和解决的良方，会因你而诞生。没准儿，你的伟大思想会彻底改变我们的生活！你要是能想象，你就尽量想象一下你能够因此而获得的关注度吧！”

“还有沮丧度，”我说。

“胡说。不可能有什么沮丧度。没有欲望，就不会沮丧。要知道，你不可能有任何的欲望。无论怎么说，不会有物质上的欲望。”

“我一定应该能记得我在这个世界上以前的生活，或许也就有欲望要返回到那种生活中去。”

“说的什么话啊，要回到那混乱不堪的生活啊！从你舒舒服服待着的盆子里出来，回到这个喧闹的世界呀！”

“再回答一个问题，”我说。“你认为，你能够让它存活多长时间？”

“是说你的大脑吗？谁知道呢？或许会活过一年又一年。存活的条件是理想中的，引起腐烂的几乎全部的因素将不复存在，这都是人工心脏的功劳。任何时候，血压保持恒定，这在现实生活里是不可能做到的，而且温度也是恒定的。血液的化学成分近乎完美，血液里没有任何的杂质、没有病毒、没有细菌，任何不利的成分都没有。要是让我猜猜活的时间长短的话，显得有点愚蠢可笑，但是，我相信在上述这些条件之下，大脑或许能活上二百年到三百年不等。告辞了，再见，”他说。“明天我顺便再来一下，到时候见。”他迅速走了出去，留下我一个人。你或许猜得到，剩下我一个人在那儿，心绪烦乱、焦虑重重。

他离开后，我的第一反应就是，对整件事情我怀有一种反感、厌恶之情。不管怎么说，这根本算不上什么好的提议。从本质上来说，这一提议有点令人厌恶、作呕。想想啊，把思维能力健全的我，竟然缩成一团小小的、黏糊糊的、灰不溜秋的东西，还放入一滩水里。这事真是骇人听闻、亵渎无耻、无法容忍。还有一点令我坐卧不安的事情就是，一旦兰迪将我放入盆中，我必定要感到孤立无助。这事只要一开始实施，那就有去无回。而且，在那种状态下，无法提出异议，更无法解释说明。只要他们让我活着，我就得任由摆布。

比方说，要是我忍无可忍，那可怎么办？最终，我要是痛苦不堪，那可怎么办？要是我火冒三丈，那可怎么办？

没有腿脚可以跑开，没有口舌可以喊叫，什么都没有，我只能咧嘴笑笑。余下的二百年里，默默忍受、毫无怨言。

甚至，也没有嘴可以咧开笑笑。

就在这一时刻，我脑子里有了一个奇妙古怪的想法，是这样的：因为手术截肢而失去一条腿的人，不是经常幻想，自己的那条腿依然健在吗？这个人不是对护士说他的脚趾痒得要命吗？但是，他的那几根脚趾早已不复存在。此类事情，不胜枚举。最近一段时间以来，我听说过类似事情。

好得很啊。在同样的前提下，我的孤零零待在那只盆子里的大脑，或许会对我的身体产生类似的幻想，这不可能吗？那样的话，我所有一般性的疼痛和痛苦就可以潮水般涌来，而我甚至用不着服一粒阿司匹林加以缓解。一会儿，我或许想象我的一条腿抽筋了，而且极其痛苦；或者，想象一下消化极其不良。再过一会儿，我或许轻而易举就感觉到我的膀胱快挺不住了，这你是知道的；它涨得满满的，要是不排空，马上就会爆炸。

上天宽恕我这些想法吧。

我在那儿躺了很长时间，脑子里尽是这些可怕的想法。接下来，大约到了中午时分，猛然之间，我的心绪开始转变了。我不怎么关心这件事情中令人不快的一面，转而从一个更合情合理的角度审视兰迪的提议了。我的大脑或许未必死掉，也未必在随后几周内消失殆尽。一想到这一点，我就问自己，难道这不能给自己带来一丝安慰吗？毕竟，会有点安慰的。我也因为我的大脑而感到十分自豪，它还是一个敏感微妙、神志清醒、孕育思想的器官，那里蕴含庞大的信息，仍然富有想象力,能提出原创性的理论。就智慧而言,大脑真是一个好东西,尽管这话是我一家之言。而我的身体,我那可怜的身体,正是兰迪想要扔掉的东西。那么,就说你吧,我亲爱的玛丽,也不得不赞同我的观点:扔掉没有什么可惜的,没有任何值得保留的价值。

我仰卧在床,正在吃一粒葡萄。葡萄香甜可口,可里面有三个小小的葡萄籽。于是,我把葡萄籽吐出来,放到盘子边上。

“我要做这件事,”我安静地说。“是的,老天在上,我要做这件事。明天兰迪再来看我的时候,我要直截了当地告诉他,我要做这件事。”

转变之快,莫过如此。从那时起,我感觉就好多了。午餐时,我狼吞虎咽吃下一大堆东西,在场的每个人都惊呆了。之后不久,你跟往常一样,进来看望我。

你当时对我说,我气色怎么那么好,怎么那么欢快愉悦、兴高采烈。发生什么事了吗?有什么好消息吗?

我说,是的,有。接着,如果你记得的话,我请求你坐下,让你放轻松、随便些。然后,我就马上开始向你解释即将发生的事情,而且尽量温柔、平和地向你解释。

哎,你一点也听不进去。还没等我细说,你就勃然大怒,说这事令人恶心、讨厌透顶、恐惧可怕、无法想象。随后,我尽力继续跟你解释,你却甩手就走,离开了房间。

噢,玛丽,你是知道的,从那时起有很多次,我尽力要与你讨论这件事。但是,你却一个劲儿地拒绝听我说话。因此,我就写了这封短信,这么做唯一的希望就是,你会有良好的感觉来阅读。更何况,我花了很长时间才写完这封信。从草草写下第一句话算起,两周时间已经过去,我现在比当时虚弱了很多。我担心,我没有力气再往下写了。当然,我也不愿意说再见,因为还有一次机会,哪怕是一次微小的机会。那机会就是,如果兰迪做成的话,过些时候我就会再次见到你了。但是,条件是,你肯屈尊前来看望我。

我一再吩咐,我死一周之后,再把这几页信纸转交给你。所以嘛,当你坐下来阅读这几页信的时候,兰迪实施这件事已经有七天啦，而你本人甚至已经知道结果如何。要是你还不知道的话，要是你有意回避、不愿意参与的话——我担心你会这样做的，那么，现在就请你改变一下主意，去拜访一下兰迪，看看我的事情进展如何。那是你起码能够做到的。我已经告诉过他，预期他能在第七天得到你的消息。

你诚挚的丈夫

威廉

附言：我死后，你要学乖些。永远记住：做寡妇不易，比做妻子难多了。不要喝鸡尾酒，不要乱花钱，不要抽烟，不要吃油腻的点心，不要涂口红，也不要买电视机。夏季，要把我的玫瑰花坛和假山园里的杂草清除得干干净净。顺便提一句，电话我再也用不着了，你就拔掉连线、取消服务吧。

阿威

珀尔太太把最后一页信纸慢慢放到身旁的沙发上。她那张小嘴向上硬硬地撅起，两只鼻孔周围泛起一层白白的痕迹。

可真是的啊！你会想到吗？这么多年熬过来，成了寡妇，才有权利享受到那么一点安宁和平静。

整件事太糟糕、太可怕，简直无法想象。既糟糕透顶，又残忍可怕，令她不寒而栗。

她伸手够自己的手提包，又找到一支烟。她点上烟，深深吸进一口，然后吐出来，一阵烟雾随即在整个屋子里弥漫开来。透过烟雾，她看到了她新买的那台可爱的电视机——崭新的、亮晶晶的，而且个头很大。电视机放在威廉以前工作用的那张桌子上面，那姿势颇具挑衅性，但也带点扭捏、难为情的样子。

她好奇地发出疑问，要是他能看到这一切，会说出什么话来？

她暂停下来。记起了最后一次他逮着她吸烟的情景，那是约一年前的事情。当时,她坐在厨房里,就坐在开着的窗户前,趁他下班到家之前,速战速决,要吸完一支烟。收音机音量开得很大,里面放着舞曲。她转身,又倒了一杯咖啡。恰巧在这时,他站到了门口,高大威猛,令人生畏。他那两只眼睛向下盯着她,眼神可怕,每只眼睛的中心都闪现出一个怒不可遏的小黑点。

那之后四周时间内,他自己亲自支付家务开支账单,一分钱也没有给她。可是,他当然不会知道,她藏匿了六英镑多的钱,藏在放肥皂片的箱子里,箱子放在水槽下的那个小储藏柜里。

“这算是怎么一回事?”有一次正吃着晚饭时,她问他。“你担心我得肺癌吗?”

“不是,”他回答。

“那么,为什么我不能吸烟呢?”

“因为我不同意,那就是为什么。”

他也不同意要孩子,结果可想而知,他们一个孩子也没有。

她的这位威廉——事事都不赞同的一个家伙,现在在哪里呢?

兰迪正期待着她打电话过去呢。她一定要给兰迪打电话吗?

哦,不一定如此。不打。

她抽完烟,马上就用上一支的烟蒂又点了一支。她看了看电话机,话机就放在工作台上,放在电视机的旁边。威廉要求她打电话,还特别做出请求,请求她一读完信,就给兰迪打电话。她犹豫不决,竭力抗拒那种由来已久、根深蒂固的责任感,但这种责任,她还不是很有胆量抖落掉。接着,她慢慢地站起身来,穿过屋子,走到放在工作台上的电话前。她在号码簿里找到一个号码,拨通后等待着。

“拜托,找一下兰迪医生。”

“你是哪位?”

“珀尔太太。我是威廉·珀尔太太。”

“请稍等。”

话音刚落,电话另一端的兰迪就开始说话了。

“是珀尔太太吗?”

“我是珀尔太太。”

稍微停顿了一小会儿。

“珀尔太太,您终于打电话了,我很高兴。希望你一切都好!”说话的声音听起来安安静静、平平淡淡、客客气气的。“不知道您愿不愿意到医院来一趟?然后,我们可以随便聊聊。我想,您一定很着急想知道结果如何吧。”

她没有应声。

“我现在可以告诉您,不管怎么说,一切进行得相当顺利。事实上,比我能够期望的要好得多。珀尔太太,它不仅活着,而且还有知觉——第二天意识就恢复了。是不是很有意思呢?”

她等着他继续往下说。

“眼睛也能看见了。对此,我们表示肯定,因为我们把东西举起、放到前面的时候,脑电描记器的偏移量立刻就发生了变化。现在,我们每天都给它报纸阅读。”

“哪家报纸?”珀尔太太尖声问道。

“《每日镜报》,大标题的字更大些。”

“他不喜欢看这份报纸。给他《泰晤士报》看。”

暂停了一下。接着,医生说:“那好吧,珀尔太太。我们就改《泰晤士报》。我们想尽我们所能,让它开开心心的。”

“是‘他’,”她说。“不是‘它’,是‘他’!”

“是的,‘他’,”医生说。“是的,请原谅。让他开开心心的。那就是我建议您尽快赶来的原因。我想,他要是见到您,会是一件好事情。您可以向他表示,又能跟他在一起,您是多么开心愉快。对他微笑,给他一个飞吻,以及做些诸如此类事情吧。有您在他旁边站着,对他一定是一种安慰。”

一阵长时间的停顿。

“好吧,”珀尔太太终于说话了,她的声音突然之间变得温和、顺从起来,显得很疲乏。“我想,我最好现在就去,看看他怎么样了。”

“很好,我知道您会来的,我在这儿等您。直接到三楼我的办公室来。再见。”

半小时后,珀尔太太到医院了。

“看到他的样子，你一定不要感到意外，”兰迪一边陪着她沿着走廊前行，一边对她说道。

“不，我不会的。”

“第一眼看上去，你一定会感到有一点震惊的。我担心，就他目前的状态而言，不会给人留下什么好的感觉。”

“医生，我嫁给他，并不是看中他的长相。”

兰迪转过身，盯着她看。他寻思着，眼前这位小个头的女人是多么的怪异啊！眼睛大大的，看起来郁郁寡欢、怨恨满腹的样子。她曾经一定有着娇美悦人的容貌，现在却荡然无存：嘴部松松垮垮、脸颊松弛、面部肌肉下垂。给人的印象是，由于受到多年享受不到欢乐的婚姻生活的影响，她整个脸部慢慢地、一点一点地塌陷，都快要成碎片了。他们继续向前走了一会，谁都没有说话。

“进去后，放松些，慢慢来，”兰迪说。“你把脸直接伸到他眼睛上方的时候，他才能知道你来了。那只眼睛总是睁着，他也没办法移动，所以，视野范围很窄。目前，我们让它一直看向天花板。当然，他什么都听不见，我们喜欢说多少话，就可以说多少。到了。”

兰迪打开一扇门，把她引入一个小小的方形屋子。

“我还不能靠得太近，”他一只手拉着她的胳膊说。“跟我一起在后边这儿待一会，完全适应下来后再靠近。”

屋子中央有一张高高的白色桌子，桌子上放了一只稍大一点的、白色的珐琅搪瓷盆，约有一个洗脸盆那么大，从盆子里伸出六条细细的塑料管，这些管子又与一整套玻璃管件相连接，可以看到血液从管子里流进心脏机器，又流出来。这台机器轻轻地、有节奏地发出搏动的声音。

“他就在那里面，”兰迪指着盆子说，但盆子放得太高，她看不到里面。“稍微靠近一点吧，但别太近。”

他带着她向前跨出两步。

现在，珀尔太太伸长了脖子，才能够看见盆子里的液体表面。液体清澈，静止不动，上面漂浮着一个椭圆形的小盒子，约有鸽子蛋那样大小。

“那里面的就是眼睛，”兰迪说。“能看见吗？”

“能。”

“就我们所知，这只眼睛状况依然完好，是他的右眼。塑料盒上装有一枚透镜，跟他过去戴的眼镜的镜片很相似。此刻，他的视力或许跟以前的一样好。”

“光看天花板，也不够看啊，”珀尔太太说。

“那用不着担心。我们正在为他制定计划，确保他有所娱乐。但是，刚开始的时候，我们不想操之过急。”

“给他一本好书看。”

“我们会的，会给的。珀尔太太，你感觉还好吧？”

“还好。”

“那么，我们再稍微向前一点，好吗？你就会看到完整的了”

他带着她向前，直到离桌子约有两三米的距离，停下来。现在，她正好能俯视盆子。

“看到了吧，”兰迪说。“那就是威廉。”

他看起来比她想象的大得多，颜色也更黑，表面布满了突起和皱褶。这模样倒让她想起了一只巨大的、腌渍的胡桃。她能够看到，四条大动脉和两条静脉的残端从底部伸出来，又规规整整地与塑料管连接起来。随着心脏机器每一次有规律的搏动，所有的管子都步调一致地急速拉动一下，血液也就随之流动开来。

“你必须把身体靠过去，”兰迪说。“然后，把你那张漂亮的脸伸到他眼睛正上方。那样的话，他就能看到你，你可以冲他微笑，来个飞吻。我要是你的话，我就会说上几句好听的。事实上，他听不见你说的是什么，但我敢肯定，大概意思他会领会得差不多。”

“他讨厌飞吻，”珀尔太太说。“要是你不介意的话，我就按照自己的方式做。”她跨步走到桌子边上，身体前倾，脸正对着盆子。然后，垂直向下看着威廉的那只眼睛。

“嗨，亲爱的，”她低声细语。“是我，玛丽啊。”

那只眼睛明亮依然。只见它瞪了她一下，目光还是那样强烈，但是样子怪怪的。

“亲爱的，你好吗？”她说。

塑料盒四周都是透明的，因此，整个眼球都是可见的。眼球底部与大脑连接的视觉神经看起来就像一小段短短的意大利式细面条。

“一切感觉还好吗，威廉？”

只能看到丈夫的眼睛，却看不到与之相配的面孔，这真是一种怪怪的感觉。她所能看的只是这只眼睛，只能一个劲儿地盯着它看。渐渐地，它变得越来个头越大。到最后，她满眼所见，只有这只眼睛了，甚至于它变得跟面孔似的。眼球的白色表面部分爬满了细细的、网状的红色静脉，冰蓝色的虹膜里有三四条相当好看的、稍微发黑的条纹沿着中心部位的瞳孔辐射开来，而瞳孔又大又黑，瞳孔的一边反射出一小点光亮。

“亲爱的，我收到你的信了。看完后，就立刻赶过来看看你。兰迪医生说，你的状况出奇的好。或许，我慢慢跟你讲话，你会看着我嘴唇的动作，明白一点我说话的意思。”

毫无疑问，那只眼睛在看着她。

“亲爱的，他们尽一切可能来照料你。这儿这个东西——这台机器总是工作不停，我敢肯定，它比我们其余那些人身上脆弱的老心脏可是强百倍了。我们的心脏随时可能垮掉，而你的将会永远工作下去。”

她仔细打量一下那只眼睛，尽量想看看它究竟有什么奇特之处，造就了目前如此这般模样。

“你看起来不错，亲爱的，还算不错。你真的不错。”

她对自己说，目前这只眼睛看起来，比他以前任何一只眼睛都要令人愉快得多。这只眼睛的某个地方有一种温柔感，还具有一种平静、友善的品质，这些她以前不曾见到。或许，这与眼睛中间的那个圆点——也就是瞳孔——有关系吧。威廉的瞳孔以前总是两个微小的黑点，就像大头针的针头一般大小，总是对着你发出微光，要穿过你的大脑，把你看个通透；总会立刻看出你在忙些什么，甚至看出你在想些什么。可是，目前她正在注视的这只眼睛的瞳孔，却是大大的、柔软的、温柔的，几乎跟牛眼睛一般。

“你是否很肯定地认为他有知觉呢?”她头也不抬地问道。

“噢,当然啦,十分肯定,”兰迪说。

“那么,她*能够*看到我吗?”

“看得十分清楚。”

“那岂不是太奇妙了吗?我期望的是,他正纳闷发生什么情况呢。”

“根本不会的。他在哪里,为什么会在那里,他再也清楚不过的啦。他是不可能忘记的。”

“你的意思是说,他*知道* 自己在盆子里吗?”

“当然的。要是他有说话的能力就好了,此时此刻他或许就能够跟你完美地、正常地交流了。就我所知,在思维方面,这儿的威廉跟你过去在家时熟悉的威廉没有半点不同。”

“我的*老天*啊,”珀尔太太说。接着,她暂停一下,思考着这个有趣的问题。

她对自己说,你知道吗?现在就看看那只眼睛的后面,使劲地看看后面那个大大的、灰灰的、多肉的胡桃,它躺在水下是多么安详、平和啊。也许,我更喜欢他目前的样子,我真的不敢说不喜欢。事实上,我相信,跟这样一个威廉生活在一起,我会感到舒适、安逸。这个威廉,我能应付得来。

“他很安静,难道不是吗?”她说。

“他很安静,这很自然。”

她想,这个威廉不会跟你争论不休,不会指指点点,不会没完没了地训斥,不会设定规则让你去遵守,不会禁止你吸烟,不会在晚上用一双不赞同的眼睛,透过书的顶部看着你,不会让你洗熨衬衫,不会让你做饭,什么都不会的。只会有心脏机器搏动的声音,但不管怎么说,那声音让人感到安慰,也不吵闹,不会影响她看电视。

“医生,”她说。“我确信,突然之间,我对他产生了极其强烈的爱恋之情。那听起来奇怪吗?”

“我想,那是相当可以理解的。”

“他躺在那儿,就在那只小盆子里,就躺在水的下面,一个人静悄悄的,显得多么孤立无助啊。”

“是的,我知道。”

“他像是一个婴儿。对,就像是一个婴儿。真的,他酷似一个小小的婴儿。”

兰迪站在她身后,一动不动地观察着。

“那么,”她看着盆子,轻柔地说。“从现在起,玛丽要亲自照料你,这个世界上你也没有什么可担心的。医生,我什么时候能把他带回家?”

“抱歉,能再说一遍吗?”

“我说的是,我什么时候能把他带回家,回我自己的家中?”

“你在开玩笑吧,”兰迪说。

她慢慢转过头来,直视着医生。“我为什么要开玩笑啊?”她问。她脸上放着光彩,眼睛睁得大大的,像两块钻石那样闪闪发光。

“他是不可能挪动的。”

“我不明白为什么不能挪动。”

“珀尔夫人,这只是一个实验。”

“但是,它是我丈夫,兰迪医生。”

兰迪的嘴上露出一半微笑,显得很好笑、又有点紧张的样子。“噢,……”他说。

“它*是*我丈夫,你是知道的,”她的声音里并没有生气的成分。她说起话来心平气和,就好像是在提醒他一个简简单单的事实。

“你说的那点很是微妙啊,”兰迪边说,边舔了舔嘴唇。“珀尔太太,你现在已经是一个寡妇了。我想,你必须接受这个事实。”

她突然从桌子那儿转过身,穿过屋子,走到窗前。“我说到做到,”她边说,边从手提包里摸出一支烟来。“我想要他回家。”

看着她把烟放到两只嘴唇之间、随即点燃的时候,兰迪想,要是他记得不差的话,这个妇女身上有点反常的地方:看到丈夫躺在那儿的盆子里,她似乎近于喜形于色。

他尽力去想象一下,要是*他妻子*的大脑躺在那里,她的一只眼睛从盒子里向上盯着他的时候,他自己的感觉会是什么样子的。

他不喜欢这种想象。

“现在去我的办公室,好吗?”他说。

她正站在窗户那儿喷烟吐雾,外表看起来相当镇静和放松。

“好的,可以。”

经过那张桌子的时候,她停了下来,又一次俯身盆子上方。“亲爱的人啊,玛丽现在要离开一会儿,”她说。“你什么都不要担心,明白吗?我们就要把你弄回家,在家里我们会尽可能快地让你得到妥当的照料。听着,亲爱的……”话说到这儿,她暂停一下,双唇夹起烟,打算吸一口。

与此同时,那只眼睛闪了一下。

她当时一直盯着它看。就在它正中间的位置上,她看到一个微小的、但却耀眼的光点;瞳孔收缩成一个极其微小的黑色小点,绝对是怒火高涨的样子。

刚开始的时候,她没有动地方,站在那儿俯身在盆的上方,手持香烟放进嘴里,观察着那只眼睛。

接下来,她慢悠悠地故意把烟放到两唇之间,长长地地吸了一口。她把烟深深地吸入,让其在肺部停留三四秒钟时间,随后,“呼”的一声响,烟就通过两只鼻孔窜出来。这时候,只见两股烟喷射到盆里的水面上,水表面翻腾起一阵浓稠的蓝色烟云,遮住了那只眼睛。

兰迪已经走到门口,后背对着她,等待着。“快来,珀尔太太,”他喊道。

“威廉,不要如此恼羞成怒啊,”她轻轻地说。“恼怒发火可是没有任何好处的。”

兰迪转过头,要看看她在干什么。

“你不能再那样了,”她低声耳语。“因为从现在起,我的宠物啊,玛丽要你做什么,你就得分毫不差地做什么。你明白吗?”

“珀尔太太,”兰迪边说边向她走去。

“所以嘛,不要再调皮捣蛋了,我亲爱的宝贝,好吗?”说完,又吸了一口香烟。“这年头,调皮捣蛋要挨重罚,你应该知道的。”

兰迪走到了她旁边,握着她的胳膊,把她从桌子那儿拽开,态度坚定,但力量不大。

“再见了,亲爱的,”她喊道。“我很快就回来。”

“可以啦,珀尔太太。”

“难道他不可亲吗?”她大声说,抬起头看了一眼兰迪。她眼睛睁得大大的,显得很明亮。“难道他不可爱吗?我就是要把他弄回家去,迫不及待了。”

第二节 《探声机器》*The Sound Machine*

罗尔德·达尔的《探声机器》(The Sound Machine)首次发表于美国一本文学性刊物《纽约客》(The New Yorker)杂志1949年9月17日出版的那期上。后来,这篇小说收录到《罗尔德·达尔短篇故事集锦》(The Collected Short Stories of Roald Dahl)、《罗尔德·达尔小说精品集》(The Best of Roald Dahl)、《五部畅销书集》(5 Bestsellers)、《如你之人》(Someone like You)、《科学事实或幻想》(Science Fact/Fiction)、《完全出人意料故事集》(Completely Unexpected Tales)、《更多出人意料故事集》(More Tales of the Unexpected)以及《幻觉之轨:科幻小说心理学》(Hallucination Orbit: Psychology in Science Fiction)等书中。另外,这部小说还被改编成电视系列剧中的一集——1981年5月17日播映的《出乎意料的故事集》(Tales of the Unexpected)第四部中的第7集(Episode 4.7),是一部很具影响力的作品。

一、原作导读

克劳斯纳尽管耳朵患有疾病,但还是潜心研究声音,已经到了入迷的程度。关于声音,他的理论就是:这个世界上有很多很多种类的声音人的耳朵是听不见的,因为它们的频率超出了人耳能够听得见的范围。他对顺路来看他的医生解释说,他发明的这台机器能调节到不同的频率上,将探测到的、人耳听不见的、不同种类的声音转换成人耳能够听得见的声音。

克劳斯纳第一次将自己发明的机器搬到室外进行实地测试时，通过耳机听到了邻居家那位主妇在自己花园剪玫瑰时，玫瑰发出的尖锐的声音——她每剪下一枝玫瑰，他就听到那种尖锐的声音。于是，第二天他试着到外面做一个更大型的实验。他抡起斧子奋力砍向一棵三毛榉树的底部，随后通过耳机他听到那棵树发出的一种轰隆隆的、音调很低的喊叫声。克劳斯纳惶恐起来，跑回家中，给他的医生打了个电话。

"斯科特医生吗？"他问。

"是啊。请讲。"

"斯科特医生，你务必马上过来——请快过来。"

"你贵姓？"

"我是克劳斯纳啊。你记得我昨晚给你讲的吧，我的那个关于声音的实验。我是多么希望我——"

"对，对，当然记得。可是，你怎么啦？生病了吗？"

"不，没生病，但是——"

"这才早晨六点半啊，"医生说，"你就给我打电话，却没有不舒服的地方。"

"请来一趟，要快。我想要人来听一下。我简直要疯掉了，我无法相信……"

"Dr Scott?" he said.

"Yes. Speaking."

"Dr Scott. You must come at once—quickly, please."

"Who is it speaking?"

"Klausner here, and you remember what I told you last night about my experiment with sound, and how I hoped I might—"

"Yes, yes, of course, but what's the matter? Are you ill?"

"No, I'm not ill, but—"

"It's half-past six in the morning," the Doctor said, "and you call me but you are not ill."

"Please come. Come quickly. I want someone to hear it. It's driving me mad! I can't believe it..."

医生最终同意来一趟,亲自听听。到来后,医生戴上了耳机,打算听个究竟。但是,就在克劳斯纳第二次抡起斧子砍向那棵山毛榉树的时候,可能是用力过猛的缘故吧,只听得"'咔嚓'一声响,树杈断裂,树叶相互摩擦,发出"唰啦啦"的声音"(the cracking sound of wood splintering and the swishing sound of leaves brushing against other leaves)。医生边跑边喊叫着让克劳斯纳赶紧跑,但是,克劳斯纳却站在原地发呆。结果,那个断裂的大树杈落到两人之间,砸坏了那台探声机器。克劳斯纳问医生听到什么声音没有,医生说什么都听到,因为当时医生撇下耳机,撒腿就跑开了。克劳斯纳大为震惊,喊着要让医生给树的"伤口"蘸些碘酒,包扎起来。

医生不知如何是好。他看了看克劳斯纳紧握斧子的双手,盘算着唯一的选择就是快跑。当然,还没有打算那么去做。

"好吧,"他说。"我用碘酒给它涂上吧。"

…………

"谢谢你,医生,"克劳斯纳说,接着又点了点头,随即扔掉斧子,突然间微笑起来,笑得有些疯狂和兴奋。医生快速走近,轻轻抓起他的胳膊,说道:"好了,现在我们必须走了。"他们两个人急速走开,默默无语、匆匆忙忙地穿越公园,横过马路,回到房中。

The Doctor hesitated. He saw Klausner's hands tightening on the handle of the axe. He decided that his only alternative was to run away, fast, and he certainly wasn't going to do that.

"All right," he said. "I'll paint it with iodine."

...

"Thank you, Doctor," Klausner said, and he nodded his head again and he dropped the axe and all at once he smiled, a wild, excited smile, and quickly the Doctor went over to him and gently he took him by the arm and he said, "Come on, we must go now," and suddenly they were walking away, the two of them, walking silently, rather hurriedly across the park, over the road, back to the house.

二、原作释读

在这部小说的阅读过程中,要从达尔细腻的描写中把握好主人公克劳斯纳的性格特点,以及他前后态度的转变。有关声音方面的物理学词汇是阅读的障碍,但通过查阅注释可以将障碍一一扫清。

The Sound Machine①

It was a warm summer evening and Klausner walked quickly through the front gate and around the side of the house and into the garden at the back. He went on down the garden until he came to a wooden shed② and he unlocked the door, went inside and closed the door behind him.

The interior of the shed was an unpainted room. Against one wall, on the left, there was a long wooden workbench③, and on it, among a littering of wires and batteries and small sharp tools, there stood a black box about three feet long, the shape of a child's coffin④.

Klausner moved across the room to the box. The top of the box was open, and he bent down and began to poke and peer inside it among a

---

① 本部小说原文出自"DAHL, R. *The Best of Roald Dahl*. London: Penguin Books Ltd., 2006"。

② shed: *Noun* a simple roofed structure, typically made of wood or metal, used for garden storage, to shelter animals, or as a workshop 棚式建筑;货棚;牲口棚;工作棚

③ workbench: *Noun* a strong worktable for a carpenter or mechanic 工作台;作业台

④ coffin: *Noun* box in which a corpse is buried or cremated 棺材

mass of different-coloured wires and silver tubes. He picked up a piece of paper that lay beside the box, studied it carefully, put it down, peered inside the box and started running his fingers along the wires, tugging gently at them to test the connections, glancing back at the paper, then into the box, then at the paper again, checking each wire. He did this for perhaps an hour.

Then he put a hand around to the front of the box where there were three dials, and he began to twiddle[①] them, watching at the same time the movement of the mechanism inside the box. All the while he kept speaking softly to himself, nodding his head, smiling sometimes, his hands always moving, the fingers moving swiftly, deftly[②], inside the box, his mouth twisting into curious shapes when a thing was delicate or difficult to do, saying, "Yes... Yes... And now this one... Yes... Yes. But is this right? Is it—where's my diagram?... Ah, yes... Of course... Yes, yes... That's right... And now... Good... Good... Yes... Yes, yes, yes." His concentration was intense; his movements were quick; there was an air of urgency about the way he worked, of breathlessness, of strong suppressed excitement.

Suddenly he heard footsteps on the gravel[③] path outside and he straightened and turned swiftly as the door opened and a tall man came in. It was Scott. It was only Scott, the doctor.

"Well, well, well," the Doctor said. "So this is where you hide yourself in the evenings."

---

① twiddle: *Verb* [with obj.] twist, move, or fiddle with (something), typically in a purposeless or nervous way(尤指无聊或紧张地)旋弄;捻弄;摆弄(e. g. She twiddled the dials on the radio. 她无聊地旋弄着收音机上的调谐盘。)

② deft: *Adjective* quick and skillful in movement 熟练的;灵巧的

③ gravel: *Noun* [mass noun] a loose aggregation of small water-worn or pounded stones 砾石

"Hullo, Scott," Klausner said.

"I happened to be passing," the Doctor told him, "so I dropped in to see how you were. There was no one in the house, so I came on down here. How's that throat of yours been behaving?"

"It's all right. It's fine."

"Now I'm here I might as well have a look at it."

"Please don't trouble. I'm quite cured. I'm fine."

The Doctor began to feel the tension in the room. He looked at the black box on the bench; then he looked at the man. "You've got your hat on," he said.

"Oh, have I?" Klausner reached up, removed the hat and put it on the bench.

The Doctor came up closer and bent down to look into the box. "What's this?" he said. "Making a radio?"

"No, just fooling around."

"It's got rather complicated looking innards."

"Yes." Klausner seemed tense and distracted.

"What is it?" the Doctor asked. "It's rather a frightening-looking thing, isn't it?"

"It's just an idea."

"Yes?"

"It has to do with sound, that's all."

"Good heavens, man! Don't you get enough of that sort of thing all day in your work?"

"I like sound."

"So it seems." The Doctor went to the door, turned, and said, "Well, I won't disturb you. Glad your throat's not worrying you any more." But he kept standing there looking at the box, intrigued[①] by the remarkable complexity of its inside, curious to know what this strange patient of his was up to. "What's it really for?" he asked. "You've made me inquisitive[②]."

Klausner looked down at the box, then at the Doctor, and he reached up and began gently to scratch the lobe of his right ear[③]. There was a pause. The Doctor stood by the door, waiting, smiling.

"All right, I'll tell you, if you're interested." There was another pause, and the Doctor could see that Klausner was having trouble about how to begin.

He was shifting from one foot to the other, tugging at the lobe of his ear, looking at his feet, and then at last, slowly, he said. "Well, it's like this... the theory is very simple really. The human ear... you know that it can't hear everything. There are sounds that are so low-pitched or so high-pitched that it can't hear them."

"Yes," the Doctor said. "Yes."

"Well, speaking very roughly any note so high that it has more than fifteen thousand. vibrations a second—we can't hear it. Dogs have better ears than us. You know you can buy a whistle whose note is so high-pitched that you can't hear it at all. But a dog can hear it."

"Yes, I've seen one," the Doctor said.

---

① intrigue: *Verb* [with obj.] arouse the curiosity or interest of; fascinate 引起……的好奇心(或兴趣);迷住(e. g. I was intrigued by your question. 你的问题引起了我极大的兴趣。)

② inquisitive: *Adjective* curious or inquiring 好奇的;好问的(e. g. He was very chatty and inquisitive about everything. 他对什么事都爱追根问底。)

③ ear lobe: *Noun* a soft, rounded fleshy part hanging from the lower margin of the ear 耳垂

"Of course you have. And up the scale[①], higher than the note of that whistle, there is another note—a vibration if you like, but I prefer to think of it as a note. You can't hear that one either. And above that there is another and another rising right up the scale for ever and ever and ever, an endless succession of notes an infinity of notes... there is a note—if only our ears could hear it—so high that it vibrates a million times a second... and another a million times as high as that... and on and on, higher and higher, as far as numbers go, which is... infinity... eternity... beyond the stars."

Klausner was becoming more animated every moment. He was a frail[②] man, nervous and twitchy[③], with always moving hands. His large head inclined towards his left shoulder as though his neck were not quite strong enough to support it rigidly. His face was smooth and pale, almost white, and the pale-grey eyes that blinked and peered from behind a pair of steel spectacles were bewildered, unfocused, remote. He was a frail, nervous, twitchy little man, a moth[④] of a man, dreamy and distracted; suddenly fluttering and animated; and now the Doctor, looking at that strange pale face and those pale-grey eyes, felt that somehow there was a-

---

① scale: *Noun* (Music) an arrangement of the notes in any system of music in ascending or descending order of pitch(音乐)音阶(e.g. the scale of C major C大调)

② frail: *Adjective* (of a person) weak and delicate(人)脆弱的;虚弱的(e.g. She looked frail and vulnerable. 她看上去弱不禁风。)

③ twitchy: *Adjective* (informal) nervous; anxious(非正式)烦躁不安的;焦急的;紧张的(e.g. She felt twitchy about the man hovering in the background. 她对背后或隐或现的那个男子感到紧张不安。)

④ moth: *Noun* an insect with two pairs of broad wings covered in microscopic scales, typically drably coloured and held flat when at rest. Moths are chiefly nocturnal, and lack the clubbed antennae of butterflies 蛾;飞蛾

bout this little person a quality of distance, of immense immeasurable distance, as though the mind were far away from where the body was.

The Doctor waited for him to go on. Klausner sighed and clasped his hands tightly together. "I believe," he said, speaking more slowly now, "that there is a whole world of sound about us all the time that we cannot hear. It is possible that up there in those high-pitched inaudible regions there is a new exciting music being made, with subtle harmonies and fierce grinding① discords, a music so powerful that it would drive us mad if only our ears were tuned to hear the sound of it. There may be anything... for all we know there may—"

"Yes," the Doctor said. "But it's not very probable."

"Why not? Why not?" Klausner pointed to a fly sitting on a small roll of copper wire on the workbench. "You see that fly? What sort of noise is that fly making now? None—that one can hear. But for all we know the creature may be whistling like mad on a very high note, or barking or croaking② or singing a song. It's got a mouth, hasn't it? It's got a throat?"

The Doctor looked at the fly and he smiled. He was still standing by the door with his hands on the doorknob. "Well," he said. "So you're going to check up on that?"

"Some time ago," Klausner said, "I made a simple instrument that proved to me the existence of many odd inaudible sounds. Often I have sat and watched the needle of my instrument recording the presence of sound vibrations in the air when I myself could hear nothing. And those are the sounds I want to listen to. I want to know where they come from

---

① grinding: *Adjective* (of a sound or motion) harsh and grating 刺耳的;吱吱嘎嘎响的(e. g. the grinding roar of the lorries 卡车刺耳的轰鸣声)

② croak: *Verb* [no obj.] (of a frog or crow) make a characteristic deep hoarse sound(蛙或鸦)呱呱叫

and who or what is making them."

"And that machine on the table there," the Doctor said, "is that going to allow you to hear these noises?"

"It may. Who knows? So far, I've had no luck. But I've made some changes in it and tonight I'm ready for another trial. This machine," he said, touching it with his hands, "is designed to pick up sound vibrations that are too high-pitched for reception by the human ear, and to convert them to a scale of audible tones. I tune it in, almost like a radio."

"How d'you mean?"

"It isn't complicated. Say I wish to listen to the squeak[①] of a bat. That's a fairly high-pitched sound—about thirty thousand vibrations a second The average human ear can't quite hear it. Now, if there were a bat flying around this room and I tuned in to thirty thousand on my machine, I would hear the squeaking of that bat very clearly. I would even hear the correct note F sharp, or B flat, or whatever it might be—but merely at a much *lower pitch*. Don't you understand?"

The Doctor looked at the long, black coffin-box. "And you're going to try it tonight?"

"Yes."

"Well, I wish you luck." He glanced at his watch. "My goodness!" he said. "I must fly. Good-bye, and thank you for telling me. I must call again sometime and find out what happened." The Doctor went out and closed the door behind him.

For a while longer, Klausner fussed about with the wires in the black box; then he straightened up and in a soft excited whisper said,

---

① squeak: *Noun* a short, high-pitched sound or cry 短促的尖叫声;嘎吱声(e. g. The door opened with a slight squeak. 门开时有点嘎吱声。)

"Now we'll try again... We'll take it out into the garden this time... and then perhaps... perhaps... the reception will be better. Lift it up now... carefully... Oh, my God, it's heavy!" He carried the box to the door, found that he couldn't open the door without putting it down, carried it back, put it on the bench, opened the door, and then carried it with some difficulty into the garden. He placed the box carefully on a small wooden table that stood on the lawn. He returned to the shed and fetched a pair of earphones. He plugged the wire connections from the earphones into the machine and put the earphones over his ears. The movements of his hands were quick and precise. He was excited, and breathed loudly and quickly through his mouth. He kept on talking to himself with little words of comfort and encouragement, as though he were afraid—afraid that the machine might not work and afraid also of what might happen if it did.

He stood there in the garden beside the wooden table, so pale, small, and thin that he looked like an ancient, consumptive①, bespectacled child. The sun had gone down. There was no wind, no sound at all. From where he stood, he could see over a low fence into the next garden, and there was a woman walking down the garden with a flower-basket on her arm. He watched her for a while without thinking about her at all. Then he turned to the box on the table and pressed a switch on its front. He put his left hand on the volume control and his right hand on the knob that moved a needle across a large central dial, like the wave-length dial of a radio. The dial was marked with many numbers, in a series of bands, starting at 15,000 and going on up to 1,000,000.

---

① consumptive: *Adjective* (dated) affected with a wasting disease, especially pulmonary tuberculosis(古旧用法)患销蚀性疾病的;身体耗损的(尤指患肺结核的)(e. g. From birth he was sickly and consumptive. 从一出生他就体弱多病,患上了肺结核。)

And now he was bending forward over the machine. His head was cocked to one side in a tense, listening attitude. His right hand was beginning to turn the knob. The needle was travelling slowly across the dial, so slowly he could hardly see it move, and in the earphones he could hear a faint, spasmodic[①] crackling.

Behind this crackling sound he could hear a distant humming tone which was the noise of the machine itself, but that was all. As he listened, he became conscious of a curious sensation, a feeling that his ears were stretching out away from his head, that each ear was connected to his head by a thin stiff wire, like a tentacle[②], and that the wires were lengthening, that the ears were going up and up towards a secret and forbidden territory, a dangerous ultrasonic[③] region where ears had never been before and had no right to be.

The little needle crept slowly across the dial, and suddenly he heard a shriek, a frightful piercing shriek, and he jumped and dropped his hands, catching hold of the edge of the table. He stared around him as if expecting to see the person who had shrieked. There was no one in sight except the woman in the garden next door, and it was certainly not she. She was bending down, cutting yellow roses and putting them in her basket.

Again it came—a throatless, inhuman shriek, sharp and short, very clear and cold. The note itself possessed a minor, metallic quality that he

---

① spasmodic: *Adjective* occurring or done in brief, irregular bursts 间歇性的;一阵阵的(e. g. Spasmodic fighting continued. 战斗时断时续地进行着。)

② tentacle: *Noun* a slender flexible limb or appendage in an animal, especially around the mouth of an invertebrate, used for grasping, moving about, or bearing sense organs 触角;触手;触须;触器

③ ultrasonic: *Adjective* of or involving sound waves with a frequency above the upper limit of human hearing 超声的;超音速的

had never heard before. Klausner looked around him, searching instinctively for the source of the noise. The woman next door was the only living thing in sight. He saw her reach down; take a rose stem in the fingers of one hand and snip① the stem with a pair of scissors. Again he heard the scream.

It came at the exact moment when the rose stem was cut.

At this point, the woman straightened up, put the scissors in the basket with the roses and turned to walk away.

"Mrs. Saunders!" Klausner shouted, his voice shrill with excitement. "Oh, Mrs. Saunders!"

And looking round, the woman saw her neighbour standing on his lawn—a fantastic, arm-waving little person with a pair of earphones on his head—calling to her in a voice so high and loud that she became alarmed.

"Cut another one! Please cut another one quickly!"

She stood still, staring at him. "Why, Mr. Klausner," she said. "What's the matter?"

"Please do as I ask," he said. "Cut just one more rose!"

Mrs. Saunders had always believed her neighbour to be a rather peculiar person; now it seemed that he had gone completely crazy. She wondered whether she should run into the house and fetch her husband. No, she thought. No, he's harmless. I'll just humour② him. "Certainly, Mr. Klausner, if you like," she said. She took her scissors from the basket, bent down and snipped another rose.

---

① snip: *Verb* sever or remove by pinching or snipping 剪

② humour or humor: *Verb* [with obj.] comply with the wishes of (someone) in order to keep them content, however unreasonable such wishes might be 纵容;迁就;迎合(e. g. She was always humouring him to prevent trouble. 她总是迁就他以防止麻烦。)

Again Klausner heard that frightful, throatless shriek in the earphones; again it came at the exact moment the rose stem was cut. He took off the earphones and ran to the fence that separated the two gardens. "All right," he said. "That's enough. No more. Please, no more."

The woman stood there, a yellow rose in one hand, clippers in the other, looking at him.

"I'm going to tell you something, Mrs. Saunders," he said, "something that you won't believe." He put his hands on top of the fence and peered at her intently through his thick spectacles. "You have, this evening, cut a basketful of roses. You have with a sharp pair of scissors cut through the stems of living things, and each rose that you cut screamed in the most terrible way. Did you know that, Mrs. Saunders?"

"No," she said. "I certainly didn't know that."

"It happens to be true," he said. He was breathing rather rapidly, but he was trying to control his excitement. "I heard them shrieking. Each time you cut one, I heard the cry of pain. A very high-pitched sound, approximately one hundred and thirty-two thousand vibrations a second. You couldn't possibly have heard it yourself. But I heard it."

"Did you really, Mr. Klausner?" She decided she would make a dash for the house in about five seconds.

"You might say," he went on, "that a rose bush has no nervous system to feel with, no throat to cry with. You'd be right. It hasn't. Not like ours, anyway. But *how do you know, Mrs. Saunders*"—and here he leaned far over the fence and spoke in a fierce whisper "*how do you know* that a rose bush doesn't feel as much pain when someone cuts its stem in two as you would feel if someone cut your wrist off with a garden shears? *How do you know that*? It's *alive*, isn't it?"

"Yes, Mr. Klausner. Oh, yes and good night." Quickly she turned and ran up the garden to her house. Klausner went back to the table. He put on the earphones and stood for a while listening. He could still hear the faint crackling sound and the humming noise of the machine, but nothing more. He bent down and took hold of a small white daisy[①] growing on the lawn. He took it between thumb and forefinger and slowly pulled it upward and sideways until the stem broke.

From the moment that he started pulling to the moment when the stem broke, he heard—he distinctly heard in the earphones—a faint high-pitched cry, curiously inanimate. He took another daisy and did it again. Once more he heard the cry, but he wasn't sure now that it expressed pain. No, it wasn't pain; it was surprise. Or was it? It didn't really express any of the feelings or emotions known to a human being. It was just a cry, a neutral, stony cry—a single emotionless note, expressing nothing. It had been the same with the roses. He had been wrong in calling it a cry of pain. A flower probably didn't feel pain. It felt something else which we didn't know about—something called toin or spurl or plinuckment, or anything you like.

He stood up and removed the earphones. It was getting dark and he could see pricks of light shining in the windows of the houses all around him. Carefully he picked up the black box from the table, carried it into the shed and put it on the workbench. Then he went out, locked the door behind him and walked up to the house.

The next morning Klausner was up as soon as it was light. He dressed and went straight to the shed. He picked up the machine and carried it outside, clasping it to his chest with both hands, walking unsteadily under its weight. He went past the house, out through the front gate, and across the road to the park. There he paused and looked a-

---

① daisy: *Noun* a small European grassland plant which has flowers with a yellow disc and white rays. It has given rise to many ornamental garden varieties. 雏菊

round him; then he went on until he came to a large tree, a beech tree[①], and he placed the machine on the ground close to the trunk of the tree. Quickly he went back to the house and got an axe from the coal cellar and carried it across the road into the park. He put the axe on the ground beside the tree. Then he looked around him again, peering nervously through his thick glasses in every direction. There was no one about. It was six in the morning.

He put the earphones on his head and switched on the machine. He listened for a moment to the faint familiar humming sound; then he picked up the axe, took a stance[②] with his legs wide apart and swung the axe as hard as he could at the base of the tree trunk. The blade cut deep into the wood and stuck there, and at the instant of impact he heard a most extraordinary noise in the earphones. It was a new noise, unlike any he had heard before—a harsh, noteless, enormous noise, a growling[③], low-pitched, screaming sound, not quick and short like the noise of the roses, but drawn out like a sob lasting for fully a minute, loudest at the moment when the axe struck, fading gradually fainter and fainter until it was gone.

Klausner stared in horror at the place where the blade of the axe had sunk into the woodflesh of the tree; then gently he took the axe handle, worked the blade loose and threw the thing to the ground. With his fin-

---

① beech or beech tree: *Noun* a large tree with smooth grey bark, glossy leaves, and hard, pale, fine-grained timber 山毛榉(树)

② stance: *Noun* the way in which someone stands, especially when deliberately adopted (as in cricket, golf, and other sports); a person's posture(板球、高尔夫球等运动用语)击球姿势;姿态(e. g. She altered her stance, resting all her weight on one leg. 她变了姿势,用一条腿支撑全身重量。)

③ growling: *Noun* a gruff or angry utterance (suggestive of the growling of an animal) 咆哮;隆隆;怒吼

gers he touched the gash[①] that the axe had made in the wood, touching the edges of the gash, trying to press them together to close the wound, and he kept saying, "Tree... oh, tree... I am sorry I am sorry... but it will heal... it will heal fine."

For a while he stood there with his hands upon the trunk of the great tree; then suddenly he turned away and hurried off out of the park, across the road, through the front gate and back into his house. He went to the telephone, consulted the book, dialled a number and waited. He held the receiver tightly in his left hand and tapped the table impatiently with his right. He heard the telephone buzzing at the other end, and then the click of a lifted receiver and a man's voice, a sleepy voice, saying: "Hullo. Yes."

"Dr Scott?" he said.

"Yes. Speaking."

"Dr Scott. You must come at once—quickly, please."

"Who is it speaking?"

"Klausner here, and you remember what I told you last night about my experiment with sound, and how I hoped I might—"

"Yes, yes, of course, but what's the matter? Are you ill?"

"No, I'm not ill, but—"

"It's half-past six in the morning," the Doctor said, "and you call me but you are not ill."

"Please come. Come quickly. I want someone to hear it. It's driving me mad! I can't believe it..."

The Doctor heard the frantic, almost hysterical note in the man's voice, the same note he was used to hearing in the voices of people who

---

① gash: *Noun* a long deep slash, cut, or wound(砍伤、割伤的深长)伤口;切口(e. g. A bad gash in one leg became infected. 一条腿上严重的伤口开始感染了。)

called up and said, "There's been an accident. Come quickly." He said slowly. "You really want me to get out of bed and come over now?"

"Yes, now. At once, please."

"All right, then—I'll come."

Klausner sat down beside the telephone and waited. He tried to remember what the shriek of the tree had sounded like, but he couldn't. He could remember only that it had been enormous and frightful and that it had made him feel sick with horror. He tried to imagine what sort of noise a human would make if he had to stand anchored① to the ground while someone deliberately swung a small sharp thing at his leg so that the blade cut in deep and wedged itself in the cut. Same sort of noise perhaps? No. Quite different. The noise of the tree was worse than any known human noise because of that frightening, toneless, throatless quality. He began to wonder about other living things, and he thought immediately of a field of wheat standing up straight and yellow and alive, with the mower going through it, cutting the stems, five hundred stems a second, every second. Oh, my God, what would that noise be like? Five hundred wheat plants screaming together and every second another five hundred being cut and screaming and no, he thought, I do not want to go to a wheat field with my machine. I would never eat bread after that. But what about potatoes and cabbages and carrots and onions? And what about apples? Ah, no. Apples are all right. They fall off naturally when they are ripe. Apples are all right if you let them fall off instead of tearing them from the tree branch. But not vegetables. Not a potato for example. A potato would surely shriek; so would a carrot and an onion and a cabbage...

---

① anchor: *Verb* provide with a firm basis or foundation 扎根(e. g. It is important that policy be anchored to some acceptable theoretical basis. 把政策建立在可接受的理论基础是很重要的。)

He heard the click of the front-gate latch and he jumped up and went out and saw the tall doctor coming down the path, little black bag in hand.

"Well," the Doctor said. "Well, what's all the trouble?"

"Come with me, Doctor, I want you to hear it. I called you because you're the only one I've told. It's over the road in the park. Will you come now?"

The Doctor looked at him. He seemed calmer now. There was no sign of madness or hysteria; he was merely disturbed and excited.

They went across the road into the park and Klausner led the way to the great beech tree at the foot of which stood the long black coffin-box of the machine—and the axe.

"Why did you bring it out here?" the Doctor asked.

"I wanted a tree. There aren't any big trees in the garden."

"And why the axe?"

"You'll see in a moment. But now please put on these earphones and listen. Listen carefully and tell me afterwards precisely what you hear. I want to make quite sure..."

The Doctor smiled and took the earphones and put them over his ears.

Klausner bent down and flicked the switch on the panel of the machine; then he picked up the axe and took his stance with his legs apart, ready to swing. For a moment he paused. "Can you hear anything?" he said to the Doctor.

"Can I what?"

"Can you *hear* anything?"

"Just a humming noise."

Klausner stood there with the axe in his hands trying to bring himself to swing, but the thought of the noise that the tree would make made him pause again.

"What are you waiting for?" the Doctor asked.

"Nothing," Klausner answered, and then lifted the axe and swung it at the tree, and as he swung, he thought he felt, he could swear he felt a movement of the ground on which he stood. He felt a slight shifting of the earth beneath his feet as though the roots of the tree were moving underneath the soil, but it was too late to check① the blow and the axe blade struck the tree and wedged② deep into the wood. At that moment, high overhead, there was the cracking sound of wood splintering③ and the swishing④ sound of leaves brushing against other leaves and they both looked up and the Doctor cried, "Watch out! Run, man! Quickly, run!"

The Doctor had ripped off the earphones and was running away fast, but Klausner stood spellbound, staring up at the great branch, sixty feet long at least, that was bending slowly downward, breaking and crackling and splintering at its thickest point, where it joined the main trunk of the tree. The branch came crashing down and Klausner leapt aside just in time. It fell upon the machine and smashed it into pieces.

"Great heavens!" shouted the Doctor as he came running back. "That was a near one! I thought it had got you!"

Klausner was staring at the tree. His large head was leaning to one

---

① check: *Verb* stop or slow down the progress of (something undesirable) 制止;控制(e. g. Efforts were made to check the disease. 人们努力控制这种疾病。)

② wedge: *Verb* [with obj.] fix in position using a wedge 楔入;楔进(e. g. The door was wedged open. 门被楔子插住开着。)

③ splinter: *Verb* break or cause to break into small sharp fragments(使)裂成碎片(e. g. The soap box splintered. 肥皂盒裂成碎片。)

④ swish: *Verb* [no obj., with adverbial of direction] move with a hissing or rushing sound 刷的(或嗖的)行进(e. g. A car swished by. 一辆汽车刷的一声开过去了。)

side and upon his smooth white face there was a tense, horrified expression. Slowly he walked up to the tree and gently he prised the blade loose from the trunk.

"Did you hear it?" he said, turning to the Doctor. His voice was barely audible.

The Doctor was still out of breath from running and the excitement. "Hear what?"

"In the earphones. Did you hear anything when the axe struck?"

The Doctor began to rub the back of his neck. "Well," he said, "as a matter of fact..." He paused and frowned and bit his lower lip. "No, I'm not sure. I couldn't be sure. I don't suppose I had the earphones on for more than a second after the axe struck."

"Yes, yes, but what did you hear?"

"I don't know," the Doctor said. "I don't know what I heard. Probably the noise of the branch breaking." He was speaking rapidly, rather irritably.

"What did it sound like?" Klausner leaned forward slightly, staring hard at the Doctor. "*Exactly* what. did it sound like?"

"Oh hell!" the Doctor said, "I really don't know. I was more interested in getting out of the way. Let's leave it."

"Dr Scott, *what-did-it-sound-like*?"

"For God's sake, how could I tell, what with half the tree falling on me and having to run for my life?" The Doctor certainly seemed nervous. Klausner had sensed it now. He stood quite still, staring at the Doctor and for fully half a minute he didn't speak. The Doctor moved his feet, shrugged his shoulders and half turned to go. "Well," he said, "we'd better get back."

"Look," said the little man, and now his smooth white face became suddenly suffused[①] with colour. "Look," he said, "you stitch this up." He pointed to the last gash that the axe had made in the tree trunk. "You stitch this up quickly."

"Don't be silly," the Doctor said.

"You do as I say. Stitch it up." Klausner was gripping the axe handle and he spoke softly, in a curious, almost a threatening tone.

"Don't be silly," the Doctor said. "I can't stitch through wood. Come on. Let's get back."

"So you can't stitch through wood?"

"No, of course not."

"Have you got any iodine[②] in your bag?"

"What if I have?"

"Then paint the cut with iodine. It'll sting, but that can't be helped."

"Now look," the Doctor said, and again he turned as if to go. "Let's not be ridiculous. Let's get back to the house and then..."

"*Paint-the-cut-with-4-iodine.*"

The Doctor hesitated. He saw Klausner's hands tightening on the handle of the axe. He decided that his only alternative was to run away, fast, and he certainly wasn't going to do that.

"All right," he said. "I'll paint it with iodine."

He got his black bag which was lying on the grass about ten yards away, opened it and took out a bottle of iodine and some cotton wool. He

---

① suffuse: *Verb* [with obj.] gradually spread through or over 逐渐扩散;布满;充满(e.g. The first half of the poem is suffused with idealism. 诗的前半部分充满了理想主义。)

② iodine: *Noun* [mass noun] the chemical element of atomic number 53, a non-metallic element forming black crystals and a violet vapour (Symbol: I); a solution of this in alcohol 碘;碘酒

went up to the tree trunk, uncorked the bottle, tipped some of the iodine on to the cotton wool, bent down and began to dab① it into the cut. He kept one eye on Klausner who was standing motionless with the axe in his hands, watching him.

"Make sure you get it right in."

"Yes," the Doctor said.

"Now do the other one—the one just above it!"

The Doctor did as he was told.

"There you are," he said. "It's done."

He straightened up and surveyed his work in a very serious manner. "That should do nicely."

Klausner came closer and gravely examined the two wounds.

"Yes," he said, nodding his huge head slowly up and down. "Yes, that will do nicely." He stepped back a pace. "You'll come and look at them again tomorrow?"

"Oh, yes," the Doctor said. "Of course."

"And put some more iodine on?"

"If necessary, yes."

"Thank you, Doctor," Klausner said, and he nodded his head again and he dropped the axe and all at once he smiled, a wild, excited smile, and quickly the Doctor went over to him and gently he took him by the arm and he said, "Come on, we must go now," and suddenly they were walking away, the two of them, walking silently, rather hurriedly across the park, over the road, back to the house.

三、翻译探索

这篇小说的翻译中，一些声音和植物方面的词汇要处理好。一

---

① dab: *Verb* apply (a substance) with light quick strokes 轻敷；轻搽(e. g. She dabbed disinfectant on the cut. 她在伤口上轻轻敷了消毒剂。)

些英制的度量衡单位在翻译过程做了“同化”处理,以给中国读者留下一个直观的印象,这一点也贯穿于这个系列翻译研究的始终。当然,个中优劣,也值得探索。

探声机器

夏季的傍晚很是温暖。克劳斯纳快步穿过前门,绕着自家房子侧面步入后面的花园。在花园里,他继续向前,停在一个小木屋前,开了门走进去,随手把门带上。

房间没有涂漆,屋内左边紧靠一面墙壁的地方有一个长长的木制工作台,台上放了个黑盒子。盒子有九十多厘米长,小孩儿棺材形状。盒子周围满是乱糟糟的电线,还有些电池和锋利的小型工具。

克劳斯纳穿越房间走到盒子跟前,盒子的顶部是开着的。他弯腰开始边拨弄,边向盒子内部观瞧:里面布满了一大堆颜色各异的电线和一些银白色的管子。盒子边放了张纸。他拿起纸来,仔细研究,然后把纸放下,再向盒内观瞧。他的手指顺着线滑动,轻轻地拽了拽,看看连接得好不好,回头再研究那张纸,然后再向盒内观瞧,接着又研究那张纸,同时挨个检查每一根线。就这样弄来弄去,他鼓弄了约一个小时。

接下来,他一只手伸到盒子前面,那里有三个控制盘。他开始转动控制盘,同时观察盒内机构的运动状况。他始终轻声自言自语,不断点头,有时候还微微一笑。他双手不停移动,手指熟练地、迅速地在盒内移来移去。一旦有哪个环节很棘手、很难弄的时候,他的嘴就会扭曲成各种形状,显示出很好奇的样子,嘟囔着:“对……对……那么,现在这个……对……对……但是,这样对吗?是否……我的示意图哪去了?噢,对……当然啦……对,对的……那没错的……那么,现在……好的……好的……对……对,对的,对的。”他聚精会神、动作敏捷。他工作起来,样子显得很紧迫,没有喘息的机会,强烈压抑着自己兴奋的情绪。

突然,屋外砾石路上传来脚步声。他直起身来,迅速一转身。门开了,进来一个高个子男子。此人叫斯科特,是个医生。进来的只有他一个人。

“喔,喔,喔,”医生说。“这就是你晚上栖身之所啦。”

“你好,斯科特,”克劳斯纳问候道。

“刚刚碰巧路过,”医生说。“所以,我就顺便拜访一下,看看你康复得怎样。你家房里没人,所以我就溜达到这里来了。你那嗓子怎么样啦?”

“还好,不错的。”

“我既然来了,就不妨给你看一下吧。”

“不用麻烦的。我恢复得相当好。我很好的。”

医生觉察到屋内气氛有点紧张。他望了眼台上的黑盒子,又看了眼屋子的主人。“你帽子还没摘呢,”他说。

“噢,是吗?”克劳斯纳伸手摘下帽子,放到工作台上。

医生靠近一些,弯腰瞧盒内。“这是什么?”他问。“你在做收音机吗?”

“不是。只是瞎捣鼓。”

“内部看起来相当复杂啊。”

“没错。”克劳斯纳似乎紧张起来,有些心不在焉。

“这是什么呀?”医生继续问。“这东西看起来相当吓人,是不是呢?”

“一个意念罢了。”

“是吗?”

“与声音有关。仅此而已。”

“我的天呐,伙计!难道你一整天都摆弄这类东西而不觉得厌烦吗?”

“我喜欢声音。”

“看起来,你是喜欢的。”医生向门口走去,接着转过身,说:“好吧,我不打扰了。你的嗓子不再令你烦恼,我很高兴。”话虽这么说,人却没挪窝,看着那盒子,心里核计:那东西内部怎么那么复杂?他很好奇,很想知道:他的这个古里古怪的病人怎么那么忙碌?“说真的,这是干什么用的?”他问。“我本来不愿刨根问底的。”

克劳斯纳低头看了看盒子，又看了看医生，然后抬手开始轻轻挠自己的右耳垂。停顿了一会儿。医生站在门口，微笑着等待回答。

“好吧。你要是有兴趣，我就告诉你。”又停顿了一会儿。医生看得出，克劳斯纳颇费周折，不知从何讲起。

他换另一条腿站着，手使劲拽着耳垂，眼睛看着双脚。最终，他慢慢地说：“嗯，是这样的……理论上，这很简单的，真的。人的耳朵……你是知道的，无法听到所有的声音。有些声音，其音调太低了，或者太高了，耳朵是听不见的。”

“是的，”医生说。“这我懂。”

“嗯，大致说来，声调要是太高，每秒振动多达一万五千次的话，我们就听不见了。狗的耳朵就比我们的耳朵灵敏。要知道，买一只哨子，声调吹得太高的话，你根本就听不到，而狗却能听得到。”

“是的，我见过哨子，”医生说。

“你当然见过的。要是提高一下音阶，比哨子更高的，有另一种声调——称作‘振动’也行，但我更喜欢叫‘声调’，你也听不到的。在那个声调之上，顺着音阶往上排，还有另一种，以及另一种……更高的声调，可以一直、一直、一直排下去，无穷尽的、无极限的声调序列。有一种声调——如果我们的耳朵能听到的话——每秒振动高达一百万次，就有另一种声调，其振动次数是前者的一百万倍……很多很多声调的。振动次数越来越高，只要数字够用，一个比一个高……无穷无尽的……永不停止的……超过了天上的繁星数量。”

克劳斯纳越来越活跃，手总是不停地移来移去。他个子矮小、身体虚弱、精神紧张、性情焦躁。他头很大，偏向左肩，就好像脖子不够壮实，无法牢固地把头部支撑起来似的。他脸很光滑，呈灰白色——近乎全白了；他双眼白中透灰，一眨一眨地透过那副钢架眼镜向外观瞧，那眼神令人困惑，很是茫然，显得距离遥远。这个小个子家伙身体虚弱、精神紧张、性情焦躁，就像一只蛾子迷迷蒙蒙、恍恍惚惚，却突然间振翅起舞，活跃起来了。现在，这位医生嘛，看了看他那张奇怪的、灰白的脸，又看了看他那两只白中透灰的眼睛，不知怎么地就感觉这个小个子病人身上有一种遥远的距离感，一种巨大的、无法测量的遥远距离感，就好像其身、心相距十万八千里似的。

医生等着他继续往下说。克劳斯纳叹了口气，两手紧紧攥到一起。“我相信，”他说，语速更慢了，“自始至终我们周围存在一个完整的声音世界——我们听不到的声音的世界。在那儿很多听不见的高音调区域里，会产生一种全新的、令人兴奋的音乐之声，那声音既有令人难以捉摸的和谐之音，又有刺耳的、无休止的不谐之音。我们的耳朵要是通过机器的调谐听到那音乐之声，那么这种力量强大的音乐就足以让我们发疯般着迷了。那个世界或许无所不有。就我们所知，那里或许有——”

“是的，”医生打断了他。“但是，这不是太可能的。”

“为什么不可能？为什么不可能？”克劳斯纳反问道，手指向一只苍蝇，那只苍蝇落在工作台上的一小卷铜线圈上。“你看到那只苍蝇了吗？那苍蝇现在发出的是什么种类的声音呢？你什么都听不见，但苍蝇听得见。就我们所知，那苍蝇或许用很高的声调在疯狂地吹口哨呢，或许正如犬吠，或许似蛙鸣，或许像鸟唱呢。它是长了嘴的，是不是啊？它还有嗓子的。”

医生看了看苍蝇，微笑一下，仍站在门口，一只手放在门把手上。“噢，”他说。“这么说，你要就此加以检验了。”

“前些阵子，”克劳斯纳说，“我做了一个简单的仪器，测试证明很多奇特的、听不见的声音是存在的。我常常坐下来，观察我那仪器的指针记录这空气中声音的振动，而我自己什么也听不到。那些振动就是我想要听到的声音。我想知道那些声音的来源，是什么人或者什么东西发出的。”

“那儿台子上的那个机器，”医生说，“是你要用来听这些声音的吗？”

“或许吧。谁知道呢？可目前为止，运气不佳。但，我对它做了些改进，今晚准备再试一次。这台机器——”他边说边用双手摸着机器，“按其设计是用来捕捉声音振动的，这些振动音调太高，人耳根本听不到。为把这些声音转换到能听得见声调的音阶上，我就调谐这台机器，就像操作收音机那样。

"你,什么意思啊?"

"一点也不复杂的。比如,我希望听蝙蝠的吱吱声——音调相当高的一种声音,振动的次数大约是每秒三万次,一般的人耳是听不到的。现在,设想有一只蝙蝠在这个屋子里飞来飞去,我就可以把我这台机器调谐到三万的刻度上,能清晰地听到蝙蝠吱吱的叫声了。我甚至能正确地听清声调——升F调,降B调,或者其他什么调,但只是以一种*低得多的声*调听到的。难道你还不明白吗?"

医生看了眼那个长长的、黑棺材盒一样的东西,问道:"那么,今晚你就用它来试?"

"是的。"

"好吧。祝你好运。"他瞥了眼自己的手表。"我的天啊!"他说。"我必须飞奔了,再见。谢谢你跟我讲。有时间我一定再来拜访,看看进展如何。"医生出去,顺手关上门。

克劳斯纳又花一些时间摆弄黑盒子里的电线,然后直起腰身,兴奋地轻声自语:"好了,再试一次……这次拿到花园里试……那时,或许……或许,捕捉效果会更好一些。现在,抬起来……小心啊……噢,我的天啊,太沉了。"他把盒子搬到门口才发现,要是不先放下盒子,根本无法推开门。于是,他把盒子搬回去,放到工作台上,再去把门推开,随即他费了九牛二虎之力才把盒子搬到花园。他小心地把盒子放到立在草坪上的小木桌上,然后返回小木屋,取来一副耳机。接着,他把耳机的接头插进机器,戴上耳机。他双手的动作既快又准,人很兴奋,呼吸起来速度很快,嘴上发出很大声音。他不断自言自语说几句来安慰自己、鼓励自己,似乎害怕什么——害怕机器不好使,也害怕机器真的不好使时,会有什么情况发生。

他站在花园的木桌旁,脸色那么灰白、个头那么矮小、身体那么瘦弱,以致整个人看起来就像一个戴着眼镜、身患肺病、老态龙钟的小孩子。此时,太阳已经落山,没有风,也没有一丁点儿声音。从站立的地方,他可以隔着一排低矮的栅栏看见隔壁花园,那里面一个女人在走动,胳膊上挎一个花篮。他观察她有一会儿了,但并没有多想什么。随后,转向桌上的盒子,按下前面板上一个开关。他左手放在音量控制钮上,右手放在一个旋钮上,那旋钮可以转动一枚指针,指针位于中心位置上一个大大的刻度盘上,就像收音机上的波长刻度盘。刻度盘上标了很多数字,是一连串的波段数字,起始点是15,000,结束点是1,000,000。

现在,他正俯身机器上方,头歪向一边,一副紧张兮兮、正在聆听的姿态。右手开始转动旋钮了,指针在刻度盘上缓慢移动——移动的速度很慢,几乎看不出指针是在移动的。从耳机里,他能听到一种微弱的、间歇式的、噼里啪啦的声音。

从噼里啪啦的声音里,他听得出有一种距离遥远的"嗡嗡"声调,那是机器本身发出的噪音,仅此而已。听着听着,他就产生了一种稀奇古怪的、莫名其妙的感觉,这种感觉就是,他的两只耳朵从头部拉伸出来,抻得很长,每一只耳朵与头部靠一根细细的、硬硬的线连接着,类似于触须。他感觉,这两根线不断变长,两只耳朵也不断向上延伸到一个隐秘的禁地,那是一个充满危险的超声波地段,那个地段耳朵从未涉足,而且无权涉足。

小小的指针慢慢地在刻度盘上移动。突然,他听到一声尖叫——令人毛骨悚然的、刺耳的尖叫。他随即跳起,松开手,紧紧抓住桌角。他盯着周围看,好像要看看发出尖叫的人。可是,除了隔壁花园那个女人,周围一个人也没有。很显然,声音不是她发出的,因为她正弯腰剪黄玫瑰,剪完放进篮子。

这声音又响起来了——不是通过嗓子发出的,也不是人发出的;这声音尖锐而短促,清晰却冷漠;这声音本身具有小调的性质和金属的质感,他以前从没有听过的。克劳斯纳环视周围,本能地搜索着声音的来源,但视线里只有隔壁花园的那个女的是个活物。他看见她弯腰,用手指捏住一枝玫瑰花茎,然后用剪子"咔嚓"一声剪断。这时,他又听到了尖叫声。

这声音正好在玫瑰花茎被剪断的当儿发出的。

就在这时,那女人直起腰身,把剪刀放入装满玫瑰花的篮子,转身走开了。

"桑德斯太太!"克劳斯纳喊道,声音由于兴奋而颤抖起来。

"噢,桑德斯太太!"

这个女人转身一看,她的邻居站在草坪上挥动手臂——古里古怪的一个小个头男子,头戴一副耳机。他正冲她喊叫,声调很高,音量很大,听得她甚至恐慌起来。

"再剪一枝！请再剪一枝！快!"

她站在原地,一动不动地盯着他看。"为什么啊,克劳斯纳先生?"她问。"怎么啦?"

"请按我的要求做吧,"他恳求。"就再剪一枝吧!"

桑德斯太太始终认为她的邻居是一个相当怪异之人,现在看起来完全疯掉了。她犹豫着是否该冲进房门,把丈夫找来。她寻思着:不,不能那样做,况且他并无恶意。我就迎合一下他吧。"当然啦,克劳斯纳先生,只要你喜欢,"她说道。然后从篮子里拿出剪子,弯下腰,"咔嚓"一声又剪断一枝玫瑰。

克劳斯纳又一次从耳机里听到那种令人毛骨悚然的、并非嗓子发出的尖叫声,而且这声音又一次正好是在玫瑰花茎被剪断的当儿发出的。他摘下耳机,跑向栅栏,那栅栏把花园一分为二。"好了,"他说。"可以了。不要再剪了。请不要再剪了。"

那个女人一手拿着黄玫瑰,一手握着剪子,站在那儿看着他。

"桑德斯太太,我要跟你说点事儿,"他说。"一点儿你难以置信的事。"他把手放到栅栏顶部,透过镜片厚厚的眼镜,目不转睛地看着她。"今天傍晚,你已经剪了整整一篮子的玫瑰。你已经用一把锋利的剪子剪断了很多活物的茎,而你剪断的每一枝玫瑰都叫得极其凄惨。你知道吗,桑德斯太太?"

"不,"她说。"我怎么可能知道?"

"你说巧不巧,事情就是这样的。"他说。他呼吸相当急促,但却尽力控制自己的兴奋。"我听到它们尖叫了。每次你剪的时候,我就听到痛苦的喊叫——音调很高的声音,约每秒振动三十万两千次。这声音你自己不可能听见的,但我,听见了。"

"真的吗,克劳斯纳先生?"她决定,五秒钟之内,冲进自家的房门。

“你或许会说，”他继续说，“一丛丛的玫瑰没有感知外界的神经系统，也没有叫出声音的嗓子。你说的没错，是没有。不管怎么说，不会跟我们人一样的。但是，*桑德斯太太，你怎么会知道*……”说到这儿，又向栅栏的上方靠了靠，用足了力气小声说：“*你怎么会知道*，当有人把玫瑰花茎一剪断成两截时，玫瑰不会感到极其疼痛呢？你怎么会知道，这疼痛就像有人用园艺剪剪短你的手腕那样厉害呢？*你怎么会知道呢*？玫瑰是*活着*的，难道不是吗？”

“是的，克劳斯纳先生。噢，你说的没错——那么，晚安。”她快速转身，穿过花园，奔向自家大门。克劳斯纳回到桌旁，戴上耳机，站着又听了一会。他还能听到那微弱的、噼里啪啦的声音和嗡嗡的机器噪音，但听不见其他声音。于是，他弯腰握住生长在草坪上的一枝小小的白色雏菊花，用大拇指和食指夹住，先慢慢向上一拔，然后向边一拉，花茎就“啪”地折断了。

从向上拔的那刻起，到花茎折断那刻止，他从耳机里清清楚楚地听到了一个微弱的、音调很高的叫声，而且说来也怪，不是动物发出的。他抓起另一枝雏菊，重复了刚才的动作，结果又一次听到了叫声。可是，他现在不敢肯定那叫声表达的是不是痛苦。不，不会是痛苦，或者表达的是吃惊？它真正表达的不是人类所知道的任何一种感觉或情感，那只不过是一声叫声——中性的、冷冰冰的叫声；那就是单一的、毫无情感而言的声调，什么意思也表达不了，跟玫瑰是一样的。所以，称它为“痛苦的叫声”是不对的。一朵花可能感觉不到痛苦，它感觉到的应是某些我们还不了解的东西，你可以叫它“张酸”“李涩”或“王苦咸辣”，或者随你怎么叫都可以。

他站起来，摘下耳机。天就要黑了，他看到周围各家各户都闪耀着一束束刺眼的灯光。他小心地从桌子上抬起黑盒子，搬进小屋，放到工作台上。接着，他出去，随手锁上门，走回家。

第二天早晨天一亮，克劳斯纳就爬起来，穿好衣服，径直走向小屋。他抬起机器往外搬。机器很重，他两只手抱着机器紧紧贴到胸部，压得他走起路来晃晃荡荡的。他走过自家房子，从前门出去，然后穿过马路，来到公园。他停了一下，往四周看了看，继续前行，走到一棵大树下,那是棵三毛榉树。他把机器放到靠近树干的地面上,然后快速回家从煤窖里拿起一把斧子,穿过马路又回到公园,把斧子放到树旁的地面上。

接着,他又看看周围,透过厚厚的镜片紧张兮兮地四面八方观望着。周围一个人也没有,才早晨六点呢。

他戴上耳机,打开机器,听了一会他熟悉的、微弱的、嗡嗡的声音。然后,拾起斧子,双腿叉开,做出站姿,接着抡起斧子奋力砍向树干的底部。斧子的刃口深深地嵌入树木,卡在那儿。就在斧子和树木碰撞的那一刻,他从耳机里听到一声噪音——非同寻常的声音。这种声音听起来很陌生,与以前他听过的都不一样。这种声音很尖锐,没有声调,而且响动巨大,是一种轰隆隆的、音调很低的喊叫声。这种声音不像玫瑰发出的声音那样急促和短暂,但却是一种拉长了的声音,像是人的抽泣声,持续了整整一分钟。斧子砍入的那一刻,这种声音的响度最大,随后逐渐变得越来越弱,直到最后消失。

克劳斯纳惊恐地盯着斧刃深嵌到树干的地方,然后轻轻握住斧柄,慢慢地把斧子松动,最后拔出来,"咣当"一声扔到地上。他用手指抚摸着斧子砍出的口子,抚弄着口子的边缘,尽量用力把口子合拢,嘴里还不断嘟囔着:"树啊……噢,树啊……很抱歉……真对不起……可是,会好起来的……会愈合得很不错的……"

他双手抚弄着大树的树干,在那儿站了一会。突然,他一转身,匆匆离开公园,穿越马路,经过前门,返回房中,奔向电话,查了下号码簿,拨了个数字,等待着。他左手紧握听筒,右手轻轻敲着桌子,一副急不可耐的样子。他听到电话另一端响起了"嘀铃铃"的声音,紧接着"咔"的一声,对方拿起了话机听筒,一个男子的声音——很困倦的声音——传了过来:"嗨,你好!"

"斯科特医生吗?"他问。

"是啊。请讲。"

"斯科特医生,你务必马上过来——请快过来。"

"你贵姓?"

"我是克劳斯纳啊。你记得我昨晚给你讲的吧,我的那个关于声音的实验。我是多么希望我——"

"对,对,当然记得。可是,你怎么啦?生病了吗?"

"不,没生病,但是——"

"这才早晨六点半啊,"医生说,"你就给我打电话,却没有不舒服的地方。"

"请来一趟,要快。我想要人来听一下。我简直要疯掉了,我无法相信……"

这位医生听出对方的语调像发了狂似的,近乎于歇斯底里了,而这种语调他早就习以为常,跟其他打来电话的人的语调是一样的:"出车祸了,快过来。"他回应道:"你真的想要我现在就爬出被窝过去吗?"

"是的,就现在,马上。拜托了。"

克劳斯纳在话机旁坐下,等待着。他尽量回忆那树的喊叫声,却想不起来了。他只记得那声音响动巨大,很是恐怖,令他不寒而栗。他尽量想象着在那种情况下,人会发出什么样的声音:把一个人固定到地面上,让其站着不动时,有人挥舞一个尖锐的东西向其腿部砍去,刀刃深深嵌入,停留在切口处。这时,人或许会发出一样的声音吗?不会的。声音完全不同的。树发出的声音比任何已知的、人类发出的声音都更糟糕,因为树的声音很是令人恐惧,没有声调,也不是通过嗓子发出的。他不知道其他生物会怎样,因为他当时就想到了一片田野里的小麦。那片黄橙橙的、活生生的小麦笔直站立着。这时,收割机驶过,切断茎秆,速度是每秒五百根——每一秒切断五百根茎秆啊。噢,我的天呐。那会发出什么样的声音啊?五百颗小麦一起发出尖叫声,而且每过一秒钟,就有另外五百颗小麦被切断而尖叫。他想,不能这样的,我不能搬着我的机器去麦田,我至此再也不吃面包了。可是,土豆会怎样?卷心菜、胡萝卜、圆葱呢?还有,苹果会怎样?啊,不要这样。苹果会没事的,因为成熟时它们会自然掉落。要是让苹果从树上自然掉落,而不是从枝条上把它们揪下来的话,它们会没事的。但是,蔬菜,比如土豆,就不会那么幸运了。土豆一定会尖叫的。同样,胡萝卜、圆葱、卷心菜……都会尖叫的。

一听见前门门闩"咔哒"一声响，他就跃身而起，奔出门去。他看见个子高高的斯科特医生走进来，手里拎个小黑包。

"哎呀，"医生说。"那么，到底出什么岔子了？"

"医生，随我来。我想让你听一听。我打电话给你，因为这事我只跟你说过。到马路对面的公园里听听。现在就来吧，可以吗？"

医生看了他一眼，发现他现在似乎镇定多了，也没有了发疯或者歇斯底里的迹象，只不过受到了惊扰而兴奋不已。

他们穿过马路，钻入公园。克劳斯纳带着医生来到那棵大三毛榉树下，树下是那台长长的、黑棺材盒似的机器——还有那把斧子。

"为什么把这玩意弄到这里？"医生问。

"我想找一棵树做实验，可花园里一棵大树也没有。"

"那斧子又是怎么回事？"

"过会儿你就明白了。现在，请带上这两个耳机听一下。听仔细些，然后准确地跟我说说听到了什么。我想彻底弄清楚……"

克劳斯纳"啪"地一下打开了机器前面板的开关，然后拾起斧子，双腿叉开，做出站姿，准备要抡起斧子。就在此刻，他暂停一下。"你能听到什么吗？"他问医生。

"我能……什么？"

"你能*听到*什么吗？"

"只有嗡嗡的噪音。"

克劳斯纳站在那儿，手持斧子准备要抡起来，可突然想到树会发出的声音，就又停顿下来。

"你在等什么呀？"医生问。

"没什么，"克劳斯纳回答，接着就举起斧子，向大树抡了下去。斧子抡下去的时候，他想自己感觉到——他可以发誓——感觉到站立的地面在移动，他感到脚下的大地有轻微的位移，就好像树根在土里行走似的。但是，这一斧子已经砍下去，要收回去，为时已晚。斧子的刃口深深地嵌入树木，卡在那儿。就在那时，听到头顶上方高处"咔嚓"一声响，树杈断裂，树叶相互摩擦，发出"唰啦啦"的声音。他俩忙不迭地抬头，医生喊道："当心！跑，伙计！跑，快！"

医生扯掉耳机，飞速跑开，但克劳斯纳却如同中了邪一般，仰头盯着那个断裂的大树杈。树杈至少有十八米长，"噼里啪啦""咔嚓咔嚓"作响，正慢慢地向其枝叶最浓密的下方坠落，碰上大树的主干，随即"唰啦"一声落下。克劳斯纳向边一跃，正好躲过。大树杈"啪嚓"落到机器上，将其砸得粉碎。

"老天啊！"医生边往回跑边喊。"真玄啊！当时我想，大枝杈砸你没商量啦！"

克劳斯纳呆呆地看着大树，他那大大的脑袋歪向一侧，平滑而刷白的脸上露出一副紧张、恐惧的表情。他慢慢地走近大树，轻轻地把斧子松动，然后从树干上拔了出来。

"你听到没有？"他边问边转向医生，声音小得几乎听不见。

由于奔跑和兴奋，医生仍然气喘吁吁。"听到什么？"

"从耳机里听到的。斧子砍进去的时候，听到什么没有？"

医生开始挠自己的后脖颈。"噢，"他说，"实际上……"他停了下来，紧皱眉头，咬着下嘴唇。"不，我不敢肯定。我不能肯定。我估计，你斧子砍进去后，我耳机戴的时间没有超过一秒钟。"

"那是，那是，可你听到什么没有？"

"我不知道，"医生回答。"我不知道我听到什么。或许听到那个大枝杈断裂的声音。"他说得很快，相当急躁。

"听起来像什么声音？"克劳斯纳身体稍微向前倾斜，眼睛一动不动盯着医生。"*准确说一下*，像什么声音？"

"啊，真见鬼！"医生说。"我真的不知道。当时，我一个心思想跑开。别说了。"

"斯科特医生，*听起来——像——什么——声音*？"

"大树的一半要压到我身上、仓皇逃命时，看在上帝的分上，我怎么能说得出来像什么声音？"当然啦，医生紧张得很，克劳斯纳感觉到了这一点。他一动不动地站着，眼睛一动不动地盯着医生，足有半分钟时间一言未发。医生动了动脚，耸了耸肩，半个身子转了过来。"那么，"他说。"我们最好回去吧。"

"听着，"小个头男子说，此时他那张光滑的、刷白的脸突然间泛起颜色。“听着，”他说，“你把这缝合一下吧。”他指向斧子在树干砍出的最后一个切口。“快点把这缝合起来吧。”

“别犯傻了。”医生说。

“照我说的做，缝起来啊。”克劳斯纳握紧斧子柄，轻声细语地说，语调怪异，几乎带有一种威胁的色彩。

“别做傻事啊，”医生说。“我没法缝合木头。别扯了，我们还是回去吧。”

“你说，你没法缝合木头？”

“没法，当然没法。”

“你包里有碘酒吗？”

“有的话，怎么样啊？”

“那就用碘酒涂抹切口。会感觉灼痛的，可又没有别的办法。”

“现在，你瞧瞧啊，”医生说完，又转过身，好像准备要走。“我们不要荒唐胡闹了，回你家，然后……”

“用碘酒——涂抹——切口。”

医生不知如何是好。他看了看克劳斯纳紧握斧子的双手，盘算着唯一的选择就是快跑。当然，还没有打算那么去做。

“好吧，”他说。“我用碘酒给它涂上吧。”

他把放在草坪上约十米远的黑包拿来，打开，取出一瓶碘酒和一些药棉。他走近树干，打开瓶塞，把一些碘酒倒到药棉上，然后弯腰，轻轻地用药棉蘸着切口，一只眼睛瞟着克劳斯纳。克劳斯纳双手握斧，一动不动站立，看着他。

“一定要把碘酒蘸进去。”

“是的，”医生说。

“现在再把另一个处理一下，就在这个的上方！”

医生照做无误。

“你看看吧，”医生说。“完事了。”

说完，直起腰，认认真真地审视起自己的工作成果。

“效果应当很不错的。”

克劳斯纳走近，一脸严肃地检查那两个伤口。

“不错，”他边说边慢慢地上下晃着他那大大的脑袋。“不错，效果会很不错的。”他向后退了一步。“明天来，再看看伤口，如何？”

“哦，可以的，”医生说。“当然可以的。”

“到时候，再上些碘酒吗？”

“如果必要，可以上。”

“谢谢你，医生，”克劳斯纳说，接着又点了点头，随即扔掉斧子，突然间微笑起来，笑得有些疯狂和兴奋。医生快速走近，轻轻抓起他的胳膊，说道：“好了，现在我们必须走了。”他们两个人急速走开，默默无语、匆匆忙忙穿越公园，横过马路，回到房中。

第四章 匪夷所思

生活中,有些人和事的确超出了一般人所能理解或想象的范畴,正所谓"匪夷所思"也。对于源自《周易·涣》(原文为:"涣有丘,匪夷所思。")的"匪夷所思",虽然据考证其本意并非如此,但是,这里还是按照流行的意义来理解,即"不是平常人所能想象的"①。梁实秋先生在《雅舍小品·偏方》中说:"有些偏方实在偏得厉害,匪夷所思",正取此意也。

1960年,人类探索的脚步迈下一万多米深的马里亚纳海沟——那是一个高压、漆黑和冰冷的海底世界,竟然有一条比目鱼和一只小红虾在那里游动!真是匪夷所思;在海拔5,000米左右靠近雪线的高山碎石坡上,盛开着一朵朵雪莲花,而周围却是白雪皑皑的世界!真是匪夷所思;埃及神话中的不死之鸟——火凤凰,是生长于阿拉伯沙漠之中的一种美丽而孤独的鸟儿,据说每500年就自焚一次,化为灰烬,再从灰烬中重生,如此循环往复而得到永生!真是匪夷所思……现在的大都市到处都是灰蒙蒙的一片,雾霾天气成为家常便饭,蓝天白云成为罕见的奢侈品!真是匪夷所思。

《圣经》(Bible)的第一卷书《创世记》(Genesis)中,大洪水的暴

① 参见"商务印书馆辞书研究中心,2002:203"。

发给人类带来了无尽的灾难,但人类还是得以拯救,这也是匪夷所思的。在作家罗尔德·达尔的笔下,一位母亲一连痛失三个亲生骨肉,而瘦弱不堪的第四个孩子——阿道夫斯,却奇迹般活了下来,这也算得上奇迹了。噢,等一等,“阿道夫斯”,这个名字听起来怎么有些耳熟?这个婴儿跟德国纳粹党的元首、第二次世界大战中种族主义政策的核心人物阿道夫·希特勒有什么关系?难道这个婴儿长大后会重现《创世记》中的“大灾难”(catastrophe)吗?这真是匪夷所思。

孩提时代是美好的,天真无邪,无忧无虑。可是,你遇到过那些专门欺负好孩子的坏孩子吗?这些坏孩子将好孩子手脚绑住,放到铁轨上,任火车呼啸而过,这本身就够令人匪夷所思的了。更有甚者,他们竟然将天鹅的翅膀砍下,绑到好孩子的双臂,要让好孩子像天鹅一样飞起来!这又让人感到匪夷所思。

走进罗尔德·达尔的世界,去看看《创世新灾》中一个婴儿降生的匪夷所思之处,去读读《折翼天鹅》中坏孩子匪夷所思的行为吧。

第一节　《创世新灾》*Genesis and Catastrophe*

罗尔德·达尔的《创世新灾》(Genesis and Catastrophe)首次发表在《花花公子》(Playboy)杂志1959年12月号上,当时的标题为《优秀之子》(A Fine Son)。后来,这个故事又收录到《罗尔德·达尔短篇故事集锦》(The Collected Short Stories of Roald Dahl)、《罗尔德·达尔小说精品集》(The Best of Roald Dahl)、《五部畅销书集》(5 Bestsellers)、《吻了又吻》(Kiss Kiss)、《罗尔德·达尔二十九篇成人故事集》(Twenty Nine Kisses from Roald Dahl)、《更多出人意料故事集》(More Tales of the Unexpected)、《后续出人意料故事集》(Further Tales of the Unexpected)以及《完全出人意料故事集》(Completely Unexpected Tales)等书中,也被改编成电视系列剧中的一集——1980年5月17日播映的《出乎意料的故事集》(Tales of the Unexpected)第二部中的第12集(Episode 2.12),可见其影响力之大。

跟达尔其他许多短篇小说不同的是，这部《创世新灾》没有出人意料的结尾，更没有惊险曲折的情节。但是，读到故事的结尾，读者也许会得到一个具有讽刺性的、震撼人心的启示吧！

一、原作导读

不久前，克拉拉跟丈夫阿劳伊斯·希特勒搬到了一个陌生的小镇居住。阿劳伊斯是“一个酒鬼、个子矮小、狂妄自大、盛气凌人、恃强凌弱”（an arrogant, overbearing, bullying little drunkard），而克拉拉，也就是希特勒夫人，则“温柔贤惠、笃信宗教”（gentle and religious）。她的孩子即将出生。

孩子出生后，年轻的母亲克拉拉有些焦虑和担心。这次生的是个男孩，是她生下的第四个孩子，前三个孩子都不幸地相继死去。医生恪尽职守，尽力安慰这位忧心忡忡的母亲。

医生弯下腰，把病人胸前的被单稍微向上拉了拉。“你没有什么好担心的，”他轻轻地说。“这个婴儿完全正常。”

“其他那几个，医生也是这么对我说的，说得一模一样。但是，医生，那几个，我都失去了。在过去十八个月的时间里，我失去了我所有三个孩子。所以，我目前这样焦虑不安，你一定不要责怪。”

“三个？”

“在四年的时间内……这是我第四个孩子。”

The doctor bent down and pulled the sheet up a little higher over the patient's chest. "You have nothing to worry about," he said gently. "This is a perfectly normal baby."

"That's exactly what they told me about the others. But I lost them all, Doctor. In the last eighteen months I have lost all three of my children, so you mustn't blame me for being anxious."

"Three?"

"This is my fourth... in four years."

医生劝慰她说，新生婴儿没有任何问题，顺便问了问她有没有给孩子起名字。她说道：

“起名字？”

“是呀。”

“我不知道，我不敢肯定。我想，我丈夫说过，如果生下的是个男孩儿的话，就叫阿道夫斯。”

“那就等于说，他将取名为阿道夫（“阿道夫”为“阿道夫斯”的简化的异体形式——译者注）。”

“A name?”

“Yes.”

“I don't know. I'm not sure. I think my husband said that if it was a boy we were going to call him Adolfus.”

“That means he would be called Adolf”

她抱起自己的小阿道夫，喜欢的不得了，而丈夫阿劳伊斯回来后就说孩子如何、如何小的不得了。这时，医生就劝他多体贴一下自己的妻子，多给她一些安慰。他最终吻了吻妻子，安慰了几句。故事的最后，克拉了说道：

“阿劳伊斯，他一定要活下来。他一定要，一定要……噢，老天啊，现在，赐予他仁慈……”

“He *must* live, Alois. He *must*, he *must* Oh God, be merciful unto him now...”

二、原作释读

这篇小说中，作家罗尔德·达尔以讽刺的手法，借助圣经中“创世记”篇及其描述的大洪水灾难为依托，描写了一对夫妇第四个孩子的降生以及降生以后的细节。难道这个孩子与历史上的一个人物有关联吗？

Genesis and Catastrophe[①]

A True Story

"This is normal," the doctor was saying. "Just lie back and relax."

His voice was miles away in the distance and he seemed to be shouting at her. "You have a son."

"You have a fine son. You understand that, don't you? A fine son. Did you hear him crying?"

"Is he all right, Doctor?"

"Of course he is all right."

"Please let me see him."

"You'll see him in a moment."

"You are certain he is all right?"

"I am quite certain."

"Is he still crying?"

"Try to rest. There is nothing to worry about."

"Why has he stopped crying, Doctor? What happened?"

"Don't excite yourself, please. Everything is normal."

"I want to see him. Please let me see him."

"Dear lady," the doctor said, patting her hand. "You have a fine strong healthy child. Don't you believe me when I tell you that?"

"What is the woman over there doing to him?"

"Your baby is being made to look pretty for you," the doctor said.

---

① 本部小说原文出自"DAHL, R. *The Best of Roald Dahl* [M]. London: Penguin Books Ltd., 2006"。

"We are giving him a little wash, that is all. You must spare us a moment or two for that."

"You swear he is all right?"

"I swear it. Now lie back and relax. Close your eyes. Go on, close your eyes. That's right. That's better. Good girl.

"I have prayed and prayed that he will live, Doctor."

"Of course he will live. What are you talking about?"

"The others didn't."

"What?"

"None of my other ones lived, Doctor."

The doctor stood beside the bed looking down at the pale exhausted face of the young woman. He had never seen her before today. She and her husband were new people in the town. The innkeeper's wife, who had come up to assist in the delivery, had told him that the husband worked at the local customs-house[①] on the border and that the two of them had arrived quite suddenly at the inn with one trunk and one suitcase about three months ago. The husband was a drunkard, the innkeeper's wife had said, an arrogant, overbearing[②], bullying little drunkard, but the young woman was gentle and religious. And she was very sad. She never smiled. In the few weeks that she had been here, the innkeeper's wife had never once seen her smile. Also there was a rumour that this was the husband's third marriage, that one wife had died

---

① customs house or custom house: *Noun* a government building at a port where, in the past, the papers for goods leaving or entering a country were checked and taxes were paid 海关

② overbearing: *Adjective* unpleasantly overpowering 专横的;蛮横的;盛气凌人的(e. g. an overbearing, ill-tempered brute 一个蛮不讲理、脾气暴躁的恶汉。)

and that the other had divorced him for unsavoury[①] reasons. But that was only a rumour.

The doctor bent down and pulled the sheet up a little higher over the patient's chest. "You have nothing to worry about," he said gently. "This is a perfectly normal baby."

"That's exactly what they told me about the others. But I lost them all, Doctor. In the last eighteen months I have lost all three of my children, so you mustn't blame me for being anxious."

"Three?"

"This is my fourth... in four years."

The doctor shifted his feet uneasily on the bare floor.

"I don't think you know what it means, Doctor, to lose them all, all three of them, slowly, separately, one by one. I keep seeing them. I can see Gustav's face now as clearly as if he were lying here beside me in the bed. Gustav was a lovely boy, Doctor. But he was always ill. It is terrible when they are always ill and there is nothing you can do to help them."

"I know."

The woman opened her eyes, stared up at the doctor for a few seconds, then closed them again.

"My little girl was called Ida. She died a few days before Christmas. That is only four months ago. I just wish you could have seen Ida, Doctor."

"You have a new one now."

"But Ida was so beautiful."

"Yes," the doctor said. "I know."

---

① unsavoury or unsavory: *Adjective* disagreeable and unpleasant because morally disreputable(品德)令人讨厌的;可憎恶的(e. g. an unsavoury reputation 坏名声。)

"How can you know?" she cried.

"I am sure that she was a lovely child. But this new one is also like that." The doctor turned away from the bed and walked over to the window and stood there looking out. It was a wet grey April afternoon, and across the street he could see the red roofs of the houses and the huge raindrops splashing① on the tiles②.

"Ida was two years old, Doctor... and she was so beautiful I was never able to take my eyes off her from the time I dressed her in the morning until she was safe in bed again at night. I used to live in holy terror of something happening to that child. Gustav had gone and my little Otto had also gone and she was all I had left. Sometimes I used to get up in the night and creep over to the cradle and put my ear close to her mouth just to make sure that she was breathing."

"Try to rest," the doctor said, going back to the bed. "Please try to rest." The woman's face was white and bloodless, and there was a slight bluish-grey tinge③ around the nostrils and the mouth. A few strands of damp hair hung down over her forehead, sticking to the skin.

"When she died... I was already pregnant again when that happened, Doctor. This new one was a good four months on its way when Ida died. 'I don't want it!' I shouted after the funeral. 'I won't have it! I have buried enough children!' And my husband... he was strolling among the guests with a big glass of beer in his hand... he turned around

---

① splash: *Verb* [no obj., with adverbial of direction] (of a liquid) fall or be scattered in irregular drops(液体)滴下;泼落;散落(e.g. A tear fell and splashed on to the pillow. 一滴眼泪掉下来,落在枕头上。)

② tile: *Noun* a thin rectangular slab of baked clay, concrete, or other material, used in overlapping rows for covering roofs 瓦(片)

③ tinge: *Noun* a tendency towards or trace of some colour 一丝;一抹(色彩)(e.g. There was a faint pink tinge to the sky. 天空有一丝淡淡的粉晕。)

quickly and said, 'I have news for you, Klara, I have good news.' Can you imagine that, Doctor? We have just buried our third child and he stands there with a glass of beer in his hand and tells me that he has good news. 'Today I have been posted to Braunau,' he says, 'so you can start packing at once. This will be a new start for you, Klara,' he says. 'It will be a new place and you can have a new doctor...'"

"Please don't talk any more."

"You are the new doctor, aren't you, Doctor?"

"That's right."

"And here we are in Braunau."

"Yes."

"I am frightened, Doctor."

"Try not to be frightened."

"What chance can the fourth one have now?"

"You must stop thinking like that."

"I can't help it. I am certain there is something inherited that causes my children to die in this way. There must be."

"That is nonsense."

"Do you know what my husband said to me when Otto was born, Doctor? He came into the room and he looked into the cradle where Otto was lying and he said, 'Why do *all* my children have to be so small and weak?'"

"I am sure he didn't say that."

"He put his head right into Otto's cradle as though he were examining a tiny insect and he said, 'All I am saying is why can't they be better *specimens*? That's all I am saying.' And three days after that, Otto was dead. We baptised[1] him quickly on the third day and he died the same evening. And then Gustav died. And then Ida died. All of them died, Doctor... and suddenly the whole house was empty..."

"Don't think about it now."

"Is this one so very small?"

"He is a normal child."

"But small?"

"He is a little small, perhaps. But the small ones are often a lot tougher than the big ones. Just imagine, Frau[2] Hitler, this time next year he will be almost learning how to walk. Isn't that a lovely thought?"

She didn't answer this.

"And two years from now he will probably be talking his head off[3] and driving you crazy with his chatter. Have you settled on a name for him yet?"

"A name?"

"Yes."

"I don't know. I'm not sure. I think my husband said that if it was a boy we were going to call him Adolfus[4]."

"That means he would be called Adolf"

"Yes. My husband likes Adolf because it has a certain similarity to

---

① baptize or bapise: *Verb* [with obj. and often with complement] administer baptism to (someone); christen 给(某人)施洗礼;洗礼时命名为(e. g. He was baptized Joshua. 他受洗礼并被命名乔舒亚。)

② Frau: *Noun* a title or form of address for a married or widowed German-speaking woman 夫人(对德语国家已婚或孀居妇女的称呼。)

③ talk your head off: (informal) talk a lot(非正式)喋喋不休;说个不停(e. g. He talked his head off all evening. 他一整晚都在喋喋不休。)

④ 根据相关的人名翻译规则,"Adolphus"这个名字可以译作"阿道夫斯",是"Adolf"的异体形式。

Alois[①]. My husband is called Alois."

"Excellent."

"Oh no!" she cried, starting up suddenly from the pillow. "That's the same question they asked me when Otto was born! It means he is going to die! You are going to baptize him at once!"

Now, now," the doctor said, taking her gently by the shoulders. "You are quite wrong. I promise you you are wrong. I was simply being an inquisitive old man, that is all. I love talking about names. I think Adolfus is a particularly fine name. It is one of my favourites. And look—here he comes now."

The innkeeper's wife, carrying the baby high up on her enormous bosom, came sailing across the room towards the bed. "Here is the little beauty!" she cried, beaming. "Would you like to hold him, my dear? Shall I put him beside you?"

"Is he well wrapped?" the doctor asked. "It is extremely cold in here."

"Certainly he is well wrapped."

The baby was tightly swaddled[②] in a white woollen shawl, and only the tiny pink head protruded. The innkeeper's wife placed him gently on the bed beside the mother. "There you are," she said. "Now you can lie there and look at him to your heart's content.[③]"

---

① 依据《人名翻译大辞典》,"Alois"这个名字应译作"阿洛伊斯",但是,为了上下文意思的衔接,这里变通性地译成"阿劳伊斯"。

② swaddle: *Verb* [with obj.] wrap (someone, especially a baby) in garments or cloth 用外衣(或布)裹(人,尤指婴儿)(e. g. She swaddled the baby tightly. 她把婴儿裹得紧紧的。)

③ to one's heart's content: to the full extent of one's desires 心满意足地;尽情地(e. g. The children could run and play to their heart's content. 孩子们能尽情奔跑玩耍。)

"I think you will like him," the doctor said, smiling. "He is a fine little baby."

"He has the most lovely hands!" the innkeeper's wife exclaimed. "Such long delicate fingers!"

The mother didn't move. She didn't even turn her head to look.

"Go on!" cried the innkeeper's wife. "He won't bite you!"

"I am frightened to look. I don't care to believe that I have another baby and that he is all right."

"Don't be so stupid."

Slowly, the mother turned her head and looked at the small, incredibly serene[①] face that lay on the pillow beside her.

"Is this my baby?"

"Of course."

"Oh...oh...but he is beautiful."

The doctor turned away and went over to the table and began putting his things into his bag. The mother lay on the bed gazing at the child and smiling and touching him and making little noises of pleasure. "Hello, Adolfus," she whispered. "Hello, my little Adolf..."

"Ssshh!" said the innkeeper's wife. "Listen! I think your husband is coming."

The doctor walked over to the door and opened it and looked out into the corridor.

"Herr[②] Hitler!"

---

① serene: *Adjective* calm, peaceful, and untroubled; tranquil 安详的;宁静的(e.g. Her eyes were closed and she looked very serene. 她闭着眼看上去很平静。)

② Herr: *Noun* a title or form of address used of or to a German-speaking man, corresponding to "Mr." and also used before a rank or occupation 先生(用于称呼说德语的男子,相当于"Mr.",亦用在头衔或职业之前。)

"Yes."

"Come in, please."

A small man in a dark-green uniform stepped softly into the room and looked around him.

"Congratulations," the doctor said. "You have a son."

The man had a pair of enormous whiskers① meticulously② groomed after the manner of the Emperor Franz Josef, and he smelled strongly of beer. "A son?"

"Yes."

"How is he?"

"He is fine. So is your wife."

"Good." The father turned and walked with a curious little prancing stride over to the bed where his wife was lying. "Well, Klara," he said, smiling through his whiskers. "How did it go? He bent down to take a look at the baby. Then he bent lower. In a series of quick jerky movements, he bent lower and lower until his face was only about twelve inches from the baby's head. The wife lay sideways on the pillow, staring up at him with a kind of supplicating③ look.

"He has the most marvellous pair of lungs," the innkeeper's wife announced. "You should have heard him screaming just after he came into this world."

"But my God, Klara..."

---

① whiskers: *Noun* the hair growing on a man's face, especially on his cheeks 胡须;髯;连鬓胡子;络腮胡子

② meticulous: *Adjective* showing great attention to detail; very careful and precise 十分注意细节的;一丝不苟的(e. g. He had always been so meticulous about his appearance. 他一直来都十分注意外表形象。)

③ supplicate: *Verb* [no obj.] ask or beg for something earnestly or humbly 恳求;哀求;祈求

"What is it, dear?"

"This one is even smaller than Otto was!"

The doctor took a couple of quick paces forward. "There is nothing wrong with that child," he said.

Slowly, the husband straightened up and turned away from the bed and looked at the doctor. He seemed bewildered and stricken[①]. "It's no good lying, Doctor," he said. "I know what it means. It's going to be the same all over again.

"Now you listen to me," the doctor said.

"But do you *know* what happened to the others, Doctor?"

"You must forget about the others, Herr Hitler. Give this one a chance."

"But so small and weak!"

"My dear sir, he has only just been born."

"Even so..."

"What are you trying to do?" cried the innkeeper's wife. "Talk him into his grave?"

"That's enough!" the doctor said sharply.

The mother was weeping now. Great sobs were shaking her body.

The doctor walked over to the husband and put a hand on his shoulder. "Be good to her," he whispered. "Please. It is very important." Then he squeezed the husband's shoulder hard and began pushing him

① stricken: *Adjective* (of a face or look) showing great distress(脸或表情)非常悲痛的;极其忧伤的;非常痛苦的(e.g. She looked at Anne's stricken face, contorted with worry. 她看着安妮那张愁得变了形的痛苦的脸。)

forward surreptitiously[1] to the edge of the bed. The husband hesitated. The doctor squeezed harder, signalling him urgently through fingers and thumb. At last, reluctantly, the husband bent down and kissed his wife lightly on the cheek.

"All right, Klara," he said. "Now stop crying."

"I have prayed so hard that he will live, Alois."

"Yes."

"Every day for months I have gone to the church and begged on my knees that this one will be allowed to live."

"Yes, Klara, I know."

"Three dead children is all that I can stand, don't you realize that?"

"Of course."

"He *must* live, Alois. He *must*, he *must* Oh God, be merciful unto[2] him now..."

三、翻译探索

本篇小说的翻译中,要处理好那几个与德语有关的人名和称呼,因为这些地方应该是作家罗尔德·达尔的用意所在,也是讽刺笔法的最初体现。除此之外,整篇翻译难度适中。

创世新灾

这是一则真实的故事。

---

① surreptitious: *Adjective* kept secret, especially because it would not be approved of 私下的;偷偷摸摸的(尤指因为不会被批准)(e.g. Low wages were supplemented by surreptitious payments from tradesmen. 商人私下付的报酬弥补了工资的不足。)

② unto: *Preposition* archaic term for "to" 介词"to"的古旧用法(e.g. Do unto others as you would be done by. 己所不欲,勿施于人。)

“一切都很正常，”医生说。“只管躺下休息便是。”医生的声音仿佛从数公里以外的地方传来，又仿佛对她大声说道：“你生了一个儿子。”

“你说什么？”

“你生的儿子很不错。我这样说，你明白的，对不对？一个不错的儿子。听到他的哭声没有呢？”

“医生，他一切还好吗？”

“当然，一切都好。”

“请让我看一眼吧。”

“一会儿你就会看到的。”

“你肯定，他一切都好吗？”

“我十分肯定。”

“他还在哭吗？”

“你尽量休息一下吧。没有什么可担心的。”

“他为什么停下来不哭了啊，医生？发生什么事情了？”

“拜托，不要激动。一切都很正常。”

“我想看一眼。就让我看一眼吧。”

“亲爱的女士，”医生边说，边轻轻拍了拍她的一只手。“你生了一个很不错的、强壮的、健康的孩子。我都这样对你说了，难道你还不相信我吗？”

“那儿有个女的，正在对他做什么呢？”

“正在给你的婴儿清理呢，好让你看到时，感觉赏心悦目，”医生说。“我们正给他稍微洗一洗呢，仅此而已。为此，你一定得给我们一时半会儿的时间。”

“你保证，他一切都很好吗？”

“我保证。现在，躺下休息吧。闭上眼睛。对了，闭上眼睛。这就对了。这样好多了吧。真乖，好样的……”

“医生，我祈祷了一遍又一遍，祈祷他活下来。”

“他当然会活下来的。你说的是什么话呢？”

“其他几个就没有。”

"你说什么?"

"医生,我生的其他几个孩子,一个都没有活下来。"

医生站在床边,低头看着这位年轻的母亲,只见她脸色苍白、精疲力竭。在此之前,他从未见过她。她跟她丈夫搬到这个城镇没有多久。旅店老板的妻子上楼来帮忙接生。她告诉他说,这位妇女的丈夫在边界处的本地海关部门工作;大约三个月前,这两个人突然而至,开着辆卡车直奔她的旅店,只带了一个手提箱。旅店老板的妻子还说,这位做丈夫的是个酒鬼,个子矮小、狂妄自大、盛气凌人、恃强凌弱,而他的妻子则温柔贤惠、笃信宗教;这个做妻子的闷闷不乐、从未笑过。她刚到的那几周时间里,旅店老板的妻子从来没有看到她微笑过一次。还有谣传说,这是这位丈夫的第三次婚姻了。前两次婚姻中,一个妻子死了,另一个因为品行方面的原因跟他离了婚。但,那仅仅是一个谣传。

医生弯下腰,把病人胸前的被单稍微向上拉了拉。"你没有什么好担心的,"他轻轻地说。"这个婴儿完全正常。"

"其他那几个,医生也是这么对我说的,说得一模一样。但是,医生,那几个,我都失去了。在过去十八个月的时间里,我失去了我所有三个孩子。所以,我目前这样焦虑不安,你一定不要责怪。"

"三个?"

"在四年的时间内……这是我第四个孩子。"

医生感到有些不怎么自在,在光秃秃的地面上换了换两只脚的重心。

"医生,我想,你不明白失去他们意味着什么——慢慢地,隔那么一段时间,一个接一个,三个孩子全都没有了。他们总是浮现在我的眼前。现在,我能清清楚楚地看见古斯塔夫的脸,好像他就躺着我的床上,躺在我的身旁。医生,古斯塔夫是个惹人喜爱的男孩儿,但是,他却病不离身。孩子总被疾病缠身,而你却无能力为、帮不上忙,那真是一件可怕的事情。"

"我知道。"

听到这儿,这位妇女睁开眼睛,盯着医生看了好儿秒钟,随后又闭上了。

“我的小女儿叫艾达,圣诞节前几天死的,也就是四个月前的事情。医生,我真的希望你能看到艾达。”

“现在,你又生了一个。”

“但,艾达太漂亮了。”

“是的,”医生说。“我知道。”

“你怎么会知道?”她大声问。

“我敢肯定,她是一个惹人喜爱的孩子,可这个新生的跟那个是一样的。”医生从床那儿转过身向窗户走去,站在窗前,向外望去。现在是四月的一个潮湿的下午,天空灰蒙蒙的。他看到对面大街上一座座房子的红色屋顶,还有大大的雨滴“噼里啪啦”洒落到屋顶的瓦片上。

“艾达当时才两岁啊,医生……她太漂亮了,从早晨我给她穿衣服起,直到晚上看着她上床安然入睡时为止,我都会目不转睛地看着她。当时,我经常生活在极度恐惧之中,担心她会发生什么不测。古斯塔夫已经去了,我的小奥托也已经去了,我就剩下她了。有的时候,我常常在夜间起来,轻手轻脚走到摇篮前,耳朵靠近她的嘴边,为的就是确定一下,她是不是还在继续呼吸。”

“尽量休息一下吧,”医生返回床边,说道。“请尽量休息一下吧。”这位母亲的脸苍白如纸,没有血色,但鼻孔和嘴的周围轻微带有一点淡淡的蓝灰色。几绺湿漉漉的头发从前额垂下,贴到了皮肤上。

“她死的时候……医生,当时我又怀孕了。艾达死时,现在出生的这个,已经怀了足足四个月了。‘我不想生下肚子里这个孩子!’葬礼之后,我喊道。‘我不愿意把这个孩子生下来!我埋葬的孩子已经够多了!’当时,我丈夫……一只手里端着一大杯啤酒,在客人中间溜溜达达……听我这么一说,快速转过身,说道:‘克拉拉,我有消息要告诉你,是好消息。’医生,你想象得出吗?当时,我们刚葬完第三个孩子,而他却手里端着杯啤酒站在那儿,说什么有好消息要告诉我。‘今天,给我调动工作了,调我去布劳瑙,’他说。‘所以嘛,你可以立刻打点行装。克拉拉,对你来说,这是一个新的起点,’他继续说。

‘到了一个新的地方,你会有一名新的医生……’”

“请不要再讲话了。”

“你就是那名新医生,是不是呢,医生?”

“说的没错。”

“现在我们已经搬过来了,在布劳瑙。”

“是的。”

“我很害怕,医生。”

“尽量不要害怕。”

“现在,第四个孩子存活的可能性有多大?”

“你必须停止那样的想法。”

“我忍不住的。我敢肯定,某种遗传的东西导致我的孩子一个一个像这样死去。一定是的。”

“你那是瞎说。”

“医生,奥托出生时,你知道我丈夫是怎么说的吗?他走进房间,看着躺在摇篮里的奥托,说道:‘为什么我*所有*的孩子都这么瘦小、虚弱呢?’”

“我敢肯定,他不会那样说。”

“他当时把头埋进摇篮,好像是在检查一只微小的昆虫,说道:‘我要说的就是,把我们的孩子制作成一个个*标本*,真的是再合适不过了。这就是我要说的。’他那话说完才三天,奥托就死了。第三天我们很快地就给奥托施以洗礼、取了名字,就在当天晚上,他就死了。接着,古斯塔夫和艾达也先后死去。三个孩子都死了,医生……突然之间,整座房子一下子空荡荡……”

“现在不要想这事儿了。”

“这一个,也是这样小吗?”

“这个孩子很正常。”

“但却很小?”

“或许,他是有点儿小,但是,小的经常比大的要更壮实。你就想象一下吧,希特勒夫人(“夫人”是用德语说的——译者注),明年的这个时候,他几乎就可以蹒跚而行了。这样想,难道不是很温馨吗?”

她没有回答。

“两年后的今天，说不定他就会没完没了地说个不停，让你发疯的。给他起好名字没有？”

“起名字？”

“是呀。”

“我不知道，我不敢肯定。我想，我丈夫说过，如果生下的是个男孩儿的话，就叫阿道夫斯。”

“那就等于说，他将取名为阿道夫(“阿道夫”为“阿道夫斯”的简化形式——译者注)。”

“是的，我丈夫喜欢阿道夫斯这个名字，因为它跟阿劳伊斯这个名字有点相似。我丈夫就叫阿劳伊斯。”

“棒极了。”

“哦，不！”她叫道，一下子从枕头上起来了。“奥托出生时，有人也问了同样的问题啊！那就意味着，他就要死了呀！你马上就要给他施以洗礼、取名字了啊！”

“喔，喔，”医生说，轻轻压着她的双肩。“你大错特错了。我保证，你说的不对。只不过是我这个人上了年纪就好奇、爱打听罢了。我也喜欢谈论名字。我想，阿道夫斯是一个相当不错的名字，也是我最喜欢的一个名字。看呐——孩子抱过来啦。”

旅店老板的妻子把婴儿高高竖立起，抱在她宽阔的胸前，穿过房间，如一艘挂帆之船，向床前驶来。“小美男来了！”她满脸堆笑，叫道。“我亲爱的，你想抱一抱吗？我把他放到你身旁，好吗？”

“包裹严实了没有？”医生问。“这里十分寒冷的。”

“当然，包得很严实。”

婴儿被严严实实地裹进一条白色的羊毛围巾中，只有那个小小的、粉粉的脑袋凸了出来。旅店老板的妻子轻轻地把他放到床上，放到了母亲的身旁。“你看呐，”她说。“现在，你可以躺在那儿，尽情看个够。”

“我想，你会喜欢他的，”医生微笑着说道。“他是一个很不错的小家伙。”

“他那双手太招人喜爱啦!”旅店老板的妻子说道。“手指这么修长啊!”

母亲没有动弹,甚至没有转头看一眼。

“快看啊!”旅店老板的妻子喊道。“他又不会咬你的啊!”

“我担心,我不敢看。我不敢去相信,我又生了个孩子,而且孩子还一切都好。”

“不要自欺欺人了。”

孩子就躺在母亲旁边的枕头上。她慢慢地转过头来,看着孩子那张小小的脸,那张脸是那样的平静,令人难以置信。

“这是我的孩子吗?”

“当然。”

“噢……噢……可是,他真的漂亮啊。”

医生转身向桌子走去,开始把东西放回自己的包里。母亲躺在床上,凝视着孩子。她一边微笑,一边抚摸着孩子,轻轻发出愉快而满足的声音。“嗨,阿道夫斯,”她小声说。“嗨,我的小阿道夫……”

“嘘——嘘!”旅店老板的妻子说。“听!我想,你丈夫来了。”

医生走过去,打开门,向走廊看去。

“是希特勒先生吗?”(“先生”是用德语说的,下同——译者注)

“是我。”

“请进。”

一名身穿深绿色制服的小个子男子轻轻跨进门,向周围观瞧着。

“祝贺了,”医生说。“你有一个儿子啦。”

这名男子的两鬓留着络腮胡子,是依照弗朗兹·约瑟夫皇帝的样式仔仔细细修剪出来的。他身上散发出浓烈的啤酒味道。“一个儿子?”

“是的。”

“他怎么样?”

“他很不错。你的妻子也不错。”

“很好。”这位做父亲的转过身,带点昂首阔步的架势走到妻子床前,走路的样子很是奇特。“那么,克拉拉,”他透过络腮胡子微笑着说道。“情况如何?”他弯腰看了看婴儿。接着,把腰弯得更低一些。他每弯一次腰,身体就停顿一下。经过一系列的停顿之后,他的腰也弯得越来越低了。最后,他的脸离婴儿的头只剩下三十厘米多一点儿的距离了。妻子枕着枕头,侧身躺着,眼睛盯着他,眼神中带有点儿哀求的意思。

“他那两片肺,奇妙无比,”旅店老板的妻子宣布。“你真应该听听他来到这个世界时的哭叫声。”

“可是,我的天啊,克拉拉……”

“亲爱的,怎么了?”

“这个孩子甚至比奥托还要小啊!”

医生快速向前迈出两三步。“这孩子没有任何问题的,”他说。

丈夫缓缓地直起腰来,从床那儿转过身来,看着医生。这位丈夫似乎困惑迷茫、痛苦忧伤。“医生,撒谎是没有任何好处的,”他说。“我知道那是什么意思,到头来,结果会如出一辙的。”

“现在,听我说,”医生说。

“可是,医生,你了*解*其他几个孩子的情况吗?”

“希特勒先生,你必须忘掉其他几个孩子的事儿,给这个孩子一个机会。”

“可是,也太小、太弱了啊!”

“我亲爱的先生,他才刚刚生下来啊。”

“即使这样……”

“你这是在干什么呢?”旅店老板的妻子叫道。“说服他进坟墓吗?”

“够了,”医生尖声叫道。

现在,母亲开始哭了起来,大声的哽咽令她的身体一抖一抖的。

医生走到这位丈夫跟前,一只手放到他的肩上。“对她好点儿吧,”医生低声耳语。“拜托了。这很重要。”接着,他使劲捏了一下这位丈夫的肩膀,开始暗暗使劲把他推到了床边。到了床边,他却犹豫再三、不肯继续。于是,医生捏得更用力了,用大拇指和手指头对肩膀的挤压示意他快点行动。最终,尽管不情愿,这位做丈夫的还是弯下身，轻轻亲了亲妻子的脸颊。

“好吧，克拉拉，”他说。“现在，不要哭了。”

“阿劳伊斯，我一再祈祷，祈祷他活下来。”

“嗯，知道。”

“好几个月以来，我每天都去教堂，双膝跪下，祈求老天让这个孩子活下来。”

“嗯，是的，克拉拉，我知道。”

“三个孩子相继死去，已经到了我能够忍受的极限了。难道你不明白吗？”

“当然明白。”

“阿劳伊斯，他一*定要*活下来。他一*定要*，一*定要*……噢，老天啊，现在，赐予他仁慈……”

第二节　《折翼天鹅》*The Swan*

罗尔德·达尔的《折翼天鹅》（The Swan）收录在《<非凡亨利>及另外六篇故事集》（The Wonderful Story of Henry Sugar and Six More）一书中，后来这篇小说被多家网络媒体引用，是一篇读后令人“惊诧不已”的小说，同时又是一篇令人感到“匪夷所思”的作品。

在研究罗尔德·达尔“非儿童类”作品的名义之下，本章所选的《折翼天鹅》其实具有“儿童类”文学作品的特点，只不过内容有些“血腥”，不太适合儿童阅读。但是，这篇是罗尔德·达尔早期短篇作品（区别于后期他所创作的诸多成功的长篇儿童文学作品，如《查利与巧克力工厂》等），因此被收录进来，作为研究的对象。

一、原作导读

笨拙而粗鲁的小子厄尼15岁生日的时候，得到的礼物是父亲送给他的一把来复枪。厄尼这小子，“在他生长的家庭环境中，身体暴力是家常便饭，就连他自己也被熏染成一个极其暴力的人”（Brought up in a household where physical violence was an everyday occurrence, he was himself an extremely violent person)。因此,他也就成了欺负其他孩子的“小霸王”,恃强凌弱。另一个孩子雷蒙德是他的伙伴,同时也成为他的“同伙”或“帮凶”。“放学后,他就抓小男生,将其胳膊扭到背后,并以此为乐。然后,他就命令小男生说些侮辱其父母的脏话”(He took great pleasure in catching small boys after school and twisting their arms behind their backs. Then he would order them to say insulting and filthy things about their own parents)。

厄尼带上作为生日礼物的来复枪,喊上雷蒙德,两人要出去打兔子。路上,他俩碰上了正在用双筒望远镜观察鸟类活动的彼得·沃森。彼得13岁,是个弱弱的小男孩儿,但他聪明,还有礼貌,却经常受人欺负。这次,他更是成为厄尼和雷蒙德这两个混混欺凌的对象了。

他俩用污言秽语侮辱彼得,还威胁说要开枪打死他,而雷蒙德则毫不示弱,说要是打死他,他俩就会得到惩罚,被送进跟监狱差不多的少年教养院。闻听此言,他俩退缩了,没有开枪,却将他摔倒在地,将他的手脚捆绑起来,拖到铁轨上,让他躺在两条铁轨之间,令他动弹不得。彼得意识到这两个家伙是玩真的,不会放自己走,于是,他就设法调整好自己的身体姿势,力求不会让呼啸而来的火车碰到自己而身亡。最终,火车呼啸而过,彼得毫发无损,躲过了这一劫。见此情景,厄尼和雷蒙德这两个混混很是失望,但仍不肯放过彼得,又心生一计,打算继续玩玩彼得。

他俩押着彼得来到附近一座湖的岸边——这个区域是水禽的自然保护区。他俩打算将彼得丢进湖中,但是,一只野鸭的出现令他俩改变了主意。厄尼举枪射击,射死了野鸭,要彼得充当猎狗去把野鸭“叼”回来。彼得不肯,厄尼就扇了他一巴掌,还威胁说要打掉他满口的牙齿,彼得不得不屈从。厄尼继续搜寻芦苇丛,要继续猎杀野鸭,但却有了新的发现:

“看那里面!”厄尼指着香蒲生长密集的一块区域,小声说。“我看见了,你看见没有?”

“哇,好家伙!”雷蒙德叫道。“太美啦!”

彼得站在稍远的距离上向灯芯草中看去,立刻认出来他们看到的是什么东西。那是一只天鹅,是一只华贵的白天鹅,正宁静地蹲坐在巢穴里,巢穴是用一大堆芦苇和灯芯草做成的,高出水面六十多厘米。这只天鹅就像一位湖中伟大的白衣贵妇人,高高地端坐在巢穴里。她的头转向湖岸那两个男孩子,机警起来,显得有所戒备的样子。

“Lookit in there!” Ernie whispered, pointing into a dense patch of bulrushes. “D'you see what I see?”

“Holy cats!” cried Raymond. “What a beauty!”

Peter, peering from a little further away into the rushes, saw at once what they were looking at. It was a swan, a magnificent white swan sitting serenely upon her nest. The nest itself was a huge pile of reeds and rushes that rose up about two feet above the waterline, and upon the top of all this the swan was sitting like a great white lady of the lake. Her head was turned towards the boys on the bank, alert and watchful.

厄尼射死了白天鹅,彼得只得奉命将其取回,却谎报实情,说没有小天鹅孵化出来。这样,小天鹅就幸免于难了。彼得将死去的天鹅扔到地上,忍无可忍,开始大骂出口,指责这两个家伙的罪恶行径,谴责这两个家伙不该射杀天鹅。听到这话,厄尼若有所思,说道:

“所以嘛,要是我能让这只天鹅复活、再度翱翔蓝天的话,那么,你就会开心。对吗?”

“又是一个问得很愚蠢的问题!”彼得叫道。“你认为你是谁呢?”

“我要告诉你我是谁,”厄尼说。“我是魔术师,那就是我。仅仅为了使你开心、满意,我即将变一个魔术,把这只死天鹅变活,并再度飞翔在天空。”

"So if I could make this swan come alive and go flyin' round the sky all over again, then you'd be 'appy. Right?"

"That's another stupid question!" Peter cried out. "Who d'you think you are?"

"I'll tell you 'oo I am," Ernie said. "I'm a magic man, that's 'oo I am. And just to make you 'appy and contented, I am about to do a magic trick that'll make this dead swan come alive and go flyin' all over the sky once again."

厄尼砍下死去天鹅的两只翅膀,跟雷蒙德一起将翅膀分别绑到彼得的两只胳膊上,然后命令他爬上湖岸一棵高高的垂柳,好让他从树上跳下,以便起飞。彼得爬上树,隐藏到垂柳的枝叶间,不肯往下跳。于是,他俩气急败坏,开始射击,一颗子弹击中了彼得的大腿,令他站立不稳,开始跌落。慌忙之中,他抓住了一根细枝,但细枝脆弱,不堪重负,就要折断。就在这一瞬间,彼得猛然醒悟,猛冲下去,展开了双翼……

就在那天的下午,正在厨房洗碗的沃森太太偶然间向窗外瞥了一眼,看见一个白色的东西"扑棱"一下,落到自家后花园的草坪上。她冲出门,奔了过去。

"哎呀,我亲爱的孩子!"她叫了起来,火冒三丈,几乎无法相信眼前所见。"我亲爱的孩子!你这是怎么了?"

"我的一条腿疼,"彼得睁开了眼睛说道。随后,他就晕了过去。

"Oh, my darling!" she cried, near to hysterics and hardly believing what she saw. "My darling boy! What happened to you?"

"My leg hurts," Peter said, opening his eyes. Then he fainted.

二、原作释读

阅读这篇小说,要充分体会好"小霸王"的种种"匪夷所思"的行为,还要注意辨别对话中一些非标准的表达形式,这应该是阅读的一个障碍。

The Swan①

Ernie had been given a .22 rifle for his birthday. His father, who was already slouching② on the sofa watching the telly③ at nine-thirty on this Saturday morning, said. "Let's see what you can pot④, boy. Make yourself useful. Bring us back a rabbit for supper."

"There's rabbits in that big field the other side of the lake," Ernie said. "I seen⑤ 'em⑥."

"Then go out and nab⑦ one," the father said, picking breakfast from between his front teeth with a split matchstick. "Go out and nab us a rabbit."

---

① 本部小说原文出自"DAHL, R. *The Wonderful Story of Henry Sugar and Six More* [M]. London: Penguin Books Ltd., 2002"。

② slouch: *Verb* [no obj., with adverbial] stand, move, or sit in a lazy, drooping way 没精打采地站(或动、坐)(e.g. He slouched against the wall. 他没精打采地靠在墙上。)

③ telly: *Noun* (Brit. informal) term for television(英国英语的非正式用法)同"television"(电视)

④ pot: *Verb* (informal) hit or kill (someone or something) by shooting(非正式)击中;射死(e.g. He was shot in the eye as neighbours potted clay pigeons. 邻居们在射泥鸽子时射中了他的眼睛。)

⑤ I seen = I have seen 这样的表达由儿童说话不标准所致。本篇小说中,有很多类似的不标准表达,读者要注意辨别。

⑥ 'em = them

⑦ nab: *Verb* [with obj.] (informal) catch (someone) doing something wrong(非正式)捉住;逮住(e.g. Olympic drug tests nabbed another athlete yesterday. 昨天奥林匹克药物检测又逮住了一个运动员。)

"I'll get yer[①] two," Ernie said.

"And on the way back," the father said, "get me a quart bottle of brown ale[②]."

"Gimme[③] the money, then," Ernie said.

The father, without taking his eyes from the TV screen, fished in his pocket for a pound note. "And don't try pinchin'[④] the change like you did last time," he said. "You'll get a thick ear if you do, birthday or no birthday."

"Don't worry," Ernie said.

"And if you want to practise and get your eye in[⑤] with that gun," the father said, "birds is best. See 'ow[⑥] many spadgers[⑦] you can knock down, right?"

"Right," Ernie said. "There's spadgers all the way up the lane in the 'edges[⑧]. Spadgers is easy."

"If you think spadgers is easy," the father said, "go get yourself a

---

① yer: *Pronoun* non-standard spelling of "you", used in representing dialectal speech(非规范的方言表达)同"you"(你,你们)

② ale: *Noun* [mass noun] (chiefly Brit.) any beer other than lager, stout, or porter(主要为英国英语表达)(除陈啤酒、浓烈黑啤酒或黑啤酒之外的)麦芽啤酒

③ gimme = give me

④ pinchin' = pinching

⑤ get (keep) one's eye in: (Brit.) become (or remain) able to make good judgements, especially visual ones, about a task or occupation in which one is engaged(英国英语)对(从事的任务或工作)目测准确;眼光准确(e.g. I've got my eye in now; I'm landing them just where I want them. 我现在对得很准,正把它们降在我想要的地方。)

⑥ 'ow = how

⑦ spadger: *Noun* a sparrow 麻雀

⑧ 'edges = hedges

jenny wren[①]. Jenny wrens is 'alf[②] the size of spadgers and they never sit still for one second. Get yourself a jenny wren before you start shootin'[③] yer mouth off[④] about 'ow clever you is."

"Now, Albert," his wife said, looking up from the sink. "That's not nice, shootin' little birds in the nestin'[⑤] season. I don't mind rabbits, but little birds in the nestin' season is another thing altogether."

"Shut your mouth," the father said. "Nobody's askin'[⑥] your opinion. And listen to me, boy," he said to Ernie. "Don't go waving that thing about in the street because you ain't[⑦] got no licence. Stick it down your trouser-leg till you're out in the country, right?"

"Don't worry," Ernie said. He took the gun and the box of bullets and went out to see what he could kill. He was a big lout[⑧] of a boy, fifteen years old this birthday. Like his truck-driver father, he had small slitty[⑨] eyes set very close together near the top of the nose. His mouth was loose, the lips often wet. Brought up in a household where physical violence was an everyday occurrence, he was himself an extremely violent

---

① jenny wren: *Noun* (Brit. informal) a wren, any of several small active brown birds of the northern hemisphere with short upright tails; they feed on insects (英国英语的非正式用法)(雌)鹪鹩

② 'alf = half

③ shootin' = shooting

④ shoot one's mouth off: (informal) talk boastfully or indiscreetly(非正式)胡吹;随便乱说

⑤ nestin' = nesting

⑥ askin' = asking

⑦ 这里的"ain't"为非标准用法,相当于"aren't"。

⑧ lout: *Noun* an uncouth or aggressive man or boy 笨拙的人;乡巴佬;举止粗鲁的人

⑨ slitty: *Adjective* (chiefly derogatory) (of the eyes) long and narrow(主要为贬义用法)(眼睛)细长的

person. Most Saturday afternoons, he and a gang of friends travelled by train or bus to football matches, and if they didn't manage to get into a bloody fight before they returned home, they considered it a wasted day. He took great pleasure in catching small boys after school and twisting their arms behind their backs. Then he would order them to say insulting and filthy things about their own parents.

"Ow[1]! Please don't, Ernie! Please?"

"Say it or I'll twist your arm off!"

They always said it. Then he would give the arm an extra twist and the victim would go off in tears.

Ernie's best friend was called Raymond. He lived four doors away, and he, too, was a big boy for his age. But while Ernie was heavy and loutish[2], Raymond was tall, slim and muscular.

Outside Raymond's house, Ernie put two fingers in his mouth and gave a long shrill whistle. Raymond came out. "Look what I got for me birthday," Ernie said, showing the gun.

"Gripes[3]!" Raymond said. "We can have some fun with that!"

"Come on, then," Ernie said. "We're goin'[4] up to the big field the other side of the lake to get us a rabbit."

The two boys set off. This was a Saturday morning in May, and the countryside was beautiful around the small village where the boys lived.

---

① ow: *Exclamation* used to express sudden pain(用于表示突然的疼痛)啊唷(e.g. Ow! You're hurting me!. 啊唷！你弄疼我了！)

② loutish: *Adjective* having the characteristics of a lout; awkward, stupid, and boorish 笨拙的;粗野的(e.g. He was not as loutish as his manner suggested. 他举止粗野,但人不是那样的。)

③ cripes: *Interjection* used to express annoyance, anger, or dismay(表示惊讶、烦恼、厌恶等)天呐;啊呀

④ goin' = going

The chestnut[①] trees were in full flower and the hawthorn[②] was white along the hedges. To reach the big rabbit field, Ernie and Raymond had first to walk down a narrow hedgy lane for half a mile. Then they must cross the railway line, and go round the big lake where wild ducks and moorhens[③] and coots[④] and ring-ouzels[⑤] lived. Beyond the lake, over the hill and down the other side, lay the rabbit field. This was all private land belonging to Mr. Douglas Highton and the lake itself was a sanctuary[⑥] for waterfowl[⑦].

All the way up the lane, they took turns with the gun, potting at

---

① chestnut or sweet chestnut: *Noun* a glossy hard brown edible nut, which may be roasted and eaten 栗子

② hawthorn: *Noun* a thorny shrub or tree of the rose family, with white, pink, or red blossom and small dark red fruits (haws). Native to north temperate regions, it is commonly used for hedging in Britain 山楂

③ moorhen: *Noun* a small aquatic rail with mainly blackish plumage 水鸡;黑水鸡

④ coot: *Noun* an aquatic bird of the rail family, with blackish plumage, lobed feet, and a bill that extends back on to the forehead as a horny shield 大(番鸟);白骨顶

⑤ ring ouzel or ring ousel: *Noun* a European thrush that resembles a blackbird with a white crescent across the breast, inhabiting upland moors and mountainous country 环颈(黑)鸫

⑥ sanctuary: *Noun* [usu. with modifier] a nature reserve 自然保护区;禁猎区(e.g. a bird sanctuary 鸟类禁猎区)

⑦ waterfowl: *Noun* [plural noun] ducks, geese, or other large aquatic birds, especially when regarded as game 水鸟;水禽

small birds in the hedges. Ernie got a bullfinch① and a hedge-sparrow②. Raymond got a second bullfinch, a whitethroat③ and a yellowhammer④. As each bird was killed, they tied it by the legs to a line of string. Raymond never went anywhere without a big ball of string in his jacket pocket, and a knife. Now they had five little birds dangling on the line of string.

"You know something," Raymond said. "We can eat these."

"Don't talk so daft," Ernie said. "There's not enough meat on one of those to feed a woodlouse⑤."

"There is, too," Raymond said. "The Frenchies⑥ eat 'em and so do the Eyeties⑦. Mr. Sanders told us about it in class. He said the Frenchies and the Eyeties put up nets and catch 'em by the million and then they eat 'em."

"All right, then," Ernie said. "Let's see 'ow many we can get. Then we'll take 'em 'ome⑧ and put 'em in the rabbit stew."

---

① bullfinch: *Noun* a stocky Eurasian finch with a short thick bill, and typically with grey or pinkish plumage, dark wings, and a white rump 红腹灰雀

② hedge sparrow: *Noun* (Animals) a small brownish European songbird, also called: dunnock 篱雀;岩鹨

③ whitethroat: *Noun* a migratory Eurasian and North African warbler with a grey head and white throat 白喉林莺

④ yellowhammer: *Noun* a common Eurasian bunting, the male of which has a yellow head, neck, and breast 黄鹀

⑤ woodlouse: *Noun* a small terrestrial crustacean with a greyish segmented body and seven pairs of legs, living in damp habitats 鼠妇;潮虫;窃虫;土鳖

⑥ Frenchy or Frenchie: *Adjective* (informal, chiefly derogatory) a French person(主要为非正式的贬义用法)法国人

⑦ Eyetie: *Noun* (Brit. informal, offensive) Italian or an Italian(英国英语非正式的冒犯语)意大利人

⑧ 'ome = home

As they progressed up the lane, they shot at every little bird they saw. By the time they got to the railway line, they had fourteen small birds dangling on the line of string.

"Hey!" whispered Ernie, pointing with a long arm. "Look over there!"

There was a group of trees and bushes alongside the railway line, and beside one of the bushes stood a small boy. He was looking up into the branches of an old tree through a pair of binoculars.

"You know who that is?" Raymond whispered back. "It's that little twerp① Watson."

"You're right!" Ernie whispered. "It's Watson, the scum of the earth②!"

Peter Watson was always the enemy. Ernie and Raymond detested him because he was nearly everything that they were not. He had a small frail body. His face was freckled and he wore spectacles with thick lenses. He was a brilliant pupil, already in the senior class at school although he was only thirteen. He loved music and played the piano well. He was no good at games. He was quiet and polite. His clothes, although patched and darned, were always clean. And his father did not drive a truck or work in a factory. He worked in the bank.

"Let's give the little perisher③ a fright," Ernie whispered.

---

① twerp or twirp: *Noun* (informal) a silly or annoying person(非正式)笨蛋;讨厌的家伙

② the scum of the earth: the worst type of people that can be imagined 人渣;社会渣滓(e. g. Drug dealers are the scum of the earth. 毒品贩子是社会的渣滓。)

③ perisher: *Noun* (Brit. informal) a term used, often affectionately, for a mischievous or awkward person or thing, especially a child(主要为英国英语的非正式表达)讨厌鬼,淘气鬼(尤指孩子,常带感情色彩)(e. g. some pushy little perisher 某个莽撞的小淘气鬼。)

The two bigger boys crept up close to the small boy, who didn't see them because he still had binoculars to his eyes.

"*'Ands*[1] *up*!" shouted Ernie, pointing the gun.

Peter Watson jumped. He lowered the binoculars and stared through his spectacles at the two intruders.

"Go on!" Ernie shouted. "Stick 'em up!"

"I wouldn't point that gun if I were you," Peter Watson said.

"*We're* givin'[2] the orders round 'ere[3]!" Ernie said.

"So stick 'em up," Raymond said, "unless you want a slug[4] in the guts!"

Peter Watson stood quite still, holding the binoculars in front of him with both hands. He looked at Raymond. Then he looked at Ernie. He was not afraid, but he knew better than to play the fool with these two. He had suffered a good deal from their attentions[5] over the years.

"What do you want?" he asked.

"*I want you to stick 'em up*!" Ernie yelled at him. "Can't you understand English?"

Peter Watson didn't move.

"I'll count to five," Ernie said. "And if they're not up by then, you get it in the guts. One...Two...Three..."

Peter Watson raised his arms slowly above his head. It was the only

---

① 'ands = hands

② givin' = giving

③ 'ere = here

④ slug: *Noun* a bullet, especially one of lead(尤指铅制的)子弹

⑤ attention: *Noun* [count noun] (attentions) a person's interest in someone, especially when unwelcome or regarded as excessive(尤指不受欢迎的或过分的)关注(e.g. His primary aim was to avoid the attentions of the newspapers. 他的首要目的是要避开报界的关注。)

sensible thing to do. Raymond stepped forward and snatched the binoculars from his hands. "What's this?" he snapped. "Who you spyin'[1] on?"

"Nobody."

"Don't lie, Watson. Them things is used for spyin'! I'll bet you was spyin' on us? That's right, ain't it? Confess it!"

"I certainly wasn't spying on you."

"Give 'im[2] a clip[3] over the ear," Ernie said. "Teach 'im not to lie to us."

"I'll do that in a minute," Raymond said. "I'm just workin'[4] meself[5] up."

Peter Watson considered the possibility of trying to escape. All he could do would be to turn and run, and that was pointless. They'd catch him in seconds. And if he shouted for help, there was no one to hear him. All he could do, therefore, was to keep calm and try to talk his way out of the situation.

"Keep them 'ands up!" Ernie barked, waving the barrel of the gun gently from side to side the way he had seen it done by gangsters on the telly. "Go on, laddie[6], reach!"

Peter did as he was told.

---

① spyin' = spying

② 'im = him

③ clip: *Noun* (informal) a smart or glancing blow(非正式)猛击;擦击(e. g. I'd give him a clip round the ear. 我要抽他一耳光。)

④ workin' = working

⑤ meself: *Pronoun* non-standard spelling of "myself", used as representative of informal speech(非规范、非正式表达)同"myself"

⑥ laddie: *Noun* (informal, chiefly Scottish) a boy or young man (often as a form of address)(主要为苏格兰的非正式用法)(常作称谓)少年;年轻人;老弟

"So 'oo[①] was you spyin' on?" Raymond asked. "Out with it!"

"I was watching a green woodpecker[②]," Peter said.

"A what?"

"A male green woodpecker. He was tapping the trunk of that old dead tree, searching for grubs[③]."

"Where is 'ee[④]?" Ernie snapped, raising his gun. "I'll 'ave[⑤] 'im!"

"No, you won't," Peter said, looking at the string of tiny birds slung over Raymond's shoulder. "He flew off the moment you shouted. Woodpeckers are extremely timid."

"What you watchin'[⑥] 'im for?" Raymond asked suspiciously. "What's the point? Don't you 'ave nothin'[⑦] better to do?"

"It's fun watching birds," Peter said. "It's a lot more fun than shooting them."

"Why, you cheeky[⑧] little bleeder[⑨]!" Ernie cried. "So you don't like us shootin' birds, eh? Is that what you're sayin'[⑩]?"

"I think it's absolutely pointless."

---

① 'oo = who

② woodpecker: *Noun* a bird with a strong bill and a stiff tail, which climbs tree trunks to find insects and drums on dead wood to mark territory 啄木鸟

③ grub: *Noun* the larva of an insect, especially a beetle 蛴螬;昆虫的幼虫

④ 'ee = he

⑤ 'ave = have

⑥ watchin' = watching

⑦ nothin' = nothing

⑧ cheeky: *Adjective* impudent or irreverent, typically in an endearing or amusing way(常指可爱有趣的)老脸皮的;目无尊长的;无礼的

⑨ bleeder: *Noun* [with adj.] (Brit. informal) a person regarded with contempt, disrespect, or pity(英国英语的非正式用法)被人瞧不起的人;被蔑视的人;可怜虫;倒霉蛋

⑩ sayin' = saying

"You don't like anything we do, isn't that right?" Raymond said.

Peter didn't answer.

"Well, let me tell you something," Raymond went on. "We don't like anything you do either."

Peter's arms were beginning to ache. He decided to take a risk. Slowly, he lowered them to his sides.

"Up!" yelled Ernie. "Get 'em up!"

"What if I refuse?"

"Blimey[①]! You got a ruddy[②] nerve, ain't you?" Ernie said. "I'm tellin'[③] you for the last time, if you don't stick 'em up I'll pull the trigger!"

"That would be a criminal act," Peter said. "It would be a case for the police."

"And you'd be a case for the 'ospital[④]!" Ernie said.

"Go ahead and shoot," Peter said. "Then they'll send you to Borstal[⑤]. That's prison."

He saw Ernie hesitate.

"You're really askin' for it, ain't you?" Raymond said.

"I'm simply asking to be left alone," Peter said, "I haven't done

---

① blimey or cor blimey: *Exclamation* (Brit. informal) used to express one's surprise, excitement, or alarm(英国英语的非正式用法)哎呀;天呐(表示惊奇、激动或惊恐)

② ruddy: *Adjective* (Brit. informal, dated) used as a euphemism for 'bloody'(英国英语的非正式古旧用法)非常的;极度的;十足的;该死的(用作 bloody 的委婉语)

③ tellin' = telling

④ 'ospital = hospital

⑤ borstal: *Noun* [mass noun] (Brit. historical) a custodial institution for young offenders(英国历史上的用法)青少年犯教养院

you any harm."

"You're a stuck-up[①] little squirt[②]," Ernie said. "That's exactly what you are, a stuck-up little squirt."

Raymond leaned over and whispered something in Ernie's ear. Ernie listened intently. Then he slapped his thigh and said, "I like it! It's a great idea!"

Ernie placed his gun on the ground and advanced upon the small boy. He grabbed him and threw him to the ground. Raymond took the roll of string from his pocket and cut off a length of it. Together, they forced the boy's arms in front of him and tied his wrists together tight.

"Now the legs," Raymond said. Peter struggled and received a punch in the stomach. That winded[③] him and he lay still. Next, they tied his ankles together with more string. He was now trussed[④] up like a chicken and completely helpless.

Ernie picked up his gun, and then, with his other hand, he grabbed one of Peter's arms. Raymond grabbed the other arm and together they began to drag the boy over the grass towards the railway lines.

---

① stuck-up: *Adjective* (informal) staying aloof from others because one thinks one is superior(非正式)高傲自大的;自命不凡的

② squirt: *Noun* (informal) a person perceived to be insignificant, impudent, or presumptuous(非正式)无足轻重的人;厚颜无耻的人;妄自尊大的人(e.g. What did he see in this patronizing little squirt? 他在这个傲慢自大的小人身上看中了什么?)

③ wind: *Verb* [with obj.] (usu. as "be winded") cause (someone) to have difficulty breathing because of exertion or a blow to the stomach 使气急;使胃部受击呼吸困难(e.g. The fall nearly winded him. 这一跌使他几乎喘不过气来。)

④ truss: *Verb* tie up (someone) with their arms at their sides 捆缚;绑(某人)(e.g. I found him trussed up in his cupboard. 我发现他被捆在他家的食柜里。)

Peter kept absolutely quiet. Whatever it was they were up to, talking to them wasn't going to help matters.

They dragged their victim down the embankment[①] and on to the railway lines themselves. Then one took the arms and the other the feet and they lifted him up and laid him down again lengthwise[②] right between two lines.

"You're mad!" Peter said. "You can't do this!"

"'Oo says we can't? This is just a little lesson we're teachin'[③] you not to be cheeky."

"More string," Ernie said.

Raymond produced the ball of string and the two larger boys now proceeded to tie the victim down in such a way that he couldn't wriggle away from between the rails. They did this by looping string around each of his arms and then threading the string under the rails on either side. They did the same with his middle body and his ankles. When they had finished, Peter Watson was strung down helpless and virtually immobile between the rails. The only parts of his body he could move to any extent were his head and feet.

Ernie and Raymond stepped back to survey their handiwork[④]. "We done a nice job," Ernie said.

---

① embankment: *Noun* a bank of earth or stone built to carry a road or railway over an area of low ground(公路或铁路的)路堤

② lengthwise: *Adverb* lengthways 纵长地;直地(e. g. Halve the potatoes lengthwise. 把土豆顺长地切成两半。)

③ teachin' = teaching

④ handiwork: *Noun* [mass noun] (one's handiwork) something that one has made or done(某人的)做的东西;作品(e. g. The dressmakers stood back to survey their handiwork. 裁缝退后几步,审视他们自己的作品。)

"There's trains every 'arf[①] 'our[②] on this line," Raymond said. "We ain't gonna[③] 'ave long to wait."

"This is murder!" cried the small boy lying between the rails.

"No it ain't." Raymond told him. "It ain't anything of the sort."

"Let me go! Please let me go! I'll be killed if a train comes along!"

"If you *are* killed, sonny[④] boy," Ernie said, "it'll be your own ruddy fault and I'll tell you why. Because if you lift your 'ead[⑤] up like you're doin'[⑥] now, then you've 'ad[⑦] it, chum[⑧]! You keep down flat and you might just possibly get away with it. On the other 'and, you might not because I ain't exactly sure 'ow much clearance[⑨] them trains've got underneath. You 'appen[⑩] to know, Raymond, 'ow much clearance them trains got underneath?"

"Very little," Raymond said. "They're built ever so close to the ground."

"Might be enough and it might not," Ernie said.

"Let's put it this way," Raymond said. "It'd probably just about be

---

① 'arf = half

② 'our = hour

③ gonna = going to

④ sonny: *Noun* (informal) used by an older person as a familiar form of address to a young boy(非正式)(年长者对小男孩的昵称)小家伙;小弟弟;宝宝乖儿

⑤ 'ead = head

⑥ doin' = doing

⑦ 'ad = had

⑧ chum: *Noun* a form of address between men or boys expressing familiarity or friendliness 朋友(用于男人或男孩间表示友好熟识的称呼)

⑨ clearance: *Noun* clear space allowed for a thing to move past or under another 移动空间(e. g. Always give cyclists plenty of clearance. 勿忘常给骑自行车者留出足够的移动空间。)

⑩ 'appen = happen

enough for an *ordinary* person like me or you, Ernie. But Mister Watson 'ere I'm not so sure about and I'll tell you why."

"Tell me," Ernie said, egging him on.

"Mister Watson 'ere's① got an extra big 'ead, that's why. 'Ee's so flippin'② big-'eaded I personally think the bottom bit of the train's goin' to scrape 'im whatever 'appens③. I'm not saying it's goin' to take 'is④ 'ead off, mind you. In fact, I'm pretty sure it ain't goin' to do that. But it's goin' to give 'is face a good old scrapin'⑤ over. You can be quite sure of that."

"I think you're right," Ernie said.

"It don't do," Raymond said, "to 'ave a great big swollen 'ead full of brains if you're lyin'⑥ on the railway line with a train comin'⑦ towards you. That's right, ain't it, Ernie?"

"That's right," Ernie said.

The two bigger boys climbed back up the embankment and sat on the grass behind some bushes. Ernie produced a pack of cigarettes and they both lit up.

Peter Watson, lying helpless between the rails, realized now that they were not going to release him. These were dangerous, crazy boys. They lived for the moment and never considered the consequences. I must try to keep calm and think, Peter told himself. He lay there, quite

---

① 'ere's = here's: here is

② flippin' = flipping: *Adjective* [attrib.] (informal, chiefly Brit.) used for emphasis or to express mild annoyance(主要为英国英语的非正式用法)该死的;讨厌的(用于加强语气或表示轻微恼怒)(e.g. Are you out of your flipping mind? 你难道真的疯了吗?)

③ 'appens = happens

④ 'is = his

⑤ scrapin' = scraping

⑥ lyin' = lying

⑦ comin' = coming

still, weighing his chances. His chances were good. The highest part of his head was his nose. He estimated the end of his nose was sticking up about four inches above the rails. Was that too much? He wasn't quite sure what clearance these modern diesels had above the ground. It certainly wasn't very much. The back of his head was resting upon loose gravel in between two sleepers. He must try to burrow down a little into the gravel. So he began to wriggle his head from side to side, pushing the gravel away and gradually making for himself a small indentation, a hole in the gravel. In the end, he reckoned he had lowered his head an extra two inches. That would do for the head. But what about the feet? They were sticking up, too. He took care of that by swinging the two tied-together feet over to one side so they lay almost flat.

He waited for the train to come.

Would the driver see him? It was very unlikely, for this was the main line, London, Doncaster①, York②, Newcastle③ and Scotland, and

---

① Doncaster: *Noun* an industrial town in northern England; pop. 284,300 (1991) 唐克斯特(英国北部一工业城镇,1991 年人口 284,300。)

② York: *Noun* a city in northern England, on the River Ouse, a unitary council formerly in Yorkshire; pop. 100,600 (1991). The Romans occupied the site, known as Eboracum, from ad 71 until about ad 400; in ad 867 it was taken by the Vikings. It is the seat of the Archbishop of York and is noted for its magnificent cathedral, York Minster 约克(英国英格兰北部城市,位于奥斯河河畔,为前约克郡的一个采取集权制市政委员会政体的城市,1991 年人口 100,600;公元 71 年至 400 年被罗马人侵占,称为伊保勒肯;公元 867 年被北欧海盗占领;约克市为约克大主教所在地,以其壮观宏伟的大教堂——约克大教堂闻名。)

③ Newcastle: *Noun* an industrial city in NE England, a port on the River Tyne; pop. 263,000 (1991). Full name Newcastle-upon-Tyne 纽卡斯尔(英格兰东北部的一个工业城市,泰恩河上一港口,1991 年人口 263,000,全称“泰恩河畔纽卡斯尔”。)

they used huge long engines in which the driver sat in a cab[①] way back and kept an eye open only for the signals. Along this stretch of the track trains travelled around eighty miles an hour. Peter knew that. He had sat on the bank many times watching them. When he was younger, he used to keep a record of their numbers in a little book, and sometimes the engines had names written on their sides in gold letters.

Either way, he told himself, it was going to be a terrifying business. The noise would be deafening, and the swish of the eighty-mile-an-hour wind wouldn't be much fun either. He wondered for a moment whether there would be any kind of vacuum created underneath the train as it rushed over him, sucking him upward. There might well be. So whatever happened, he must concentrate everything upon pressing his entire body against the ground. Don't go limp. Keep stiff and tense and press down into the ground.

"How're you doin', rat-face!" one of them called out to him from the bushes above. "What's it like waitin'[②] for the execution?"

He decided not to answer. He watched the blue sky above his head where a single cumulus[③] cloud was drifting slowly from left to right. And to keep his mind off the thing that was going to happen soon, he played a game that his father had taught him long ago on a hot summer's day when they were lying on their backs in the grass above the cliffs at Beachy

---

① cab: *Noun* the driver's compartment in a lorry, bus, or train(卡车、汽车或火车的)驾驶室

② waitin' = waiting

③ cumulus: [mass noun] (Meteorology) cloud forming rounded masses heaped on each other above a flat base at fairly low altitude(气象学)积云

Head[①]. The game was to look for strange faces in the folds and shadows and billows of a cumulus cloud. If you looked hard enough, his father had said, you would always find a face of some sort up there. Peter let his eyes travel slowly over the cloud. In one place, he found a one-eyed man with a beard. In another, there was a long-chinned laughing witch. An aeroplane came across the cloud travelling from east to west. It was a small high-winged monoplane with a red fuselage. An old Piper Cub, he thought it was. He watched it until it disappeared.

And then, quite suddenly, he heard a curious little vibrating sound coming from the rails on either side of him. It was very soft, this sound, scarcely audible, a tiny little humming, thrumming[②] whisper that seemed to be coming along the rails from far away.

That's a train, he told himself.

The vibrating along the rails grew louder, then louder still. He raised his head and looked down the long and absolutely straight railway line that stretched away for a mile or more into the distance. It was then that he saw the train. At first it was only a speck, a faraway black dot, but in those few seconds that he kept his head raised, the dot grew bigger and bigger, and it began to take shape, and soon it was no longer a dot but the big, square, blunt front-end of a diesel express. Peter dropped his head and pressed it down hard into the small hole he had dug for it in the gravel. He swung his feet over to one side. He shut his eyes tight and tried to sink his body into the ground.

---

① Beachy Head: *Noun* a chalk headland in Southeastern England, rising to 162 metres (531 ft) above sea level 白垩峭壁(海拔 162 米[531 英尺]高,位于英格兰东南沿岸。)

② thrum: *Verb* [no obj.] make a continuous rhythmic humming sound 低沉地嗡嗡作响(e. g. the boat's huge engines thrummed in his ears. 船上的巨型发动机在他的耳边嗡嗡作响。)

The train came over him like an explosion. It was as though a gun had gone off in his head. And with the explosion came a tearing, screaming wind that was like a hurricane blowing down his nostrils and into his lungs. The noise was shattering. The wind choked him. He felt as if he were being eaten alive and swallowed up in the belly of a screaming murderous monster.

And then it was over. The train had gone. Peter opened his eyes and saw the blue sky and the big white cloud still drifting overhead. It was all over now and he had done it. He had survived.

"It missed 'im," said a voice.

"What a pity," said another voice.

He glanced sideways and saw the two large louts standing over him.

"Cut 'im loose," Ernie said.

Raymond cut the strings binding him to the rails on either side.

"Undo 'is feet so 'ee can walk, but keep 'is 'ands tied," Ernie said.

Raymond cut the strings around his ankles.

"Get up," Ernie said.

Peter got to his feet.

"You're still a prisoner, matey①," Ernie said.

"What about them rabbits?" Raymond asked. "I thought we was goin' to try for a few rabbits?"

"Plenty of time for that," Ernie answered. "I just thought we'd push the little bleeder into the lake on the way."

"Good," Raymond said. "Cool 'im down."

"You've had your fun," Peter Watson said. "Why don't you let me go now?"

---

① matey: *Noun* used as a familiar and typically hostile form of address, especially to a stranger(用于故作亲近但有敌意的称呼,多对陌生人)伙计;朋友

"Because you're a prisoner," Ernie said. "And you ain't just no ordinary prisoner neither. You're a spy. And you know what 'appens to spies when they get caught, don't you? They get put up against the wall and shot."

Peter didn't say any more after that. There was no point at all in provoking those two. The less he said to them and the less he resisted them, the more chance he would have of escaping injury. He had no doubt whatsoever that in their present mood they were capable of doing him quite serious bodily harm. He knew for a fact that Ernie had once broken little Wally Simpson's arm after school and Wally's parents had gone to the police. He had also heard Raymond boasting about what he called "putting the boot in①" at the football matches they went to. This, he understood, meant kicking someone in the face or body when he was lying on the ground. They were hooligans, these two, and from what Peter read in his father's newspaper nearly every day, they were not by any means on their own. It seemed the whole country was full of hooligans. They wrecked the interiors of trains, they fought pitched battles② in the streets with knives and bicycle chains and metal clubs, they attacked pedestrians, especially other young boys walking alone, and they smashed up roadside cafés. Ernie and Raymond, though perhaps not quite yet fully qualified hooligans, were most definitely on their way.

Therefore, Peter told himself, he must continue to be passive. Do not insult them. Do not aggravate③ them in any way. And above all, do

---

① put the boot in (into) someone: (Brit. informal) kick someone hard when they are on the ground(英国英语的非正式用法)(在对方倒地后)狠狠踢上一脚

② pitched battle: *Noun* a violent confrontation involving large numbers of people 酣战;激战

③ aggravate: Verb (informal) annoy or exasperate (someone), especially persistently(非正式)(尤指不断地)激怒(某人);使恼火

not try to take them on physically. Then, hopefully, in the end, they might become bored with this nasty little game and go off to shoot rabbits.

The two larger boys had each taken hold of one of Peter's arms and they were marching him across the next field towards the lake. The prisoner's wrists were still tied together in front of him. Ernie carried the gun in his spare hand. Raymond carried the binoculars he had taken from Peter. They came to the lake.

The lake was beautiful on this golden May morning. It was a long and fairly narrow lake with tall willow trees growing here and there along its banks. In the middle, the water was clear and clean, but nearer to the land there was a forest of reeds and bulrushes①.

Ernie and Raymond marched their prisoner to the edge of the lake and there they stopped.

"Now then," Ernie said. "What I suggest is this. You take 'is arms and I take 'is legs and we'll swing the little perisher one two three as far out as we can into them nice muddy reeds. 'Ow's② that?"

"I like it," Raymond said. "And leave 'is 'ands tied together, right?"

"Right," Ernie said. "'Ow's that with you, snot-nose③?"

"If that's what you're going to do, I can't very well stop you," Peter said, trying to keep his voice cool and calm.

"Just you try and stop us," Ernie said, grinning, "and then see what 'appens to you."

"One last question," Peter said. "Did you ever take on somebody

---

① bulrush or bullrush: *Noun* a tall reed-like water plant with strap-like leaves and a dark brown velvety cylindrical head of numerous tiny flowers 香蒲

② 'Ow's = How's: How is

③ snotnose or snot-nose: *Noun* (Derogatory) a young child; a relatively young person(贬义)小子;年轻人

your own size?"

The moment he said it, he knew he had made a mistake. He saw the flush coming to Ernie's cheeks and there was a dangerous little spark dancing in his small black eyes.

Luckily, at that very moment, Raymond saved the situation. "Hey! Lookit① that bird swimmin'② in the reeds over there!" he shouted, pointing. "Let's 'ave 'im!"

It was a mallard③ drake④, with a curvy spoon-shaped yellow beak and a head of emerald⑤ green with a white ring round its neck. "Now those you really can eat," Raymond went on. "It's a wild duck."

"I'll 'ave 'im!" Ernie cried. He let go of the prisoner's arm and lifted the gun to his shoulder.

"This is a bird sanctuary," Peter said.

"A what?" Ernie asked, lowering the gun.

"Nobody shoots birds here. It's strictly forbidden."

"'Oo says it's forbidden?"

"The owner, Mr. Douglas Highton."

"You must be joking," Ernie said and he raised the gun again. He

---

① lookit: *Verb* [with obj., in imperative] look at 看(e.g. Hey, lookit that! 嘿,看那个!)

② swimmin' = swimming

③ mallard: *Noun* the commonest duck of the northern hemisphere and the ancestor of most domestic ducks, the male having a dark green head and white collar 绿头鸭

④ drake: *Noun* a male duck 雄鸭

⑤ emerald: *Noun* a bright green precious stone consisting of a chromium-rich variety of beryl 翡翠;绿宝石

fired. The duck crumpled[①] in the water.

"Go get 'im," Ernie said to Peter. "Cut 'is 'ands free, Raymond, 'cause then 'ee can be our flippin' gun-dog[②] and fetch the birds after we shoot 'em."

Raymond took out his knife and cut the string binding the small boy's wrists.

"Go on!" Ernie snapped. "Go get 'im!"

The killing of the beautiful duck had disturbed Peter very much. "I refuse," he said.

Ernie hit him across the face hard with his open hand. Peter didn't fall down, but a small trickle of blood began running out of one nostril.

"You dirty little perisher!" Ernie said. "You just try refusin'[③] me one more time and I'm goin' to make you a promise. And the promise is like this. You refuse me just one more time and I'm goin' to knock out every single one of them shiny white front teeth of yours, top and bottom. You understand that?"

Peter said nothing.

"Answer me!" Ernie barked. "Do you understand that?"

"Yes," Peter said quietly. "I understand."

"Get on with it, then!" Ernie shouted.

Peter walked down the bank, into the muddy water, through the reeds, and picked up the duck. He brought it back and Raymond took it from him and tied string around its legs.

"Now we got a retriever dog with us, let's see if we can't get us a

---

① crumple: *Verb* [no obj.] (of a person) suddenly flop down to the ground so that their body appears bent or broken(人)(突然)倒下

② gundog or gun dog: *Noun* A dog trained or bred to assist hunters, as in flushing or retrieving game 猎犬

③ refusin' = refusing

few more of them ducks," Ernie said. He strolled along the bank, gun in hand, searching the reeds. Suddenly he stopped. He crouched. He put a finger to his lips and said, "Sshh!"

Raymond went over to join him. Peter stood a few yards away, his trousers covered in mud up to the knees.

"Lookit in there!" Ernie whispered, pointing into a dense patch of bulrushes. "D'you see what I see?"

"Holy cats①!" cried Raymond. "What a beauty!"

Peter, peering from a little further away into the rushes②, saw at once what they were looking at. It was a swan, a magnificent white swan sitting serenely upon her nest. The nest itself was a huge pile of reeds and rushes that rose up about two feet above the waterline, and upon the top of all this the swan was sitting like a great white lady of the lake. Her head was turned towards the boys on the bank, alert and watchful.

"'Ow about that?" Ernie said. "That's better'n③ ducks, ain't it?"

"You think you can get 'er④?" Raymond said.

"Of course I can get 'er. I'll drill a 'ole right through 'er noggin⑤!"

Peter felt a wild rage beginning to build up inside him. He walked up to the two bigger boys. "I wouldn't shoot that swan if I were you," he said, trying to keep his voice calm. "Swans are the most protected birds in England."

---

① Holy cats: *Noun* (Slang) used to express surprise, wonder, or confusion (俚语)哎呀!好家伙!(表示强烈的惊讶、愤怒或高兴)

② rush: *Noun* a marsh or waterside plant with slender stem-like pith-filled leaves, widely distributed in temperate areas. Some kinds are used for matting, chair seats, and baskets, and some were formerly used for strewing on floors 灯芯草

③ better'n = better than

④ 'er = he;

⑤ noggin: *Noun* (informal) a person's head(非正式)人头;脑袋

"And what's that got to do with it?" Ernie asked him, sneering.

"And I'll tell you something else," Peter went on, throwing all caution away. "Nobody shoots a bird sitting on its nest. Absolutely nobody! She may even have cygnets① under her! You just can't do it!"

"'Oo says we can't?" Raymond asked, sneering. "Mister bleedin'② snotty-nose Peter Watson, is that the one 'oo says it?"

"The whole country says it," Peter answered. "The law says it and the police say it and *everyone* says it!"

"I don't say it!" Ernie said, raising his gun.

"Don't!" screamed Peter. "Please don't!"

Crack! The gun went off. The bullet hit the swan right in the middle of her elegant head and the long white neck collapsed on to the side of the nest.

"Got 'er!" cried Ernie.

"Hot shot!" shouted Raymond.

Ernie turned to Peter who was standing small and white-faced and absolutely rigid. "Now go get 'er," he ordered.

Once again, Peter didn't move.

Ernie came up close to the smaller boy and bent down and stuck his face right up to Peter's. "I'm tellin' you for the last time," he said, soft and dangerous. "Go get 'er!"

Tears were running down Peter's face as he went slowly down the bank and entered the water. He waded out to the dead swan and picked it up tenderly with both hands. Underneath it were two tiny cygnets,

---

① cygnet: *Noun* a young swan 幼天鹅

② bleedin' = bleeding: *Adjective* [attrib.] (Brit. informal) used for emphasis, or to express annoyance(英国英语的非正式用法)(用于加重语气或表示恼怒)该死的;该诅咒的;完全的;彻底的;非常(e. g. The watch was a bleeding copy. 这手表是该死的仿冒品。)

their bodies covered with yellow down. They were huddling together in the centre of the nest.

"Any eggs?" Ernie shouted from the bank.

"No," Peter answered. "Nothing." There was a chance, he felt, that when the male swan returned, it would continue to feed the young ones on its own if they were left in the nest. He certainly did not want to leave them to the tender mercies① of Ernie and Raymond.

Peter carried the dead swan back to the edge of the lake. He placed it on the ground. Then he stood up and faced the two others. His eyes, still wet with tears, were blazing with fury. "That was a filthy thing to do!" he shouted. "It was a stupid pointless act of vandalism! You're a couple of ignorant idiots! It's you who ought to be dead instead of the swan! You're not fit to be alive!"

He stood there, as tall as he could stand, splendid in his fury, facing the two taller boys and not caring any longer what they did to him.

Ernie didn't hit him this time. He seemed just a tiny bit taken aback at first by this outburst, but he quickly recovered. And now his loose lips formed themselves into a sly, wet smirk② and his small close-together eyes began to glint in a most malicious manner. "So you like swans, is that right?" he asked softly.

"I like swans and I hate you!" Peter cried.

"And am I right in thinkin'③," Ernie went on, still smirking, "am

---

① tender mercies: used ironically to imply that someone cannot be trusted to look after or treat someone else kindly or well(讽刺)听天由命;任人摆布(e. g. They have abandoned their children to the tender mercies of the social services. 他们遗弃了孩子,任其在社会福利中听天由命。)

② smirk: *Noun* a smug, conceited, or silly smile 得意的笑;傻笑(e. g. Gloria pursed her mouth in a self-satisfied smirk. 格洛瑞亚紧闭嘴巴,心满意足地笑。)

③ thinkin' = thinking

I absolutely right in thinkin' that you wished this old swan down 'ere were alive instead of dead?"

"That's a stupid question!" Peter shouted.

"'Ee needs a clip over the ear-'ole[1]," Raymond said.

"Wait," Ernie said. "I'm doin' this exercise." He turned back to Peter. "So if I could make this swan come alive and go flyin'[2] round the sky all over again, then you'd be 'appy[3]. Right?"

"That's another stupid question!" Peter cried out. "Who d'you think you are?"

"I'll tell you 'oo I am," Ernie said. "I'm a magic man, that's 'oo I am. And just to make you 'appy and contented, I am about to do a magic trick that'll make this dead swan come alive and go flyin' all over the sky once again."

"Rubbish!" Peter said. "I'm going." He turned and started to walk away.

"Grab 'im!" Ernie said.

Raymond grabbed him.

"Leave me alone!" Peter cried out.

Raymond slapped him on the cheek, hard. "Now, now," he said. "Don't fight with auntie, not unless you want to get 'urt[4]."

"Gimme your knife," Ernie said, holding out his hand. Raymond gave him his knife.

Ernie knelt down beside the dead swan and stretched out one of its enormous wings. "Watch this," he said.

---

① ear-'ole = ear-hole or earhole: *Noun* (informal) a person's ear(非正式)耳朵(e.g. a clip round the earhole 一记耳光)

② flyin' = flying

③ 'appy = happy

④ 'urt = hurt

"What's the big idea?" Raymond asked.

"Wait and see," Ernie said. And now, using the knife, he proceeded to sever the great white wing from the swan's body. There is a joint in the bone where the wing meets the side of the bird, and Ernie located this and slid the knife into the joint and cut through the tendon[①]. The knife was very sharp and it cut well, and soon the wing came away all in one piece.

Ernie turned the swan over and severed the other wing.

"String," he said, holding out his hand to Raymond.

Raymond, who was grasping Peter by the arm, was watching fascinated. "Where'd you learn 'ow to butcher up a bird like that?" he asked. "With chickens," Ernie said. "We used to nick chickens from up at Stevens Farm and cut 'em up into chicken parts and flog 'em to a shop in Aylesbury[②]. Gimme the string."

Raymond gave him the ball of string. Ernie cut off six pieces, each about a yard long.

There are a series of strong bones running along the top edge of a swan's wing, and Ernie took one of the wings and started tying one end of the bits of string all the way along the top edge of the great wing. When he had done this, he lifted the wing with the six string-ends dangling from it and said to Peter, "Stick out your arm."

"You're absolutely mad!" the smaller boy shouted. "You're de-

---

① tendon: *Noun* a flexible but inelastic cord of strong fibrous collagen tissue attaching a muscle to a bone 腱

② Aylesbury: *Noun* a town in south central England, the county town of Buckinghamshire; pop. 50,000 (1985) 艾尔斯伯里(英格兰中南部城市,白金汉郡首府,1985 年人口 50,000。)

mented[①]!"

"Make 'im stick it out," Ernie said to Raymond.

Raymond held up a clenched fist in front of Peter's face and dabbed it gently against his nose. "You see this," he said. "Well I'm goin' to smash you right in the kisser[②] with it unless you do exactly as you're told, see? Now, stick out your arm, there's a good little boy."

Peter felt his resistance collapsing. He couldn't hold out against these people any longer. For a few seconds, he stared at Ernie. Ernie with the tiny close-together black eyes gave the impression he would be capable of doing just about anything if he got really angry. Ernie, Peter felt at that moment, might quite easily kill a person if he were to lose his temper. Ernie, the dangerous backward child, was playing games now and it would be very unwise to spoil his fun. Peter held out an arm.

Ernie then proceeded to tie the six string ends one by one to Peter's arm, and when he had finished, the white wing of the swan was securely attached along the entire length of the arm itself.

"Ow's that, eh?" Ernie said, stepping back and surveying his work.

"Now the other one," Raymond said, catching on to what Ernie was doing. "You can't expect 'im to go flyin' round the sky with only one wing, can you?"

"Second wing comin' up," Ernie said. He knelt down again and tied six more lengths of string to the top bones of the second wing. Then he stood up again. "Let's 'ave the other arm," he said. Peter, feeling sick and ridiculous, held out his other arm. Ernie strapped the wing

---

① dement: *Verb* (Obsolete) (used with object) to make mad or insane 使发狂

② kisser: *Noun* (informal) a person's mouth(非正式)人的嘴(e.g. I belted him one, right on the kisser. 我狠狠打了他一下,正好打在嘴上。)

tightly along the length of it.

"Now!" Ernie cried, clapping his hands and dancing a little jig[1] on the grass. "Now we got ourselves a real live swan all over again! Didn't I tell you I was a magic man? Didn't I tell you I was goin' to do a magic trick and make this dead swan come alive and go flyin' all over the sky? Didn't I tell you that?"

Peter stood there in the sunshine beside the lake on this beautiful May morning, the enormous, limp and slightly bloodied wings dangling grotesquely at his sides. "Have you finished?" he said.

"Swans don't talk," Ernie said. "Keep your flippin' beak shut! And save your energy, laddie, because you're goin' to need all the strength and energy you got when it comes to flyin' round in the sky." Ernie picked up his gun from the ground, then he grabbed Peter by the back of the neck with his free hand and said, "March!"

They marched along the bank of the lake until they came to a tall and graceful willow tree. There they halted. The tree was a weeping willow[2], and the long branches hung down from a great height and almost touched the surface of the lake.

"And now the magic swan is goin' to show us a bit of magic flyin'," Ernie announced. "So what you're goin' to do, Mister Swan, is to climb up to the very top of this tree, and when you get there you're goin' to spread out your wings like a clever little swannee-swan-swan and you're goin' to take off!"

"Fantastic!" cried Raymond. "Terrific! I like it very much!"

"So do I," Ernie said. "Because now we're goin' to find out just

---

① jig: *Noun* a lively dance with leaping movements 吉格舞;快步舞

② weeping willow: *Noun* a Eurasian willow with trailing branches and foliage reaching down to the ground, widely grown as an ornamental in waterside settings 垂柳

exactly 'ow clever this clever little swannee-swan-swan really is. He's terribly clever at school, we all know that, and 'ee's[1] top of the class and everything else that's lovely, but let's see just exactly 'ow clever 'ee is when 'ee's at the top of the tree! Right, Mister Swan?" He gave Peter a push towards the tree.

How much further could this madness go? Peter wondered. He was beginning to feel a little mad himself, as though nothing was real any more and none of it was actually happening. But the thought of being high up in the tree and out of reach of these hooligans at last was something that appealed to him greatly. When he was up there, he could stay up there. He doubted very much if they would bother to come up after him. And even if they did, he could surely climb away from them along a thin limb that would not take the weight of two people.

The tree was a fairly easy one to climb, with several low branches to give him a start up. He began climbing. The huge white wings dangling from his arms kept getting in the way, but it didn't matter. What mattered now to Peter was that every inch upward was another inch away from his tormentors below. He had never been a great one for tree-climbing and he wasn't especially good at it, but nothing in the world was going to stop him from getting to the top of this one. And once he was there, he thought it unlikely they would even be able to see him because of the leaves.

"Higher!" shouted Ernie's voice. "Keep goin'!"

Peter kept going, and eventually he arrived at a point where it was impossible to go higher. His feet were now standing on a branch that was about as thick as a person's wrist, and this particular branch reached far out over the lake and then curved gracefully downward. All the branches

① 'ee's = he's: he is

above him were very thin and whippy[①], but the one he was holding on to with his hands was quite strong enough for the purpose. He stood there, resting after the climb. He looked down for the first time. He was very high up, at least fifty feet. But he couldn't see the two boys. They were no longer standing at the base of the tree. Was it possible they had gone away at last?

"All right, Mister Swan!" came the dreaded voice of Ernie. "Now listen carefully!"

The two of them had walked some distance away from the tree to a point where they had a clear view of the small boy at the top. Looking down at them now, Peter realized how very sparse and slender the leaves of a willow tree were. They gave him almost no cover at all.

"Listen carefully. Mister Swan!" the voice was shouting. "Start walking out along that branch you're standin'[②] on! Keep goin' till you're right over the nice muddy water! Then you take off!"

Peter didn't move. He was fifty feet above them now and they weren't ever going to reach him again. From down below, there was a long silence. It lasted maybe half a minute. He kept his eyes on the two distant figures in the field. They were standing quite still, looking up at him.

"All right then, Mister Swan!" came Ernie's voice again. "I'm gonna count to ten, right? And if you ain't spread them wings and flown away by then, I'm gonna shoot you down instead with this little gun! And that'll make two swans I've knocked off today instead of one! So here we go, Mister Swan! One!... Two!... Three!... Four!... Five!... Six!..."

---

① whippy: *Adjective* flexible; springy 柔韧的；易弯曲的；有弹性的（e. g. new growths of whippy sapling twigs 新长出的柔软的嫩枝）

② standin' = standing

Peter remained still. Nothing would make him move from now on.

"Seven... Eight!... Nine!... Ten!"

Peter saw the gun coming up to the shoulder. It was pointing straight at him. Then he heard the *crack* of the rifle and the *zip* of the bullet as it whistled past his head. It was a frightening thing. But he still didn't move. He could see Ernie loading the gun with another bullet.

"Last chance!" yelled Ernie. "The next one's gonna get you!"

Peter stayed put①. He waited. He watched the boy who was standing among the buttercups② in the meadow far below with the other boy beside him. The gun came up once again to the shoulder.

This time he heard the *crack* at the same instant the bullet hit him in the thigh. There was no pain, but the force of it was devastating. It was as though someone had whacked③ him on the leg with a sledgehammer④, and it knocked both feet off the branch he was standing on. He scrabbled with his hands to hang on. The small branch he was holding on to bent over and split.

Some people, when they have taken too much and have been driven beyond the point of endurance, simply crumble and give up. There are others, though they are not many, who will for some reason always be

---

① stay put:(of a person or object) remain somewhere without moving or being moved(人或物)留在原地不动

② buttercup: *Noun* a herbaceous plant with bright yellow cup-shaped flowers, which is common in grassland and as a garden weed. All kinds are poisonous and generally avoided by livestock 毛茛;金凤花(e. g. The fields were golden with buttercups. 田里是一片金黄色的金凤花。)

③ whack: *Verb* [with obj.] strike forcefully with a sharp blow 用力打;猛击(e. g. His attacker whacked him on the head. 攻击者猛击他的头部。)

④ sledgehammer: *Noun* a large, heavy hammer used for such jobs as breaking rocks and driving in fence posts(用于锤岩石和篱笆打桩的)大锤

unconquerable. You meet them in time of war and also in time of peace. They have an indomitable spirit and nothing, neither pain nor torture nor threat of death, will cause them to give up.

Little Peter Watson was one of these. And as he fought and scrabbled[1] to prevent himself from falling out of the top of that tree, it came to him suddenly that he was going to win. He looked up and he saw a light shining over the waters of the lake that was of such brilliance and beauty he was unable to look away from it. The light was beckoning him, drawing him on, and he dived towards the light and spread his wings.

Three different people reported seeing a great white swan circling over the village that morning, a school-teacher called Emily Mead, a man who was replacing some tiles on the roof of the chemist's shop whose name was William Eyles, and a boy called John Underwood who was flying his model aeroplane in a nearby field.

And that morning, Mrs. Watson, who was washing up some dishes in her kitchen sink, happened to glance up through the window at the exact moment when something huge and white came flopping[2] down on to the lawn in her back garden. She rushed outside. She went down on her knees beside the small crumpled figure of her only son. "Oh, my dar-

---

① scrabble: *Verb* [no obj.] scratch or grope around with one's fingers to find, collect, or hold on to something(为找到、收集或抓牢而)抓;摸(e. g. She scrabbled at the grassy slope, desperate for purchase. 她在青草坡上乱抓,拼命想抓住一个受力物。)

② flop: *Verb* [no obj.] [with adverbial] fall, move, or hang in a heavy, loose, and ungainly way 沉重下坠;笨拙移动;垂落(e. g. Black hair flopped across his forehead. 黑发在他额前甩来甩去。)

ling!" she cried, near to hysterics[①] and hardly believing what she saw. "My darling boy! What happened to you?"

"My leg hurts," Peter said, opening his eyes. Then he fainted.

"It's bleeding!" she cried and she picked him up and carried him inside. Quickly she phoned for the doctor and the ambulance. And while she was waiting for help to come, she fetched a pair of scissors and began cutting the string that held the two great wings of the swan to her son's arms.

三、翻译探索

这篇小说的翻译中，儿童语言在风格上的传达，应该是翻译的重中之重。但是，对于这样风格的传达，总会有所遗失的。有的地方，译者干脆做了一般性的调整，风格的对等体现也就有所欠缺了，这方面的翻译有待进一步探索。

折翼天鹅

厄尼得到的生日礼物是一支"点22"口径的来复枪。今天是周六，上午九点半的时候，厄尼的父亲就已经躺在沙发上看电视了，边看边对孩子说："小子，让我们看看你能打到什么。不要当废人，给我们带回一只兔子晚上吃啊。"

"湖的另一边，那一大片田野里有兔子，"厄尼说。"我看到过，有很多呢。"

"那就去，打一只回来，"父亲说着，用一根劈开的火柴棍将门牙间吃早餐时塞进去的东西往外抠。"走出去，给我们打一只兔子回来。"

"我给你们打两只回来，"厄尼回答。

---

① hysterics: *Noun* being extremely upset and angry 极其愤怒(e.g. My mum will have hysterics when she sees the colour of my hair. 妈妈看到我头发染成这种颜色会火冒三丈的。)

“回来的路上,”父亲说,“顺便给我打一小瓶棕色麦芽酒。”

“那得给我钱,”厄尼说。

这位做父亲的从衣兜里摸出一英镑钞票,眼睛却始终没有离开电视。“不要再像上次那样,将找头悄悄留下不交啊,”他警告说。“要是那样,你的耳朵就得给打肿了,还关系到生日礼物的问题。”

“别操心,”厄尼说。

“那支枪,你要是想练习一下、打得准的话,”父亲说,“鸟是最佳目标。看看你能打落多少只麻雀,好不好?”

“好的,”厄尼说。“沿着小道走,树篱里尽是麻雀,打麻雀很轻松。”

“要是你认为打麻雀很容易、不值得的话,”父亲说,“那就去打只雌鹪鹩回来。雌鹪鹩的体型是麻雀的一半,总是跳来跳去,无片刻停歇。趁你对自己的聪明劲儿还没有达到吹破牛皮的程度,就打一只雌鹪鹩回来证明一下。”

“听着,艾伯特,”他妻子从水池那儿抬起头说道。“孵化季节打小鸟,可不怎么好。打兔子我不介意,但是,孵化季节打小鸟就完全另当别论啦。”

“闭嘴,”父亲说。“没有人要你发表意见。小子,听我的,”他说。“不要在大街上将那东西挥来舞去的,因为你没有持枪许可证。把它塞到裤管里,到了乡野再拿出来,明白了吗?”

“别操心,”厄尼说完,拿起枪,带上那盒子弹,出了家门,看看有什么能打的。厄尼是一个大块头的男孩子,笨拙而粗鲁,这个生日他正好十五岁。他长着一双小小的、细长的眼睛,那双眼睛在鼻子顶端紧紧地相互靠在一起,跟他当卡车司机的父亲的眼睛如出一辙;他的嘴巴很松弛,两只嘴唇总是湿乎乎的。在他生长的家庭环境中,身体暴力是家常便饭,就连他自己也被熏染成一个极其暴力的人。多数星期六的下午,他都跟一帮朋友坐火车或者公共汽车去参加橄榄球比赛。每次比赛回来,要是没有想方设法打斗一番,他们就认为那天是白白浪费掉了。放学后,他就抓小男生,将其胳膊扭到背后,并以此为乐。然后,他就命令小男生说些侮辱其父母的脏话。

“啊唷！厄尼，求求你别这样！求求你！”

“快说，否则我就扭断你的胳膊！”

小男生每次都要说那样的脏话，说完后，他就将小男生的胳膊再扭一下，然后将其放走，小男生一边走，一边眼泪汪汪地哭着。

厄尼最好的朋友名叫雷蒙德，住在离厄尼家隔着四户人家的地方。就其年龄而言，他也是一个大块头的男孩子，但是，与胖重、笨拙而粗鲁的厄尼不同的是，雷蒙德瘦高、强壮。

在雷蒙德家房子外面，厄尼将两根手指放入口中，长长地吹了一阵口哨，雷蒙德应声而出。“看啊，我生日得到了什么礼物，”厄尼一边显摆枪，一边说。

“哇呀！”雷蒙德叫道。“我们可以好好玩耍一番啦！”

“那就快来啊，”厄尼说。“我们到湖那头那大片田野里去，打只兔子回来。”

两个孩子出发了。当时是五月份的一个星期六的上午，他俩住的小村子周围的景色美极了。栗子树开满了花，沿着树篱排列的山楂树一片白色。要想到达那大片有兔子的田野，厄尼和雷蒙德首先要沿着狭窄的、两边布满灌木树篱的小径走上四百米，然后必须穿过铁道线，绕着大湖走，湖里有野鸭子、雌红松鸡、白骨顶水鸟以及环颈黑鸫。在湖以远的地方，越过一座小山，山的另一侧就是兔子生长的那片田野。这是一块完全属于私人的土地，主人是道格拉斯·海顿先生。这个湖本身是水禽的禁猎区。

沿着小径走的途中，他俩轮流拿枪，不时地射击树篱里的小鸟儿。厄尼射中一只红腹灰雀，还有一只篱雀。雷蒙德也射中一只红腹灰雀，还射中了一只白喉林莺和一只黄鹀。每射死一只鸟，他们就将其腿部绑到一根线上。雷蒙德只要出门，夹克衫的兜子里总要揣上一大团线和一把小刀。现在，那根线上已经栓上五只小鸟儿了。

“你知道吧，”雷蒙德说。“这些鸟我们可以吃掉。”

“不要说傻话，”厄尼说。“一只鸟身上的肉还不够一只小土鳖吃的。”

“还是有肉的，”雷蒙德说。“法国佬吃，意大利那帮家伙也吃，是课堂上桑德斯先生说的。他说,法国佬和意大利那帮家伙支起网捕鸟,成百万只捕,然后就吃掉。”

“那么,好吧,”厄尼说。“瞧瞧我们能打到多少,然后拿回家,放进兔子肉里炖。”

他俩一边沿着小径走,一边开枪打鸟,见一只打一只。到达铁路线的时候,那根线上已经吊着十五只小鸟了。

“嘿,看呐!”厄尼挥动长长的手臂指着一个方向,小声说。“看那儿啊!”

铁路沿线两边布满了树木和灌木丛,其中一堆灌木丛旁边站着一名小男孩,正通过双筒望远镜向一棵古树上方的树枝观瞧。

“你知道那小子是谁吗?”雷蒙德低声问。“就是那个小蠢蛋沃森。”

“没错!”厄尼小声说。“就是他,一个人渣!”

彼得·沃森总是他人攻击的目标。厄尼和雷蒙德十分憎恨他,因为他几乎样样都行,而他俩却一无是处。他身体矮小、人很脆弱,脸上长了雀斑,戴着一副眼镜,镜片厚厚的。他是一名成绩优异的小学生,尽管年仅十三,却已经进入学校高年级学习。他喜爱音乐,钢琴弹得很不错,但却不擅长游戏活动。他沉默寡言却彬彬有礼。他穿的衣服尽管补了又补、织了又织,却总是干干净净。他的父亲既不是卡车司机,又不是工厂工人,而是银行的职员。

“我们好好吓唬吓唬这个小蠢蛋吧,”厄尼小声嘀咕着。

这两个大块头的男孩子蹑手蹑脚地靠近了这个小男孩,但这个小男孩并没有看见他们,因为那只双筒望远镜还架在眼睛上。

“手举起来!”厄尼用枪指着,喊道。

彼得·沃森吓了一跳,只见他放低望远镜,透过眼镜盯着这两个不速之客。

“快!”厄尼喊道。“举起来!”

“我要是你,就不会用枪指着人,”彼得·沃森说。

“这块地盘,得听我们的命令!”厄尼说。

“所以,举起来,”雷蒙德说,“否则,你就是想让肚子挨枪子儿!”

彼得·沃森站在那儿,一动不动,双手在胸前举着望远镜。他先看了看雷蒙德,又看了看厄尼。此时,他并不害怕,但是,他清楚得很,在这两个家伙面前,不能莽撞行事,这些年以来,这两个家伙没少欺负他,也让他吃了不少苦头。

"你到底想干什么?"他问。

"我要你举起手来!"厄尼冲他吼道。"难道你不懂英语吗?"

彼得·沃森并没有挪动半步。

"我数到五,"厄尼说。"如果数完,手还没有举起来,你的肚子就得挨枪子儿。一……二……三……"

彼得·沃森将双臂慢慢地举过头顶,只有这样做才是明智之举。于是,雷蒙德向前跨出一步,从他手中一下子夺走了望远镜。"这是什么?"他厉声问道。"暗中监视谁呢?"

"没有监视谁。"

"说实话,沃森。这东西是监视用的! 我敢说,你在监视我们! 我说的没错,是不是呢? 快承认!"

"我当然不是在监视你们。"

"照他耳朵狠狠扇一下,"厄尼说。"教训他一下,省得跟我们撒谎。"

"马上就扇,"雷蒙德回应。"我先简单做一下扇前准备。"

彼得·沃森考虑了一下,看看试图逃走的可能性有多大。他所能做到的就是转身就跑,但那样做毫无意义,不出几秒的工夫,他俩就会抓住他。要是他大喊救命的话,也不会有什么人听见的。因此,他所能做到的就是保持冷静,设法用语言使自己摆脱险境。

"双手举起来!"厄尼不断轻轻地挥舞着枪管吼叫着。这种行为,他只是在电视上看到歹徒做过。"快啊,小老弟,举起来!"

彼得照做了。

"那么,你在监视谁呢?"雷蒙德问。"快说出来!"

"我是在观察一只绿色的啄木鸟,"彼得回答。

"一只绿色的什么?"

"一只绿色的公啄木鸟,它正在啄那棵老树的树干找虫子吃呢。"

“鸟儿在哪儿？”厄尼举起枪，厉声问道。“我要逮住它。”

“不，不能逮，”彼得一边说，一边看了眼从雷蒙德肩上耷拉下来的那根线，上面挂了几只小鸟。“但是你一喊，他就飞走了，啄木鸟胆子非常小。”

“你观察它干什么？”雷蒙德带着怀疑的口吻问。“有什么意义？难道你没有更好的事儿去做吗？”

“观鸟很有意思，”彼得说。“观鸟比射鸟要有意思得多。”

“哇，你这个目无尊长的小倒霉蛋儿！”厄尼叫道。“那么说，我们射鸟你不喜欢啦，是吗？你说的是这个意思吗？”

“我认为，射鸟绝对是没有任何意义的。”

“我们做什么，你都不喜欢，难道不是吗？”雷蒙德问。

彼得没有回答。

“好吧，我也跟你说道说道，”雷蒙德继续说。“你做的事情，我们也没有一样喜欢的。”

彼得的双臂开始疼痛起来，他决定冒一下险。他慢慢地将双手放低，放到身体两侧。

“举起来！”厄尼大喊。“手举起来！”

“要是我不举呢？”

“哇呀呀！你胆子不小啊，是不是？”厄尼说。“我最后一次警告你啊，要是你不举起来，我就扣动扳机！”

“那将是刑事犯罪行为，”彼得说。“警察会立案侦查的。”

“你将会受伤入院！”厄尼说。

“赶紧开枪吧，”彼得说。“然后，警察就会将你送进少年教养院，那个地方可是和监狱差不多。”

他看到，厄尼开始犹豫起来。

“这可是你要求开枪的，是不是？”雷蒙德说。

“我只是要求放开我，”彼得说。“我没有对你们造成任何伤害。”

“你是一个高傲自大的小人，”厄尼说。“高傲自大的小人，这样说，再恰当不过了。”

雷蒙德倾斜着身体，小声在厄尼耳边嘀咕着什么，厄尼则专心地听着。然后，他一拍大腿说道："我喜欢！好棒的主意！"

厄尼把枪放到地上，向小男孩走去，一把将他抓住，将其摔倒在地。雷蒙德从衣兜里掏出那卷线，剪下来一段。接下来，他俩一起强行将小男孩的双手拉到身前，将两个手腕紧紧绑在一起。

"现在，该绑腿了，"雷蒙德说。彼得奋力抗争，结果胃部却猛地挨了一拳。这一拳令他喘不过气来，一动不动地躺在那儿。紧接着，他俩用更长的线将他的脚踝部绑到一起。至此，他就像一只被捆绑起来的鸡，不由自主、束手无策。

厄尼一只手拿起枪，另一只手死死抓住彼得的一只胳膊，雷蒙德则抓住另一只胳膊。然后，他俩将小男孩拖过草地，向铁道线拽去。

彼得完全不敢吱声了，不管他们有什么企图，跟他们说这说那，看来是无济于事、于事无补了。

他俩拽着可怜兮兮的彼得沿着路堤一直走到铁轨上。然后，他俩一个扯着双臂，一个扯着双腿，将小男孩抬起，接着再放下，但这次是将其横着放在两条铁轨之间。

"你们两个疯子！"彼得喊道。"你们不可以这样做！"

"谁说不可以？这只是我们给你的一个小小的教训，省得你高傲自大。"

"再来些线，"厄尼说。

雷蒙德拿出那团线，于是，两个大块头家伙继续捆绑可怜兮兮的小男孩，一直绑到他无法将身体从铁轨间扭开为止。他们的做法是，将线绕着每只胳膊一圈圈地缠，再将线系到两只铁轨的下方。对于身体的中间部位和脚踝部位，他们也如法炮制。做完之后，彼得·沃森被绑得无计可施，整个人横在两只铁轨之间几乎动弹不得。他的身上能够四处动弹的部位就只剩下头和双脚了。

厄尼和雷蒙德向后退去，打量着他们的手工杰作。"我们干得不赖，"厄尼说。

"这条线路每半小时就有一趟车经过，"雷蒙德说。"我们用不着等多长时间的。"

“这是谋杀!”躺在铁轨间的小男孩喊道。

“不,不是,”雷蒙德对他说。“这与你说的不搭边。”

“放开我! 请放开我! 要是火车开过来,我就没命了!”

“小家伙,*要是* 你死了,”厄尼说,“那全是你自己的过错,我告诉你缘由吧。到时候,如果你就像现在这样把头高高抬起,那么,小朋友,你就死定了! 将头向下放平,或许幸免一死。另一方面,你或许不会有什么事儿,因为我没有把握,也不确切知道火车跟下方地面之间有多大空隙。雷蒙德,没准儿你知道的,它们之间有多大的空隙呢?”

“很小,”雷蒙德说。“建造的时候,跟地面就贴得很近。”

“空隙或许足够,或许不足,”厄尼说。

“让我们这么说吧,”雷蒙德说。“对于像厄尼你或者我这样的*一般* 人来说,那空隙或许刚刚够,但是,对于这里这位沃森先生,空隙够不够,我没有把握。告诉你其中的原因吧。”

“跟我说说其中的原因,”厄尼怂恿他继续往下说。

“这里这位沃森先生,其头部大得出奇,这就是原因所在。他那只大脑袋大得要命,我个人认为,要是有事儿的话,火车的底部就会刮到他。提醒你注意的是,我不是说,火车会将他的脑袋刮掉。事实上,我十分肯定的是,火车不会将脑袋刮掉,但是,会将他的脸刮蹭一番。这一点,你丝毫不用怀疑。”

“我想,你说的没错,”厄尼说。

“脑袋是刮不掉的,”雷蒙德说,“躺在铁道上,一辆火车向你驶来,即使你的脑袋因为充满了智慧而肿胀,块头变得很大,也不会刮掉的。说的对吧,厄尼?”

“说的对,”厄尼接着说。

这两个大块头的男孩子爬回到路堤上,坐在灌木丛后面的草地上。厄尼掏出一盒烟,他俩各自点燃香烟。

彼得·沃森横躺在铁轨间,无计可施。现在,他意识到,这两个家伙是不会放开他的。这两个是疯子,是危险分子。他们只图暂时的愉悦,从来不考虑后果如何。彼得对自己说,我必须保持冷静、认真思考。他躺在那儿,纹丝不动,盘算着胜算的几率会有多少。结果是,几率不小。他的头部最高的部分是鼻子,他估计,鼻子尖向上竖起,高出铁轨十厘米多一点。这个高度太高了吗?他不敢肯定,现代柴油机车跟地面之间有多大空隙。当然,间隙不会很大。他脑袋的后部靠在两根枕木间松散的砾石上,所以他必须将脑袋使劲往下面的砾石里钻进一点。于是,他将脑袋从一侧向另一侧蠕动起来,把砾石挤走,一个小小的凹陷处渐渐地被他弄了出来,也就是说,他为自己在砾石中弄出了一个坑。最后,他估计自己的头部放低了五厘米。这样,头部就没有问题了。可是,两只脚怎么办?脚也是向上竖起的啊。他仔细转动两只紧紧绑在一起的脚,转向一侧。这样,两只脚几乎就是平放的啦。

他等着火车驶来。

司机会看到他吗?可能性很小,因为这是一条主干线路,途经伦敦、唐克斯特、约克、纽卡斯尔以及苏格兰,采用的是很大、很长的机车,机车很靠后的位置才是驾驶室,司机就坐在驾驶室里,眼睛只注视各种信号灯。在这条铁路的这一地区,火车的时速约一百二十八公里,这一点彼得了解。有很多次,他坐在路堤上看着火车经过。他还很小的时候,常常在一个小本子上记录火车的编号,有时候,引擎的侧面还有用金字写下的火车的名字。

他对自己说,不管是火车的噪音还是时速,都将是一件可怕的事情。噪音会把耳朵震聋的,一百二十八公里的时速带来的"飕飕"的风声也不会是什么好玩儿的事情。有那么一瞬间,他甚至突发奇想:火车在他上方疾驰而过之际,火车底部会不会生出某种真空旋涡,一下子将他吸上去呢。很有可能吧。所以,无论发生什么,他必须全神贯注,将整个身体贴向地面,不能松弛下来,要将身体绷直、绷紧,往下压,贴近地面。

"还好吧,鼠脸小弟!"其中一个家伙从上方的灌木丛那儿喊道。"等待判处的滋味如何?"

他决定不予理睬。他看着头顶上方蓝蓝的天空,那里有一朵积云,正慢慢从左向右飘移。为了让自己的思绪避开即将发生的一幕,他玩了一个游戏,这个游戏是很久以前一个炎热的夏天,他父亲教给他的。当时他跟父亲仰面躺在白垩峭壁上方的草地上。游戏的内容就是,在一朵积云的皱褶处、阴影里、翻腾处寻找千奇百怪的面孔。他父亲说过,要是用心寻找的话,总是会在那上面找到某种类型的面孔。彼得的眼睛慢慢在云彩上移动着。在其中一个地方,他发现一个长胡子独眼男子,而在另一个地方,他又发现了一个长长下巴的女巫正哈哈大笑。一架飞机穿越积云自东向西飞去,那是一架小型单翼飞机,机身是红色的。他想,那是一架老式的派珀小熊飞机,并一直看着它消失不见了。

接下来,突然之间,他听到一种奇怪的、微小的震动声音从两侧的铁轨传来。这种声音很是轻微,几乎听不见,是一种微弱的、轻微的、低沉的、嗡嗡作响的声音,似乎沿着铁轨从很远的地方传过来。

他对自己说,那是火车的声音。

这种沿着铁轨传来的震动声音越来越响、越来越响。他抬起头,向长长的、笔直的铁路线看去,铁路一直向远方延伸,足足延伸有一公里半才消失不见。就在铁轨消失的地方,他看见了火车。刚开始的时候,火车还只是一个小点点——很远很远处的一个小黑点,可是,就在他抬起头那几秒钟的时间里,那小点点越来越大、越来越大,继而呈现出轮廓来,很快就由一个小点点变成柴油机车那大大的、方形的、平直的火车头。彼得将头放下,使劲挤进起先在砾石中弄出来的凹形坑,再扭动双脚转向一侧。他紧紧闭上双眼,努力使身体向地面沉下去。

火车从他身体上方驶过,好似爆炸物"轰"的一声炸响,又好似枪在脑袋里"砰"的一声回荡。随着这声巨响,一阵风撕扯着、咆哮着,迎面而来,如同一股飓风,沿着两个鼻孔吹入肺部。噪音撕心裂肺,大风令他窒息难耐,感觉自己好像被活生生吃掉,被一只厉声尖叫、凶残无比的怪兽吞到肚子里。

然后,一切都结束了,火车已走远。彼得睁开双眼,看见了蓝蓝的天空,还有大朵的白云依然在头顶上方飘动。现在,一切都结束了,他胜算、幸免一死。

“火车没有压着，”一个声音响起。

“有些可惜，”另一个声音回应。

他向旁边瞥了一眼，看见那两个大块头的、粗鲁的家伙俯身在他上方。

“把他松开吧，”厄尼说。

雷蒙德将铁轨上与他身体相连的线切断。

“把他腿上的线松开，好让他能够走路，但手还是要绑着，别松开，”厄尼吩咐道。

雷蒙德将他脚踝部位的线切断。

“起来，”厄尼说。

彼得站了起来。

“小老弟，你还是囚犯一个，”厄尼说。

“兔子还打不打？”雷蒙德问道。“我想，我们是要去打几只兔子，对吗？”

“打兔子，时间有的是，”厄尼回答。“我刚刚想到，我们顺路把这个小倒霉蛋儿推进湖中。”

“好，”雷蒙德回应。“让他凉爽一下。”

“你们已经快活够了，”彼得·沃森说。“为什么现在不放我走？”

“因为你是一名囚犯，”厄尼回答。“况且，你还不止是一个普普通通的囚犯，而是一个间谍。你知道间谍被逮住会怎么样吧，难道不知道吗？靠墙站立，然后枪毙。”

听到这些，彼得不再多说什么了，刺激、惹怒这样两个家伙毫无意义。他的话语越少，对他们的抵制情绪越少，越有机会避免受到伤害。他对他们目前的情绪状态没有一丝一毫的怀疑：他俩有能力对他造成相当严重的身体伤害。很清楚的一个事实就是，有一次放学后，厄尼扭断了小沃利·辛普森的胳膊，沃利的父母还报了警。他也听过雷蒙德吹嘘有一次参加橄榄球赛做过的事儿，就是所谓的“在对方倒地后还狠狠踢上一脚”这件事儿。对于这件事儿，他的理解是：对方躺倒在地，雷蒙德还照其脸部或者身体踢上一脚。他们就是无耻之徒,就是眼前这两个家伙。彼得从父亲几乎每一天都要阅读的报纸上看到,这些无耻之徒绝不是单打独斗、独立行动的,整个国家似乎到处都是这样的无耻之徒。他们毁坏火车内部的东西,手持刀具、自行车链条、金属棒等在大街上激战,攻击行人——特别是那些独自行走的小孩子,还砸坏路边小餐馆什么的。尽管厄尼和雷蒙德或许算不上正儿八经、合格胜任的无耻之徒,但极为明确的是,他俩却向着这个方向发展了。

因此呢,彼得对自己说,他必须继续保持被动、低调的状态,不能侮辱他们,也绝不能激怒他们。重中之重的是,不能试图跟他俩发生肢体上的冲突。那么,到了最后,他们就有望厌烦这个恶意的小游戏,转而去打兔子了。

两个大块头男孩子每人揪住彼得一只胳膊,押着他,穿过那片紧挨着的田野,向湖的方向走去,被押者的手腕在身体前部仍然被绑在一起。厄尼空闲的那只手拿着枪,雷蒙德空闲的手则拿着从彼得那儿抢来的望远镜。他们三个来到了湖边。

现在是五月里一天的上午,湖面金光闪闪,很是漂亮。整座湖很长,但十分狭窄。湖岸各处生长着高高的柳树;湖中央,水清澈、明净,但是,较靠近岸边的地方则生长着一丛丛芦苇,还有一簇簇香蒲。

厄尼和雷蒙德押着囚犯走到湖边,停了下来。

“那么,现在,”厄尼说。“我的意见是这样的:你扯着他的胳膊,我拉着他的腿,然后我们喊‘一、二、三’将这个小讨厌鬼尽可能远地荡进湖中,丢进芦苇丛下的烂泥里。我的想法怎么样?”

“我喜欢这主意,”雷蒙德回答。“不把他的双手解开,对吗?”

“对的,”厄尼说。“你小子觉得怎么样呢?”

“要是你想那样做的话,我也阻止不了,”彼得说,尽量使自己的声音听起来平缓、冷静。

“你就阻止我们一下,试试看啊,”厄尼露齿一笑,说道,“看看结果会怎么样呢?”

“最后问一个问题,”彼得说。“你是否跟与你一般大小的较量过呢?”

问题一出口,他就意识到自己做错了,他看见厄尼的脸颊一下子红了,那双小小的黑眼睛里跳跃着小小的火花,预示着危险的来临。

所幸的是,就在这一关口,雷蒙德挽救了局面。“嘿,看啊,那儿的芦苇丛中有一只鸟儿在游动!”他用手指着,喊道。“我们把它逮住吧!”

那是一只绿头公鸭,黄色的喙部呈勺子形状,曲线优美,头部是翡翠绿色,脖子上长有一圈白色的羽毛。“现在,这是真正能吃的东西,”雷蒙德继续说。“是野鸭啊。”

“我要打它!”厄尼叫道。他放开囚犯的胳膊,将枪举到肩上。

“此处禁止猎鸟,”彼得说。

“禁止什么?”厄尼将枪放低,问道。

“谁都不能在此射鸟,绝对禁止。”

“谁说禁止的?”

“这儿的主人,道格拉斯·海顿先生。”

“你一定是在开玩笑,”厄尼说完,又举起了枪,开了火。鸭子应声倒入水中。

“去取来,”厄尼对彼得说。“雷蒙德,把他的双手松开,他要充当我们的猎犬,我们射中后,帮我们取回猎物。”

雷蒙德拿出刀,将小男孩手腕缠的线割断。

“快!”厄尼厉声喊道。“去取回来!”

猎杀野鸭这件事已经搅得彼得心神不安了。“我不去,”他说。

厄尼亮出手掌,狠狠地在彼得脸上横扇一掌。他没有倒下,但是一股血液的细流从一只鼻孔流淌出来。

“你这个下贱的小讨厌鬼!”厄尼出言不逊。“你再拒绝我一次试试,我向你保证,我保证会这么做:要是你再拒绝我一次,我就敲掉你嘴里的每一颗雪白、闪亮的门牙,敲完上面的,再敲下面的。你明白了吗?”

彼得没有吱声。

“你明白了吗?”厄尼吼道。“回答!”

“是的,”彼得悄声说。“我明白。”

“那么,去取!”厄尼喊道。

彼得走下湖岸,踏入布满烂泥的水中,穿过芦苇丛,捡起了鸭子。他将鸭子带回来,雷蒙德从他手里接过来,用线拴住了鸭腿。

“现在,我们俩有一只猎犬帮我们找回猎物啦,那就看看我们能否再多打几只鸭子吧,”厄尼说。他手里拎着枪沿着湖岸溜达,搜寻着芦苇丛。突然间,他停下脚步,蹲伏下来,一只手指放到嘴唇上,说道:“嘘!”

雷蒙德走过去要看个究竟,而彼得则站在几米远的地方,裤子从裤脚一直到膝盖,沾满了烂泥。

“看那里面!”厄尼指着香蒲生长密集的一块区域,小声说。“我看见了,你看见没有?”

“哇,好家伙!”雷蒙德叫道。“太美啦!”

彼得站在稍远的距离上向灯芯草丛中看去,立刻认出来他们看到的是什么东西。那是一只天鹅,是一只华贵的白天鹅,正宁静地蹲坐在巢穴里,巢穴是用一大堆芦苇和灯芯草做成的,高出水面六十多厘米。这只天鹅就像一位湖中伟大的白衣贵妇人,高高地端坐在巢穴里。天鹅的头转向湖岸那两个男孩子,机警起来,显得有所戒备的样子。

“那只怎么样?”厄尼问。“那可比鸭子好多了,不是吗?”

“你认为你能射中它吗?”雷蒙德问。

“我当然能射中,而且能穿过它的头射出一个洞!”

彼得感到体内的一股狂怒越来越膨胀起来。他走近那两个块头比自己大一些的男孩子。“我要是你的话,我就不会开枪射击那只天鹅,”他说,并尽量使自己的声音平静下来。“在英国,天鹅是最受保护的鸟类。”

“那与这只有何相干?”厄尼问道,嗤之以鼻。

“我给你讲讲相干的吧,”彼得继续说,将所有的谨慎都抛到了脑后。“没有人会对正在孵蛋的鸟儿开枪的,绝对不会有人这样做!它身底下或许孵出了小天鹅!你不能那样做!”

“谁说我们不能?”雷蒙德问,嗤之以鼻。“是彼得·沃森先生你这个该死的小老弟说的吧?"

"全国的人都这样说,"彼得回答。"法律这样说,警察这样说,*每个人*都这样说!"

"我不这样说!"厄尼举起枪说道。

"不要啊!"彼得叫道。"请不要这样做!"

"砰"的一声,枪响了!子弹正中天鹅那优雅的头部,那只长长的白色脖子倒向巢穴的一边。

"射中啦!"厄尼叫道。

"神枪手!"雷蒙德喊道。

厄尼转身看着彼得,彼得则僵直地站在那儿,显得弱小无比,脸色苍白。"现在,去取回来,"他命令道。

彼得又一次没有动地方。

厄尼走近这个弱小的男孩儿,俯下身去,将脸紧逼到对方的脸上。"我对你说最后一次,"他说,声音平和却满是危险的气息。"去取回来!"

彼得慢慢地走下湖岸,踏入水中,眼泪顺着面颊流淌。他蹚水走近死去的天鹅,用双手将她轻轻捡起,发现她身底下有两只小小的天鹅,身上长满黄色的绒毛。两个小家伙在巢穴中央挤到了一块儿。

"有鹅蛋吗?"厄尼从湖岸那儿喊道。

"没有,"彼得回答。"空空的。"他感觉,将小天鹅留在巢穴中,公天鹅返回巢穴时,很有可能继续独自承担起抚养小天鹅的义务。他当然不想将小天鹅交给厄尼和雷蒙德、任由他俩糟蹋。

彼得将死去的天鹅带到湖边,放到地面上。他的双眼由于哭泣仍然湿湿的,充满愤怒的光芒。"这是卑劣的行径!"他喊道。"这是野蛮的行为,愚蠢而荒唐!你们是一对无知的蠢货!该死的是你们,而不是天鹅!你们不配活在这个世界上!"

他站在那儿,尽量让自己站得高大一些。面对两个高个子家伙,他愤怒起来也辉煌无比,也不再去在意他们会对自己怎么样了。

这一次,厄尼没有打他。开始的时候,他的这种突如其来的行为似乎有点让厄尼惊呆了,但是很快就回过神来。现在,厄尼松弛的、湿润的嘴唇改变了形状，形成了一种狡黠的、得意的笑容，一双小小的、紧靠在一起的眼睛也开始闪烁着不怀好意的光亮。"那么说，你喜欢天鹅，对吗？"他轻声问道。

"我喜欢天鹅，但憎恨你！"彼得叫道。

"我可不可以这么想，"厄尼仍然得意地笑着，继续说，"我认为，你希望躺在地上的这只老天鹅是活着的，而不是死的。我想的是否绝对正确呢？"

"这个问题问得很愚蠢！"彼得喊道。

"他的耳朵欠抽了，"雷蒙德喊。

"等等，"厄尼说。"我要做做这样的尝试。"他转回身体看着彼得。"所以嘛，要是我能让这只天鹅复活、再度翱翔蓝天的话，那么，你就会开心。对吗？"

"又是一个问得很愚蠢的问题！"彼得叫道。"你认为你是谁呢？"

"我要告诉你我是谁，"厄尼说。"我是魔术师，那就是我。仅仅为了使你开心、满意，我即将变一个魔术，把这只死天鹅变活，并再度飞翔在天空。"

"胡说八道！"彼得说。"我要走了。"他转身走开。

"抓住他！"厄尼说。

雷蒙德一把将他抓住。

"放开我！"彼得喊了起来。

雷蒙德扇了他脸颊一下，狠狠地扇了一下。"走啊，走啊，"他说。"还敢跟大爷我斗啊，除非你想挂点彩。"

"把你的刀给我，"厄尼伸出一只手，说道。

厄尼跪在死去的天鹅旁边，将天鹅的一只大翅膀伸展出来。"看看这个，"他说。

"有什么奇思妙想？"雷蒙德问。

"等着瞧吧，"厄尼说。现在，他用这把刀将大大的白色翅膀从天鹅身上往下切割。天鹅骨头上有一个关节将翅膀跟身体侧面连接起来，于是，厄尼就找到这个关节，将刀伸进去，切断了肌腱。刀很是锋利，切得很利索。没用多久，翅膀就完整地切割下来了。

厄尼将天鹅翻了过来，然后切掉了另一只翅膀。

“线拿来，”他把手伸向雷蒙德，说道。

雷蒙德拽着彼得的胳膊，看得入了迷。“像那样切割鸟儿，你是从哪儿、怎么样学到的？”他问。

“切割过鸡，”厄尼说。“我们过去经常在史蒂文斯农场杀鸡，然后剁成鸡块，卖给艾尔斯伯里的一家商店。把线给我。”

雷蒙德把那团线给了厄尼，厄尼接过线，切断六根下来，每根九十多厘米长。

每只天鹅翅膀的上端都排列着一根根结实的骨头，厄尼拿起其中一只翅膀，将那几根线的一头沿着大翅膀的上端系了上去。系完后，他把翅膀举起来，六根线头就从翅膀上悬垂下来。他对彼得说：“把胳膊伸直。”

“你绝对是疯了！”弱小的男孩子喊道。“你发疯了！”

“让他把胳膊伸直，”厄尼对雷蒙德吩咐道。

雷蒙德在彼得眼前举起一只攥紧了的拳头，轻轻接触一下他的鼻子。“看到这个了吧，”他说。“好吧，要是你不听话，我就用拳头砸烂你的嘴巴，明白了吗？现在，伸直胳膊，你就是一个乖小子啦。”

彼得感到自己的抵抗力垮了下来，再也无法跟这样的人对抗了。他盯着厄尼看了好几秒钟的时间。两只微小的、黑黑的眼睛长得紧靠在一起的厄尼给人的印象是：他要是真的发起火来，差不多什么事儿都能做得出来。在这一时刻，彼得感到：要是厄尼发脾气的话，或许轻而易举就会杀掉一个人。厄尼是个危险分子，是个鲁莽的坏孩子，现在正在玩游戏呢，扫他的兴是很不明智的举动。于是，彼得伸直了一只胳膊。

接着，厄尼开始将六根线头一根一根系到彼得的胳膊上。系完后，天鹅的白翅膀就牢牢地绑到了彼得整只胳膊上。

“感觉怎样，好吗？”厄尼问，向后退去，打量着自己的成果。

“现在，另外一只，”雷蒙德说，领会了厄尼的所作所为。“只有一只翅膀，无法期望他能翱翔蓝天，对吗？”

"第二只翅膀就要搞定了，"厄尼说。他又跪下来，将另外六根线系到第二只翅膀上端的骨头上。然后，他又站了起来。"我们绑另一只翅膀吧，"他说。这时候，彼得伸直了另一只胳膊，感到既恶心又好笑。厄尼沿着彼得的整只胳膊牢牢地绑好了翅膀。

"看呀！"厄尼叫道，同时拍着双手，在草地上轻轻跳起了快步吉格舞。"看看，我们又有了一只活着的真天鹅！难道我没有告诉你，我是一位魔术师吗？难道我没有告诉你，我要变一个魔术，让这只死天鹅复活、翱翔蓝天吗？那话，难道我没有告诉你吗？"

五月份的这个景色美丽的上午，彼得站在阳光下的湖边，身体两侧是大大的、松弛低垂的翅膀，还轻微滴着血，显得滑稽可笑、荒诞不经。"弄完了吗？"他问。

"天鹅是不会说话的，"厄尼说。"闭上你该死的鸟嘴！节省点精力，小老弟，因为你要竭尽全力翱翔蓝天啦。"厄尼一只手从地上拾起枪，另一只手抓住彼得的后脖颈，命令道："走！"

他们沿着湖岸行走，一直走到一棵高高的、枝条婀娜的柳树下面才停了下来。这是一棵垂柳，长长的枝条从很高的地方垂吊下来，几乎碰到了湖面。

"现在嘛，这只魔力天鹅要向我们展示魔力飞行技术了，"厄尼宣布。"所以，天鹅先生，你要做的就是，爬到这棵树的顶部。一到顶部，你就伸展双翼，就像聪明的小小天鹅宝宝那样，然后你就起飞。"

"太棒了！"雷蒙德叫道。"太棒了！我很喜欢！"

"我也喜欢，"厄尼说。"因为从现在起，我们就要见证一下这只聪明的小小天鹅宝宝到底有多聪明。我们都知道，他在学校聪明透顶，在班级名列前茅，在其他所有美好的事情上他都处处领先。但是，我们倒要看看爬到树的顶部，他到底会有多聪明啊！天鹅先生，好吗？"他将彼得往树跟前推了一下。

彼得想知道：这种疯狂程度还会持续多久？他也开始感觉自己也有点疯狂起来了，就好像一切都不再真实、都没有发生似的。可问题是，有一种想法极力地吸引着他：爬到高高的树上，最终会摆脱这两个无耻之徒。一旦爬上顶部，他就可以待在那儿不下来了。他想，他们不大可能不嫌麻烦而爬上来追赶的。即使他们追着爬上来，他也能爬到一根细枝上摆脱他们，因为所选的细枝只能承受一个人的重量。

这棵树爬起来也十分容易，有几根低矮的枝杈可以作为攀登起点。于是，他开始爬了。胳膊上垂下来大大的白色翅膀总是碍事，但并不至关重要。对彼得来说，至关重要的是，每向上爬一厘米，就离开下面折磨他的人远一厘米。他从来都不是什么爬树能手，也不特别擅长爬树，但是，没有什么东西能阻止他爬到这棵树的顶部。他寻思着，一旦爬上顶部，他们甚至没都不可能看见他了，因为树叶很稠密。

"再高一点儿！"厄尼的声音喊道。"继续爬！"

彼得不停地爬，最终爬到了一个地方，从那地方起，再也无法向上爬了。现在，他的双脚踩在一根树枝上，这根树枝大约有一个人手腕那么粗。奇特的是，这根树枝向湖面上方远远伸过去，然后才曲线优美地向下垂去。他上方所有的枝条都很稀疏、柔嫩，可是，他双手拽住的那根却相当结实，好像是专门为他攀爬准备好的。他站在那儿，不爬了，开始休息。他第一次向下看去，发现自己爬得很高了，至少有十五米，也看不见那两个家伙了。树的底部没有发现那两个家伙，他俩是否有可能最终走开了呢？

"好了，天鹅先生！"此时，传来了厄尼那可怕的声音。"现在，听好啦！"

这两个家伙已经走到离树有一些距离的地方，为的是能够清楚地看到树顶部的小男孩儿。现在，彼得向下看去，看到了他们。他这才意识到，一棵柳树的叶子是多么稀疏和纤细，几乎无法将他遮掩。

"天鹅先生，听好了！"那声音喊道。"从你站立的那根枝条上，开始往外走！一直走，走到正对着你下面烂泥水面的地方！然后，你就起飞！"

彼得没有动弹。现在，他在他们上方有十五米高呢，他们再也够不着他啦。下方那儿，有很长时间没有声音传来，或许有半分钟的时间吧。他眼睛盯着下方田野里两个遥远的身影，两个家伙一动不动地站着，抬头看着他。

“那么，好吧，天鹅先生！”又传来厄尼的声音。“我数到十，好吗？要是到时候你还没有展开翅膀飞翔的话，我就用这支小枪把你打下来！那样的话，我今天射中的就不是一只天鹅，而是两只啦！那么，天鹅先生，我们开始！一！……二！……三！……四！……五！……六！……”

彼得依然没有动弹。从现在起，他是雷打不动啦。

“七！……八！……九！……十！”

此时，彼得看见那支枪举到了肩上，径直瞄向了他。接着，他听到“啪”的一声来复枪响，还听到“嗖”的一声，子弹从他的头顶呼啸而过。太可怕了，但是，他仍然没有动弹。他看见厄尼又装上一颗子弹。

“最后一次机会！”厄尼大喊。“下一颗会射中的！”

彼得按兵不动，等待着。他看到大下方有一个男孩子站在草地里盛开的金凤花之中，旁边站着另一个男孩子。此时，枪又一次举到了肩上。

这一次，在他听到“啪”的一声的瞬间，子弹也射进了他的大腿。没有疼痛感，可是冲击力却不可小觑，就好似有人用一把大锤子使劲猛击腿部，力量如此之大，他被撞得双脚离开了站立的树枝。他双手胡乱抓着，要将自己吊住，可是慌乱中抓住的小树枝却被拽弯，继而断裂开来。

有那么一些人，要是承受的太多、被逼得超过了容忍限度的话，就会轰然垮掉、落荒而逃。还有那么一些人——尽管数量不多，出于某种原因，总是击不垮。这样的人，在战争年代你能遇到，在和平时期你也能遇到。他们具有不屈不挠的精神，没有任何东西能让他们落荒而逃，哪怕是痛苦、折磨，或者死亡的威胁。

小小的彼得·沃森就是后者之一。当他在奋争、乱抓，免得自己从树顶掉落的时候，突然间想到：自己要赢了。他抬起头，一束光从湖面反射上来，这束光壮丽非凡、优美斑斓，令他无法视而不见；这束光在向他召唤，吸引他靠前，于是，他猛冲下去，展开了双翼。

分别有三个人报告,说他们那天上午看见一只大大的白色天鹅在村子上空盘旋。这三个人中,有一个是学校教师,名字叫艾米丽·米德;另一个是名男子,名叫威廉·艾尔斯,当时他正在药店的屋顶上更换瓦片;还有一个是名小男孩,名叫约翰·安德伍德,他在附近的田野里放模型飞机玩呢。

就在那天上午,沃森太太正在自家厨房的水池边洗碗,凑巧抬头向窗外瞥了一眼,正好看见一个大大的、白色的东西"扑棱"一下落到她家后面花园的草坪上。她赶忙向门外冲去,双膝跪到她唯一的儿子身旁,他的儿子身材瘦小,瘫倒在地。"哎呀,我亲爱的孩子!"她叫了起来,火冒三丈,几乎无法相信眼前所见。"我亲爱的孩子!你这是怎么了?"

"我的一条腿疼,"彼得睁开了眼睛说道。随后,他就晕了过去。

"腿在流血啊!"她大叫,随即抱起孩子,冲进屋子。她立刻打电话给医生,并叫了救护车。趁着等待救援到来的工夫,她取来一把剪子,将线剪断,也就是剪断了将两只大大的天鹅翅膀绑到儿子胳膊上的线。

参考文献

[1] DAHL R. The Wonderful Story of Henry Sugar and Six More [M]. London: Penguin Books Ltd., 2002.

[2] DAHL R. The best of Roald Dahl [M]. London: Penguin Books Ltd., 2006.

[3] DAHL R. The Collected Short Stories of Roald Dahl [M]. London: Penguin Books Ltd., 1992.

[4] Dictionary. com LLC's. Dictionary. com [DB/OL]. Oakland, CA: Dictionary. com LLC's Online, http://dictionary. reference. com/

[5] Farlex, Inc. The Free Online Dictionary [DB/OL]. Huntingdon Valley, PA: The Free Online Dictionary by Farlex, Inc. http://www. thefreedictionary. com/

[6] HOWARD, K. Roald Dahl Fans [Z/OL]. Sydney: http://www. roalddahlfans. com/ (1996 – 2013)

[7] Merriam-Webster, Incorporated. Merriam-Webster [DB/OL]. Springfield, MA: Merriam-Webster Online, http://www. merriam-webster. com/

[8] Oxford University Press. Oxford Dictionaries [DB/OL]. Oxford: Oxford Dictionaries Online, http://www. oxforddictionaries. com/

[9] Wikimedia Foundation, Inc. Wikipedia [DB/OL]. http://en. wikipedia. org/

[10] 陈钰. 畸形精神世界的工笔画家——谈罗尔德·达尔的小说

创作特色[J].外国文学研究，1985(4)：66－69.

[11] 金山软件. 金山词霸2009牛津版[CP]. 北京：北京金山软件有限公司，2008.

[12] 刘卫东. 意识流文学综述[J]. 安徽文学，2009(5)：95.

[13] 屈光. 中国古典诗词中的意识流[J]. 中国社会科学，2000(5)：155－156.

[14] 吴锡民. “意识流”流入中国现代文坛论[J].外国文学研究，2002(4)：110－111.

[15] 新华社译名室. 世界人名翻译大辞典[M]. 北京：中国对外翻译出版公司，2007.

[16] 曾艳兵. 意识流：从西方“流”到中国[J].文艺理论与批评，2004(01)：120.

[17] 周定国. 世界地名翻译大辞典[M]. 北京：中国出版集团，中国对外翻译出版公司，2008.

后 记

我们对罗尔德·达尔“非儿童类”短篇故事(小说)进行研究和翻译已经持续了四个年头了。其间,因教学和其他科研的缘由,有所间断,但多数时间是在研读和翻译达尔的这部分短篇小说中度过的。所研读、翻译的达尔这部分短篇作品共计六十篇。

在研究和翻译罗尔德·达尔这部分作品过程中,历尽了艰辛,特别是在翻译过程中,不时会遇到这样或那样的“坎坷”。达尔在写作过程中,时常会“卖弄”自己所掌握的某些专业方面的知识,如葡萄酒、收藏、音乐、医学等,这就逼着译者硬着头皮去熟悉相应的知识。另外,达尔还偶尔会“显摆”一下自己英语之外的词汇,如法语、拉丁语等,这对于译者来说,未免有些“捉襟见肘”了——有的词,任凭怎么查也不得结果。达尔原文中的某一段有时会罗列出若干的专有名词,本着一丝不苟的研究态度,翻译过程中译者对它们均一一查证——哪怕对其中某些表达已经相当熟悉了。对于这样的“坎坷”,下笔前会来回踱步、反复思量、仔细斟酌,正如鲁迅先生在译完《死魂灵》谈到翻译时所言:“我向来总以为翻译比创作容易,因为至少是无须构想。但到真的一译,就会遇着难关,譬如一个名词或动词,写不出,创作时候可以回避,翻译上却不成,也还得想,一直弄到头昏眼花,好像在脑子里面摸一个急于要开箱子的钥匙,却没有。”(鲁迅《“题未定”草·且介亭杂文二集》)

在研究和翻译罗尔德·达尔的这部分作品过程中，还会遇到语言及文化差异方面的“绊脚石”，处理起来颇费脑筋，正如严复在他翻译的《天演论》（译例言）中所言：“新理踵出，名目纷繁，索之中文，渺不可得，即有牵合，终嫌参差，译者遇此，独有自具衡量，即义定名。”另外，在翻译中对于查询无果的地方，也得认真加以思考，甚至经过了很长时间才“创造性”地下笔定论，可谓“一名之立，旬月踟蹰。我罪我知，是存明哲”（严复《译例言》）。由此可见，译事之难，不亚于李太白笔下的“蜀道之难，难于上青天”了！

幸运的是，在对罗尔德·达尔这些“非儿童类”短篇小说进行研究和翻译过程中，我们得到了许多朋友和同事热情的帮助和有力的支持，感激之情无以言表。

对罗尔德·达尔短篇小说的研究和翻译源于英国朋友马礼（他的英文原名叫“Jonathan Rackham”，时任渤海大学外籍英语教师）2009年赠送给著者的一本书，书名叫《罗尔德·达尔小说精品集》（*The Best of Roald Dahl*）。在阅读这本书的过程中，得到了启发，萌生了要研究并翻译作家罗尔德·达尔“非儿童类”短篇小说的念头。我们于2010年9月开始动笔，从此一发而不可收。在对原文理解过程中所遇到的难题，得到了马礼耐心而细致的解答，甚至在他回到英国后，还继续通过电子邮件、越洋电话等方式给予我们热情的解答。在此，衷心感谢好友兼同行的马礼，感谢他的热情帮助！

译文从初稿到成稿，虽经数次校正和修改，仍然存在不少问题。此时，我们的学长兼兄长又兼同事和朋友的刘恩东先生及时伸出了援助之手，对最终的成稿在“忠实”的基础上进行了“通顺”方面的梳理。刘恩东先生虽身为渤海大学英语教师，但是，其汉语功力不可小觑，令吾等外语研究者难以望其项背，特别是他古汉语的功力，甚至超出很多古汉语的专业研究者。有了我们兄长对书稿的梳理和理顺，毛坯一样的成稿方焕发出光彩。兄长对书稿的修改，虽然有时只是增填一个字，或者是删除一个词，但却救译文于“水火”之中。可以说，没有兄长对书稿的理顺，名为“成稿”的译文只能如同一个咿呀学语、走路不稳的婴儿。在此，衷心感谢刘恩东先生，感谢他辛苦的付出！

研究伊始，一个偶然的机会，我们搜索到克里斯廷·霍华德(Kristine Howard)创建并维护的网站“罗尔德·达尔粉丝网”(Roald Dahl Fans. com)，并就罗尔德·达尔有关问题联系过霍华德女士，收到了她及时的回复。整个研究也因霍华德女士的网站而受益匪浅。在此，衷心感谢克里斯廷·霍华德女士，感谢她在网站里所提供的全面而翔实的资料！

同时，我们十分感谢渤海大学外语教研部和渤海大学外国语学院领导和同事给予我们热情的帮助和有力的支持！十分感谢哈尔滨工业大学出版社田新华主任在出版方面提供的有力支持！同时感谢为本书的出版而忙碌的所有编辑人员和工作人员！同时，我们十分感谢为本研究提供帮助的所有朋友和同仁！

当然，由于时间和能力所限，错误在所难免，还望读者赐教、斧正，并多提宝贵意见。

对罗尔德·达尔“非儿童类”短篇故事(小说)研究、翻译所成之书，难免泛泛而论，甚至是流于平庸，但是，我们本着扎实做学问、做学问如做人的思想，从起点出发，稳扎稳打，力戒浮躁之风，勿求好高骛远。

记得《礼记·中庸》里有言：“君子之道，譬如行远，必自迩，譬如登高，必自卑。”愿以此语共勉。

单 畅 王永胜
2014 年金秋于渤海大学